'YOU'LL LIKE HIM. I KNOW YOU WILL.' SHE WAS UNAWARE OF THE PLEADING NOTE IN HER VOICE. 'IF HE'S YOUR CHOICE, I'LL LIKE HIM, LASS . . . JUST BE CAREFUL FOR THE TIME BEING, THAT'S ALL I ASK . . .'

Well, it was bound to have happened eventually . . . but how was Davie going to take this? They fought hard enough anyway, but this was something different . . . There was something badly wrong with his grandson, something unnatural, disturbing. He'd seen it grow through the years, aye, he had . . . there'd been something born in the lad, a perversion, a sickness, and right or wrong no one would ever convince him different . . .

ABOUT THE AUTHOR

Helen Brooks was born and educated in Northampton, where she met her husband at the age of sixteen. Three beautiful children and several dogs later, they are on the verge of celebrating their silver wedding anniversary. Being a committed Christian and fervent animal lover, she has little spare time, but since writing her first book, a romantic novel which was was published in 1992, she indulges her love of writing and reading, calling it work! She has had seventeen books published since 1992 but still finds moments for long walks in the country with her dogs, trips to the theatre, and cosy evenings at home with her husband.

HELEN BROOKS

THE TWISTED CORD

A SIGNET BOOK

SIGNET

Published by the Penguin Group
Penguin Books Ltd, 27 Wrights Lane, London W8 5TZ England
Penguin Books USA Inc., 375 Hudson Street, New York, New York 10014, USA
Penguin Books Australia Ltd, Ringwood, Victoria, Australia
Penguin Books Canada Ltd, 10 Alcorn Avenue, Toronto, Ontario, Canada M4V 3B2
Penguin Books (NZ) Ltd, 182–190 Wairau Road, Auckland 10, New Zealand

Penguin Books Ltd, Registered Offices: Harmondsworth, Middlesex, England

Published in Signet 1995
1 3 5 7 9 10 8 6 4 2

Typeset by Datix International Limited, Bungay, Suffolk
Filmset in 10/12pt Monophoto Plantin
Printed in England by Clays Ltd, St Ives plc

For my dear husband, Clive, and our precious children,
Cara, Faye and Benjamin.

ACKNOWLEDGEMENTS

Thanks to my editor and friend, Luigi, who has given me nothing but encouragement since our first meeting.

My thanks also to Eugenie and the team at the Kingsthorpe library for their assistance in digging for background information.

And last but not least, my gratitude to my Maker for His gift.

Contents

Dark hidden life in nature's womb,
What wiles and twists of fate is theirs
As deep within their cryptic lair
The bond is forged and fused with blood,
And memories, what place have they,
When torn asunder into light
Another twisted cord displays
The black satire of devil's love.

Anon.

Part One
The Awakening
1947–60

CHAPTER ONE

'Come on, lass, *push* . . . That's it, that's right, push, girl. Don't give up now, Jenny love. Just a bit more and it's over.'

'I can't . . .'

'You can, lass, you can, you're nearly there. One more time . . . That's it, here it is, love. It's over, Jenny, can you hear me?'

It was strange, this feeling that was running through her body. The pain had eased, now, that unbearable savage pain that had reached every part of her and turned her into a panting animal with no thought in its head but that the unbelievable torture had to end. She knew the baby had been born but there was no sound, no cry. Surely that wasn't right? She turned her head slowly on the old bolster, seeking her mother's eyes.

'Mam?'

'Yes, lass?' As Mary Longbridge looked down into the exhausted waxen face, she forced her voice to sound normal, bright even. 'I'm here, my love.'

'The baby? Is the baby all right?'

Mary glanced down to the foot of the bed where old Sarah was preparing to wrap the small lifeless body in an old square of rough linen and, as she met the midwife's eyes, Sarah gave an imperceptible shake of her head.

'Sarah's seeing to it, Jenny.' She pulled the breath hard into her lungs before smiling down at the young girl on the bed. 'It's a boy, a little lad.'

'A boy? . . .' The cloudy eyes closed for a moment and then opened again. 'Can I see him?'

'See him? In a minute, lass, in a minute. Let Sarah

see to things for now.' Dear God, what should she say? Did she tell her? How – The faint mewing cry from the tiny scrap of humanity in Sarah's large red hands surprised both the older women, and as Jenny's damp head turned instinctively to the sound, Sarah hastily uncovered the minute face that she had shrouded in cloth and, stepping forward, handed the child to Mary.

'Here, show her while I see to the rest of it.' She hadn't liked the look of that afterbirth and she liked it still less now. Sarah's none-too-clean face wrinkled into more creases as she frowned at the great red mass of tissue in her hands. It had separated, damn it, and by the look of the bleeding there was a sight more left in than she'd have liked.

'Mary?' As Mary turned to her Sarah flicked her eyes downwards at Jenny's spread-eagled legs. 'Put the bairn down an' help me here a minute. No, don't give 'im to the lass, she's still some work to do yet.'

'What is it?' As Mary deposited the now silent child on a piece of torn blanket on the floor her gaze was anxious on Sarah's face. 'What's wrong?'

'There's more to come.' Sarah dropped the torn placenta into the enamel dish at the side of the bed. 'It ain't come away clean and she's bleedin'.'

'Mam?'

'Don't worry, love.' Mary's heart missed a beat as Sarah placed one hand on Jenny's swollen, blue-veined stomach and inserted several fingers into her daughter's body, causing her to groan and twist in protest.

'Steady, lass, steady . . .' Sarah spoke automatically, her face preoccupied with the manipulation of the young body under her experienced fingers. 'It's bulky . . .' She raised her face and gave another slight shake of her head at Mary. 'I reckon there's another 'un in there.'

'Another? . . .' Mary felt her throat constrict in protest. Twins? Please, God, no. This was judgement on her. Judgement for the relief she had felt when that first tiny rib-cage had been still, the minute eyelids closed tight. And now that first one was breathing and there was another. *Please, God*. She shut her eyes tight for a second as Jenny moaned in pain under Sarah's ministration. Forgive me, Father, but they would have been better dead than born into this. But they couldn't live anyway, could they? This first one was so small, like a little skinned rabbit.

'Mam, Mam . . .' Jenny screwed her buttocks into the bed in an attempt to escape what the midwife was doing to her. 'Please, it's hurtin'.'

'We've got to get the other'n out, Mary.' Old Sarah's voice was flat and grim. 'An' she's stopped workin'. Come on, lass.' She raised herself to stare into Jenny's sweat-soaked face. 'You've got to push, girl. There's a load of mess left in there an' the little 'un can't fight through that. You've got to help me, lass.'

'*I can't . . .*' The words were a high-pitched wail of pain and Sarah flicked her head at Mary who was frozen with fear at her daughter's side. 'Get Georgie to go for Doctor Mead, Mary, an' quick. An' I hope to 'ell 'e's there.'

Mary flew to the door and wrenched it open, stepping on to the small square of landing beyond and shouting down to her husband in the room below, before hurrying back to Sarah. 'He's goin'.'

Sarah nodded without raising her head, one hand working outside Jenny's body as the other moved inside until Mary thought she would go mad at what was happening to her lass, her lovely young bonny lass. And still there was no baby. 'You're sure there's another one?' she asked quietly when she couldn't stand it any longer.

'Aye.' Sarah was almost mouthing the words at her, so soft was her voice. 'But the other 'un's done for it, I reckon. It'll be suffocated in there with the rest of that.' She indicated the placenta in the dish by the bed and it was almost in the next moment that Jenny made a sound in between a groan and a snarl as her body went into another violent contraction.

'That's it, me lass, that's a good girl . . .' The old midwife was crooning gently as the head emerged in a gush of blood and tissue, to be followed a few moments later by a tiny body that slithered on to the wet sheets. Sarah had cut the umbilical cord, whisking the limp, doll-like baby upside-down and smacking its bottom before Mary could blink but there was no movement in the tiny chest. 'Give me that.' Sarah reached for a piece of torn sheet and wiped the encrusted face, inserting her finger into the minute mouth as she tried to clear blocked passages. It was a full minute later before the child made a strangled, choking gasp for air and even then the clogged passages and congested chest were full and stifled.

'I've done what I can.' As Sarah laid the second child alongside the first she glanced across at Mary, who had just raised her gaze from Jenny's white, bloodless face, and the midwife's eyes spoke their own message.

'What is it?' Mary asked flatly.

'A little lassie.' Sarah looked down at Jenny, who had lain still and motionless, eyes closed, since the second twin had been born. 'You'll have to wake her, Mary.'

'Mam?' Jenny's eyes were huge and glazed with

exhaustion when Mary gently shook her awake. 'Is it over?'

'It's over, love.' The second child was snuffling like a little pig as she spoke. 'You've got one of each, a boy and a girl.'

'I'm tired, Mam . . .'

That feeling was back again but stronger this time, a deep sticky warm feeling that had her wanting to close her eyes and drift into the comforting darkness that was pulling her down. She wanted to go into that darkness. Oh, she did. She didn't want to have to think again, to feel, to face the sly spiteful whispers and the knowing looks. It had been so hard.

'Jenny?' Her mother's voice was low but of a quality that forced her heavy eyelids open. 'He's got two bairns now, responsibilities. Tell me his name, love. I promise you I won't let your dad do anything silly.'

'I can't, Mam.' She was weary, so weary of it all.

'You can, lass, *you can.*' Mary's voice broke and then she forced herself to go on. 'Look what you've just been through, how you've suffered. He should at least be made to pay –' She stopped abruptly. 'He should know about the bairns, Jenny,' she said more softly. 'He should at least know.'

'It wouldn't make any difference.'

'It would.' Mary shut her eyes tight for a moment and then looked at Sarah who was standing to one side of the bed, her face tender with sympathy. 'It would.'

'Come on, lass.' Sarah moved to her side and took her arm. 'I know what you've gone through but now's not the time.' She flicked her head to one side and as Mary's eyes followed the gesture and she saw the ever-widening red stain under her daughter's sprawled limbs she felt her blood run cold. 'I hope your

Georgie's quick,' Sarah said quietly. 'We need that doctor. We ain't had no afterbirth at all from this 'un.'

'Jenny?' Mary knelt down by her daughter's face, stroking the damp brow that was turning cold. 'Jenny listen to me. You've got to push again, love, you understand?'

No, no, she didn't understand. She didn't want to understand. It was so good to sink into the soft, all-enveloping darkness that soothed her body of all feeling, a thick blanket of heaviness drawing her down into the bed, and still further . . . This was all she wanted. But there was one thing, what was it? She had to try and remember, to speak. Oh yes, that was it. She knew now . . .

'Mam?' The words were a mere whisper through lips that were colourless. 'You'll look after 'em? It wasn't their fault.'

'I know that, love.' Mary squeezed her daughter's hand but there was no response in the limp fingers, the same fingers that had gripped her hand for most of the twenty-four-hour ordeal like bands of steel, and the gut-wrenching fear that twisted Mary's insides paralysed her throat.

Not her Jenny. *Please, God, no*. Take the bairns, they wouldn't live anyway, but spare her beautiful Jenny. She had sinned, she knew her daughter had sinned, but at fifteen, when the blood is singing warm and sweet through the veins and the summer nights are soft . . .

Who was he? She stared blindly into space. They still didn't know who had done this to their only child, who was nowt but a bairn herself. They didn't even know if she had been willing . . . Why wouldn't the lass say his name? What power did this man have over her that in spite of all she'd suffered in the last twenty-four hours she was still protecting him?

By the time George returned with the doctor his only daughter was dead and the two tiny babies looked as though they would follow on the next breath.

'I'm sorry, Mary.' Doctor Mead rested his hand on the shoulder of this woman who had borne so much over the last few years. First the death of her son in a freak drowning accident down in the Sheaf, then old George losing his job at the steelworks just a couple of days ago and it being a tied house too, but the thing that had aged her far beyond her thirty-eight years was the shame the young girl lying there so still had brought on her mother's head. 'Did she say a name?'

'No, Doctor.' The voice was blank and so were the eyes as they lifted slowly and stared into his. 'And now he's got away with murder.'

'Mary, Mary . . .' Doctor Mead rubbed his hand comfortingly over the thin bony shoulder. 'Don't look at it like that.'

'*Don't look at it like that?*' It said a lot for her state of mind that Mary would raise her voice to this man whom she had respected and revered all her life, the awe she felt for him being just a little less than that she held for the priest, Father Michael. 'She's not sixteen for another four months, she's still a bairn!' Her voice was a harsh scream of protest.

'I know, Mary, I know.' As he heard George thunder up the stairs at the sound of his wife's voice, Doctor Mead closed his eyes for an instant. How was George going to take this final knock? Jenny had been his pride and joy, the sun had shone out of her big blue eyes for her father from the minute she had been born. He sighed softly. Even the shame and humiliation of the last few months hadn't killed the love within this close-knit little family. He knew of hundreds who would have thrown the girl out within minutes of finding out she was going to present them with a bastard grandchild, but he doubted if it had even occurred to Mary and George. There weren't many like them among his patients in this hard northern town where the daily fight for food and the basic necessities soon ground all thoughts of love and charity into the ground.

'Mary?' As the big man in the doorway stood transfixed, unable to take in the sight in front of him, Doctor Mead moved quickly to cover the lower part of Jenny's body with a blanket and close the still partly open eyes. There was so much blood. Even though he had been a doctor for over twenty years it still amazed him where all that vital, life-giving liquid came from, and the haemorrhaging had been severe, the worst he'd seen in years. Things were getting better, and not before time in his opinion; maybe this idea of a National Health Service would make life for such as Mary and George easier, but in this year of 1947 he still had damn little to fight the results of poverty and ignorance with. And this was the sad consequence.

'Oh, Georgie . . .' For the first time since he had come into the room Doctor Mead saw a spark of life in Mary's eyes, and as the burly six-footer in the doorway opened his arms, the tears streaming unashamedly down his pock-marked cheeks, his wife flew into them like a homing pigeon.

'Take her downstairs out of this, George.' Doctor Mead's voice was brusque but as he met the eyes of the younger man, his face was gentle. 'I'll be down in a minute.'

When it was just the two of them the doctor turned to the midwife with another deep sigh. 'Well, Sarah?' He indicated the two tiny babies lying silently side by side wrapped in an old sheet on the bare floor. 'What do you think? Any chance?'

'No, Doctor.' Sarah Millett shook her grey head as she washed her hands in the bowl of cold water that was already stained a bright red, rubbing them dry on a piece of old cloth that did as a towel. 'The wee laddie didn't breathe at first and in being born he almost choked the lassie. On top of that they're two months early. The kindest thing would be to put 'em under the blanket at the bottom of the bed for a few minutes . . .' She sniffed grimly. 'There'll be no milk and the weather's agen 'em, they won't last above an hour or two, poor little mites.' She hitched her ample bosom up with her forearms as the doctor still didn't speak. 'An' Georgie's gotta be out of this place at the end of the week. Criminal, I call it, when I think of some of the scroungers who work in that place. All he did was talk a bit easy, like.'

'He was talking union talk, Sarah,' Doctor Mead said quietly. 'And he'd been warned before. Now I don't say I approve of what they've done.' He raised a hand as Sarah opened her mouth to protest. 'But there it is, it's done now and Mary and George will have to make the best of it.' He turned to glance at the two tiny babies again and shook his head slowly. 'And you're right, they couldn't last but maybe it's for the best, all things considered. Can I leave you to clear up?'

Sarah nodded without speaking. She knew what he meant. Funny thing about these doctors, the squeamish side they had to 'em with something like this. But then – her slack lower lip curled slightly as her thoughts sped on – they were gentry. When had any of them been hungry and cold and watched their kiddies go out on the slack heaps in the middle of winter searching for bits of coal with numb hands and bare feet? She sniffed a self-righteous sniff before turning away. Doctor Mead was a good 'un all right, one of the best, but he was still one of them when all was said and done, the gentry. And theirs was a different world. 'I'll see to everything, Doctor,' she said quietly now. 'Don't you worry.'

Don't worry? Arthur Mead stared down at the babies one more time before leaving the room. Don't worry? He found his teeth were clamped together as he left the cheerless little house that was nevertheless as clean as a new pin. All the years at medical school and in the job hadn't hardened him to the despair he felt at times such as this. He was supposed to *save* life, dammit, and he'd left those two new-born infants with that woman knowing full well what she was going to do. But what was the alternative? He stood for a moment, breathing in the grimy air in the street outside. There wasn't one. It was as simple as that.

When she was alone Sarah glanced down at the babies still lying on the floor. She hadn't bothered to wrap them up well, although the small damp room was chilly. No point in the circumstances, she thought stolidly. She bent down and pushed the nearest baby with the back of her hand and knew a moment of relief when it didn't open its eyes.

The cold often took 'em in the first few minutes when they were as small as this, she told herself flatly. And these two had come from a body that was as thin and light as any of those poor blighters that'd come back from the prisoner-of-war camps. It was a crying shame, she'd been a bonny lass. Well, she'd tidy her up for Mary, make her presentable, like, and just to make sure the little 'uns could go under the blankets heaped at the bottom of the bed while she worked.

It was as she lifted the first baby that the tiny blue-grey eyes opened wide to stare straight into hers and for a moment she almost dropped the child so great was her shock. The baby's gaze was unblinking and cold, almost as if it knew what she was about to do, and although she knew it was impossible, the thought sent an icy shiver flickering down her spine. 'Don't be silly, girl,' she told herself out loud as she placed the small bundle jerkily on the top of the bed and stepped back a pace. 'You're a sight too long in the tooth to start imagining things now.' Nevertheless, as the child continued to stare at her, she couldn't bring herself to pick it up again. The other baby was grunting softly, making small sucking sounds with its mouth, and as she bent to unwrap the tiny limbs from their scant covering she saw it was the girl who was a good pound or so heavier than her brother. And yet . . . She turned back to the child on the bed and crossed herself quickly. There was something about this one that wasn't quite right, it seemed to have a strength that was nothing to do with its body. Perhaps it was just a will to live? She glanced nervously round the room to avoid meeting that blue-grey gaze.

The thick cloying smell of blood was heavy in the still air and as she moved to open the small sash-window that overlooked the street below she saw the old drawer in a corner of the room that was to have been the baby's cot. It was lined with brown paper, a few scraps of blanket resting on top, and her glance flickered back to the bed again. 'I'll put 'em both in there.' She nodded to herself. Yes, that's what she'd do. It wouldn't hurt and they'd only last an hour at most if she left the window open so the room was aired a bit. No one could blame her for that.

When Sarah walked down the narrow stairs some

twenty minutes later Mary opened swollen eyes as she raised herself from the chair. 'Thanks for what you've done, Sarah.' She indicated George sitting in stunned silence in front of the heavily banked meagre fire. 'We're grateful.' As she pressed some money into Sarah's hand the old midwife nodded slowly.

'I've left it tidy, and the bairns are in the drawer for now. All right, lass?'

'The bairns?' Mary's voice was flat. 'Wouldn't they have been better with Jenny? All going together, like?'

'They're still alive, Mary.' As she saw the bewilderment in the grief-stricken face in front of her, Sarah blinked quickly.

'But Doctor Mead?' Mary swung her head to George's stiff back and then back to Sarah's face. 'He said they'd gone.'

'We thought they'd gone,' Sarah lied uncomfortably. 'But you can't always tell when they're so little, lass. I don't think it'll be long any roads but I wasn't quite sure where to put 'em . . .' She let the words dwindle away as Mary pushed past her, moving swiftly up the stairs that led directly to the room overhead. 'I don't think it'll be long,' she repeated uneasily to George, who nodded, empty-eyed, before turning his gaze back to the glowing embers of the fire, his hands hanging loosely over his knees and his head drooping apathetically.

'I'll let meself out, then.' As she left the small house, Sarah sighed heavily with relief. There had been something about this whole thing she couldn't rightly explain, she told herself shakily. Something strange . . . She wasn't normally given to fancies, but the way that afterbirth had been torn . . . It'd been almost as though the first 'un had been trying to keep his sister in the womb, suffocating the life out of her before she'd had a chance to be separate . . . She shook her head at her own foolishness. Eeh, they'd be locking her away at this rate, aye they would. To let a little bairn put the 'eebie-jeebies up her at her age! But she couldn't laugh at her imagination, not with the feel of those cold blue-grey eyes still on her flesh.

She'd get a jug of stout on the way home, aye she would. She nodded to herself as she looked at the money in her hand. Mary had been generous, she'd always been one to pay her way, had Mary. Aye, she'd get the stout and put her feet up, there'd be none who could say she hadn't earned it the day.

Alone in the room that was her marital bedroom, Jenny having slept on the cracket to one side of the fireplace in the room downstairs, Mary gazed silently at the two tiny screwed up faces of her grandchildren as they mewed softly in the cold air. 'Jenny, oh Jenny lass . . .' She shivered in an agony of grief, her eyes shifting to the lifeless figure on the bed and then back to the babies as the crying became more plaintive. Landsakes, the chill in here was enough to take your breath away, what had Sarah been thinking of? She moved to the window and closed it quickly before turning to gaze down into the drawer again.

This, then, was all that she had left of her Jenny, her beautiful vibrant Jenny with eyes the colour of cornflowers and hair like ripe wheat. She'd always marvelled that such an enchanting creature could have come from her body but her daughter had been too beautiful. She shut her eyes tightly. Right from the moment she could toddle the boys had been after her in their droves. The number of times their David had had to fight them off before he – she shut her mind from the path it was following as she crossed her forearms against her waist, swaying back and forth in her grief. She couldn't think of her son now, her precious first-born, not with his sister lying there so still. Why both of them? A suffocating thickness rose up in her head before one of the babies gave a sharp whimper, dispelling the darkness. What was she thinking of? She couldn't give way now, she had to pull herself together, there were these bairns to see to.

'A boy and a girl.' She spoke out loud as she bent down to peer at them more closely. When David had been drowned nigh on three years ago Jenny had become her whole world, but now – she stretched her eyes wide as her thoughts raced on. God was good. *Oh, He was*. 'The Lord giveth and the Lord taketh away, blessed be the name of the Lord.' The priest's words at David's funeral burnt in her brain. He had given her them back, two bairns for the ones He had taken.

Jenny wasn't built to stand the shame of bringing up an illegitimate child, let alone two, she thought frenziedly. The last few months had all been but a build-up to this day, the spark of life slowly extinguishing in her daughter as her stomach had swollen. She had seen it but she hadn't wanted to acknowledge it. But God had given her back her children in the forms of her grandchildren. She crossed herself before reaching down and picking up the drawer, which was disturbingly light. They were so tiny, so frail. She sent up a swift urgent prayer as she carried the drawer out of the room and down the stairs into the dimly lit room below.

'Go and get our Martha, Georgie. She should be home from the works by now.' As Mary placed the drawer on the old clippie mat in front of the fire, George stared at his wife, his mouth agape. The defeated, broken woman who had been in the room a few minutes before was gone and in her place was his old Mary, strong and fierce and determined, taking charge like she'd always done when times were hard. 'And tell her to bring those eye-drop bits she had for her Bill and Sally when they had measles last year, and the two big jugs, the ones she uses when she makes her lemonade for the bairns.' As Mary was speaking she felt the inside of the big bread oven, which was warmed by the fire. 'Go on, Georgie, now.'

As George ran to fetch her younger sister from a few streets away, Mary's mind was moving rapidly. They'd need to keep them warm and fed, that was all that mattered. The rest would take care of itself. The oven would double as a mother's warmth and, if they wrapped them up and slid them into the big earthenware jugs tilted on their side and fed them with the little droppers . . . One of the babies gave a wah of a cry as the tiny mouth searched the air hungrily for sustenance, but already the sound was weaker. *And the nights were so cold and they had but a few pieces of coal left and they had to be out at the end of the week.* No. She shook her head fiercely, forcing the panic that had gripped her throat to subside. She wouldn't think of all that now. All that mattered was David and Jenny, she couldn't worry about anything else. David and Jenny . . .

Martha's pretty wide-eyed face, so unlike that of her sisters, was flushed and pink when she came darting in with George a few minutes later, but she had brought all that Mary had asked, along with a full jug of fresh creamy milk and a half-sack of coal.

'Bless you, Martha.' As the two sisters embraced, Mary felt her lips quiver but resolutely took a grip on her emotions. There was no time for that now, and tears were weakening. She of all people knew that. She glanced at George who stood looking at them both and her voice was sharp as she brushed him aside. 'Mind out of that, there's work to do the night.'

The night was long and hard but at the end of it, as a weak watery dawn filtered in through the narrow window, the babies were still alive and had taken a little milk hour by painstaking hour from the small droppers squeezed gently into their searching mouths.

'I'll have to go now, Mary.' As Martha wearily drained the last dregs from the mug of strong sweet tea George had placed silently in front of her, she carefully adjusted the small bundle on her lap before placing the tiny body carefully into the warmed jug, which was like a heated cocoon in the depths of the oven. 'I'll be back tonight, pet, and I'll have a word with Frank if I get the chance. Put in a word for Georgie and explain things like.'

'What's this?' George reared up from his seat at the side of the hearth. 'I want no favours from Frank Malley, woman, foreman or no foreman. I tell you –' The piercing stare that Mary sent his way silenced further protest but his face was dark as he glared at them both.

'We want all the favours we can get,' Mary said flatly, lowering her gaze to the baby on her lap. 'If they'll take you back on, we can keep the house and there'll be money for milk and coal. You'll crawl, beg, plead, lie, anything, George Longbridge, to keep these bairns alive.'

As her voice broke, George and Martha's eyes met over Mary's head and as Martha dropped her gaze, turning quickly away, George ran his hand over his face before he spoke again, and this time his voice was quiet. 'All right, lass, all right. Don't take on.' His eyes flickered towards the stairs and the room at the top of them where the stiff, cold body of his daughter lay. 'We'll see what we can do, eh?'

'I'll send my Rosy round when I get back, Mary.' Martha stood by the door and her voice too was quiet. 'She'll already have the young 'uns up and ready for school if I know anything and she can take 'em afore she nips back here. She'll be glad of an excuse not to go herself, and I can't see learning is much good for a lass anyway.'

'Are you sure?'

'Aye. She might not have a lot up top but she's a marvel with little 'uns an' you can't manage here by yourself. If I can square things for Georgie, he might get the afternoon shift anyway.'

'Be careful, Martha.' Mary's voice was low and, as the sisters' eyes met for a long moment, Martha nodded slowly at the unspoken warning before looking away, and she pulled open the door, stepping out into the street beyond, which was deserted and grey in the biting early morning chill.

'You shouldn't let her do it, Mary.' George's voice was tight and strained when next he spoke. 'That Frank Malley has been looking for a way in since Bill died, you know it. This'll give him the lever he needs, an' being the man he is he'll take full advantage, that he will. He's nothing but a –'

'That's enough.' Mary's voice was sharp but her tired eyes pleaded for understanding as she smoothed back a wisp of downy hair from the forehead of the child on her lap. 'I had to let her try, Georgie, there's no other way. You need work, we need a roof over our heads more than ever now, and even if Frank does take you back on it don't mean our Martha has to get friendly with him, does it? She's been without a man nigh on six years now and there's been others interested, as you well know.'

Their eyes held for a full minute but it was George who looked away first, turning and standing with his back towards her as he stared down into the fire. 'An' what does that mean?'

'Martha's a lovely-looking woman.' Mary's voice was tight. 'John Turner, Michael Patterson, Jim Cullen, they've all been after her in their time but she would have none of it. Why should Frank Malley be any different?'

'Because them others aren't like Malley an' you know it.' She couldn't know, he thought guiltily as he licked the little beads of moisture on his top lip. He was reading more into her words than was there. And there wasn't anything to know anyway, was there? Nothing had happened. Not really. But to think of Martha with Malley. He ground his teeth, the gnawing ache that always accompanied such thoughts gripping his stomach. And he knew why Martha hadn't looked the side any of those blokes were on. Oh yes, he knew, heaven help him. 'Malley's a boss's man,' he said grimly without turning. 'A sly creeping vine that's choked many a good man out of a job in order to curry favour with old McQueen. I've only lasted as long as I have because Martha's me sister-in-law and he's carried a torch for her for years. You know full well he was after her even before Bill died.' He'd seen the way those narrowed black eyes followed Martha round the factory, seen the way he sidled up to her at every opportunity. And now Mary had sent her sister like a lamb to the slaughter and if Frank agreed to take him back on . . .

George breathed deep in his chest. Could you love two women at the same time? He shook his head at his thoughts. Don't be daft, man, asking the road you know. He was living proof of it, wasn't he? And somehow, somehow he felt Malley knew. Whether it was his obsession with Martha that made him particularly intuitive where she was concerned, he didn't know, but the way the foreman looked at him sometimes . . . And if Malley took him back on, what then? He'd have to keep his mouth shut and his eyes closed, he'd be little more than an emasculated bullock. Could he stand it? He turned and glanced across to where Mary was kneeling in front of the oven, testing the warmth of the interior with her hand as she placed the other baby gently in its jug, her plain face anxious and weary. He had no choice, dammit. There was another funeral to get through now, as though their David's hadn't near broke her, and if these little 'uns could stop her cracking up then he had to do all he could. The knowledge was thick bile in his throat.

For the next three months Mary rarely changed her clothes or ate without one of the babies tucked under her arm, and never once went upstairs to the room she had shared with her husband for twenty years of married life. Her whole existence, every second she was awake, and even when she slept if the patchy catnaps could be called sleeping, was geared to the two tiny infants who had taken their mother's life in their entrance into the world. And gradually, despite all the odds stacked against her, she pulled them away from the very brink of death, assisted by Martha and Rosy.

In spite of the fact that the girl child was bigger and therefore stronger than her brother, it had been she who had caused the most worry, catching a cold within the first week of life that, along with her delayed entrance into the world, had threatened several times to snuff out the feeble fight for survival. But the boy was different . . .

Mary glanced at him now as she sat in the last of the daylight from the small window, shelling peas at the scrubbed wooden table. For some reason she had never been concerned for him in the same way. It wasn't that he was stronger physically or more alert than Jenny but there was something, a determination, a tenacity to hold on to the root of life, that defied the outward shell of tiny helpless limbs and underdeveloped lungs. He had accepted milk from the bottle weeks before his sister, struggling with the cumbersome teat as he pulled the liquid into his mouth but persevering until he was full, whereas Jenny – Mary's eyes turned to her sleeping grand-daughter lying in the corner of the settle on a folded blanket – Jenny wasn't a fighter.

'What, then.' It was George's customary greeting when arriving home, which had never varied in all their years of marriage, but now, as he entered on a burst of thick hot air from the dusky June evening outside, she didn't raise her eyes or smile as she had always done before. Something had changed in the last three months, something precious and undefinable, but she was powerless to set it right. No. She shook her head mentally as she silently corrected the thought. If she was honest, she didn't want to think about what was wrong, the price might be too high.

'They been feeding all right?' The tone, like the question, was automatic without real interest, and her voice was the same as she replied with the stock answer.

'They'll do.'

He passed her without looking at her, walking into the stone-floored scullery that led from the room directly adjoining the street with his face straight and his mouth grim. A bowl of warm water and a dry rough towel were waiting for him and as he washed his hands and arms Mary busied herself fetching the teapot from the hob and setting two plates on the table after placing a linen table-cloth on top of the piece of oil cloth.

'Your Martha been in the day?'

'No.'

This growing animosity between them that took its form in a flat hard abruptness worried her when she had time to think about it, which wasn't often. The babies took all her time and attention and they had to come first. Rosy only came for an hour after school now and Martha rarely called in. Martha – She forced her mind away from her sister. The relationship between Martha and Frank Malley, begun just after the twins were born, was another nail in her coffin as far as George was concerned. She pushed the shadow of suspicion to the back of her mind when her thoughts would have gone on. George just hated Frank, that was all, he always had. But the obsession had got worse in the last few weeks, although she had had no part in that. He couldn't blame that on her, could he? And Martha was comfortable, even happy about Frank.

'He's ever so different to what you'd expect, Mary.' Her sister's voice had been quiet and soft on her last visit some ten days ago, when George was on a different shift. She rarely came when he was home now. 'Real caring, like, and the kids love him.'

'I'm glad.' Mary had reached out a hand and enclosed one of Martha's. 'It was hard for you when Bill was killed so young. War is a terrible thing.'

'It is that.' Martha sighed deeply. 'An' I know some

women can go through life alone, some even like it, but I'm not like that, Mary. I need someone.'

'I know, lass, I know. So you're all right, then?'

'Aye.'

She had tried to tell George about the conversation thinking to make things easier but he would have none of it. In fact it had made things worse. But she had wanted him to know how Martha felt, that she wanted Frank Malley. The familiar flicker of unease that she couldn't put a name to, dare not, was back. Why did he have to make life even more difficult at the moment anyway? Couldn't he see she had enough on her plate?

'I'm waitin'.' She came back to the present to find George seated at the table, his face aggressive. 'I've been hard at it all the day and I don't expect to have to wait for me dinner.' He eyed her morosely and the temptation to reply in like manner was hot and strong before she choked the angry words back. A few months ago he'd never have spoken to her like that. What was happening to them?

'Here.' As she ladled out two steaming platefuls of rabbit stew and dumplings from the large pot that had been simmering on the stove all afternoon, she pushed his over to him jerkily, her face tight. 'The bread's in front of you.'

'I've got eyes.'

She glared at him, hard, before sitting down and beginning her own meal, but had barely taken more than a few mouthfuls when a hungry cry from the settle brought her rising instantly to her feet.

'Leave it.'

'What?' She spoke absent-mindedly, her attention already centred on little David as he squirmed in his corner, searching the air for food.

'I said, leave it.' George too had half-risen but with

the intention of pushing his wife down in her seat, which he did with more force than was merited. 'We're eatin' a meal and they can wait. They're not so small now.'

'Georgie?' She stared at him in amazement as she looked at him, really looked at him, for the first time in weeks. The furious tone of voice, the darkness in his square face were all new to her and in all their years of marriage he had never manhandled her like that. What did he think he was about?

'I mean it, Mary.' He eyed her tightly but she noticed his face had a dry, bleached look, the broken veins on his large nose standing out in vivid contrast. 'I've had all I'm going to take, an' if they're stayin' –'

'If they're staying?' She glared at him now as though he had gone mad. 'What do you mean, if they're staying? They are our grandchildren, man, where do you think they would go if not here?'

'An' I expect you to remember just that.' As he sat down heavily in his seat without taking his eyes off her, both the infants began to wail loudly, disturbed by their raised voices. 'By, lass, you never jumped to when our own yelled, not like you do now. You didn't bear these ones, Mary, you aren't their mam. You can't replace what's gone.'

'Replace?' He had her full attention now. 'What are you going on about? They're our Jenny's bairns, all we've got left. Do you want to turn your back on 'em? Is that it?'

'Don't be such a damn fool.'

She remained absolutely still for a moment as their eyes met, her expression as angry as his, and when she went to rise again he bit her name into the space between them with such ferocity that she sank back into her seat, her hand going to her throat.

'An' I'm telling you something else. You're sleepin' back up there, with me.' He flicked his head upwards towards the ceiling, his movements jerky. 'All this nurse-maidin' has gone on long enough.'

So that was what this was all about? His rights? His husbandly rights? The tide of burning rage that swept through her took her breath away and she had to breathe in, very slowly, before she could speak. 'I'm not.' She stared at him grimly. 'They need me still.'

'That's as may be.' His voice wasn't the voice of the man she had known most of her life, the partner she had cried and moaned with on the death of their son and drawn strength from when their only daughter was took down by goodness knows who. No, this man was a stranger. A cold, hostile stranger whose eyes looked through her. 'But from now on, I'm tellin' you, they'll fit in with me. I've sold me soul for 'em and I'll be master in me own home if nowhere else. Understand this. If they stay, they stay under my protection. Without me the three of you'd be out on the streets.'

'The three of us?' She was frightened now, frightened and unbelieving of where they had sunk to. She reached out a hand across the table but he sat stone cold and unmoved, his face rigid. 'But we're a family, Georgie, you, me and them. Surely you can see that?'

He looked back into her face and for a moment she saw a weary kind of pity mixed with the pain and bitter anger before he shook his head slowly, his eyes narrowing. 'You don't see, do you? You really don't see.' As the noise from the babies grew louder he leant across and moved her plate nearer to her. 'You'll eat it, all of it, before you see to 'em, and after they go in the crib Martha gave us.' His lip curled over her sister's name as though it was repugnant to him. 'And they'll sleep down here. If it was good enough for our own bairns, it's good enough for Jenny's.'

'Don't be like this.' Her voice was flat now and as cold as his. 'Don't make me hate you.'

'Eat your meal, Mary.'

For a moment she thought of defying him, of tipping her plate across the table and gathering up the crying babies in her arms, but the truth of his words had registered. They *were* dependent on him but, oh, the unfairness of it!

'I don't understand you any more.' Her voice was low and harsh. 'What's the matter with you anyway? Anyone'd think they weren't your own flesh and blood.'

He stared at her silently for a long considering moment as he methodically chewed a mouthful of food and then, after swallowing, turned in his chair to glance across at the two infants who had settled down into hiccuping sobs. 'You don't understand me?' He gave a hard bark of a laugh before turning to face her again. 'You understand me all right, lass.' His eyes were hard gimlets boring into hers. 'I *know* you understand me but it suits your purposes to let things be, let 'em ride. Least said soonest mended, eh?' It was so near the truth that she could only blink at him. 'Well, I've done what you wanted. I crawled back, tail atween me legs, to the boss-man your sister is whorin' for and now I'm sayin' I want to eat with me wife and lay with her. Is that so bad?'

'It wasn't like that with our Martha, you know it wasn't. She isn't –'

'Don't give me that. That's exactly how it was and is. There isn't a man at the steelworks that doesn't know how I got me job back and how I get the pickings for overtime, but bad as that is I could have stood it except for seeing your Martha getting further and further down the road. Frank Malley had been waitin' for years and you handed her to him on a plate and what's more you did it with your eyes open –'

'She likes him.' Mary's face was as white as a sheet. 'I told you the other night, she said she likes him. He's good to her and the bairns and you can't argue with that, George Longbridge. It's not natural for someone like our Martha to be without a man and Bill has been dead the last six years. Just because you don't like Frank Malley –'

'No, lass, I don't.' His voice was quiet, unnaturally so. 'An' you know why? Because he's the type of scum who'd sell his own mother for a shillin' and that's the truth. He might be good to Martha now while he's gettin' his portion but when he tires of her she'll be out on her ear, maybe me 'n all. Have you thought of that in your schemin'? That this might all be to nought? That we might still have to get out?'

'The bairns will be older then.' She had answered before she considered her words, lulled into a false sense of security by the quietness of him, but as soon as the words had left her lips she knew she had made a grave mistake.

He nodded his big head slowly, pressing his lips tightly together before he spoke softly, almost conversationally.

'You'd sell us all for 'em, wouldn't you, lass? You've changed, by, how you've changed.'

As his lips moved away from his teeth she wanted to cry out to him, to beg him to understand, to tell him that the only thing keeping her halfway sane was the knowledge that there was something left of her children after all. But even as the words hovered on her lips, she knew she couldn't speak. His bitterness about her sister had caused all the old half-buried suspicions to rear their heads again and she felt sick, sick to her soul. One half of her mind told her she was wrong, criminally, dangerously wrong, that George and Martha were just in-laws to each other, family, but the other . . . The other remembered that day in this very house, four years after Bill had been killed, when her sister and Jenny had entered on a noisy gust of hilarity that had caused her and George to glance up enquiringly.

'You'll never guess, Mam.' Jenny had been giggling helplessly as she held on to her aunty's arm. 'You know that new lot down the road, them at number 64? Well the woman was sitting on her doorstep with her youngest an' we got chatting, trying to be friendly, like, and she thought –' Here Jenny had poked her aunty in the ribs teasingly. 'She thought me an' Aunty Martha were sisters. *Sisters!* She couldn't believe it when I told her she was me aunty and had three kids of her own. She said she don't look old enough to have one bairn, let alone three.'

'I did have our Rosy when I was eighteen, you know,' Martha retorted with mock severity before the two of them fell against each other again in another burst of shared laughter. 'An' I'm only twenty-eight now. Some folks'd consider that just out of nappies.'

'Oh Aunty Martha, the things you say.' Jenny had walked into the scullery to get a drink of water from the jug Mary kept cool on a big marble slab, and as Mary had raised her eyes from the mending on her lap, intending to make some laughing remark, the words had died in her throat. Her husband and her sister were looking at each other in such a way – the way that a courting couple did when they were fair gone on each other, or like them young newly-weds, Pam and Wilfred at the end of the road, them that were always having the mickey taken out of them for being so soft.

The incident had only lasted a few seconds. They had seen her watching them and George had lowered his head as Martha had followed Jenny into the next room, but from that point on – Mary shut her eyes tightly for a second. From that point on she'd had no peace.

'Eat your dinner, Mary.' George's voice was harsh as it snapped her eyes to his, and when, without a word, she picked up her fork and began to eat, he did the same. And later, when he moved the old wicker crib from the corner of the room and brushed it down she silently fetched the babies' blankets and placed them inside, her face grim and her mouth tight. How would they sleep without her warmth? she asked herself bitterly. She had got into the habit of sleeping in the old easy chair close to the fire with a baby nestled in each arm, their small bodies lying across her chest. It had made life easier in the first few weeks, when the hourly feeding had exhausted her to the point where she had begun to have hallucinations, but then as they had got stronger there had always been a reason, one of them had a sniffle or the other was restless, to avoid returning upstairs.

'You'll be up shortly.' It was a statement, not a question, and for a second she felt a shaft of hate so strong it stopped her breath. How could he do this? Make her leave them when they were still so small, so vulnerable? And the night feed – she always fed them at two o'clock. What if she didn't hear them cry? She didn't know him, perhaps she'd never known him, maybe the last twenty years had been a mass of lies and hidden thoughts and actions? Perhaps Martha – *No*. Please, God, no. She wouldn't believe that, she couldn't. Help me, Mary, Mother of God, she prayed silently as she settled the infants more upright in their separate corners of the bench and fetched their bottles, kneeling down on the floor in front of them as she inserted a rubber teat into each mouth. She had perfected this method of feeding once Jenny had accepted the bottle and it had cut down on the time she spent feeding them enormously. Bring me some peace . . .

She smiled at them now in spite of her misery as two pairs of round bright eyes surveyed her over the top of the bottles. They were so ridiculously alike and so good . . . She bit her lip hard as the smile turned shaky. She'd done the right thing, the only thing she could have done, and she hated him, she did.

George was waiting for her when she entered the small bedroom some time later, the weak glow from the oil lamp illuminating his stiff features into a devil's mask. He said nothing while she undressed and neither did she, but she suddenly felt painfully shy as she unlaced her boots and slid under the covers in her thin cotton shift. She found she was holding her breath and exhaled softly as she lay rigidly by his side, tensing when he moved to extinguish the lamp.

'Good night, Mary.' As he turned over and settled into the lumpy mattress with his back towards her, her mouth opened in a little 'o' of surprise in the darkness. She had expected – she caught hold of herself abruptly. Well, whatever she had expected this suited her just fine. If he wanted to carry this thing on and on, then so be it. One thing was for sure, she wouldn't be the one to lie awake half the night. She hadn't realized how the days and weeks of sleeping downstairs in a constant semi-doze, ever-conscious of the two little mites at her side had tired her, but now, as she began to relax, she felt as though she could sink through the mattress with the heaviness in her body.

Would she hear the bairns if they cried? It was her last coherent thought before the thick deep layers of sleep swamped her.

When she awoke to bright sunlight filtering in through the grimy panes in the window she didn't panic, not at first. Her mind was numb, dulled by the unaccustomed luxury of hours and hours of uninterrupted sleep and as she lay in the comforting warmth of the big bed her only thought was that she must be slipping, that window had never been dirty in all her years of marriage. What on earth had she been thinking of to let it get into that state?

And then she shot bolt upright, her heart pounding. *The twins*. The brightness of the sunlight told her it was late morning, and as she flung back the bedclothes and almost fell out of the bed she felt a sick raw fear claw at her throat. What had happened to them? They would have cried in the night, they must have, and if she hadn't heard them? Her blood ran cold. And George, where was he? He wouldn't do anything . . . No. He wouldn't, would he? Not his own grandchildren. He wouldn't hurt his own grandchildren in spite of what she had forced him to do for them. Please, God, she prayed frantically, don't have let him do anything . . .

She didn't stop to dress, stumbling out of the room in her shift and on to the tiny square of landing that overlooked the small room below. And then she stood quite still, her face unsmiling and her mind stunned.

It was Sunday. For some reason that thought was uppermost as she stared downwards. It was Sunday and she'd missed the early and the late mass. Father Michael would be round to see what was what . . .

As she continued to stare into the room beneath her George stirred slightly on the settle and opened his eyes, the babies that were tucked protectively in the crook of his arms and half across his broad chest stirring too as an empty bottle rolled off the bench and on to the floor below with a dull thud.

'Georgie?' Her whisper was soft but he heard it, his eyes meeting hers as he looked upwards.

'They're all right, just asleep.' He answered the question she hadn't asked with the ghost of a smile touching his mouth. 'How you've done this every night is beyond me, lass. Come and take one of 'em off me, they weigh a ton.' He winced as cramped muscles objected. 'I can't feel me right arm.'

She flew down the stairs and when she lifted David from George's chest the baby gave a tiny squawk of protest, minute fingers grabbing at the air.

'He's a lad and a half, that one,' George said quietly as she gazed at him over the infant's small bald head. 'No one'll put anythin' over on him, that's for sure.' He smiled at her, his eyes soft now in a way they hadn't been for a long time, and the love in his face was her undoing. As she sank to the floor, the tears and pain and misery exploding from her eyes and mouth in an unstoppable flood, she felt George take David from her and then he had pulled her into himself, cradling her in his arms while they sat on the floor rocking gently, the room alive with her gasping sobs. How long she cried she didn't know but with the release came a sort of peace, a quiet, still acceptance of that which couldn't be changed.

'All right, lass?' When at last she raised her head from George's chest to look into his clear blue eyes she knew a deep sense of shame. She had nearly lost him, she knew that now, and if she had she wouldn't have known how to continue. As fresh tears welled he pulled her close again, his voice gruff with emotion while he fought a personal battle of guilt and remorse that could never be voiced. 'That's enough now, me lass, that's enough.'

He pushed her from him slightly as he nodded towards their grandchildren lying fast asleep in the crib where he'd hastily placed them a few minutes before. 'The bairns'll want feeding soon and there's somethin' we have to do first.'

'There is?' She stared at him dazedly, the force of her recent emotion leaving her trembling and shaken, and then as he grinned and gestured towards the room upstairs with a flick of his head she eyed him in horror.

'Georgie! It's a Sunday morning.'

'Aye, lass, that it is.' He stood up slowly, pulling her with him. 'An' that being the case there's nought to stop us as far as I can see. The good Lord knew what He was about when He put the feelin' there and it's been a long time . . .' He had been walking to the stairs as he spoke and she followed silently, suddenly weak as her flesh responded to what was about to happen. In all the years they had been married their love-making had been carried out under cover of darkness and never, ever, spoken about beforehand.

This was all wrong, she ought to be feeling bad, dirty, but – but she didn't. The thought stretched her eyes wide open. She didn't. Dear God . . . She found herself talking to the Creator in her mind as she was wont to do in moments of deep joy or crisis. We're man and wife joined in your sight. Please, please, make everything all right again.

As she followed George into the bedroom he turned and shut the door carefully, his eyes hungry. 'You're me wife, Mary, and I want no other. I don't understand you, mind.' He cupped her face in his hard calloused hands. 'But you'll do for me, lass.'

She knew it was his way of saying he loved her and a deep thankfulness caught the breath tight in her chest, constricting her throat.

'We'll look after the little 'uns together, bring 'em up right like we did our own, but they've got to know their place, mind, and I won't have you spoilin' 'em.'

She looked deep into his face, her neck muscles tense and her throat so blocked she couldn't say the words she wanted, *needed* to say, to this man she had hurt so badly over the last few months. The main thing that had grieved him was unchanged, she knew that, but she hadn't meant to bring him so low, to humiliate him so badly. As God was her witness, she hadn't meant to.

'Georgie?' She wanted to set it right, to tell him that he could leave the steelworks and Frank Malley, that they would manage somehow, even if it meant one room somewhere, but before she could say more than his name he placed a finger on her lips and shook his head gently.

'We'll take it a day at a time, lass, what's done's done.' He moved her slowly on to the bed, raising the loose shift from her flesh, his eyes lingering on her small firm breasts and still slim waist as love for her flooded his loins. And he did love her, in spite of that other weakness. His desire for her sister had never touched the love he had for his wife, he told himself painfully, but the feeling he had for Martha was mesmerizing, fierce. The more so since he had realized she felt the same, although never a word had been spoken of it. And never would.

He stripped off his own clothes quickly and joined

her on the bed, turning her face, which she had shyly averted as he had undressed, to his as his other hand caressed the smooth skin of her upper arms. 'But there's one thing, lass, one thing I'll say now and not mention again,' he said quietly. 'When I find out who took our Jenny down I'll have me day with him. You understand me lass?'

She flung her arms round his neck, suddenly frightened by the darkness in his face.

'An' I will find out, Mary. I'll ask me questions till the day I die and beyond and if there's any justice then I'll get me time with that scum. A young lass, barely fifteen, a good girl –'

'I know, Georgie, I know –'

'And Frank.' He paused and looked her straight in the face. 'I want no truck with the man. He's a wrong 'un, Mary, I know it in here.' He thumped his chest hard. 'If I have to work with him, so be it, but I won't have him setting foot over this threshold an' I want your word on that. Your Martha, she's welcome and the bairns, but not him. Not now, not ever. You understand me, lass?'

She nodded quickly.

'Aw, Mary lass, I've missed you . . .' As he moved over her she shut her eyes, a sudden hotness flushing her cheeks scarlet. Here she was, a grandmother at that, and she was allowing her man to take her in broad daylight like any quay-side trollop. It wasn't right. But then when he moved in the old familiar rhythm she opened her body wide to receive him, clasping her arms tight round his back as she drew him deeper inside her.

Maybe it wasn't right but she didn't care. She loved him. She hadn't known how much until just this moment. She needed the comfort only he could give, and the way ahead was going to be hard with two young bairns to clothe and feed.

She was often to think, in the long grinding years that followed, that it was as well only Almighty God had the power to read the future, because her heart would have failed her if she had known how hard that road was going to be.

CHAPTER TWO

'Grandma. Davie says I can't go to the brook with them. Tell him, tell him it's not fair.'

As Mary turned from the stove to glance at Jenny standing in the doorway, big grey eyes bright with indignation, she felt her breath catch in her throat. There were times when her twelve-year-old grand-daughter looked so much like her mother that it twisted something deep inside until it became a physical pain. And yet it shouldn't be so, not really. When you took each delicate feature separately the resemblance shouldn't be so strong . . . But it was.

Her grand-daughter's hair was the same rich deep gold as her mother's, but whereas the older Jenny's had been straight and sleek like raw silk, her grand-daughter's was thick and curly with a mind of its own. And the eyes. Her Jenny's had been a startlingly vivid blue from the day she was born, but the young girl staring at her so angrily now had eyes of smoky grey that seemed to change colour with her moods. But the shape of the face was the same and the beauty was breathtaking.

'*Grandma* . . .' The high clear voice was full of righteous indignation. 'I can go, can't I? Tell him I can go.'

'Steve Baker is going and some of the older lads.' David joined his sister in the doorway, his small stocky body held tight and his grey eyes, so like his twin's, meeting his grandmother's with a message in them that was far beyond his years. 'They'll likely go skinny-dipping.'

Mary nodded slowly in answer to the words he

hadn't spoken. This grandson of hers was a comfort she couldn't have explained to anyone. Almost from the moment he could toddle he had taken charge of his sister with such a fierce, protective love that it was no wonder Jenny often rebelled against it. He had been born knowing the ways of the world and Mary was grateful for it. Aye, that she was, she thought silently as the small boy inclined his head back at her. She couldn't be with them in their play and she had seen how some of the older lads stared at Jenny, and her still just a bairn. There was hunger in those young male eyes, a craving that chilled her blood so she lay awake at night with a thick fear clawing at her insides. But Jenny was safe when she was with David. She knew that with no doubt whatsoever and it brought an ease to her mind.

'Of course you can't go, pet.' Mary indicated with a turn of her head for David to disappear, which he did with a relieved grin. 'There's the taties to peel yet, and your grand-dad'll want his dinner on the table when he comes in the night. He's going to the allotment after.'

'Aw, Gran . . .' The words were drawn out with a twist to the small rosebud mouth. 'Go on. I never have any fun, I don't. All the others are going, even Sarah Fisher and you know what her mam is like. Please . . .'

'I said no, Jenny.' She tried to soften the refusal with a smile but the small face in front of her was having none of it. Your grand-dad is hoping you'll go with him the night,' she added casually. 'He's callin' in at the big house on the way back.'

'An' I can go?' The diversion succeeded.

'We'll see. If those taties are done properly, mind.'

The big house was the magnificent Jacobean mansion dominating the small village of Holstone they had moved to eight years ago, the house itself and its vast grounds with the farm and allotments providing considerable employment for the Kent villagers, men and women.

During the Second World War much of the surrounding grassland had been ploughed up and requisitioned for an army camp, and part of the house turned into a military hospital, but the Maine family had come through that time relatively unscathed and still had a tight hold on the village, commanding utter and unswerving loyalty as befitted such an old and noble family.

Mary had no complaints, although there were plenty who had. Since Doctor Mead had recommended George for the job as head gardener, despite his only experience of working on the land being the large allotment he had had since a boy, which had seen them through many desperate times, her life had taken a turn for the better.

Doctor Mead was an old friend of the Maine family and they trusted his judgement. The previous gardener had been sacked for supplementing his income with produce acquired from the Maine gardens that he had sold in nearby towns, and they had been quite happy to give this newcomer a try after Doctor Mead had assured them George was as honest as the day was long. And George hadn't let the good doctor down. He had worked sixteen hours a day those first months, determined to prove himself even though he had two young lads to do the donkey work.

Doctor Mead was a good man. Mary's thoughts wandered on as she settled Jenny in a corner of the room on a small stool with the pile of potatoes on one side. Just after Martha had married Frank Malley and sent George half-mad in the process, he had provided this escape route. And an escape route wasn't too strong a term either and no mistake. Look at the way things were going in the towns and such like, Mary thought with a very real burst of indignation. Bairns scarcely older than David were full of this Teddy-boy rubbish, looking like something left over from the Edwardian era with their disgustingly tight drainpipe trousers and long drape jackets, although there was nothing Edwardian about their manners, more's the pity. It was all very well for the Prime Minister to tell the population that 'they had never had it so good' but when was the last time Harold Macmillan had tackled a bunch of yobs out on the rampage? Mary's thoughts opened her mouth. 'You know I don't like you being around some of those older lads, Jenny, now then.'

'Aw, Gran . . .' Jenny's voice did little to reassure her grandmother.

'And don't use that tone either.'

'Well, I can't do anythin'!' Jenny said militantly. 'You don't even like me goin' round to Sarah's to watch Juke Box Jury on her telly, and everyone watches that now, Gran, everyone, even Mrs Fisher.'

'That's as may be.' Mary sniffed her disapproval of the Fishers' lowering of standards. Getting one of those infernal television sets was bad enough, but to allow programmes into the home that gave approval to this wild rock 'n' roll rubbish was sheer criminal. How could that Mrs Fisher go on about juvenile delinquency and that dreadful Elvis Presley and the like, and then encourage her child to listen to noises (she refused to use the word music even in her mind) that were downright disgusting?

'But I don't want you watching such things. No good can come of it, no good at all. You mark my words, lass.'

Silence reigned in the room for a full minute.

'I didn't really want to go to the brook anyway, Gran . . .' Jenny's voice was verging on tears now.

'No?' Mary turned from the saucepan of bubbling jam she was stirring at the black-leaded range. 'And why is that, pray?'

''Cos our Davie is always on at me in front of the others, that's why. Rotten spoilsport.' A derisive sniff followed which Mary ignored. 'He don't like Steve Baker, he don't like anyone.'

When this loaded statement got no reaction from her grandmother Jenny moved from the stool with a quick flick of her slender body and came to stand closer to Mary, eyeing the remaining blackberries at the bottom of the stained enamel bowl hopefully before she spoke again. 'Davie says I'm more trouble than I'm worth and he wished I was a boy.' This time the young voice held hurt beneath the indignation that Mary recognized with a little pang. What now? The two always seemed to be at each other's throats these days.

'He don't mean anything, pet. You know that.'

'He does 'n all.' Jenny nodded her head vigorously, setting the blond curls bobbing. 'An' just 'cos he had a scrap with Steve and Micky Amos and they made his nose bleed he blamed me. It was his fault and I told him so. He shouldn't pick on 'em.'

'It's not like Davie to make trouble, Jenny,' Mary said slowly. 'And why with two lads?'

''Cos they were playin' with me and not him,' Jenny answered smartly. 'He always has to be first, he never lets me play.'

'What were you playing?' Mary asked carefully.

'Mothers and fathers.' Mary felt her stomach muscles jerk in protest but forced a non-committal nod as she kept her eyes on the sweet-smelling jam. 'There was me 'n Sarah Fisher. She was the nurse and Steve was the doctor and me 'n Micky were the mother and father. We used Sarah's doll for the baby but its head kept falling off, and then Micky tried to catch Sarah's cat and wrap that up but it bit him.'

'Uh, huh . . .' Don't say a word, Mary, she warned herself tightly. It might just be bairn's play, innocent like. But Steve Baker and Micky Amos were hardly bairns any more, her mind argued violently. They were both big lads for fifteen and when did lads of that age play mothers and fathers?

'Anyway, Steve said I had to put the doll up me dress as I was the mother and then he made me lie down so he could feel me tummy. He was the doctor, see . . .'

'I see.' The hot tide of fear and blinding anger that swept over Mary caused her to feel faint momentarily.

'An' then our Davie come flyin' into Sarah's garden and started shoutin' and carryin' on, and then her mam came out and made us all go in the back lane. Then Davie went for Steve, he went mad, Gran.' Jenny's voice held a touch of awe now. Steve Baker was three years older than her twin and big with it. 'Kickin' and bitin', and then Micky joined in until Sarah's mam came out again and threw a bucket of water over the lot of 'em.'

'When was this?' Mary asked quietly.

'Last Sunday.'

'Last Sunday?' Mary glanced at her grand-daughter sharply. 'When Davie fell into the beck? I take it that was a bit of fancy, then?'

'Davie said I hadn't to tell you, Gran.' Jenny fiddled with a lock of hair as she realized too late where all the confidences had led. 'He said it'd worry you, like, and that we weren't really fibbing 'cos he did fall in the beck . . . later.'

'Accidentally on purpose?' Mary asked grimly, but her heart wasn't in the admonishment. It had started already, then? Just like with her daughter. She had thought they would be safe here in Holstone, in the small village where everyone knew everyone else, but it wasn't to be. They might have a new queen on the throne, buses might have replaced the solid trams she had grown up with, and the country might be enjoying a time of affluence the like of which she had never expected to see in her lifetime, but men were still the same the world over, thinking of one thing and one thing only even before they were out of short pants. Bitterness was tart on her tongue.

'Are you cross, Gran?'

She ignored the question, taking the jam off the stove and placing it carefully on the large wooden table before turning to her grand-daughter as she kept her face blank by sheer willpower. 'Like I've said before, Davie was right to say you couldn't play with the older boys, Jenny, and you know it. You're growing into a big girl now and I've told you time and time again, haven't I? Haven't I?' she repeated softly when the child still didn't speak.

'Aw, Gran . . .' Jenny kicked the toe of her thick brown shoe against the black grate. 'It weren't my fault, honest. Me 'n Sarah were playin' and they come along the lane and started talkin' to us and then Sarah said they could come in. I didn't even want to play mothers and fathers anyway, it's a little kid's game. I'm a teenager next year –'

'An' you can stop that talk as well.' Mary's voice was so sharp it made Jenny jump. 'I've never heard the like, teenager indeed! There was never any talk of "teenagers" when I was a young girl. We were straight out of school and earning our money like our parents, I'm tellin' you, lass. This new-fangled expression of "teenagers" is givin' rise to most of the trouble that's about in my opinion, making out the young people are something special, givin' 'em ideas and encouraging 'em to go mad. I don't hold with it.' As Jenny went to flounce away Mary caught her arm, her expression softening when she looked into the young face. 'Listen, listen to me, lass.' She dropped to her haunches and took her grand-daughter's hands in her own. 'When you were playing, were the boys nice to you? Did they do anything you didn't like, that made you feel . . . funny?' Dear God, don't let anything have happened, she prayed silently. Let it be all right.

'No.' Jenny stared unwaveringly into her face. 'We'd only just started when our Davie come in and spoilt everythin'. Well, he *does*, Gran . . .' She turned away now in a little huff, feeling her grandmother's sympathies were all with her brother. 'It's not fair. All the other girls go down to the brook when it's hot to paddle, even Millie Halliday and she's only six. We don't go near the river where the boys go swimming except when it's time to go home.'

The naturalness of the answer combined with the unswerving conviction that she had been poorly treated convinced Mary all was well and she sank back on her heels with a soft sigh. It was time to have that talk with her grand-daughter she had been putting off for months. She could see now it wasn't fair on David to keep his sister ignorant of the facts of life any longer, but she'd wanted to keep her a bairn as long as possible, heaven knew that was difficult enough in this modern age in which they had been thrust seemingly all of a sudden. Still . . . She looked hard into the beautiful delicate face and sighed deeply again. Now was the time. There was no need to explain anything to David. His intuitive knowledge added to his sharp eyes and logical mind had seen to that. How could two bairns born of the same mother be so different? It was a question she had asked herself time and time again in the early days, when she had searched her grandchildren's faces for a clue to their paternity. But Jenny had taken her secret to the grave and in spite of George's exhaustive enquiries, there it remained.

But there was something about David at odd moments. A certain look in his eyes, a turn to his head, that reminded her of someone, but she couldn't think who. Not Jenny. Oh no. Now her grand-daughter was all her mother, but David . . .

Anyway, all that was by the by. She glanced across at Jenny sitting in sulky silence as she peeled the potatoes. 'Jenny, I've got something I want to talk to you about . . .'

Later that evening, when dinner was over and George had left for the allotments, Mary glanced at Jenny sitting quietly in the corner of the room, doodling aimlessly on her school exercise-book. 'You didn't want to go with your grand-dad, Jenny?' The child had been subdued since their chat but maybe that was no bad thing.

'No . . .' Jenny shook her head without looking up and David raised questioning eyes to his grandmother, who shook her head in silent warning.

'I'm goin' over to the farm in a while to get the eggs, OK?' David said to the room in general when a few more minutes had elapsed. Normally Jenny would have been at his side begging to come, but tonight her head remained bowed. 'Do you want to come, Jen?'

'Me?' Jenny raised her head slowly and looked straight at her grandmother. 'Can I?'

'Course you can, pet.' Mary smiled warmly. 'You'll be with Davie, won't you?'

Davie, Davie, Davie . . . Suddenly the resentment that had been growing all evening was almost too much and she lowered her head again quickly. Her brother wasn't the be-all and end-all, whatever her gran said, and she wasn't going to let him boss her around, she *wasn't*. This . . . thing that was going to happen to her which meant she could have babies, well, it hadn't happened yet, had it? And anyway she saw lots of the bigger girls out on their own. She was fed up with everyone, she was. And she liked Steve Baker. He made her laugh and he was always nice to her. Not like their Davie.

'Come on, then.' When she looked up David was waiting for her in the doorway, his face impatient. 'If you get a move on, we might be able to see the chicks. You'd like that, wouldn't you?'

She stared hard at her brother as she joined him outside. She wasn't a baby. Why did he always have to treat her like a baby? She wouldn't be surprised if he expected her to listen to Uncle Mac and *The Children's Hour* on the radio, still. 'Are you sitting comfortably? . . . Then we'll begin,' she muttered angrily.

'What?' David stared at her in surprise. 'What are you babbling on about now?'

'You're only a few minutes older'n me,' she said waspishly as they tramped down the village street of half-timbered cottages that backed on to the gently undulating Kent countryside. 'There's no need for you to be so bossy all the time.'

'I'm not bossy.' David answered automatically. He was used to this conversation, having had it more times than he could remember. 'Just 'cos Gran wouldn't let you go to the brook you're sulkin', aren't you?'

'No . . .' As they turned into a lane, its verges starred with daisies and buttercups, Jenny glared at him furiously. 'No, I'm not. It's just that –'

'Come on, I'll race you to Hawthorn Wood.' Her brother cut the imminent quarrel short by diving through a hole in the hedgeside and into the hop field on the other side, causing a host of rooks in the trees overhead to protest with harsh deep caws as he raced off towards the wood in the distance as fast as his stocky but powerful young legs could carry him.

'That's not fair! Davie, it's not fair, you've had a head start!' Jenny forgot her grievances for a few minutes as she concentrated on catching him up, her longer legs fairly flying over the uneven ground and her hair a blaze of gold in the last of the dying sun. She reached the wood just as David did and they both sank laughing on to the rough bracken amid a cluster of wood-betony, the purple-headed flowers bright between the dark shiny leaves.

They lay there panting for some minutes before David heaved himself up and brushed down his khaki shorts. 'Come on, lazy-bones.' He glanced down at his sister sprawled at his feet. 'I ain't got all day.'

The authoritative cocky tone immediately set Jenny's hackles rising. 'In a minute.' She rolled over on to her stomach, resting her head on her arms, knowing the pose would inflame his quick temper. 'I'm tired.'

'Awkward more like.' He waited a few more seconds and then poked her with the toe of his boot. '*Come on*, Jen, I'm tellin' you. It'll be gettin' dark soon and you know Gran don't like . . . us out in the dark.' The brief hesitation was not lost on her and she knew he had been about to say 'you' before he changed it to 'us'.

''Course it won't.' She raised her head to stare into his irritable frowning face. It was all right for him, wasn't it? He didn't have to be in before it was dark and always say where he was going and who with. If it wasn't her gran spoilin' her fun, it was Davie, but more often Davie. If it had been left to him, she wouldn't have any friends. She knew they all laughed at her, as it was because of his control over what she could do and not do. It just wasn't *fair* . . .

'Anyway, why can't I wait here?' she asked moodily. 'It's only another five minutes to the farm, it won't take you long to get back. I want to stay here.' She knew she was being difficult but the combination of her grandmother's talk and the knowledge of how her impending womanhood would limit even the little freedom she got now, added to David's dogged and inflexible authority over her, which her grandmother endorsed with such fervency, had brought all her rebellious tendencies to the surface.

'Don't be so stupid.' David glared at her now, his body tense. 'You know Gran wouldn't like it.'

'Oh, Gran . . .' Jenny shrugged provokingly. 'Who's gran's little blue-eyed boy, then? Anyway, she won't know, will she? Unless you go and blab.'

'Get up, Jen.' The urge to haul her to her feet and give her a good shake for defying him was strong but he knew he couldn't drag her the whole of the way. 'I didn't beg you to come, did I? You knew how far it is and you said you wanted to come.'

'Well, I've changed me mind.' It was suddenly vitally important to make some sort of stand although if anyone had told her she was fighting against being smothered, swallowed whole by her twin's compulsive love for her, she wouldn't have believed them. 'You go.'

'Jen . . .'

'I'm not coming.'

'I'll belt you one.'

'You just try 'n all.'

When he swore, softly and succinctly with an intensity that was strange in such a young boy, she raised superior disapproving eyebrows and whistled quietly through her teeth in an effort not to show how his intimidation was affecting her. 'I'm telling grand-dad. You know what he said the last time you swore.'

'You –' Words seemed to fail him as he glared down at her, his eyes fiery. 'Well, stay here, then, see if I care. I'm fed up with you anyway.'

'An' I'm fed up with you.'

'You just dare move, Jen, and I'll kill you.' So saying he stumped off along the path that skirted the wood and led to the farm, his back straight and furious and his head high with injured pride.

She raised herself slightly and watched him go. She shouldn't have done it. For a moment as she stared at her brother's stiff back the urge to run and catch up with him was paramount. He'd be mad with her for days now and make her suffer as only he could, and she'd certainly catch it from her gran when she got in. She always took Davie's side without fail. The thought quelled her sympathy for David at the position she had put him in and sent her lying on the grass again as she gazed up into the branches of the silver birch overhead. He had to make a fuss about everything, always make her do what he wanted. She was only going to wait here for him. That wasn't a crime, was it?

The September day had been one of intense heat with deep-blue skies and no breeze, and now the drone of lazy insects was pleasant as she lay in the sheltered copse. When a minute or two later she heard the snap of a twig underfoot she felt a moment's panic before smiling to herself slowly. Davie had come back. Of course, she might have known he would.

'Davie?' When her brother didn't appear immediately she felt a little thud in her chest before calling more urgently. 'Davie? Aw, don't play games. I'm sorry, I'll come now.' She sat up quickly. 'Come on, Davie –'

'Hallo, Jenny.' As Steve Baker stepped out from behind a tree she knew a moment's blinding relief. For a minute she'd begun to think – 'What you callin' for Davie for?'

She shrugged slowly. 'I'm not really. I heard someone and I thought it was him. He's gone to get some eggs from the farm.'

'I know.' Steve laughed softly at her surprised face and then came and threw himself down on the bracken beside her. 'I watched him go. I followed you from home.'

'Did you?' She stared at him in bewilderment. He was close, very close, so close she could see the point where his fair spiky eyelashes grew out from his eyelids and the faint pock-marks on his cheeks left from the chicken-pox epidemic the year before. 'Why?'

'No reason.' He smiled again but she began to feel faintly uneasy. 'I like to look at you, that's all. I look at you all the time, but Davie doesn't like me, does he?'

'I dunno.' She shrugged again and dropped her eyes to her knees as she clasped her arms round them and lowered her chin to rest on their bony shelf.

'Yes you do.' The older boy's voice was soft and thick. 'He doesn't like me 'cos I like you. He doesn't like any of the lads who like you. Do *you* like me, Jenny?'

''Course I do.' She wanted to edge away a bit but with all this talk of liking she didn't want to offend him, so she sat where she was and let her thick fall of hair hide her face from his gaze. And he was right about one thing, she thought nervously. Davie didn't like him.

'Good.' He stood up suddenly and offered her his hand as he stood looking down at her, his face flushed and his eyes hooded. 'Come for a walk in the woods, then. I can show you a badger's hole if you like but it's a secret. Come on quick before Davie comes back.'

'I can't.' She stood up quickly, ignoring his proffered hand and looked the way David had gone. 'I've got to wait for Davie.'

'Who says?' Steve's voice was slightly belligerent now.

'He said –'

'*He* said, *he* said.' The mockery was light but she sensed something else, something she didn't like, and as her face straightened his attitude underwent an immediate change. 'Aw, don't get mad, Jenny.' His voice was wheedling now. 'I just wanted to show you the badger's hole, that's all. You'll be all right with me, honest. You don't have to do everything Davie says, do you?'

'No.' She gave him a long straight look before sitting down on an old tree trunk facing the path to the farm. 'But I want to wait here.'

'All right, all right.' He walked a few steps and glanced that way before moving to sit by her side, his thigh pressing against hers. 'You're very pretty.' There was that thickness in his voice again that made her uneasy. 'I think you're the prettiest girl in the village.'

'Sarah Fisher's got longer hair than me.' She didn't look up as she spoke. Suddenly his nearness was threatening, although he hadn't said or done anything to frighten her. She couldn't quite understand what was wrong, but she knew all was not well.

'She's nothing.' There was silence for a moment and then he spoke again, his voice still soft but with a little tremor in it that made her feel funny. 'You ever kissed anyone before, Jenny?'

'Kissed anyone?' She looked at him in surprise. Well, of course she'd kissed someone. Her grandma, her grand-dad, their Davie . . .

'A lad. You ever kissed a lad?' His tongue came out and wet his lips and the panic returned, stronger this time.

'I think I oughta go and meet Davie now.' As she made to rise he put out an arm and stopped her, squirming round so he forced her off the log and on to the ground, his torso the length of hers as he pressed her into the grass. 'Don't –'

'Shut up.' She tried to struggle but his mouth fastened on hers, moist and warm, and it was only when she kicked hard with her legs that he released her with a little yelp of pain, sitting up quickly and running a hand through his carefully styled ginger hair with its Teddy boy's quiff as he kept his eyes tight on her. 'Don't yell, Jenny, you'll like it. I won't hurt you –'

'You shouldn't have done that.' She rubbed her hand hard across her mouth as she sprang to her feet with a swiftness that caught him by surprise, her stomach churning. This wasn't right, she knew it wasn't right and when he'd held her, just for those few seconds, something hard in his trousers had pressed against her thigh. Her eyes followed her thoughts and she saw the mound was still there, fierce and stiff. Her grandmother's words flew into her mind and in the same instant she turned and ran, flying along the path towards the farm with panic screaming in her ears and her breath coming in harsh sobbing pants.

She heard him call her name once, but didn't stop or turn round and as she turned a corner in the path and saw David's small solid shape in the distance she knew such a relief that for a moment she thought she was going to wet her knickers.

'Jenny?' David had raised a casual hand at first but now she saw him drop the basket and begin to run as he saw the look on her face. 'Jenny?' Just before she reached him she stumbled and fell but he caught her before she hit the ground, the momentum of her body sending them both to their knees. 'What's the matter?' As she burst into a storm of weeping he shook her, his face dark with fright. 'Jenny! What's the matter?'

It took her a few minutes to gain control but in that time she knew she couldn't tell her brother or anyone else about what had happened. Davie would go for Steve, he'd done it before, and the older boy was so much bigger and heavier than him, and so was Micky Amos and the rest of Steve's cronies. She shut her eyes tightly. And it must have been her fault, for Steve to do what he did. He must have thought she wanted him to. A tear squeezed under her eyelashes. What had she said or done to make him think she wanted him to kiss her? And with his mouth wide open and his tongue sending spittle into the back of her throat? She nearly retched at the memory but controlled the impulse just in time.

'Jenny?' As David shook her again she opened her eyes slowly and pulled away from him, rubbing her wet nose with the back of her hand. 'What happened?'

'I got scared by meself.' She took a corner of her floral-print dress and dried her face with it as she sat huddled on the ground. 'I kept hearing things.'

'What things?' David was looking at her through narrowed eyes and as his gaze flickered towards the wood she knew he had to believe her. There would be all sorts of trouble if he didn't.

'I dunno.' She sniffed again and rose shakily to her feet, managing a small smile now the danger was past. 'Rustlings and things. I kept remembering that story Grand-dad told us about the werewolf, when it jumped on that man in the woods and ripped him all to pieces.'

'Oh, for goodness sake, Jen . . .' As David's face relaxed she breathed out silently. 'You're so stupid. That was just a story for bairns, you know it was. If I've broke them eggs because of you . . .'

When they retrieved the basket six of the twelve eggs were broken and that fact kept David's mind occupied all the way home.

'Davie?' A harvest moon was already shining in the dusky sky as they walked along the village street and although she wanted to keep peering over her shoulder, her flesh creeping as she sensed eyes watching her in the looming shadows, she kept her eyes straight ahead and her face blank. 'What are you going to tell Gran?'

As her brother stopped dead and turned to look at her, his eyes suddenly suspicious again, she continued hastily before he could speak. 'She'll go for you if you say you left me and I'll get it 'n all. Can't we say I was carrying the eggs and I fell over? Eh?' She forced a grin to her face which she hoped was natural. 'An' Grand-dad will be in trouble, too. You know what she said the last time he told us one of his stories and I daren't go to the bottom of the garden to the lav by meself.'

'Yeh . . .' David's face relaxed again as she reminded him of her very real fear on that occasion. 'Well, this is all your fault anyway, so it won't hurt you to take the blame for once. I told you you should've come with me, didn't I?'

'I know.' The meekness was suspect, and as she saw David's eyes flash to her face she forced a note of defiance back into her voice. 'But you shouldn't go on at me all the time.'

'Don't start on that.'

When they reached the cottage door she pushed ahead of David and started on the explanations as soon as she was past the threshold, but later that night, as she lay on the small narrow bed to one side of the big oak chest that separated David's space from hers and gave a certain degree of privacy, she re-lived the scene in the woods over and over in her mind until her head was spinning.

That was how babies were made, then. That . . . thing was pushed up inside the woman and later a baby was born. But she wasn't a woman and Steve Baker wasn't a man, so he shouldn't have done it. Tried to make her – She shut her eyes tight but the feeling that she was dirty, filthy, wouldn't go away. She wanted to wash herself from head to foot, especially her inner thigh where she had felt the contact, but it wasn't bath night till Friday and if she asked her grandma to pull out the old zinc bath they used in front of the range before that, she'd want to know why. How could anyone *like* that happening? She recalled the feeling of the avaricious wet mouth on hers and shuddered as her stomach turned. He was horrible, that Steve Baker, and she had thought she liked him.

It took her a long time to get to sleep that night, and the next, but gradually, over a period of weeks and months, the incident began to fade from her mind.

She was careful to stay with the other girls now, or David, and when she saw Steve Baker and his cronies she ignored them as far as she could. She knew Steve didn't like it. More than once he had tried to get her alone but her fear made her too clever for him, and with the onset of winter, the worst for some years, the opportunity to play out became less and less frequent, and for this she was thankful.

Chapter Three

The spring of 1960 saw several changes in Jenny's life but none more important, at least as far as she was concerned, than the blossoming into womanhood her grandmother had spoken about, which occurred just after her thirteenth birthday. During the preceding months her breasts had grown, her waist narrowed, and her body filled out in such a way that she looked far older than her thirteen years, a fact that caused her grandmother considerable anxiety. Mary looked at her now as she twisted and turned in front of the old mirror on the wardrobe door, her face animated with pleasure over her new dress.

'Here, let me do that, lass.' She took the two ends of the sash in her hands, tying it carefully round the slender waist, even as she regretted her impulsiveness in making the frock in the first place. She should have chosen a more subdued style, something a little less well-fitting, she thought worriedly as she glanced again at her grand-daughter in the pure-white dress of fine bleached cotton, the little border of blue cornflowers standing out in vivid contrast to the snowy white. But no, the lass had had to have a new dress for the Sunday-school picnic. It only happened once a year and everyone wore their best togs. 'There.'

Jenny pirouetted in front of the cloudy glass again, satisfied with what her eyes told her. She wished she'd had a new pair of shoes, too, instead of her old brown ones. She glanced down at her small feet in the shapeless leather and then felt immediately guilty. Oh, what was she thinking, she was an ungrateful one. Here was her grandma having made her the best dress in the world and she was moaning about her shoes. 'It's lovely, Grandma, absolutely lovely.' She spun round and gave her grandmother a quick hug before turning to look in the glass again. 'Do I have to wear me cardy with it?'

'Not if you don't want to, love.' Mary looked out of the window at the blazing sun set high in a sky of transparent blue. 'It looks like the weather'll hold a day or so more yet.'

The April of that year had been a tempestuous month but May had been gentler and the last few days had seen a heatwave that had melted the Tarmacked roads and played havoc with George's allotment. Mary followed Jenny out of the bedroom now to where her husband was sitting, waiting for them with David by his side. As she caught her grandson's eye, and noticed his narrowed glance at Jenny's new dress, she felt a moment's piercing guilt at what she had revealed to him a few days before. But it had been necessary, *necessary*, she told herself fiercely, as she busied herself fixing the big straw hat on top of her head. She had seen the way the lads were looking at her Jenny, even with David always at her side, and you couldn't be too careful . . . But perhaps she shouldn't have been so brutal in the telling?

'Davie, I want a word with you while we're by ourselves, lad.' She had taken the opportunity, while Jenny was with George at the allotment watering the wilting vegetables, to get David on his own. She knew her husband disapproved of the defensive, protective love she had towards young Jenny, he even called it an obsession at times, and still more he blamed her for the way she had purposely indoctrinated their grandson into the same way of thinking. But he didn't *know*, he didn't understand. He still looked on their grand-daughter as a child, a bairn, but he was wrong. She was a woman now, and even in this quiet little back-water where she had thought Jenny would be safe from the influence of the more modern towns, she had seen the way the boys ogled her.

'You're old enough now to be told the truth, lad.' She had sat him down next to her and his face, wide-eyed and slightly frightened, had almost caused her to hold her tongue, almost . . . 'Your mam . . .' She had paused, but there was no nice way to tell it. 'She wasn't married when she had you and Jenny.'

'Wasn't married?' He had echoed her words without understanding them. 'I know. Me dad had died, hadn't he? You said –'

'I know what we said, Davie.' Her tone was too sharp and she tried to moderate it before she spoke again. 'But it wasn't like we told you, not some of it. The thing is, we never knew who took your mam down, she wouldn't say, but the result of it was you and our Jenny. She was just a young lass when it happened, Davie, barely fifteen, and I'd always had it in my mind that she was willing, but the more I've thought about it over the years the more I think I was wrong. There was a time, before we found out about her trouble, when she wouldn't leave the house for weeks on end. Terrified, she was.'

'You think she was forced?' His face had a sickly grey to it now but there was something in the depths of the dark-grey eyes that stopped Mary reaching out a comforting hand to him. Something hot and explosive.

'I do, lad, I do. She wasn't a bad lass, and I think she was more sinned against than sinful, but she was beautiful, Davie, very beautiful. You know what I'm sayin'?'

'Like Jenny,' he said flatly.

'Aye, lad, like Jenny.'

'Did you try and find out who –' He stopped and breathed deeply before speaking again. 'Who did it?'

'Your grand-dad didn't leave a stone unturned, but it was no good.' She had moved to touch his hand, then, but he recoiled from her as though from a blow, his face white.

'Who knows?'

'Who knows?' She stared at him puzzled.

'About me and Jen, about our mam? Does Steve Baker and all that lot?'

'I don't know, lad.' She shook her head slowly. 'We told the village the same story we told you and Jenny, that your dad died afore you were born and your mam in having you. But people draw their own conclusions –'

'They know.' He looked sick. 'An' what they don't know they've made up.'

'You can't stop people talking, lad.' She wished to high heaven she hadn't started this, but it was too late now and, anyway, he'd have had to know sometime. Already he'd been asking more and more about his dad. He wasn't like their Jenny, he didn't accept things easy. Perhaps they shouldn't have made up the story in the first place, but it had seemed the right thing to do at the time.

'There are some men, lads too, who will use a girl for their own relief and then skitter off without a thought for the trouble they leave behind. You know what I'm saying? I don't want history to repeat itself, Davie, and your sister is a fine-looking lass and getting better. I know you watch out for her, it's eased my heart many a time, lad. But she's older now and they might think they've got more of a chance because she's got no mam and dad to watch her.'

'You mean because we're bastards –'

'No, Davie!' She was shocked at the hardness of her grandson's face. He didn't look like a boy any more, his mouth stiff and square as he stared into her eyes with a venomous rage behind the narrowed gaze that would have been chilling enough in a man, but from a lad of thirteen . . . 'That's not what I meant at all.'

'But it's what they think.' His lips drew back from his teeth in something resembling a snarl. 'I know 'em. I've seen 'em looking at Jenny as though they could eat her alive.'

'Well, that's why you'll have to be there for her, even protecting her from herself if it's necessary. You know what I mean?'

He nodded slowly. 'I know what you mean. Oh yes, I know what you mean all right.' And, God forgive her, she had been glad at the way he had spoken in spite of its menacing coldness, which had sent a chill running right through her. He was a barrier between her Jenny and the rest of the world, and that was exactly how she wanted it.

'First of June tomorrow.' Sarah Fisher had oohed and ahed over her new dress but Jenny had known she was put out, and the thought gave her a guilty dart of pleasure. Sarah was the only child in her family in a community where the norm was at least five or six, and with her dad being the head groom at the big house her friend had new clothes nearly every week. And shop-bought, too, she thought enviously. She was spoilt rotten, her grandma was always saying it, but all the spoiling in the world couldn't get rid of Sarah's sallow spotty skin and pug nose, and Jenny always felt sorry for her. The new dress she had on today, with its flounces of ruched lace and velvet-trimmed bows, sat on the plump body like a sack, and Jenny's heart had sunk when she saw it. She just hoped Steve Baker and that lot didn't take the mickey out of Sarah like they always did, in such a way that Sarah thought they were being nice, which always made it so much worse. She cringed inside when they did that. They were mean, the lot of them.

'My mum says we're in for a hot summer this year with it being so nice this early,' Sarah continued in her high mincing voice, which was another thing the boys made fun of. 'It'll be nice, won't it? Steve Baker says he's getting his uncle's Lambretta when he gets a car but my mum says he won't. She says he's too young and it'd drive his mum mad with worry. What do you think?'

Jenny shrugged without replying as she walked by Sarah's side in the big crowd making for the manor house. The Maine family had the Sunday-school picnic in their grounds every year, even when the war had been going on, so she understood. Charles Maine had said that he had no intention of letting a jumped-up little dictator like Hitler alter an Englishman's tradition. She smiled to herself at the thought. She'd only seen the illustrious head of the Maine family once but she could imagine him saying that. He looked, and sounded, imposing.

'Hallo, Jenny.' Steve's voice just behind her made her stumble but she righted herself quickly and replied without turning her head.

'Hallo.'

'New dress?'

Sarah turned round and smiled at him as Jenny had known she would. She'd had a crush on Steve since she was a toddler. 'Mine's a new dress too, Steve.'

'Very pretty.' Jenny heard Micky Amos snigger to

the right of her and the urge to turn round and hit him full across the face burnt hotly for a moment, before she forced it to the back of her mind. As long as Sarah didn't see that they were teasing her it didn't matter, did it? And they weren't worth bothering about. Not one of them.

'Don't you think Sarah's dress is pretty, Micky?' Steve drawled lazily, drawing level with Jenny and looking down at her as she kept her eyes straight ahead.

'Yeh . . .' Another snigger followed.

'My mum got it in London, when she went up with my dad to visit the Planetarium,' Sarah continued importantly, oblivious to the undercurrents swirling about her. 'That's an astronomical exhibition, you know,' she added loudly, it being a point of some consequence that it was only her parents in the whole of the village who had reached such giddy heights.

'Is that so? . . .' Steve's voice assumed an exaggerated air of innocence that brought Sarah's eyes shooting to his face as the laughter behind her penetrated even her thick skin. 'Well, well, you learn something every day, don't you, lads . . .'

'Yes, well . . .' The look in Sarah's eyes as Jenny glanced swiftly her way reminded her of a little puppy that had been kicked, hard, and she could have killed Steve Baker for putting that whipped bewilderment on her friend's plump face. 'My mum said it was lovely.'

'Did she?' Steve asked gravely. 'Well, it must have been, then, mustn't it, lads, if Sarah's mum said so.'

'Leave her alone!' Jenny turned on him so savagely that she saw him actually start before he controlled the gesture. 'Go and annoy someone else. You lot want to grow up, you're pathetic. At least Sarah's mam has been to London, which is more than you have.'

'Is that so?' Steve stared at her for a long hard moment, his face perfectly straight now as his pale blue eyes took in every detail of her angry face before moving to the cloud of golden blond hair about her shoulders.

'Yes, it is.' She held his glance with a defiance she was far from feeling, as his eyes seemed to lick around her face, but when he signalled to his cronies with a tight jerk of his head and disappeared into the crowd she rubbed her mouth harshly as though she would wipe away every trace of his glance from her skin.

'He's sixteen, now.' Sarah's voice was wistful and for a moment Jenny could have shaken her, in view of all that had gone on. 'I reckon he looks a bit like Tommy Steele, don't you?'

'Not really.' Jenny had no intention of wasting the day talking about Steve Baker and changed the subject abruptly. 'I wonder what we'll have to eat this year. Do you remember those big hams and sides of beef last year? I couldn't believe how much I ate. I had a job to walk home after the dance, even with our Davie helping me.'

'I know.' Sarah giggled, Steve forgotten for a moment as she considered her other favourite topic, food. 'I split my dress, do you remember? And my mum was so mad 'cos she'd got it special from that posh shop.'

'That was when you lifted your arm when we were doing the rock 'n' roll.' Jenny giggled too as she recalled the ensuing rumpus when Sarah's dress split from arm-hole to waist.

'An' Steve and Micky and the lads did that skiffle number with their mums' washboards and the tea-chest double-bass, and the vicar said it was devil's music.' Sarah clutched hold of Jenny in her mirth but Jenny's laughter was forced. Since that day in the woods any mention of Steve's name caused her to tense and she remembered how he had watched her as he had played, showing off to the villagers, his hair, with its Teddy-boy flick, falling over one eye and his mouth wet and smiling. She must have been mad to think she liked him. 'I think they thought they were Buddy Holly or the next Billy Fury,' Sarah continued, giggling again. 'But they were good. Don't you think so?'

'They were all right.' Jenny caught hold of her friend's hand and pulled her along more quickly. 'Come on, I want to sit near me grandma while we eat. Last year we got stuck next to old Mrs Betts and her false teeth kept slippin'.'

The two girls sat with Mary and George to eat at the long trestle tables covered by oil cloths that had been placed in rows along the bottom field, where daisies and buttercups provided a carpet of white and gold, but straight after the meal joined the other girls, who were wandering about in twos and threes watching the boys who were playing a game of cricket.

'Jenny, look, there's Mr Lawrence.' Sarah's whisper was loud enough to wake the dead, and as Jenny glanced the way her friend was pointing the tall slim man some way in front of them turned round, his thick black brows raised enquiringly.

'Oh, Sarah, he heard you.' Jenny dropped her eyes immediately but not before she'd gained an impression of large, velvet brown eyes in a long thin face that was undeniably handsome. She'd seen the youngest son of the Maine family once or twice before when she was younger, but he had been away touring in Europe, if village gossip was to be believed, and she wouldn't have recognized him. The boy had gone, to be replaced by the man, and the man was almost a carbon copy of his father, tall and broad-shouldered, with the slightly superior expression that spoke of public schooling and unlimited wealth.

'So what if he heard me?' Sarah giggled noisily. 'The cat can look at the cream, can't it?'

'Come on, you, let's go for a walk before you say anythin' else.' She hadn't glanced Lawrence Maine's way again but was conscious of him watching her as she took Sarah's hand and almost dragged her in the opposite direction, and her cheeks were hot. Fancy Sarah embarrassing them like that, and with Lawrence Maine, of all people!' The Maine family had always seemed something apart from normal life, enchanted beings who weren't plagued by the ordinary trials and tribulations of the daily grind and who existed in a state of permanent blessedness. She knew it was silly. As she had grown she had accepted they were flesh and blood like everyone else, but still something of that feeling remained, and now all she wanted to do was to put as much space between her and Lawrence Maine as she could.

'He's only been back home a week or two, so my mum says,' Sarah puffed at Jenny's side, her round face perspiring under the cloudless summer sky. 'My dad thinks the sun shines out of his behind 'cos he loves horses, he's horse-mad. His fiancée is too, though, so that's all right. He's engaged to be married to a lord's daughter or somethin'.'

'Is he?' Jenny wasn't really listening. The sun was warm on her face, she had on a new dress that she knew she looked bonny in and there was going to be the dance later that she'd looked forward to for months in the old disused granary that had been decked out with streamers and paper chains. She was suddenly filled with a sense of joy, of well-being, that she hadn't felt since that day in the woods, and she slipped her arm in Sarah's as they reached the bottom of the field and began to wander along the river bank a little way, taking care to avoid the boggy ground at the side of the path.

She shouldn't really be this far from the others. She remembered her promise to Davie as the meal had finished and she'd announced her intention to join the other girls. 'You'n Sarah stay close, mind,' he'd warned quietly when she'd risen from her seat.

'Why?' She couldn't help it, but her chin had raised itself immediately as she'd felt the old antagonism flare at his high-handedness.

''Cos some of the lads sneaked in some home-made cider on the quiet,' he said softly, glancing over towards the sound of raucous laughter in the distance, trying to be big shots with their Elvis haircuts and flick knives.'

'That's nothing to do with me.' The proprietorial manner still got under her skin but as she saw his eyes darken and his mouth tense she reached out a conciliatory hand. She didn't want a row, not today, and she did love him, but why did he always have to spoil her fun? 'I'll be with Sarah,' she placated quickly, 'and all the others, all right?'

'Just make sure you are.' He didn't smile when she stuck out her tongue at him, and that hard look she hated was on his face as she and Sarah had made their escape.

'Let's sit down here, Sarah.' Some of the children were paddling in the shallows a little way off as they sat down on an old dry log in the shade of a weeping willow, and watched the sparkling ripples on the water. 'It's so hot . . .'

'At least you still look nice when you're hot,' Sarah

said grudgingly as she glanced at Jenny's clear translucent skin, which was already turning honey-brown in the warmth of the last few days. 'I just go red and shiny –'

'Well, an' what have we got here?' The sound of Steve's voice just behind them made both girls start, Sarah almost disappearing backwards as her legs shot up in the air to reveal a cloud of lace petticoats.

'Steve . . .' Sarah sounded relieved. 'You made us jump.'

As Micky Amos and the rest of Steve's cronies appeared from the small copse of trees to their right Jenny looked straight at Steve and she knew, she just knew, he had followed them, waiting for his chance to get her alone like a big patient spider. But she wasn't alone, was she? She took hold of Sarah's hand and pulled her up. 'Come on, we're goin' back.'

'Not before I have a little talk with you.' Steve motioned with his hand and the others darted to her left, blocking their path. 'No one can ever get near you with that brother of yours acting the way he does. Me and the boys have just about had a bellyfull of him, haven't we, lads?'

As the others murmured their agreement, the inevitable snigger coming from Micky Amos's direction, Jenny said nothing. If she didn't antagonize him, they might just let her go.

'An' like I said, I want to ask you somethin'.'

'Ask, then.' She tried to sound defiant but she was frightened, badly frightened, the more so as she noticed the children had disappeared and there was only Sarah between her and the look in Steve's eyes.

'Not here.' He glanced at the other boys and nodded towards the sound of voices in the distance coming from the field adjoining the house. 'Take Sarah up there, and me 'n Jenny'll come in a minute.'

Micky Amos sniggered again and that sound, more than anything else, set Jenny's heart thudding.

'Sarah *and* me are goin'.' She eyed him coldly. 'Aren't we, Sarah?' She nudged her friend hard in the ribs.

'You savin' me a dance tonight, then, Sarah? Been brushing up on your rock 'n' roll, eh?' As Steve turned his attention to her friend, Sarah blushed bright red with pleasure. 'You are comin', aren't you?'

''Course I am.' Sarah wriggled her plump body in a little giggle, her tone coy.

'Good.' He smiled slowly. 'An' you don't mind if I have a little chat with Jenny for a minute, do you? We've got somethin' that needs sortin' out.'

'Well . . .' Sarah glanced at Jenny dubiously. 'If she don't want –'

'I don't.' Jenny stared straight into Steve's face. 'I'm goin' back with Sarah.'

'Go on, Sarah, go with the others.' Steve's voice was cool now and Sarah's face straightened with disappointment at the tone. 'An' I'll catch you up in a minute, have a chat about the dance, eh? That's if you want to go with me?' He stared unblinkingly at the other girl as he laid out the blatant ultimatum, and after a long moment of staring back at him Sarah moved away without a word.

'Sarah.' As her friend joined the others without looking back, Micky Amos winked and grinned at Steve, and in the same instant that Jenny tried to avoid him Steve took her arms in a firm grip, his voice low.

'I just want to talk with you a minute, Jenny, don't

be stupid now,' he said thickly as his eyes fastened on her mouth.

'Well, I don't want to talk to you,' she hissed back angrily. 'And let go of me.'

She saw the others reach the bottom of the field in the distance and then disappear from sight as they turned from the path, and the sudden realization that she was in real danger made her lash out at Steve, who was still holding her arms in a bruising grip. 'I said, let go of me, what do you think you're doing!'

'Jenny –'

'I'll scream, I mean it.' As she opened her mouth to prove she meant what she said he put his hand over her face at the same time as twisting her body round so her back was against the wall of his chest. In the next instant he had picked her up bodily, his thick sinewy arms like bands of steel across her face and round her waist, and was carrying her towards the small copse as though she weighed no more than a child. His hand was across her nose as well as her mouth, and as she struggled for breath, desperately trying to draw air into labouring lungs, she felt the world begin to spin and dive and then everything went black.

Chapter Four

She came to to the feel of brutal fingers fumbling with the tiny buttons on the front of her bodice before the petticoat top was torn impatiently aside to reveal her breasts, and the knowledge that she was half-undressed sent a burst of adrenalin surging through her inert frame. 'No!' As she lashed out with her fists Steve fell on her from his kneeling position at her side, his hand clamping across her mouth and his voice thick and excited.

'This is your fault, it's all your fault.' His hot breath stank of cider, warm and sticky. 'I just wanted you to be nice to me that day in the woods, let me talk to you and make you understand how I feel, but you won't let me get near you, will you? That brother of yours always watchin', watchin' . . .'

As he spoke his other hand had moved up under the torn skirt of her petticoat to the mound between her legs where his fingers probed painfully. She couldn't scream, the weight of his body on hers was grinding her into the rough ground and his hand on her mouth was like a vice.

'I can't think about anythin' else but how you'd feel, what I want to do to you, but you walk by with your head in the air, and what are you! What are you!' Saliva was spraying from his mouth and his eyes were crazed, filled with an exultant feverish elation she had never seen before in another human being's face. 'Nought but a bastard, a dirty little bastard child, but I don't care, I want you. I'd marry you if you want, anythin', but I'm going to have you.'

She bit into his hand with such force that he groaned

but in the next moment he had slapped her across the face with a ferocity that made her ears ring and the world go black again. She could feel his mouth at her breasts now, his leg forcing her thighs apart as his other hand fumbled with his trousers and she summoned up all her remaining strength to scream her brother's name, but the sound emerged as a tortured moan.

She twisted and writhed as she fought unconsciousness but his sheer bulk had pinned her to the ground more securely than any weights. He was going to take her. Out here. In the open. 'Davie . . .' His name was just a faint whisper against the horror that was going to happen to her but when in the next instant she felt Steve's weight lifted from her and the sound of hard bone against bone, she knew Davie had come. She was dimly aware of a furious fight to the side of her but her head was spinning so badly she fell back against the ground as the dizziness made her nauseous, and just before she lost consciousness for the third time in as many minutes she felt someone fall heavily across her legs and heard the sound of running feet.

'Jenny?' She could hear Davie's voice but couldn't quite reach it, the heavy darkness that was holding her down making speech impossible. 'Jenny? Open your eyes. Come on, open your eyes.'

She forced her eyelids open, gasping air and saw her brother's eyes an inch from her own as he bent over her, his face white and blood-stained. 'Davie, oh Davie . . .' He had been right. All along he had been right. She should have listened to him, she shouldn't have wandered from the others. 'Has . . . has he gone?'

'He's gone.' She saw him take several deep breaths

before he spoke again and then his voice was tight and strained. 'How – How badly are you hurt?'

As she struggled to sit up his arms went round her and when she was leaning against his shoulder she found the world had stopped spinning, although the nausea was acute. 'I don't know . . .' She shut her eyes for a moment, her head pounding like a sledgehammer. 'I want to go home, Davie, I want me gran.'

'I know, I know –'

'I'm hurtin' and I want me gran . . .' Her voice trailed off as she gasped again and then deep heaving sobs shook her frame as she started to cry, the sound a wretched painful whimpering that filled the tiny copse.

'Jenny lass, Jenny, don't, don't . . .' He sat holding her for some time and when eventually she was quiet his own face was wet with tears. 'Can you walk?'

'Yes, I want to go home.' She struggled to her feet with his help and saw her dress lying to one side of them, spread out carefully as though it had just been ironed by an industrious housewife who didn't want a crease to mar its smoothness. It chilled her, the almost reverential care with which the white dress had been treated when all the time he had been going to rape her.

'He must have taken that off after I fainted when he carried me here.' Her voice was stiff now as shock swiftly set in. 'He's an animal, he treated me like an animal, Davie –'

He stopped the words with a soothing hand on her lips, touching the swollen cheek where Steve's handprint was vivid against her white skin. 'It's all right, it's all right. Come on, we're going to put your dress on now.' She lifted her arms obediently and he slid the dress over her head, the clean white material covering the torn fragments of her petticoat and the marks left on her skin from Steve's mouth and hands.

'I want you to stay here while I go and get Gran,' Davie said softly as she stood shivering in the humid air. 'He won't come back, I've made sure of that and I'll only be a minute –'

'No!' She clutched hold of him fearfully, her eyes desperate. 'No, I don't want to stay here by meself and I don't want people to see –' She shook her head helplessly. 'I want to go home, Davie, take me home and then you can come and get Gran.' She was trembling so violently the tremors were shaking his body through hers. 'Please . . .'

'All right, Jenny, anythin' you want. But do you think you can make it home?' he asked quietly, still in the same soft almost sing-song voice he had used since her bout of weeping.

'Yes, yes.' She nodded wildly. 'If you help me. I just want to get home before anyone sees me. Please, Davie . . .'

The journey home along the river bank was a nightmare for them both, but they were forced to go the long route rather than the path that led more directly to the village through the Maine grounds to avoid meeting anyone. They didn't speak. All David's energies were concentrated on half carrying the stumbling shaking body of his sister over the uneven ground without having her faint on him again, and Jenny herself felt half-dead and sick with shock.

Her whole body was aching and she felt despoiled and dirty, filthy . . . As she staggered along, her mind was re-living the sensation of Steve's groping rough hands on her flesh as he squeezed and probed her most intimate parts, and she felt she wanted to die. He had done things, said things she couldn't believe. Is this what boys grew up into, then? These half-crazed creatures with wet hot mouths and hard hands? She never wanted another lad to touch her again in all her life, she didn't.

'We're nearly there.' As David spoke she turned to him, her face wet with tears again. 'Come on, you're doing fine, just a few more yards.'

Mercifully they had met no one beyond the odd cat basking in the sun. The whole village had turned out for the annual picnic and the streets were deserted in the shimmering heat. She stumbled through the door of the small cottage and collapsed in her grand-dad's chair, drawing her feet up under her and beginning to rock herself quietly back and forth in the foetus position as she whimpered softly.

'I'm goin' to get Grandma.' David moved round to stand in front of her and as she raised her head she shrank back in the chair at the look in his eyes.

'Don't look at me like that, Davie. It wasn't my fault, please, I didn't –'

'I know it wasn't your fault.' In an instant he was her brother again, her other half, and he knelt down in front of her and took her dirty hands in his, his eyes holding hers. 'You think I don't know that? I've seen how that scum looks at you, and I should have done somethin' about it afore this day. But I didn't think even Baker would take a young lass of thirteen against her will –'

'He didn't take me, he didn't. You came before –'

'I know, Jenny, I know.' He stood up after placing her hands in her lap. 'An' he's not goin' to get the chance to try again, I'm tellin' you.' The rigid control that had been evident since his fight with Steve slipped for just a moment and she saw murder in his eyes before he blanked them again, turning quickly and striding out of the door as she called his name.

'Davie! *Davie!*' She fell out of the chair in her haste to follow him, scrabbling on her hands and knees before she righted herself and reached the door to scream his name again, but he didn't pause in his sprint down the road, turning into the lane that was a short cut to the big house even as she called.

'Davie, Davie, oh Davie . . .' She found herself whimpering his name and stumbled back to the chair. What was he going to do? But she knew what he was going to do . . . She must get her grandfather to stop him, keep him here when they came back. 'Oh, Davie . . .' He'd get hurt, she knew it. Steve Baker was so strong and tall, with a man's body even at sixteen. Davie wouldn't stand a chance against him.

Her grandparents burst through the open doorway some minutes later, clearly having run all the way from the house, and came to an abrupt halt in the middle of the room as she sprang from the chair, her eyes wild. 'Where is he?'

'Where is he?' Mary walked slowly towards her, her hands outstretched. 'We don't know where he is, lass, Davie says he ran off –'

'*I mean Davie.*' She took a deep breath and fought for control. 'Where's Davie? You didn't let him go, did you? You've got to keep him here, Gran, he's goin' to find Steve –'

'What will be, will be, lass. He's your brother, you can't stop him –'

'Can't stop him?' Jenny's voice rose to a shriek and she stared at her grandmother as though she was a stranger, her eyes boring into the lined face in front of her while she searched the familiar features for understanding. 'He'll be hurt, I tell you, you've got to find him. Steve is twice our Davie's size. Grand-dad?' She flung herself round to face him. 'You've got to find him *now*, please, Grand-dad.'

'Don't fret, lass, I'll find him.' George nodded at his grand-daughter as he patted her arm ineffectually. He had expected to find her distraught and crying, her clothing ripped to bits or at least dishevelled from what their Davie had flung at them a minute or two before he'd taken off again, but her dress looked fine, fine . . .

Perhaps it wasn't as bad as they'd thought? Davie was always one to take things to heart where his sister was concerned, and he knew where the blame lay for that. Mary had had too much sway with the lad.

'I'll go now and bring him home, all right, me lass?' Jenny nodded silently and George smiled at her, patting her arm again. 'That's right, you stay with your grandma and she'll get you a sup of something. I won't be long.' As her grandfather left, shutting the cottage door carefully after him, Jenny sank down to the floor, her legs finally giving way.

'I feel sick, Gran.'

'Hold on, lass.' But even as she spoke Jenny began to retch and heave, emptying the contents of her stomach over the skirt of her new dress, unable to hold back the waves of nausea any longer.

After Mary had wiped her grand-daughter's face she helped Jenny to her feet, shaking her head slowly as she surveyed her white face. 'Let's get you to bed, lass, and then you can tell me all about it. We'll have that dress off first and I can put it to soak straight off.'

It was as she lifted the dress over Jenny's quivering shoulders and saw the state of her petticoat that Mary's heart rose up in her mouth. The front of her grand-daughter's chest and her upper arms covered in scratches, red with congealed blood, and if she wasn't very much mistaken there were bite-marks on the bruised surface of the young breasts. The petticoat bodice hung in shreds, the skirt ripped from hem to waist as though an animal had been tearing at it with its claws. 'Jenny? . . .' There was a constriction in her throat and a lead weight stopping her breath as her hands fell limply to her sides. 'What in the name of –'

'He hurt me, Gran.' Jenny swayed slightly, her hands tearing at the petticoat and pulling the scraps of material off her. 'I need to wash meself. I want to wash meself all over –'

'Wait, lass.' She had to set this right. Somehow she had to set this right. Dear God, Father in heaven, holy Mary, Mother of Jesus, don't let him have penetrated her. Not at thirteen. Oh dear God, no, not at thirteen. Her mind was racing as she fetched a blanket from her bed and wrapped it round her grand-daughter's shivering body before pulling out the old zinc bath in the scullery and beginning to fill it with cold water. 'I'll boil some water –'

'No.' Jenny's teeth were chattering but the tone was adamant. 'I want to wash now, Gran.'

Perhaps this was her fault? Mary felt sick with rage and fear and recrimination as she filled the bath. They hadn't had to come here, she'd pushed for it, like she'd pushed their Martha to get wed, because . . . But here her mind wouldn't go any further. No. It could have happened anywhere, with Jenny looking like she did. Beauty like hers would always draw 'em. She was like a pure delicate flower on top of a dunghill and the filthy scavengers would always want to destroy what they couldn't possess. But perhaps he had possessed her?

Jenny let the blanket slip, pulling the tattered

remains of her knickers off her lacerated legs before she sat down in the icy-cold water, and Mary forced herself to ask the question she dreaded the answer to. 'How much did he hurt you?' Even to herself her voice sounded cold and blunt, but there was a feeling on her, a dark raw feeling that perversely had her wanting to shake and shake her grand-daughter till her teeth rattled. She had warned her, time and time again she had warned her. She couldn't go through it again, God knew she couldn't. She'd stood enough. Couldn't He see she'd stood enough?

Jenny began scrubbing herself with the hard round piece of soap and old flannel that Mary had passed to her and flinched as the soap stung the deep scratches on her upper body and legs. A particularly nasty one on the inside of her thigh, where Steve's fingernail had ripped her skin, was feeling as though it was having acid poured in.

'Jenny?' Mary tried to moderate her tone. 'I have to know exactly what happened, lass.' She shook her head when Jenny winced as she drew the flannel across her torn breasts. 'And you wanted me to stop Davie going after him? When he's done this?'

'I don't want Davie hurt –'

'You just forget about Davie for a minute and tell me about you. All of it, mind.'

When Jenny finished speaking, more tears mingling with her words now and again, Mary left the scullery and stumbled across to George's chair in the other room, groping at the chair arm as she sank into the seat. So he hadn't violated her? She was safe. She was still safe. Thank God. As she offered up a stunned prayer of thankfulness, in another part of her mind she was thinking quite coldly about the lad who had done this to their Jenny. She hoped George hadn't seen

Davie, hadn't pulled him back from what he intended, oh she did . . . She hugged the violent hate to her as though it was a live thing. She wanted her grandson to find Steve Baker, find him and teach him a lesson he would never forget. She didn't want him ever to be able to look at another lass again.

She recalled the look on Davie's face as he had left them at the big house, having garbled some explanation as to why they had to leave, and a savage desire for blood made the darkness against her closed eyelids red. She wanted Steve Baker dead. She wanted him to rot in everlasting hell . . . A deep exhaustion filled her at the same time as the pains in the chest she'd been having of late made their presence known.

But she couldn't sit here thinking thoughts when she needed to be in the scullery seeing to Jenny. She forced herself to rise slowly but the pain increased to a solid band that rose up into her throat and down her arm cutting off her breath as though with a knife. She fell sprawling to the floor, the thick choking sound coming from her throat causing Jenny to spring from the tub and rush to her grandmother's side, careless of the fact that she was as naked as the day she was born.

'But where do you think he is, Grand-dad?' George's heart went out to his grand-daughter as her swollen eyes met his over the head of his sleeping wife. They were sitting each on one side of the bed and had been for the last few hours, and now the night sky was as black as pitch.

'I don't rightly know, lass.' He shook his grizzled head slowly. 'But he'll be all right, you know our Davie can look after himself. It's you that needs to rest now, else you'll end up in the same state as your grandma.' He looked at her white drawn face, his eyes soft with pity. What a day . . . And it wasn't over yet. His young bairn had been practically raped, his wife taken bad and looking like death, and now his grandson out goodness knows where, and it past midnight. 'Go and lie down, Jenny lass, you're doing no good sittin' there.'

'Not till he's back.' She clasped her hands together, her eyes pleading with him. 'You don't think he's found Steve? What if Steve's hurt him and he's lyin' somewhere?'

'Put them ideas right out of your head,' George said abruptly. 'Steve Baker is no fool, lass, he's always been a sly one. He won't let Davie find him. No, knowin' Steve he'll lie low for a time and then stroll back as bold as brass once he thinks Davie's cooled down.'

At least he hoped the other lad would have the sense to keep out of Davie's way, he thought grimly as Jenny sank back in her chair and closed her eyes again. He too had recognized the murderous intent in Davie's eyes and it'd do no good if he went down the line for scum like Steve Baker. And somehow, in spite of Steve's superior height and weight, he didn't doubt for a minute that he would come off worst if Davie found him. Not that he didn't want the older boy to pay for what he'd done to their lass . . . He too closed his eyes, his mind weary. He'd never forget the shock he'd had when he opened the cottage door to see Mary lying on the floor and Jenny bending over her with marks on her young body that could have come from an animal. And that's all the scum was. No . . . He corrected himself bitterly. He was insulting the animal kingdom when he put it on a level with Steve Baker and the like. But he didn't want Davie to take the law into his own hands. There was something about his grandson, something dangerous and primitive, where his love for his sister was concerned. They'd get hold of the constable in the morning, let him sort out what was what, but by gum, he'd make sure the book was thrown at that young maniac. He wouldn't touch another young lass for a good many years.

'Did anybody see? . . .' Jenny's voice brought his eyes wide open and he saw her face was tight with humiliation and pain. 'I mean, does anyone know about what happened?'

'No, lass, no.' George reached out a hand and grasped one of hers over the bed as he leant forward. 'But you know we'll have to call the constable in the mornin'. Make it official, like. You can't let him –'

'No!' Her voice was shrill with protest and she glanced quickly at her grandmother before lowering her tone as she spoke again. 'I don't want anybody to know Grand-dad, I don't. I couldn't bear it –'

'Jenny, lass, you have to.' As she pulled her hand from his and lowered her head he didn't try to touch her again, but even through the pity that was twisting his guts inside out he knew he had to be firm. 'You have to, lass,' he repeated softly. 'Don't you see? He can't be seen to get away with it.'

'But you said no one knows.' She raised her head now, her eyes swimming with tears. 'You *said* . . .'

'Jenny, you know. He knows. You don't think feelin' as he does he'll let you alone? You'll never know a moment's peace –'

'But he was drunk,' she said desperately. 'That was why he did it. The lads had brought cider in, I could smell it on his breath when he –' She gulped and lowered her head again, moving it in a small, almost imperceptible gesture of abasement.

'An' you don't think he'll drink again?' George asked

quietly. 'A young lad of sixteen out to prove himself a man? Think, girl, think.'

'But everyone will look at me . . .' She gripped the top of her blouse with her hand, working the material in her fingers as she swayed back and forth. 'They'll know, they'll know where he touched me, what he did . . . I couldn't bear it Grand-dad, I couldn't, I'll kill meself –'

The opening of the cottage door cut off the reply he had been about to make and brought both their pairs of eyes to the doorway as they heard footsteps in the room outside. When David appeared in the doorway, his face expressionless, Jenny felt such a tide of relief that she sagged back in the chair with it before springing up and hugging her brother's stiff body tight. 'Davie, Davie . . .' She found she couldn't say anything but his name as she clung to his chest. 'Oh, Davie . . .'

'What's the matter with Gran?' He moved her carefully from him, his eyes going to the inert figure in the bed. 'What's happened?'

'She's had some sort of attack, lad.' George gestured for them all to leave the room and shut the door quietly before he spoke again. 'I came back from lookin' for you to find 'em in a right pickle with your grandma on the floor and lookin' as though she were about to breathe her last. We'll have the doctor in the mornin' but she's sleepin' now, which is what this one should be doin'.' He gestured at his grand-daughter without taking his eyes off Davie's curiously blank face.

'Grand-dad's right, you should be in bed.' As Davie glanced her way, his voice flat and even, Jenny felt the hairs on the back of her neck prickle with foreboding. There was something wrong. Something terribly wrong. She knew it, she always knew it with Davie.

Telepathy, call it what you will, she *knew*. And it worked both ways. Look at this afternoon, he had known she was in trouble.

'Did you find him?' She couldn't bring herself to say Steve's name. Even that brief informality was too intimate.

'No.' He turned from her as he spoke, busying himself with untying his boots, which were covered in thick red mud, before taking them through to the scullery and beginning to scrape them clean on the old clippie mat in front of the deep-set square sink.

'I'll go and sit with your gran, lass, you get to bed.' George nodded at her before walking into the bedroom and shutting the door firmly behind him. There was something wrong with their Davie but he was blowed if he was going to drag it out of the lad now. He was bone tired, bone tired and filled with a deep, sick kind of pain at this thing that had happened to their lass. And there'd be more trouble to come in the morning with this business of the constable. But he'd have to be told. There was no two ways about it.

'Davie?' Jenny followed her brother into the scullery and stood looking at his bent head as he cleaned the boots. 'What happened? What really happened?'

'Nothin'.' He didn't raise his head.

'Your shirt's wringing.' She suddenly realized the upper part of his clothing was soaking wet. 'An' there's all pink on it.'

'That's nothin'. I slipped on the river bank and got all mud on me shirt so I just washed it off, that's all. You all right now?' He still didn't look at her and, ignoring the last few words, she knelt down beside him on the floor.

'Did you find him, Davie?'

'I told you.'

'An' I don't believe you.' Now he did swing to face her but his face expressed none of the hostility that should have been present with her calling him a liar, and this fact alone told her she was right. 'You saw him, didn't you? You found him. I know you did.'

'Then you know more 'n me.'

'You aren't going to tell me?'

'Nothin' to tell,' he answered quietly without a trace of emotion in his voice. As he finished scraping the last boot he picked the mat up and went to shake it outside the back door, returning a moment later and walking into the small alcove to the side of the sink where he placed the boots neatly side by side on the stone floor.

'Davie –'

'Leave me alone, Jen.' She stared at him, her mouth slightly open. If he had shouted at her, lost his temper, that she could have understood, but this coldness, this unnatural control scared her half to death. And his voice. He hadn't sounded like a lad, her brother, when he had spoken to her just then, he'd sounded like a man . . . In all their quarrels, in all the fierce bickering that went on between a brother and a sister, she had never heard that particular note in his voice before.

'Don't.' She stood up and took a step backwards, her hand to her mouth. 'Don't be like this, I want to know –'

'No, you don't.' As her eyes still continued to cling to his he turned away abruptly, his voice gruff. 'It'll be all right, Jen, I've told you. I won't let him hurt you again. Now go to bed and we'll talk in the mornin'.'

'But –'

'In the mornin'.'

*

The morning brought nothing more from him, as she had known it wouldn't, but within minutes of her grandfather waking her just before six she was busy seeing to her grandmother, who was too ill to get out of bed.

'I'll have to go to work, lass, can you cope?' George's eyes were red-rimmed, which showed he'd had little sleep. 'I'll be back just after three 'n then we'll have to talk, you know what I mean?'

She knew what he meant all right, Jenny thought desperately as she escaped to the lavatory halfway up the small garden, shutting and bolting the door before putting the lid down and sitting on the flat surface, swaying with her head in her hands. He was going to tell the constable. He was. And there'd be questions, lots of questions, and she'd have to tell a stranger exactly what Steve Baker had done . . . Her head felt as though it was going to burst with the images that flashed through it. The whole of her body was sore and bruised, everywhere hurt to touch, but she could have coped with that side of things if it wasn't for the fear that Steve Baker had taken over her mind, that he was sending her mad . . . She couldn't have explained to anyone just how she felt but the dark rage and fear and burning desire to hurt him like he'd hurt her were so stark and clear that she could almost see and smell him, and it terrified her.

'Jenny?' Her grandfather called her from outside in the garden. 'I'm off now. Davie is goin' to stay and help you with your gran, an' I'll let the school know you're both down with a tummy upset, all right?' He waited a moment but she couldn't reply, her stomach churning with a panic that rendered her dumb. 'I'll see you later, love.'

A few more minutes ticked by and she knew she'd

have to go in the house, her grandma would be wanting her and Davie couldn't help her wash or get the breakfast. Oh, Oh . . . She wrung her hands until it hurt. Why had this happened to her? What had she done? She'd tried to stay away from Steve Baker, she'd told him she didn't want anything to do with him . . .

As she went about cleaning the cottage and preparing the vegetables for dinner some time later while Davie sat with their grandmother, she couldn't rid herself of the impression that they were all waiting – waiting for something without knowing what it was. Her grandmother had raised herself to drink a little soup that morning before falling back to sleep again almost immediately, but she could hear her murmuring to Davie in the bedroom, and she found she didn't want to go in and join them. There was something strange happening, something that was making her visit the lavatory every ten minutes . . . And when, just after two, a knock came at the cottage door it was almost a relief to answer it, although her face was tight with apprehension.

'Hallo, missy.' The village constable was vaguely known to her as a distant figure on his bike as he made his rounds, his little terrier dog trotting at his side most days. He was a large man with a ruddy face and a cheerful expression, but there was no smile on his face today as he looked down at her, his helmet barely fitting his big head. 'Not at school today, then?'

'No. I'm feelin' bad and me grandma's ill in bed too.' Some instinct she couldn't have explained made her keep the door half-shut as she faced him. She could just hear Davie's voice from the bedroom and hoped it wasn't audible to the big man outside. For some reason she didn't want the constable to know her brother was here too.

'Can I have a word with your grandma? It is important –'

'You can't.' She interrupted him before he could finish, her voice trembling but her face resolute. 'Me grand-dad said she'd to be kept quiet till he comes back.'

'Is that so?' For a moment she thought he didn't believe her but then he smiled quietly, his eyes kind. 'And when will your grand-dad be back, then?'

'Tea-time.' She fiddled with the top button of her blouse, lowering her head as the astute gaze in front of her fixed on the bruise covering the whole of her cheekbone, which was already a faint blue.

'Hurt yourself, missy?' He touched his own red-veined cheek lightly.

'I fell over.' She couldn't meet his eyes as she lied and could feel her face burning. 'Banged meself on our grate. Me grandma's always saying I've two left feet.'

'Is that so? Well, never mind, love, with a face as pretty as yours it doesn't matter over much about your feet, does it?' He gave her one more long stare before he turned and walked towards his bike, the rest of his words floating over his shoulder. 'I'll be back round about tea-time to have a word with your grand-dad, then. One of the local lads is missing, didn't come home after the jollifications up at the manor yesterday, so I understand. His mother's half-mad with worry and I'm just checking as to who saw him last.'

'Oh . . .' She wanted to ask who it was but the words wouldn't force themselves past the thick blockage in her throat. But it didn't have to be him, 'course it didn't. There'd been lots of lads at the picnic, all the village had turned out. It could be anyone.

'See you later then, missy.' As he mounted his bicycle the little dog appeared from nowhere yapping and barking at his side, and the constable rode away down the quiet village street. She saw Mrs Fisher, Sarah's mother, in the distance and shut the door quickly, her heart thudding.

Davie, oh Davie . . . She stood swaying slightly with her arms tight round her middle before walking through to the bedroom where her brother was sitting by the side of the bed. 'Who was that?' It was the first time he had spoken to her of his own volition the whole day and as he raised his eyes she saw, just for a second, that he knew exactly who had been at the door.

'The constable.' Her voice was as flat as his.

'The constable?' Mary raised herself slightly on to her elbows and her voice too was low and even. 'What did he say, lass?' The slight exertion made her pant and Jenny pushed her back down into the bed before she answered, adjusting the bolster and easing the pillows round her shoulders and neck before she walked across to the doorway and stood facing them both.

'He wants to talk to Grand-dad.'

'What about?' Her grandmother's voice was weak but determined, the white face still and watchful.

'He said one of the lads has gone missing.' She couldn't keep her eyes on Davie as she said this, she didn't know why, she just couldn't.

'Who?'

'He didn't say.' She raised her head just in time to see the look that flashed between them.

There was dead silence in the room for a few moments and then her grandmother spoke again. 'Well, I dare say we'll find out tonight, that's if he doesn't turn up aforehand, of course. You know what these lads are when they've been at the drink. Davie tells me there was cider brought in yesterday.'

'Yes.' She wanted to say more, ask more, but she couldn't.

'He's likely sleeping it off somewhere, whoever he is.' The matter-of-fact tone reassured Jenny somewhat. She was imagining things, of course she was. What was the matter with her anyway? It didn't have to be Steve Baker, did it? 'Make me a cup of tea, lass. I could do with something wet and warm.'

'Yes, all right.' As she turned her grandmother's voice came again, soft and quiet.

'How you feeling, Jenny?'

'I'm all right, Gran.' She wasn't, she was dying inside but she couldn't very well say so, could she?

'Your grand-dad thinks we ought to tell the constable about what happened yesterday. How do you feel about it?'

'I don't want to.' She turned quickly, sensing that her grandmother wasn't altogether in favour of the idea, although her voice hadn't indicated it. 'I don't want to, Gran,' she repeated, her voice urgent. 'I'd hate it, everyone knowing, and there's no need. He didn't –' She stopped abruptly, waving her hand helplessly. 'He didn't, you know, so it's all right then, isn't it?' She caught the note of pleading in her voice and tried to calm herself. She had to be rational, convince her grandma it was the best thing. If she got her on her side, her grand-dad wouldn't go against his wife, she knew it.

'All right, Jenny, all right.' Mary nodded gently. 'If you don't want to, we won't.'

It was too easy, the capitulation was too easy, she had been right. Her grandma didn't want the constable told any more than she did, but why? She shut the door on them both and made the pot of tea, sitting down at the table for a minute while the tea mashed, her mind going backwards and forwards in a series of questions and answers that made her head spin. Her grandma knew something, Davie too. The sick thudding in her chest started before transferring to her stomach, so she knew she'd have to pay a visit outside again. She was wrong to doubt Davie like this, suspect him. He had said he hadn't seen Steve and she believed him, she did. He loved her and he wouldn't hurt a fly, not their Davie. *He wouldn't*.

Her grandmother and David were sitting in silence when she entered the bedroom a few minutes later with the tea but she knew they had been talking a second before she had opened the door.

'Thanks, lovey.' As Mary took the mug from Jenny's hand she looked up into her grand-daughter's face and said confidentially, 'I've just been thinking, lass. This policeman who called? Now supposing, just supposing, the lad that's missing *is* Steve Baker. Now I know it's a long shot, and there's plenty of others who were drinking well yesterday, but just supposing for the sake of argument it is Steve, it might be a good idea to let it be known that our Davie was home last night, all night. It's not a secret that the two of 'em didn't get on and you know what people are for putting two and two together.'

Jenny stared at her grandmother for a full minute before turning to look her brother directly in the face. 'Did you see Steve last night, Davie?' she asked quietly. 'I want to know.'

She saw her grandmother move to say something but Davie raised his hand to stop her and he rose, coming to stand in front of her with his eyes wide and clear as they looked into hers. 'I didn't see him, Jenny, I swear it,' he said softly. 'Now you believe me, don't you? I'm your brother, Jenny. I wouldn't lie to you, would I?'

Yes, if you decided it was best for me, you would. She didn't know where the thought came from and thrust it back into her subconscious as something unclean. She wanted to believe him, she did. He was her Davie, the other part of her, she couldn't think – *She wouldn't*. 'I believe you if you say so, Davie.' She saw the flash of something bright in his eyes but then he had turned back to her grandmother, who spoke quickly.

'The thing is, lass, as far as we know no one knows what went on yesterday afternoon atween you and him, but what if there's some talk, gossip, like. Davie says it was fair knowledge Steve was mad on you.' Jenny nodded slowly. 'Now Steve had been drinking cider all afternoon, which probably accounts for the way he was with you. Not that I'm excusing it, mind – ' Mary raised a hand as Jenny went to speak. 'But that being the case, he was probably none too steady on his pins when he took off like a jack rabbit after Davie had got him off you. There's no knowing where he went. If he *is* the lad that's missing he could still be wandering about, most likely, thinking to stay well away until our Davie's cooled down, you see what I mean? It'll save a lot of awkward questions, keep things simple, if we say we were home all evening.'

'You mean Davie.'

'Aye, lass, that's exactly what I mean.' The blue eyes looked hard into Jenny's and she blinked uncertainly.

'All right, but what if it slips out –'

'It won't.' Her grandmother's voice was still quiet

but with an inflexion that made Jenny lick her lips nervously. 'I know the law from old, lass. They start asking one question and afore you know it they've wormed all sorts of things out of you. Now you say you don't want no one to know what went on yesterday and I'm not opposing that, not for a minute, but think on. Least said, soonest mended, eh?'

Jenny stared at her grandmother as she spoke and there rose in her a feeling, a bad feeling, towards this woman without whom she wouldn't be here now. She manipulated them, especially Davie. She had influenced and directed their minds according to what she thought best from the moment they were born, she had never seen it so clearly. But all mothers, grandmothers, had sway over their children, she thought quickly as overwhelming guilt at her ingratitude brought a flush to her cheeks. Her grandma loved her and their Davie, what was she thinking of to think the way she just had? Everything was going topsy-turvy and it was all Steve Baker's fault. Oh she hated him, she hated him so much. She wished he was dead.

'I'm going to meet Grand-dad, you stay with Grandma.' Davie had pushed past her before she could react and as she went to follow him into the other room her grandmother's voice checked her.

'Let him go, Jenny. I want him to see your granddad afore he comes home through the village, put him in the picture, so to speak, so he knows what to say.'

So he knows what to say? There was a bitterness in her she didn't understand, not when it was directed against her grandma, whom she loved all the world. 'I'll start on the dinner.' So saying she left the room quickly but not quickly enough. Davie had already gone.

CHAPTER FIVE

It was well past his usual time when her grandfather walked in the door and immediately she knew something was terribly wrong. Davie was just behind him and, although he seemed subdued, she recognized the air of defiance in his stance.

'Is your grandma awake, lass?' There was no hallo, no how are you, and Jenny answered in the same straight tone.

'Yes, Grand-dad. She's waitin' for you.'

As the door closed behind her grandfather Jenny glanced across at David while she stirred the stew simmering on the stove. 'You're late.'

'Grand-dad wanted to find out who was missin'.'

'And?'

'It's Steve Baker.'

She had known, all along she had known, but hearing it spoken out loud made her heart thud violently. 'Why is Grand-dad in such a tear?' she asked, forcing her voice to sound normal. 'Have you two had a row or something?'

'Oh, it's nothin'.'

'Don't be stupid, of course it's something,' she snapped, her tone bringing his eyes up to meet hers.

He shrugged slowly, his eyes narrowed on her face. 'Don't take on, Jen, you're doing fine.'

He could be thirty instead of thirteen, she thought wildly as she stared into the face she would have sworn she knew better than any other but which now appeared as a stranger's to her. And doing fine? She ached all over, the constant throbbing in different parts of her body reminding her every minute of what that . . . that animal had done to her. He had seen her body. Touched her where only married people were supposed to touch. Bitten and sucked at her breasts . . . She shut her eyes tight as she forced the screaming in her head back into the dark recesses of her mind. And he'd look at her knowing he'd done all that, imagining her as she was when she was laid out there on the grass, helpless . . . How would she be able to face him? Ever hold her head up again? And where was he? Hiding somewhere? Perhaps one of the other boys had taken him in. Maybe he'd told them what he'd done, boasted about it even? . . .

She took a deep breath and opened her eyes, and continued stirring the stew. But even all that would be better than this other shadow that kept jabbing at her mind, the shadow that involved her grandma and Davie. They could leave here. She needn't ever see Steve Baker again. Hating him as she did, it was madness to want him here, this minute, but she did. It was the only thing that would banish this shadow of suspicion and make the nightmare stop.

'You never liked Steve, did you? Not even when we were little?' she asked now.

'No.' David threw himself down in a chair. 'An' if you're waitin' for me to say I'm sorry he's gone missin', you'll wait a long time. He was bad all through from the day he was born, to my reckoning.' His voice was cold, hostile.

She turned back to the stove. It hurt her to look at him, she didn't know why, but it did. 'Why?'

'Why?'

'Why didn't you like him?'

'You know why,' he said flatly. 'The others would stay in their place but not him. He always had to touch you, to try and talk to you, to get me out of the way –' He stopped abruptly. 'An' look where it led.'

'But perhaps if you hadn't always been on at him –'

'The end result would have been the same.'

'He said he wanted to marry me.' She could feel him stiffen rather than see it as she kept her back towards him, stirring the stew mechanically now. She couldn't bring herself to mention the other thing that had been tormenting her since the day before. Bastard. It was an ugly word but she had known, the second she had heard it, that that was what she was. Her and Davie. She thought now she must have always known because it wasn't the shock it should have been. She didn't take into account that with all the other happenings her mind had gone into a state of stunned acceptance as it dealt with the immediate problems.

One thing was for sure, she wouldn't want anyone to feel like she was feeling now. She knew she'd never feel clean again, bright, like she had yesterday morning. *Yesterday morning*. It seemed a million miles away now, another lifetime. Now everything was concentrated into this sick fear and panic that had her wringing her hands like poor old Nessie Betts, her that had been born an idiot . . .

'He would never have married you.' David's voice was as hard as stone and as cold. 'I wouldn't have let him.'

'But –'

'Never, do you hear?' She could hear the deep throb in his voice but dare not turn round to face him. 'He wasn't worthy to look the way you were, none of 'em are.'

'Davie –'

A loud knock at the door interrupted further conversation but later she was to remember his use of the past tense and wonder . . .

'That's likely the constable.' Jenny felt herself begin to tremble. 'He said he'd be back.'

'You'd better let him in, then.'

'Yes . . .' She looked straight at her brother now. 'I'm frightened, Davie –'

'Don't be daft.' He stood up and the air of defiance she had noticed earlier was stronger. 'You've got nothin' to be frightened about, have you? None of us have. Go and let him in.'

'Hallo, missy. Your grand-dad in now?' The constable smiled at her but almost immediately his eyes had gone past her into the room.

'Yes, come in.' She had opened the door wide but for the life of her she couldn't return the smile, although her instinct told her it was the best thing, the natural thing to do. 'He's with me grandma, I'll just get him.'

'Thanks, missy.' He walked past her, taking off his helmet as he passed through the low doorway and looking with keen narrowed eyes at David sitting to one side of the black-leaded range. 'Hallo, young man.' He nodded at David who nodded back in turn. 'You'll be Davie, I'll be bound?'

'I'm David Longbridge, yes.'

What was he doing taking that tone with the policeman? Jenny asked herself desperately, knocking on the door of her grandparents' bedroom. It would only put his back up, and there was no need to be so sullen, so uncivil.

At the sound of her grandfather's voice from within the room she opened the door and stepped through quickly, shutting it behind her. 'It's the constable, Grand-dad. He's –'

'You haven't left him with Davie?' Her grandmother reared up in the bed and as Jenny nodded the older woman gestured to her husband agitatedly. 'Go on, Georgie, quick. Go and sort it out.'

Jenny was aware of her grandfather giving his wife a long hard look but she was already opening the door again, frightened by her grandmother's tone, and stepping into the room beyond.

'An' you know why I'm here?' The constable was speaking directly to David, and although the boy's eyes flickered to the opening door the policeman didn't move a muscle. 'Well?'

'Yes.' David stared back at him, his face blank and controlled. 'Steve Baker's missin'.'

'Just so.'

'Me grand-dad's just comin'.' Her voice was too high and she bit on her lip nervously as the big man turned to face her. 'He's just comin,' she repeated, the beating of her heart making her feel sick. 'He's just seein' to me grandma, you see, she's still poorly.'

'I'm sorry to hear that.' There was no smile this time but his eyes were gentle as they took in her white face, her eyes so wide they looked ready to pop from her head. Something had frightened this young girl, if he wasn't much mistaken, and that bruise across one side of her face looked suspiciously like the sort of mark he was used to seeing on some of the older women's faces after the men got paid on a Friday night. He could be wrong . . . He looked at her silently as she stood, wringing her hands without saying any more. But he doubted it.

'How can I help you, Constable Haines?' As she heard her grandfather's voice just behind her Jenny felt so relieved she went giddy. 'I understand from my Jenny that you called earlier?'

'Good evenin', Mr Longbridge.' The other man

held out his hand. 'I'm sorry to hear your wife's not well.'

'Aye . . .' George nodded slowly. 'Well, have a seat and tell me what the trouble is.'

'Nothing that affects you, probably.' The constable sat down heavily on one of the straight-backed wooden chairs either side of the small chest of drawers and placed his helmet on the floor at his feet. 'But as you may have heard, there's a lad missin', Steve Baker. Now it could be he's off somewhere on business best known to himself, he's a big lad for sixteen and looks a good deal older, which is a mixed blessin' at that age if you know what I mean, but his mum is fair going out of her mind, so I said I'd look into it.'

'I see.' George seated himself on the wooden settle facing the policeman. 'Would you like a cup of tea?'

'Wouldn't say no, Mr Longbridge, it's been a long day.'

As Jenny busied herself making the tea, her back turned to the others, she listened intently to every word of their conversation, her heart in her mouth.

'Did you see the lad at all yesterday, Mr Longbridge?'

'Can't say I noticed him, but there was a lot going on and bairns scampering all over the place. Get over-excited, they do, especially the under-fives.'

'And you, young man?' She heard the constable shift slightly in his seat. 'Did you see Steve Baker yesterday?'

''Course I saw him,' David said quietly. 'He was with his usual mates, Micky Amos and the like. They'd brought in a load of cider they were drinkin' on the quiet.'

'Ah yes, the cider.' There was a brief pause and then, 'He'd had a skinful, had he? Steve Baker?'

'I dunno.' She turned with the heavy pottery teapot in time to see David shrug calmly. 'He's no friend of mine, that's common knowledge. I was playin' cricket with the other lads but we could hear Steve and his lot kicking up a racket, probably drinkin' themselves stupid, if I know 'em.'

'But you don't know for sure?'

'No. Like I said, I was with the other lads.'

'And you don't like Steve Baker?'

'No –'

'What's my grandson likin' or not likin' this lad got to do with anythin', Constable?' Her grandfather's voice was still pleasant but with a slight edge that spoke of irritation, nothing more. Jenny gazed at him in admiration for a second as she poured the tea. She knew he didn't approve of what her grandmother had decided to say and do over all this but he was playing his part all right.

'Just getting some background, Mr Longbridge, that's all.' As Jenny handed the policeman a mug of strong tea he looked straight up at her, nodding his thanks. 'An' you, missy? Do you like Steve Baker?'

'Me?' She swallowed nervously and resisted the impulse to press her fingers tight over her eyeballs. 'I dunno. I've never thought about it.'

'But he likes you,' the big man said quietly. 'I understand from his pals that he's been sweet on you for some time.'

'Lots of the lads are sweet on Jenny.' David's voice was harsh. 'Don't mean she has to like 'em back.'

'Look . . .' George's voice was steady, thoughtful. 'Pass me my tea, lass, and let's all have a think. When did you see Steve last?' he asked his grandson. 'At the meal?'

'Aye, yes.' David nodded without looking away from

the constable. 'An' then he went off with that little gang of his.'

'And you, missy?' The constable's voice was pleasant but as he looked at her Jenny felt a little ripple of awareness steal over her body.

He knew. He knew about the meeting in the woods. Did he know about . . .? But he couldn't. No one did, no one except her and Davie and their grandma and grand-dad. Of course, the other boys, and probably Sarah too, they'd have said about them all meeting on the river bank but that was all any of them could know. She pulled herself together and forced herself to speak rationally. 'I saw him a bit later, after the meal. Me 'n my friend went for a walk and we saw Steve and the others.'

'This'd be Sarah, your friend?'

She was right, he had known.

'Yes, Sarah Fisher.' She took a sip of her tea, cupping the mug between her hands and letting the fall of her thick golden hair hide her face from his gaze. 'Steve said he wanted to talk to me for a minute and the others went off but after that I didn't see him again.'

'What did he want to talk to you about?'

She felt a little quiver in her stomach. He didn't believe her. She knew he didn't believe her. 'He wanted me to be his lass, start courtin', like.'

'And what did you say to that?'

'That me gran would never let me.' She raised her head and met the narrowed eyes now. 'I'm only thirteen and me gran'd go mad, wouldn't she, Granddad?'

'That she would, lass.' George smiled with his mouth only.

'And did the lad accept that?'

'Accept it?' During the long afternoon she had rehearsed what she was going to say over and over in her mind but now she found herself stuttering as her mind went blank. 'He – I think so. I dunno –'

'He didn't get awkward with you?' She saw him looking at her marked cheek and knew a moment of utter panic.

'Look, what's the point of all this?' George had seen the look on his grandson's face and wouldn't have been surprised if he'd sprung at the constable. His love for his sister would be the death of him. 'You don't think our Jenny is hidin' the lad, do you?' he asked with heavy humour.

'No, I don't think that.' The constable hadn't taken his eyes off Jenny. 'How's the face this evening, missy?'

'All right.' The breath stilled in her body. He couldn't know, he was guessing. 'It's me own fault anyway. I was rushin' about looking after me gran and didn't look where I was goin'.'

'She was took bad at the do yesterday,' George said, taking his cue from his grand-daughter. 'We all had to come home. Well, the bairns didn't have to but they were worried about their grandma.'

'So you were all together, then?' the constable asked quietly. ' At the grange and then here?'

'Aye.'

'Good. Well, that makes things simple, doesn't it Mr Longbridge.' The constable rose from his seat as he picked up his helmet. 'No doubt the lad'll turn up the worse for wear anytime now and get a right scrubbin' from his mum in the bargain. Don't you think so, Davie?'

'Me?' David hadn't been expecting the sudden swing to him. 'I suppose so.'

'An' there's nothing more you can add to what's been said, lad?' David shook his head in sullen silence. 'Any of you?' the big man added as his gaze moved to encompass Jenny and her grandfather. 'Then I'll be on my way. Thanks for the tea, missy.' He walked slowly to the door. 'An' I hope the wife'll be right soon. What's the trouble?'

'I don't rightly know.' An expression of concern shadowed George's face. 'I'll likely have the quack tomorrow mornin' if she's no better.'

'Yes, I'd do that.'

When the door closed behind the policeman Jenny stood with her back against it, her fingers pressed tight on the wood, feeling such relief she was almost light-headed. He'd gone. He'd gone . . . But then, as she turned to take in her grandfather and brother the look on their faces made her stomach jump into her mouth. There was something frightening in their eyes as they stared at each other across the room, something she'd never seen before. She suddenly remembered the tragic Munich air crash two years before, when seven Manchester United footballers had been killed, the team that Davie and her grandfather supported. They had sat in stunned silence then as they had listened to the radio, but it hadn't been like this. Then their eyes had been wet and their faces shocked, and she recalled that George had comforted his grandson, taking him in his arms in a rare show of affection. But now . . . now their silence was chilling, aggressive.

But Steve Baker would turn up soon, she *knew* he would. And then that would be the end of this thing that had come upon them. She rubbed her upper lip, which was damp with perspiration. And Davie would make it clear to Steve that he hadn't to come near her again, and if she didn't look at him, pretended he didn't exist, she would get through. She'd have to. She nodded to herself mentally. He would turn up soon.

Steve Baker turned up the next day. Two poachers, about their business in the depths of Hawthorn Wood, came across his stiff, broken body at the bottom of a mud-filled gully rough with gnarled tree roots and boulders. His neck had been broken and it looked as if something, an animal of some sort, had been about him during the night. With the thick red mud caking his body and the dried blood, he wasn't a pretty sight.

It was the considered opinion of the villagers that, intoxicated with cider, he must have fallen, and hit his head on the large blood-stained boulder that was found just near his body, it being the means of breaking his neck too.

His poor mother went half-mad for a time but, as folk said, what can't be changed must be accepted, and accidents happen to high and low alike.

After all, who would want to harm a nice young lad like Steve Baker? He hadn't an enemy in the world.

Part Two

Jenny

1967–8

CHAPTER SIX

'Well, I'm sorry but I think you're barmy, clean round-the-bend barmy.'

'I know you do.' Jenny smiled at her cousin's indignant face. At just seventeen Connie was an interesting mix of her parents, Martha and Frank Malley, having the former's clear creamy skin and thick blond hair and her father's dark eyes and aggressive jaw, which at the moment was stretched out as far as it could go. 'But it won't be for ever –'

'Who says it won't?' Connie asked militantly. 'You've hardly stepped a foot out of that house except to come round here since you left school, Jen. Can't you *see* what David's idea is, and Aunt Mary's, if the truth be known?'

'Connie –'

'Don't Connie me.' Connie almost stamped her foot in frustration as she glared at Jenny sitting on her bed. 'You've got to stand up for yourself, Jen. Aunt Mary could be left for part of the day at least and Uncle George would pay for old Mrs Brown to come and sit with her in the afternoons till you all got home, you told me that yourself.'

'And I also told you that Grandma would hate it,' Jenny said flatly.

'Tough.' Connie slanted her eyes at the delicately beautiful face in front of her. 'You'll be twenty-one in March, for crying out loud. Don't you *want* to see something other than those four walls in Crown Street, Jen? You can't be content to be buried alive in that dump.'

'Connie, that's my home you're talking about.'

'No, it isn't, it's your prison,' Connie stated emphatically. 'And it'll carry on being your prison unless you do something about it. Look, I'm not suggesting you move away from home or fly off to the other side of the world, for goodness' sake. It's just a part-time job in a little corner shop for three days a week, but it'd mean we were working together and we'd have such a laugh, Jen, you know we would.'

Yes, she knew they would. As Jenny gazed at her cousin's face the feeling that had been growing of late, the painful, angry feeling, which must be similar to that of a caged wild animal, threatened to emerge from the deep recesses of her mind. Connie would never know how she longed to take that job, to escape the suffocating, claustrophobic confines of no. 14 Crown Street where the minutes and hours of every day were regulated to such an extent she thought she would go mad at times. If it wasn't for the evenings she spent at her Aunt Martha's house, and this fierce, funny and very determined individual in front of her now, she wouldn't be able to stand it. There wasn't a day that went by that she didn't thank her Maker for Connie, not a day.

'Look, just put it to them.' Connie unbuttoned the flowered pink overall she wore for her job in the corner shop and threw it in the direction of her bed, where it landed on Jenny's lap – before opening her wardrobe and eyeing the contents with a frown. 'You won't have to do any evenings. Mr Slater never asks me to stay late, so he wouldn't expect a part-timer to, and the money's not bad. At least you'd be able to get a few decent clothes.' She turned round and glanced disparagingly at Jenny's jumper and skirt. 'Something a bit more modern.'

'I'm not into miniskirts, Connie, you know that –'

'Or make-up, or anything else that the gaoler doesn't approve of.' Connie sighed as the closed look that always followed her nickname of David spread across her cousin's face. 'Jen, he's your *brother*, not your husband, you know. You don't have to do what he says. Not that I'd do what my husband wanted if I didn't feel like it,' she added immediately with a nod in Jenny's direction. 'You have to keep men in their place. Give 'em an inch and they take a mile. Look at my mam and dad, he's crazy about her but half of that is because she's always stood up to him. He's never wanted her to work since they got married but she went back as soon as I started school and I don't blame her. Can you see David staying at home all day, stuck in with Aunt Mary? Well, can you?'

'That's different–'

'Don't be so *daft*. This is 1967 not 1867! Now, which of these dresses looks best for the do tonight? The red or the green?' She held up two minuscule pieces of material that didn't look as if they would cover a small child. 'I wish you were coming as well, Jen. Mick paid a fortune for those Rolling Stone tickets, they're like gold dust.' Jenny smiled but said nothing. How could she explain to someone who didn't know the meaning of the word fear, the sick dread that filled her mind at the thought of a confrontation with Davie? And there would certainly have been one if she had even suggested she accompany Connie and her friends to the pop concert in the heart of Sheffield that evening. He loathed Connie with an intensity she just couldn't understand and her cousin's friends even more.

'Well, red or green?'

'Green.' She watched as Connie slipped on the dress, the skirt of which barely covered her bottom, before selecting a pair of bright green plastic earrings that were outrageous but suited the younger girl perfectly.

'My white boots, I think.' Connie nodded at her reflection in the mirror as she applied a thick pale-pink lipstick and false eyelashes with an ease that spoke of experience. 'An' I'll have my hair loose. Mick reckons I look like Marianne Faithfull when I have it loose.'

'Does he?' Jenny wasn't really listening to the other girl's chatter as she watched her get ready. Why couldn't she be more like Connie? The thought brought her chin down into her neck for a moment. Why couldn't she stand up to life more, be her own person? The familiar churning in her stomach brought her hands into fists on her lap before she consciously relaxed them, one finger after another, but even then she didn't acknowledge that 'life' was in the form of a tall, broad-shouldered individual with dark-blond hair and eyes the colour of a cloudy day. Davie loved her, he did. She told herself the same words she had repeated so often over the years without questioning why she had to recite them with such force. He wanted the best for her, any brother would for his sister, wouldn't he? And like he said, her grandmother wouldn't live for ever, she could go any time, with her heart so bad, and he knew she'd never forgive herself afterwards if she hadn't done all she could. But . . . She tried to force the thought back but it had taken solid form. She needed to be with other people sometimes, people her own age. That wasn't bad was it? So why did he make her feel as though it was?

'You know they don't deserve you, Jen, none of them do.' Jenny's eyes snapped up to see Connie looking at her with a unusual seriousness straightening her young face. 'I couldn't stand what you do, I don't think any other young girl could. This is supposed to be the summer of love, if all the newspapers are right about the hippies and everything, and everywhere things are changing, everywhere . . .' She flung her hands out dramatically, causing Jenny to grin in spite of herself. 'Everywhere except 14 Crown Street,' she finished tartly. 'They are making you old before your time, before you've even lived.'

'Oh, Connie –'

'You might well say, oh, Connie, but I mean it! Look at the carry on there was when I bought you the *Sergeant Pepper* album. You'd have thought it was packed in cannabis the way David and Aunt Mary went on. I know the Beatles signed that advert in *The Times* calling for the legalization of marijuana, but that doesn't mean their music is any less good. I've never heard such a rumpus about a flippin' record. There was David accusing me of taking LSD and saying I was trying to turn you on to the psychedelic scene, and Aunt Mary all but banning me from the house –'

'Oh, she didn't, Connie, you know she didn't.'

'She'd have liked to.' Connie eyed her sourly. 'Honestly, Jen, they're not normal.'

'They just worry about me.'

'There's worrying and worrying,' Connie said darkly, 'and how they are goes way beyond it. It's not as if they've got anything to worry about with you anyway. Now if it was me I could understand the panic.' She grinned and Jenny smiled back.

'Now, Jen, will you promise me you'll mention to them about the job and make it clear it's yours if you want it? Tell Uncle George first, I'm sure he'll want you –'

'It won't do any good, Connie, but yes, I'll mention

it. I promise.' She rose slowly from the bed. What would her cousin say if she told her that at this moment the urge to walk out of this house and keep on walking, walking until the steelworks of Sheffield were miles behind her, was so fierce it was a physical ache? That soft, gentle Jenny, as she knew Connie thought of her, had thoughts in her head at times that were anything but soft and gentle, thoughts that sent her to confession with Father Michael with her head bowed and her heart sick? How much longer could she put up with it? Life seemed to have stopped since that day they arrived back in Sheffield from the Kent countryside where she had spent her childhood, arrived back to the three-up, two-down, back-to-back house just two streets away from this one, where the only view of the sky was from the tiny paved backyard that stank of urine from the lavatory in the adjoining yard, where those filthy Mulgatties lived.

It had been useless to tell herself that she had to get used to it, that her grandmother needed to be close to her sister now she was so ill, that she was lucky, *lucky*, to have a bedroom all to herself when all the girls she went to school with had to share with one, sometimes two or three, brothers and sisters. And her grandma had gone on and on, saying that the house was a palace to the one she and Davie had been born in, that they had landed on their feet with their Uncle Frank getting Grand-dad a good job at the works. She didn't know now how she'd got through that time, with the horror of the nightmares coming every night as regular as clockwork and her grand-dad looking as if he had died and Davie – Again she stopped her mind from continuing down the path it seemed set on. She wouldn't think of it, of how he'd changed since Steve's death, of how those terrible suspicions that had emerged from deep in her subconscious in screaming nightmares had shadowed her days with a greyness that had taken every spark of joy and happiness from her life.

'Have a good time, Connie.' She smiled at the younger girl as she reached the bedroom door. 'And for goodness' sake, be careful, you know what I mean.'

'Yes, Mother.' Connie wrinkled her nose as she giggled. 'I'll be careful 'cos it's a dead cert I can't be good.'

'Oh, you . . .' Jenny shook her head, her frown of deprecation only half-feigned. She wished Connie hadn't told her she was sleeping with her boyfriend. It made her feel responsible somehow, as if she'd given her seal of approval, although her cousin knew she didn't agree with it. They were so young . . .

'You going home? I was going to put me new Stones record on –'

'I'll have to, Connie.' She glanced at her watch quickly. 'Grand-dad and Davie'll be back any time now and they like their dinner on the table, and I said to Gran I'd only be ten minutes, but, Connie?' She smiled as the younger girl turned to her again. 'Thanks, thanks for everything,' she said softly. 'I'll let you know about the job, but whether anything comes of it or not, I appreciate you thinking of me.'

'Go on with you.' Connie flapped her hand at her in a gesture that was all her mother's. 'Send David round to me if he objects, I'd soon take the wind out of his sails.'

'If anyone could, you could. I'll see you tomorrow, and watch yourself.' She was smiling at the unladylike retort that had reached her ears as she left the room, but her amusement vanished when she reached the bottom of the stairs and the front door opened and Connie's father walked in.

'Hallo, there.' His smile was wide and he stood aside for her to precede him into the small kitchen where her Aunt Martha was stirring something on the stove, his small black eyes tight on the back of her head.

'Hallo, Uncle Frank.' On entering the kitchen she walked straight over to the back door and stood with her hand on the handle as she smiled across at Martha. 'I'm off now, Aunty. I'm sorry to come at dinner-time but Connie sent a message with the lad next door that she wanted to see me before she went out.'

'Did she indeed?' Frank's voice was jocular. 'Quite the madam, isn't she, giving her orders. Don't let her start that game, Jenny, but you know you're more than welcome here anytime, anytime at all. Isn't that right, Martha?'

'Jenny knows that.' Martha's voice was quiet and after smiling once at her niece she turned back to the saucepan of soup without glancing at her husband.

'Connie was only trying to help, to do me a favour,' Jenny said quickly in the uncomfortable pause that followed. It was always like this when her aunt and uncle were together, and yet Connie seemed oblivious to the undercurrents that swirled about this house, even when Jenny's toes were curling with embarrassment, like now. 'Mr Slater wants a part-timer in the shop as well now his wife can't help out any more. Connie thought I might like to try for it.'

'Did she . . .' This time her aunt did turn to look at Frank and he returned the glance without saying anything. 'And what did you say to that?'

'I don't think it's possible.'

'Anythin' is possible if you want it badly enough, lass.'

Jenny stared at her aunt in astonishment. There had

been a note in her voice she didn't understand, a throb of emotion that was unusual for this quiet, withdrawn woman. Her grand-dad had once told her, a few years ago now, that in the old days before their family had moved to Kent, her aunt Martha had been known for her vitality and sense of fun. She hadn't believed him at the time and she wasn't sure if she did now, but just for a second she felt she had glimpsed a different woman under that beautiful creamy skin.

'Let the girl make up her own mind, Martha.' Frank's voice was tight and Jenny knew why, oh yes, she knew. She gazed at this man who was Connie's father, her aunt's husband, and who had shown her nothing but kindness from the day they had met on the family's return to Sheffield seven years ago, and whom she disliked and distrusted without knowing why. But the feeling was powerful and she avoided Frank Malley whenever she could. He made her flesh creep. She dropped her eyes as he glanced her way. And he was Davie's ally, oh he was certainly that. Her jaw clenched at the thought. Since he'd got their Davie that job at the steelworks when her brother had left school, it'd been all Uncle Frank this, and Uncle Frank that, and her poor grand-dad –

'I'd better be going.' She opened the back door abruptly.

When her husband had spoken, Martha had stared at him hard for a long moment before turning back to the stove, a look he had returned with equal intensity, and now her aunt merely nodded without looking at her again. 'Bye, lass, give me love to your grandma.'

Once outside in the small backyard that boasted its own gate leading on to what the residents of Baker Street insisted on calling a lane, but in reality was little more than a rough dirt track between the next few rows of back-to-back houses, Jenny took a deep breath of the hard northern air. People. The world would be a lovely place if only there weren't people in it. She shook her head at her own cynicism and walked across the square flagstones towards the gate, shivering suddenly as the cold November evening penetrated her jumper and skirt after the warmth of the house.

Why did Davie and her Uncle Frank get on so well? The thought wasn't new to her, and she wrinkled her brow as she walked swiftly down the dark greasy track and out on to the pavement at the other end, where the street lamps provided some illumination. She knew her grandfather thought Frank's championing of his grandson was more to spite him than anything, she had heard him say it to her grandmother often enough, but that still didn't explain her brother's side of things, and besides . . . She looked up into the star-studded sky overhead as she came to the top of Crown Street. She didn't think it was just that. Frank really liked their Davie, loved even.

Back in the kitchen at 60 Baker Street Martha was saying much the same thing to Frank, her voice tight and cold and her eyes narrowed. "Let the girl make up her own mind." She brushed back a wisp of hair from her forehead, her movements jerky with suppressed rage. 'I thought that whatever else you were, you weren't stupid, but then it suits you to send her back into that, doesn't it. It's what David wants. Precious David. You don't look at it from the lass's point of view, that she's stuck in that house day after day with no life of her own. No, if David wants her there, then that's all right by you. He can't do no wrong in your eyes, can he?'

'Don't be stupid.' Frank slung the rucksack containing his bait tin and flask on the kitchen table and in turn glared back at his wife. 'It ain't nothin' to do with us is it? And Connie shouldn't have poked her oar in.'

'Why not?' Martha rounded on him furiously. 'Why shouldn't she tell her cousin there's a job going? What's wrong with that? It's perfectly normal. But that's the trouble, isn't it? Because that household isn't normal, or certainly one person in it.'

'Here we go. It don't take much to set you off these days, does it? What the hell has the lad ever done to you anyway to make you carry on the way you do?'

'I don't like him.' Martha's voice was quiet now and flat. 'You know I don't like him, and the power he's got over that lass is unnatural, never letting her out of his sight and always wanting to be near her –'

'She's his sister, for crying out loud, his twin –'

'I know what she is!' It was so unusual for Martha to raise her voice that Frank stared at her with his mouth partly open for a good few seconds before rallying sufficiently to shout back.

'Dammit, woman! I've come home for me dinner and what do I get? Nothin' but abuse from the minute I put me head through the door –'

She cut into his blustering with a lift of her head and a straightening of her back as she glared at him long and hard. 'You encourage him round here all the time, don't you? In spite of knowing that this is the one place Jenny can come to for a bit of a break. And he hates Connie. How can you stand by and let him talk to her the way he does sometimes, your own daughter?'

'That's just bairns' talk –'

'David is nearly twenty-one years old, Frank, he's no bairn. I don't think he's ever been a bairn.'

'He's got as much right to come here as Jenny, ain't

he? What do you want me to do, ban the pair of 'em?' He moved across to the deep-set stone sink and turned his back on her as he washed his hands under the tap, rubbing them dry on an old towel before turning back to the table and pulling out a chair.

Martha in the meantime had ladled out three bowls of soup from the pan on the stove before going to the bottom of the stairs and calling for her daughter. He wouldn't see reason, he'd never see reason where David was concerned. Anything that boy did was all right as far as her husband was concerned. She shut her eyes tightly for a moment before opening them and walking back into the kitchen as she heard Connie leave her bedroom. But there was something badly wrong with David, something . . . Her mind refused to accept the word evil and substituted strange instead. Anyone else and she'd be down on her knees thanking them for deflecting her husband's attention from her to some extent. When she remembered how it had been before Mary and George moved back up here . . . She felt the panic claw at her throat before she took a hold of herself and sat quietly at the table without looking at the figure opposite. But it'd been weeks since he'd wanted . . . that. The days at the steelworks and the drinking with David after they left here of a night made him fit for nothing when he finally came up to bed and she was thankful, oh so thankful for it.

'I'll have to be quick, Mam, Mick's picking me up at seven.' Connie grinned at them both as she took her place at the kitchen table, not in the least deterred by her father's scowl.

'You'll eat your dinner first, and what the hell do you call that?' Frank indicated the minidress with a wave of his hand. 'There's no way you're leavin' this house dressed like that my girl, so think on.'

Connie raised her pencilled-in eyebrows at her mother, made a rude face at her father and began on the soup without replying.

She'd wear the dress. Martha looked at her daughter and not for the first time felt a dart of admiration for the tenacity and determination in that 5′ 2″ frame. Small she might be, but she knew she'd never have to worry about the world treating Connie badly. It'd be the other way round if anything. She had all of Frank's single-mindedness but not, thank God, that other side of her husband's nature, the dark side. The good Lord had known what He was doing when He gave her a daughter and not a son. She offered up a small prayer of thanks with open eyes. He had that.

Chapter Seven

'Where've you been?'

Jenny knew, as soon as she entered the house and saw David's face, that her brother knew exactly where she had been.

'Didn't Gran tell you?' She walked past him in the dark, brown-painted hall, intending to enter the front room, which overlooked the narrow street and had been converted to a bedroom for her grandmother, but he caught her arm before she could open the door.

'She said you'd gone to Connie's, that she'd sent you a message with Timmy to say she had to see you urgent.'

'Well, so you do know where I've been, then.' She stared up into his face as she spoke. It was a good-looking face. The deep grey eyes, thick blond hair and fine, even features meant half the girls hereabouts were gone on him, but he never seemed to look the side they were on. Funny that. But he was so straight-laced. Always going on about the moral decline of the age, the abomination of the birth pill, the depravity of the pop scene, everything. And when the Government had made abortion legal a few weeks ago she had really thought he was going to explode with his fury. She still could picture him stomping about her grandmother's room as he had ranted and raged for a good hour. Not that she really agreed with it, what good Catholic could? And yet . . . There were times when she could see it might be necessary. David should have been a priest, she decided suddenly. Her gran would have loved that . . .

'What are you smiling about?' His voice was rough

now, with that edge she recognized with a dart of apprehension. Oh she hated him when he was like this, she did.

'I was just thinking you ought to have been a priest, our Davie.' She took advantage of his surprise to push past him into the room beyond to find her grandmother sitting as she had left her just half an hour before in the big easy chair close to the window. 'Hallo, Gran.'

'What did Connie want?'

From the abruptness of her grandmother's tone Jenny knew her brother had been working on her in her absence, reminding the older woman about Connie's short skirts and heavy eye make-up, her boyfriends and the like. It was a trick of his that he did very well but tonight she wasn't in the mood for conciliation and her voice was equally abrupt when she spoke. 'I'll tell you later, I'd better see to the dinner.'

'Jenny? . . .' Mary's voice had softened instantly as she caught her grand-daughter's mood. 'I'm sorry, lass. I've been in a bit of pain tonight and sitting at the window watching 'em all scurrying here and there made me feel a bit . . . useless.'

'Oh, Gran.' Jenny felt immediately guilty, an emotion that was ever-present these days, even as the suspicion first prompted by Connie that her grandmother wanted just that very thing crossed her mind.

'Now come and sit down a minute and tell me all about it.' Mary patted the thick wooden arm of the chair as she smiled up at her grand-daughter, her lips carrying the faint blue tinge of heart disease. 'The dinner'll keep, it's only steak and kidney pudding isn't it? And your grand-dad and Davie have only just got in themselves.'

'Here.' As her grandfather pushed past Davie who

was leaning against the wall just inside the room, she saw he was carrying a tray with four cups of tea and the guilt intensified. Moments like this were rare these days. Her grand-dad and Davie always seemed to be at each other's throats and her grandparents rarely talked at all, at least to each other, and now she was going to spoil this brief lull in the storm. Because they wouldn't like it when they heard what Connie had wanted her for, she knew that.

'Well? It's not a secret, is it?' David's eyes were tight on his sister's face and there was no softness in them.

'No, it's not a secret.' She had snapped at him and now she took a long deep breath before she continued. Trust their Davie to start her off on the wrong track like that. She'd wanted to be calm and matter of fact when she broached the matter of the job, composed.

'Here, lass.' Her grandfather passed her her cup of tea and handed one to his wife as David took his from the tray, and then they were all looking at her and she just didn't know where to start.

'I was going to tell you after dinner –'

'I knew it! I knew what that loose piece was about! The bloo –'

'*David!*' Mary's voice was sharp. 'I won't have bad language in this house.'

'Well, I told you, didn't I?' He levered himself off the wall, spilling most of the tea in his saucer. 'Frank said Connie was going with that boyfriend of hers and a few others and she'd just love to get Jenny matched up with one of them. Well, wouldn't she?' He glared at Jenny now, his mouth hard. 'She asked you to go to that Rolling Stones concert, didn't she? In the middle of Sheffield? Well, no way! No way are you going there with that crew.'

'What crew? They're perfectly ordinary people, Davie, if you took the trouble to get to know them, and anyway I'm not –'

'They're scum, the lot of 'em, the whole lot of 'em.' David was breathing hard, his eyes almost black with dark emotion. 'Those blokes, with their velvet trousers and hair as long as lassies' –'

'They're not all like that and you know it.'

'You think I don't know what goes on at those concerts? The drugs, the pills, and I'll tell you somethin' else for nothing, those cigarettes that Mick of hers smokes aren't bloo –' He stopped abruptly as his grandmother stiffened. 'Aren't Woodbines, are they? You tried one of those?'

'I don't know what you're on about.' She didn't, but she did know that if he kept on much longer she was going to do or say something she'd bitterly regret. Why did everything have to end in a confrontation, everything? Other brothers weren't like this, they couldn't be.

'Make sure you keep it that way –'

'*Shut up, shut up, shut up!*' If a choir of heavenly angels had suddenly filled the little room with their presence singing *Ave Maria*, David couldn't have looked more surprised as she jumped up to face him. 'I can't stand this any more! I've had enough, do you hear? You don't like Connie, well, fine, but I do and I'll tell you this, I shall see her when I want to and go where I want to and I don't have to ask your permission neither. I'm not a child. I'm not going to that concert tonight, but I wish I was, I do. If it wasn't too late, I'd go round there now –'

'Over my dead body –'

'An' perhaps that's not a bad idea –'

'*David!*' As David moved to stand in front of her,

glaring down into her white face, George moved quickly but she wasn't afraid, not of physical violence. Davie wouldn't hit her, he wouldn't ever hit her, she knew that. And with the knowledge, the strength to defy him drained away. What were they doing fighting like this? She loved him and she hated him and she wished she were dead. She couldn't stand her life any more, she couldn't . . . As she put her hands over her face George's elbow came out quickly to knock David aside when he would have taken his sister in his arms, and instead the older man pulled her to him, glaring at his grandson over her bent head as she sobbed against his chest. If he wasn't badgering the lass until she was half frantic, he was wanting to touch her. 'Satisfied?' His angry gaze encompassed both his grandson and his wife before he led Jenny from the room, but his voice was soft and low as he took her through into the kitchen at the back of the house and pushed her down into the old easy chair at one side of the big black range. 'C'mon, me lass. C'mon, it's not as bad as all that now. You'll make yourself ill if you carry on like this.'

But it was a good five minutes before Jenny could control herself sufficiently to raise her head from its sanctuary in the old lumpy cushion and meet her grandfather's eyes as he crouched down in front of her. 'I'm sorry, Grand-dad . . .'

'What for? For speakin' your mind, lass? Seems to me you should've been doin' that a long time ago. The pair of 'em have had it too much their own way, but there's nothin' I can do if you're not willin' now, is there? It's not natural for a young lass of your age to be cooped up all day and night, I've said it all along, and I told you old Mrs Brown would be able to come of an afternoon. She needs the money, poor old soul, and it'd give you a chance of a bit of life outside these four walls.'

'But Gran said she'd hate it –'

'Aye.' George's voice was grim. 'Aye, I know what your gran said, lass, and this is the result.' He waved at her red eyes and blotchy face. 'But just think on a minute. The old girl often comes round for a bit of a natter with your gran as it is. She's been here twice this week that I know of, so what harm would it do to make it on a regular basis? An' I know your gran's poorly, I'm not decryin' that, but there's worse than her left all day on their own I can tell you.'

'Davie'd go mad.'

'David would do what he's told. If he's that concerned about your gran, he can stay here himself. You've had nigh on six years of it, lass, you've done your share.'

'Grand-dad?'

'Aye, lass?'

'What Connie wanted me for this evening? It was about a job at her place, that corner shop at the end of Baxter's yard. Mr Slater is looking for a part-timer to do three days a week and Connie wants me to go for it.'

'An' you? What do you want to do?'

She raised liquid eyes to his and they stared at each other in perfect understanding.

'Then do it, Jenny. Life's too short and no one knows what's round the corner. It's doin' you no good stayin' here, and what's more it's doin' David no good either. He's got to see –' He stopped abruptly as the door to the kitchen opened and his grandson walked in, his face surly.

'It's time for Gran's medicine.' David spoke directly

to Jenny without looking at his grandfather, but while George straightened from his crouching position at Jenny's side he waved Jenny back as she prepared to rise too.

'So?' The word was harsh and brought David's eyes to his. 'Give it to her.'

'What, me?'

'Yes, you. You've got hands, haven't you? If it comes to that there's no reason why your gran can't have her pills and potions by the side of her in that front room and dose herself. She's not a bairn.'

David's eyes narrowed at his grandfather's tone and Jenny prepared herself for the blast but instead, after one long cold look, her brother walked over to the shelf and, after selecting a bottle from among the many there, walked back out of the room without another word to either of them.

'You see?' George nodded at his grand-daughter. 'You've got to let them see you won't stand for any more monkey business, lass, it's gone on long enough. An' I'm as much at fault as anyone, I know that. I should've put me foot down years ago instead of standin' by and lettin' you become an unpaid servant to us all, by, I should that. From now on we all take a turn and do our bit and Mrs Brown'll stand in of an afternoon.'

'Oh, Grand-dad . . .'

'An' that's enough of that, too, no more tears. Now you see about dishing up the dinner, I'm not up to that yet,' he grinned at her and she forced herself to smile back, although she had never felt less like smiling in her life. 'An' then when I've helped your gran to the table and we've set to, you speak your piece. All right, lass?'

'All right, Grand-dad.' She nodded more vigorously

now. She would, she had to, she couldn't go on like this.

'Good girl.' He smiled at her one more time and then walked out of the room, shutting the door quietly behind him, but before moving down the narrow hall he shut his eyes for a moment and let his body sag against the wall. That poor lass, that poor little lass, and he was right in saying that he was as much to blame as anyone for their present predicament. He shook his head slowly as shame and remorse churned in his stomach. He knew what that pair in there were up to, he'd known for years, and what had he done about it? A few half-hearted attempts to break their hold on the lass but that was all. And why? His lips drew back from his teeth in self-disgust. Because of his own guilt, that was why. Guilt that he hadn't got to the bottom of that business with the lad, Steve Baker. Guilt that he didn't like his own flesh and blood, the more so since he'd taken up with that scum Frank Malley. Guilt that he could hardly bear to look at Mary these days, that everything about the woman she had become repulsed him, and most of all . . . He opened his eyes wide as he stared at the opposite wall. Most of all the guilt he felt about his wife's sister.

Martha . . . Just her name set off a fire in his loins he couldn't control. As his feeling for his wife had died that for her sister had grown, he'd known it from the first day they had arrived back in Sheffield and Martha had come round to help with the moving in, her face pale and set and her eyes deep pools of sadness. He'd sensed then that, whatever else, her marriage wasn't a happy one, and the force of his emotion had terrified him. How many times had he wished her dead rather than married to that scum?

Hundreds. He knew why she'd married him, it didn't take a genius to put two and two together when Connie was born a few months after the wedding. But what he didn't know was how she could have stood him touching her in the first place. He moved his lips one over the other and then levered himself off the wall. Enough. Enough of that. It was the little lass he had to concentrate on now, because when those two in there heard what she was planning there'd be all hell let loose, if he knew anything about his wife and grandson.

By the time everyone was seated at the kitchen table Jenny's earlier high resolve to state her case firmly and calmly had dwindled into sick apprehension. All the time she had been placing the food on the plates she'd been telling herself she was in the right. All she was asking for was three days out of the house and she'd be earning a good wage to boot, able to provide for her own clothes and things. And it wasn't good for her grandmother to lie in bed or sit at the window all day, that new young doctor had been quite emphatic about that when he'd called some weeks ago. He'd even advised a little gentle exercise. But when she'd repeated his words to David her brother had cluck-clucked before putting his arm round her shoulders and telling her, very quietly and in a voice full of sympathy and concern, that she had to realize Doctor Penn was trying to encourage her along, to bear up, but the truth of the matter was that their grandmother was very, very ill. She should know how she felt, shouldn't she?

She glanced at David now and it was as if his eyes had been waiting for her. 'I'm sorry, Jen, blowing my top like that.' His voice was soft and full, that special voice he kept just for her. 'It's just that I've been around a bit more than you have and I know how things can turn from good to bad in minutes. They could have trouble at that place tonight –'

'I told you, I had no intention of going with Connie.' Her voice was stiff but she couldn't help it, every nerve in her body felt as though it was raw and exposed and she couldn't afford to weaken now. It wasn't as though she didn't love them. She did, and she knew they loved her, but lately she'd begun to feel as though she was being sucked dry of every little thing that made her her and it was frightening, terrifying. 'She'd asked me weeks ago and I said no then.' She took a deep breath and kept her voice flat and even as she continued. It was better she told them before they asked and they'd ask, she knew they'd ask. 'It was about a job actually, what she wanted to see me about.'

'A job?'

It was as though she'd said something obscene, but before David could say any more her grandmother silenced him with one glance before turning to Jenny, her mouth smiling but her eyes sharp. 'A job, lass? What sort of a job and for who?'

'Me.' She heard the note of pleading in her voice and despised herself for it. 'At the corner shop where Connie works.'

'Slater's?' Her grandmother again motioned her grandson to silence when he would have spoken with an abrupt motion of her hand. 'Is Connie leaving, then?'

'No, no, she's not leaving.' She found herself gabbling and forced herself to slow down. 'Connie would still be there but Mrs Slater's having a baby at the end of December and he doesn't want her working in the shop any more. He just wants a part-timer for the end of the week when it's busy. Thursday, Friday and Saturday, just three days a week.'

'And Connie thought you'd be interested in a job?' Mary said stiffly.

'Yes.' She wanted to back down, to say it didn't matter, but it did matter, it mattered desperately. 'Especially as one of the days was Saturday when Davie and Grand-dad are home at midday. She thought –'

'I know what the little bitch thought –'

'David!' The fact that Mary gave her grandson his full name as much as the tone of voice cut off David's growl in mid flow. 'I'll deal with this.' There followed an exchange of glances that brought David to his feet with a muttered oath before he stamped out of the room, banging the door behind him. The front door followed suit in the next second or two, and when the three of them were alone Mary leant back in her chair without taking her eyes off her grand-daughter's face. 'And what about Thursday and Friday?' she asked quietly, 'when Davie and Grand-dad aren't home at midday?'

'Ethel'd be glad to come in and sit.' George came into the conversation for the first time. 'She spends half her time round here any road from what I can make out.'

'You've asked her that?' Mary's eyes were lethal as they fastened on her husband's face.

'I don't have to. She has a job to manage on what she gets, you know that as well as I do, and the lass'd be prepared to make it worth her while.'

'You have been busy, haven't you?'

It was as though she wasn't in the room. Jenny dropped her eyes to her congealing dinner when the sight of their faces became too painful. She should never have started this, never have mentioned about the job. *Yes, she should*. The words were fierce in her mind. Yes, she should. If she didn't, she'd live and die an old maid within these four walls, she knew she would.

'The lass needs to have her own life, Mary. Dammit, woman, you must be able to see that? You're expectin' too much –'

'Oh, am I? Well, there's nothing more to be said, then, is there? Anyway, as far as I know I haven't raised any objections. Have I said I don't want you to take the job, lass?' The sudden assault in her direction brought Jenny's eyes snapping upwards.

'N-no –'

'There you are, then.' Mary swung back towards her husband, her face vicious. 'She knows she's free to do what she wants. Same as you.'

'An' what does that mean?'

'Whatever you want it to mean.'

'I don't understand you, woman. As God is my witness, I don't. What are you so scared of, you and the lad? She's a grown woman of twenty, Mary, not a young bit of a bairn of thirteen. I'm tellin' you –'

'Aye, you're telling me, you're telling me.' Mary glared across the table. 'And that's supposed to be all right, is it? You walk about with your eyes closed and your ears blocked and I'm supposed to feel reassured when you tell me somethin', am I?'

'For cryin' out loud –'

'Can't you see what things are like? Can't you?' Mary hissed. 'No. Why am I even askin' the road I know anyway? As long as you've got your darts and your football you couldn't care less about anythin' else. When Britain won the World Cup last year, that was your world put in order, wasn't it? Geoff Hurst became your God and God to plenty more besides. It didn't matter that that filthy law came into operation around the same time, did it? Homosexuality legalized!' Her lips drew back from her teeth in something resembling a snarl.

'Dammit, woman, I've never said I agree with that –'

'The streets aren't safe for decent folk any more and no one will convince me but that it's violence encouraged by the films and suchlike causing it. Young girls like our Jenny can't safely be out after dark, and the authorities encourage it –'

'Of course they don't.' George stared hard at his wife, wondering for a moment if she was going mad. 'You're talking rubbish.'

'Am I! Am I? Then how do you explain this new Radio One pop channel that's come about? If that isn't a slippery slope, I don't know what is, pandering to the worst in the youngsters –'

'It's just music, Mary, that's all –'

'Music? Pah!' She rose but her gaze was on Jenny as she spoke. 'I know what it is, encouraging lads and lasses to go wild, that's what it is, and some are more easily led than others. I'm going back to my room. There's a news item I want to see on the television that Davie bought for me.' She laid slight emphasis on her grandson's name as her eyes flicked across George's face before returning to Jenny's bent head. 'About this Dr Christiaan Barnard and some new heart work he's doing. Perhaps in time to come people like me won't have live a life without hope and with nothing to brighten their days.'

When Jenny didn't move or raise her head, her gaze fixed on her plate, George felt like applauding her for her courage in holding out. And it would have taken some courage with his lass's soft heart. When those twins were born something had got all mixed up, he told himself grimly, as he watched his wife shuffle from the room. A man couldn't be soft, weak, of course he couldn't, but a little tenderness now and again didn't go amiss. But his grandson was hard right through, like stone, and that measure of softness worked double in his grand-daughter, bless her. And his wife hadn't been slow to capitalize on it, keeping the lass so close to her you'd think she was still milk-fed.

'Well, you won that battle, lass, but there's still the rest of the war.'

'Oh, Grand-dad . . .' As Jenny lifted her eyes to him he saw her face was streaming with tears. 'She sounded so . . . unhappy, bitter.'

'I don't care how she sounded. Your grandma is a very strong woman, lass, in her mind.' He could have said a lot more, detailing his wife's iron determination to move them back to this town within weeks of the Steve Baker incident seven years ago, the fact that she wouldn't consider any other place, even Rotherham, a few miles away. No, it had to be here, where he was guaranteed a job because of the strings Frank Malley could pull and everything was laid on tap. She'd even planned, at that early date, to have David in the steelworks alongside him as soon as the lad left school. He had argued and shouted, pleaded and raged for hours, days, but she'd used her illness to trap him and wrap him up as securely as a fly caught in a web. He leant forward abruptly, his eyes hard and tight. 'Now mind you don't weaken, girl, whatever they use against you.' He was suddenly quite sure they hadn't heard the last of this little lot. 'You understand me? You hold out for what you want now or you'll never have another chance.'

'I know, Grand-dad.' Jenny rose slowly, looking at the full plates of food left on the table. 'I know.'

It was after midnight when she heard David's key in the lock downstairs and as she expected he went straight in to her grandmother, the murmur of their voices barely audible as she lay wide awake and wretched upstairs. Almost half an hour passed before she heard him walk through to the kitchen, presumably to make her grandmother a hot drink, from the sound of the saucepan being set on the stove, and then some time later she heard his heavy footsteps mounting the stairs. They paused for a second outside her door and then continued to his room at the far end of the landing, her grandfather's bedroom being between hers and David's. She still didn't relax, lying taut and rigid under the bedclothes, her hands clenched and her eyes straining wide in the darkness. She lay like this for what seemed like hours but in reality was no more than twenty or so minutes before a severe bout of cramp in the calf of her right leg brought her sitting upright and rubbing at the offending muscles, the pain excruciating.

Once the spasm eased she lay back again, sleep a million miles away. She'd love a hot drink herself. She twisted restlessly in the bed. But Davie might follow her down . . . She didn't pursue the thought, pushing the unease she felt, if she was alone with her brother these days, to the back of her mind.

At some point in the night she must have drifted into a light doze because when the sound of breaking glass brought her sharply awake it was early morning. 'What? . . .'

She heard a door open and then the sound of running feet, and she had just reached her bedroom door, knotting the belt of her dressing gown tightly round her waist, when the sound of David's voice calling her name made her pull open the door and leap out on to the landing, her heart thudding.

'What's going on?' Her grandfather called her as she flew down the stairs, but she didn't wait, replying over her shoulder as she went.

'I don't know. I think it's Gran.'

No. George stood just outside his bedroom door and the feeling inside him was such that he couldn't have explained it to anyone. He'd been expecting something but not this early. No, he thought she'd have had the sense to leave it a few days. And had the lad been in on it? He rubbed his hand across his face, dragging the skin round his eyes. Probably. Aye, probably. *Dammit all, what was he going to do?*

He had to force himself to put one foot in front of the other when Jenny's voice floated up to him. 'Grand-dad? Grand-dad, quick.' Quick? There's no need to be quick, lass. The unspoken words were bitter on his tongue. She'd have this down to a fine art. Poorly, a bad turn, but not too bad that she couldn't recover nice and slow with plenty of care and attention. By, women were the devil. The very devil. And his grandson . . . *What was he going to do?*

As it happened, he was able to do very little. The doctor was called, and George knew the cards were well and truly stacked against his grand-daughter when he saw Doctor Mead walk through the door some minutes later. If it had been Doctor Penn he might have been able to make a few pertinent comments to set the doctor on the right track, but as far as Doctor Mead was concerned his wife could do no wrong. 'A grand woman.' How many times had he heard him say it? 'Oh she's a grand woman, George, one of the best, but then I don't have to tell you that, do I?' No, he didn't need anyone to tell him what Mary was like because the old saying 'You have to drink from a well to know its water' was never more true than in his wife's case.

By the time the doctor left Jenny's fate was as good as signed and sealed. 'Plenty of rest and quiet, no excitement or exertion of any kind, light tasty meals several times a day, and don't let her get depressed or anxious.'

The brief fight to break free was finished, he could see it in the weary line of Jenny's shoulders and the tightness to her mouth, but he still had one last attempt at a rallying cry when he followed Jenny and David into the kitchen once Mary was asleep.

'You aren't thinkin' of putting off that job, are you, lass? You know your gran will be fine in a few days –'

'I don't believe this!' David reared up in his seat, glaring at his grandfather as his fist thumped on the table. 'You've seen what she's like –'

'Aye, I have, lad.' There was something in the older man's voice that stopped David in his tracks, the grey of his eyes turning black as they narrowed and held faded blue. 'An' I'll ask again, you're still takin' the job, lass?'

'I can't, Grand-dad.' There was a dead note to Jenny's voice, and in the second that it took for the bright burning triumph in David's eyes to be masked George knew such a murderous rage that he had to leave the room quickly without saying another word.

CHAPTER EIGHT

'Jenny . . . Hallo, love, how's your grandma?'

'Not too bad, Aunt Martha.' It had been a week since she had been in this kitchen but it seemed like a year.

'Connie's upstairs if you want to go up, messing with her hair. You know she's had it all cut off?'

'Her hair?' Jenny was genuinely shocked. Connie's hair had been waist-length, thick and shiny. 'What for?'

'Got some idea she wanted to look like that model, Twiggy, is it?' Martha asked grimly. 'The one that's all eyes and bones. Her dad fair hit the ceiling when she walked in tonight but there it is, she can't stick it back on. Anyway, one thing led to another and she gave him a lot of cheek so she's in tonight, not that it'll stop her bunch, I suppose. They'll all come round here as usual. Go on up anyway, lass, and I'll pop round and see your gran once I've done the dinner things. Is your grand-dad with her?' she asked casually as she turned back to the full sink. ''Cos David's gone with Frank to that darts match, hasn't he?'

'Yes.' It was an answer to both questions and Martha took it as such. 'I'll go up, then.'

When she entered her cousin's room after knocking once she didn't know quite what to expect, but nothing had prepared her for the elfin look of the girl who turned to face her. And Connie was right. The straight blond hair cut close to her head with two long curls resting on her cheeks did make her look like Twiggy, although her cousin's shape was quite different from the painfully thin model's.

'Dad went mad.' Connie grinned at her as Jenny's fascinated gaze moved from her hair to her face. 'But I like it. What do you think?'

'I –' Jenny paused and then smiled for the first time in days. 'I reckon it's brilliant. I reckon *you're* brilliant.'

'Groovy, eeh . . .' Connie giggled as she reached out and pushed her cousin down on to the bed. 'My hair'll be shorter than Mick's now!' She turned and wagged her head at the reflection in the mirror.

'Has he seen it?'

'No. He's coming round later with one or two of his mates and we were all going to go down the pub, but Dad's turned awkward just because I told him it's nothing to do with him how I have me hair done, so we'll have to stay here.'

'It is a bit . . . extreme, Connie. I suppose it'll take Uncle Frank a bit of time to get used to it.'

'He can take all the time he needs, I couldn't care less. I'm sick of –' Connie stopped abruptly. 'Oh, Jenny, I'm sorry, how's Aunt Mary? And how are you coping?' She sounded penitent now.

'She's –' Jenny went to give the stock answer and then bit her lip, shaking her head from side to side as she shut her eyes tightly. Her grandmother. Oh, oh, her grandmother . . .

'She's not worse –'

'No, no, it isn't that.' There was a moment's pause and then she opened her eyes to stare straight into her cousin's face. 'I don't know how she is, Connie, not really, you know what I mean? I thought at first she was really bad . . .'

'You'd told them about the job?' Connie's voice was flat. 'Before?' she added meaningfully.

'Uh, huh.'

'Oh, Jenny . . .'

'I'm not saying she isn't bad, but there's been times over the last week –' She stopped and the sound she made was indecipherable but Connie nodded in answer. 'And then I feel awful, wicked, that I could think such things but . . . But I do.'

'And Uncle George? What does he think?'

'We haven't discussed it.' Jenny raised her head, which had been bent almost to her chest. 'But I don't think he believes she had an attack.'

No, I bet he doesn't, Connie thought. Her Uncle George was nobody's fool. And from what she'd heard her mam saying when she was rowing with her dad a few nights ago, when they didn't know she'd come in, her mam was of the same opinion and she'd gone one step further to state that David was at the bottom of it all. Not that her dad would have that, but then he wouldn't, would he? Not with David. Would David put Aunt Mary up to something like that? Yes, of course he would. The fact that she could even ask such a question compressed her lips into a thin cynical line. You only had to look at David when he was near his sister to see how things were. He was hell-bent on keeping her in that house shut away from everyone, hell-bent. She wasn't so daft that she didn't know the reason he hated her either. He didn't like anyone Jenny liked, anyone that took his sister's attention away from himself.

'What are you going to do, Jen?'

'What can I do?' Jenny shrugged as she stood up and walked over to the little window that overlooked the street. 'Just put up with it for the time being.'

'The time being?'

'Well, what would you suggest?' Jenny swung round at the caustic note in her cousin's voice. 'Go out and leave her? Is that it? You think I haven't thought of that, Connie? It's there in the back of my mind night and day, but what if she wasn't putting it on? What then? Would you be prepared to have someone's death on your conscience?'

'It wouldn't be like that –'

'And how do you know? How on earth do you know that? It's all very well for you to look down your nose at me and think what you'd do in my shoes, but it'd be a different story if you were actually in them. I know you think I'm a coward –'

'I don't –'

'Yes, you do, I know you do.' As Jenny sank down on the bed again she covered her face with her hands, the tears spurting from her eyes. 'Well, I do at any rate.'

'Oh, Jen . . .' Connie pulled Jenny into her arms and let her cry her fill, her eyes narrowing as she thought of what she would like to do to David. She'd met some selfish swines in her time but he took the biscuit, he really did. 'C'mon, it'll be all right.'

'I'm sorry, Connie, to take it out on you like that. I didn't mean to.' Jenny sat up, scrubbing at her face with her handkerchief.

'I know, I know, that's half your trouble anyway. You've got no one to talk to and you keep everything bottled in, you always have. Look, like you said, put up with it for a while and see how things go, nothing's lost.'

'Has the job gone at the shop?' Jenny's voice was small.

Connie nodded silently. 'But it's not the only one about,' she said quickly. 'Something else'll turn up when you're ready. Come on, Jen, keep your end up.'

'Oh, Connie . . .' Jenny let out a long, weary sigh before continuing. 'I don't mean to be nasty but you don't understand, you couldn't. Everything's gone all right for you, and I don't grudge you that, I promise you I don't, but –' She paused for a moment. 'It hasn't been like that for me.'

'It might not be like that for me much longer.'

'What?' For the first time since she had come into the room Jenny forgot her own troubles and really looked into her cousin's face, noticing for the first time the sign of strain in the dark brown eyes. 'What do you mean?'

'Oh, nothin' . . .' Connie shrugged and smiled her cheeky grin and the illusion was shattered. 'It's probably nothin', I'll tell you if it's not.'

'If what's not?' Jenny asked anxiously.

'Connie!' The sound of Martha's voice calling up the stairs finished the conversation abruptly. 'Mick's here. Are you and Jenny coming down?'

'Yes, hang on.' Connie turned to Jenny after a quick glance in the mirror. 'Think he's ready for the new me?'

'If he could handle the old one, I don't think a change of hairstyle is going to put him off,' Jenny said dryly. 'Do you want me to wait up here, or will he stay?'

'I dunno. Come down anyway. Mam said I could have the front room once Dad'd gone so Mick'll probably stay. If his mates stay'n all, we could have a party, how about that?'

'You're in enough trouble with your dad as it is.'

As they made their way downstairs Mick was waiting in the hall in the full glare of the light overhead, his two friends standing to one side in shadow. 'Bloomin' 'ell, what on earth –' He stopped at a warning cough from Jenny, but then couldn't help continuing, 'your mam said I'd get a surprise, Con, but . . . Bloomin' 'ell.'

'Blooming hell apart, do you like it?'

'Well –' Something in his girlfriend's face must have warned the blunt, stocky individual to go carefully because he smiled weakly. 'Yeh, yeh, course I do. It's . . . Well, it's . . .'

'Different?' Jenny put in helpfully.

'Yeh, different, that's it.' The diversion was obviously welcome as he looked up at Jenny. 'Sorry about your gran, Jen.'

'You stopping?' Connie indicated the front room with a wave of her hand. 'Mam said you could.'

'I –' He clearly found it difficult to tear his gaze away from her shorn head but after another incredulous glance he gestured to the two figures behind him. 'Mark 'n Peter are here.'

'Don't worry about us.' The taller of the two lads moved into the light just as Connie moved off the bottom step of the stairs into the hall. 'We can go to the pub –'

'Well, come in the front room for a minute anyway.' Connie pushed past Mick and opened the door. 'There's not room to swing a cat in the hall.'

Jenny went to follow Connie and as the tall boy to the side of Mick stepped back for her to precede him, she glanced up to smile her thanks at the courtesy and almost stumbled on meeting the intent scrutiny of a pair of very piercing blue eyes which seemed to hold her to the spot for a moment before she recovered herself and walked past. She found she was shaking slightly with the force of her feelings as she sat herself down on the big pouffe in the corner of the modern, nicely furnished room but when she raised her face a few seconds later she found those eyes were still tight on her. And now she saw he wasn't the young lad she had first assumed him to be. The big, broad-shouldered body was that of a man of twenty-three, twenty-four maybe, and the square face, in which the blue of the eyes made a startling contrast to the blunt, somewhat craggy features, was tanned as though he'd been abroad recently.

'I don't think we've met.' He was looking directly at Jenny as he spoke but it was Connie who answered, and Jenny had never been more grateful for her cousin's dominant bouncy personality, as she tried to pull herself together and act normally.

'Oh sorry, Peter, I forgot you haven't met Jenny yet. Peter, Jenny, Jenny, Peter. Will that do?' She flapped her hand at the three lads. 'Sit down, sit down. Me mam paid enough for this new three-piece so you might as well use it. Who wants coffee?'

'You're a friend of Connie's?' Peter had moved across to stand in front of her even before Connie had finished speaking, and as Connie raised her eyebrows at Mick and inclined her head slightly, Jenny caught the action out of the corner of her eye and blushed painfully.

'No, well, yes – I mean, I am her friend but I'm her cousin too . . .' She had never felt so naïve, even stupid, in her life. But then she'd never met anyone like this man standing in front of her either. He was – Well, he was –

'Her cousin?' The deep voice was not from these parts, it was almost accentless, cultured. 'Ah yes, I can see a faint resemblance,' he said slowly with a slight lift of his eyebrows.

'Can you?' She smiled nervously.

'Yes, in your build and your hair. At least . . .' He

smiled as he glanced round at Connie. 'When you had hair, that is.'

'Oh, you! I'll go and get the coffee –'

'Not for me, thanks.' Jenny rose quickly, a tight smile on her face as she glanced round at everyone generally, taking great care not to meet those vivid blue eyes again. 'I'd better get back.' She needed to escape. She didn't know why, she just did.

'Not yet, Jen, surely. Mam's just gone round your place to see Aunt Mary so she'll be all right. Come and help me make the coffee, c'mon.' Connie took the initiative out of Jenny's hands by simply pushing her out of the room and into the small kitchen down the hall, leaving the three males alone. 'What's the matter with you?' As soon as they were alone she looked her cousin straight in the face. 'Bolting like that!'

'Bolting? I wasn't bolting, I was just –'

'Huh!'

Jenny felt herself rearing slightly but as always her innate sense of honesty won through and brought a warmth to her cheeks.

'What did you think of him, then, Peter?' Connie plugged in the kettle and fetched five mugs from the cupboard. 'He's just moved next door to Mick. He's lodging with Mrs Anderson and you'll never guess what he does, for a living I mean.'

'Won't I?' Jenny wasn't going to try.

'He's a teacher!' It was almost as if Connie had pulled a rabbit out of a hat. 'You know, a proper teacher. Apparently he's been to university and everything and he's left London where he was living and come up here for some reason, but he can't get a full-time job yet. He's doing some nights at the college, Mick said, teachin' maths and something else, I can't remember now. Nice though, isn't he?'

'He seems all right,' Jenny said carefully, her voice bland.

'He was very struck with you –'

'Oh, Connie, don't start that.'

'I'm not startin' anything. But he was, you could see it a mile off, and don't pretend you didn't notice, Jen, 'cos I know you did. Didn't you like him, then?'

'I don't know him now, do I? And I said, he seems all right.'

'Big deal.' Connie sniffed with great feeling. 'Well, I think he's lovely. If I hadn't got Mick I'd have made a play for him, I can tell you. He's twenty-four 'n all, nice age for a bloke, I always think. They're ready to settle down at twenty-four and don't mind putting their money where their mouth is.'

The boiling kettle brought her cousin's attention to the coffee and Jenny took the opportunity to take a few deep breaths to try to bring her racing heart under control. What on earth was the matter with her? She was acting like a skittish schoolgirl, for goodness' sake, he'd think she was ridiculous – She shut her eyes tightly for one second as she fought for calm. But it was the way he'd looked at her – No, it wasn't just that. It was everything about him . . . She was saved the necessity of trying to find words to describe Mrs Anderson's lodger by the opening of the door.

'Con?' Mick's whisper was centre-stage volume. 'You got anything you could put in a sandwich for Peter but without letting him know you've done it special? He was goin' to get pie and chips before we went in the pub 'cos Mrs Anderson don't feed him enough to keep a kitten alive, but they'll be shut in ten minutes.'

'Course.' Connie had just filled the mugs, and after putting the sugar bowl and some spoons on the tray she handed it to Jenny. 'Take that in, would you, and you can spread some bread, Mick. The marge is in the bread bin.'

'I –' Jenny looked at her cousin and Connie stared back, her dark eyes determined.

'Go on, he won't eat you.'

He didn't eat her but by the end of the evening Jenny wasn't quite sure what he had done to her. She had never felt so alive, so . . . aware in all her life, and although it wasn't a comfortable feeling it was exciting. *Exciting!* She mentally shook her head at her own naïvety. Well, it was for sure she wouldn't appear that way to him. Dull as ditch-water, more like. She watched him as he leant across Mick to answer something Mark had said to him and her heart hammered against her ribs. And she'd been here too long, far too long, but she hadn't wanted to leave. She stood up quickly now, her face betraying her agitation.

'I'll have to go, Connie. Your dad'll be home soon.'

Connie didn't make the obvious retort that her father wouldn't mind finding Jenny here because she knew exactly what Jenny was really saying. David had a way of appearing when he was least wanted, like an old flame at a wedding, and an uncanny knack of honing in on Jenny's mind. She looked at her cousin and nodded quickly. And if he saw Peter, and noticed the way he looked at Jenny . . . And he'd notice. If there was one thing that was for certain it was that. He missed nothing where Jenny was concerned.

'I'll walk you home.' Peter had stood up the moment she had risen, his gaze holding hers.

'No.' It was almost as though David was in the room with them, and she couldn't soften the refusal with a smile, her face felt stiff with panic. 'No, it's all right. It's only the next street but one.'

'I'm going that way anyway.'

She hadn't indicated in which direction she was going, she realized before she shook her head again. 'No, really.' She saw his face straighten but there was no way she could explain, and she bit tightly on her lip for a second before leaving the room, Connie close on her heels as she reached the back door.

'I'll tell him, Jen.' Connie nodded at her rapidly. 'Explain. You go.'

'I –' She wanted to say there was nothing to explain, to defend Connie's unspoken criticism of the way her brother was, but in the same instant the little voice inside her head that was making itself heard more and more these days, upbraided her bitterly. Who are you kidding? Who *are* you kidding? Start facing facts, girl, or you'll never be free of it all. You don't want Davie to see him, not yet, do you? It might be nothing. Peter probably wasn't remotely interested in a girl like her, who'd done and seen nothing when he'd been to university and France and all those other places he'd been telling them about, but if Davie saw him now everything, the whole magical evening, would be tarnished. He'd go on and on, like he had done several times in the past when he'd caught one of Connie's friends looking at her a fraction too long, detailing how men wanted just one thing, the way they viewed women, how their minds worked, until she felt dirty and soiled. And she couldn't stand that this time, not this time.

'Bye, Connie.' She slipped out of the little backyard quickly and fairly flew down the alley into the lights of the street at the other end where she hurried along, head bent, as she made for home. She reached the house two or three minutes before David, to find her grandfather had already retired upstairs and her Aunt Martha was just leaving.

'Hallo, lass.' Martha smiled at her niece's flushed face as she poked her head round the sitting-room door. 'Been having a good old chin-wag with Connie, then? I've just been tellin' your grandma what she did with her hair and how her dad kept her in the night. Still, it won't do her any harm not to see that boyfriend of hers for a night or so.' It was a definite lead and Jenny took it as such. So her aunt Martha had paved the way. She smiled at the older woman now, a little glow in her heart at the unexpected support. 'Well, I'd better be goin', Mary lass. I'll pop round sometime over the weekend and see how things are.'

'Not to worry, Martha, don't fret yourself. I'm looked after right well, aren't I, Jenny?' Mary nodded at her grand-daughter, her eyes narrowing suddenly at the light in the young girl's face. What had she been up to? She caught herself quickly at her own thoughts. Eeh, no doubt the lass had just been rabbiting on with Martha's young 'un. She always came back full of it from there. She felt a moment's guilt at the confines of her grand-daughter's life but it didn't last. She knew what was right for the lass, that she did. Hadn't it been learnt the hard way? But he'd got what he deserved, that Steve Baker. God won't be mocked. Aye, he'd got what he deserved and while she'd got breath in her body she'd make sure Jenny was kept as she should be.

'Hallo, David.' Martha had just reached the front door when the sound of a key turning in the lock made her step back to face her nephew. How could someone who was so handsome, and he *was* handsome, she admitted to herself as she stared up into his face, how could he repel her so utterly? 'I'm just going.'

He nodded without speaking, his heavy-lidded eyes cold and unblinking, and she brushed past him and stepped into the street. Sullen, morose individual . . . Martha's mouth was grim as she walked swiftly down the street. She felt sorry for that young lass in there, by, she did. To be stuck in the house with her sister all day was bad enough, especially with it furnished the way it was, but to have to put up with that one on top of everything else! And George, how did he tolerate the set-up in that house? Her stomach muscles clenched at the name. Come to that, how did she put up with her lot? She didn't know at times. She had imagined it would get easier with the passing years but she had been wrong, quite wrong.

Oh, George . . . She stood still for a moment and hugged herself tightly, her head bowed. Well, they'd paid for their feelings, that much was for sure, and were still paying . . .

'You been out?' David smiled at his sister as she walked out into the hall but his eyes narrowed on the coat that she hadn't had time to slip off, and they didn't leave her as he kicked the front door shut.

'Connie's.' She glanced at him briefly before turning her gaze away.

'Oh, aye, Frank said there'd been something of a rumpus the night. He was steaming mad. What's her hair look like, then?' He had followed her into the kitchen as he spoke and now sat on the edge of the kitchen table watching her making her grandmother a mug of cocoa, a practice of his that always made her uncomfortable.

'I liked it.' She shrugged without turning round.

'Aye well, she's a pretty lass. I dare say she could carry off being bald if she wanted.'

She gave him a quick smile before taking the milk off the stove, and as always his eyes were ready to meet hers, their grey soft and warm. He was trying to be nice about Connie, she thought, for her sake. Since the night of her grandmother's attack he had been thoughtfulness itself, insisting she put her feet up in the evening while he did the dishes, carrying the laundry basket down each night in preparation for the washing the next day, fussing that she wasn't eating enough, doing the hundred and one things that ought to make her feel grateful but instead made her want to scream, adding, as they did, to the ever-present feeling of being suffocated. This tender side of him, which he kept just for her, unnerved her, it always had, even as she told herself that she had no reason to feel uneasy, threatened. He was her brother. He was just protective, concerned for her, and that . . . incident when they were thirteen had made him more so. It was understandable, perfectly understandable.

As though her next words were a continuation of her thoughts she turned to him and said. 'You never bring anyone home, Davie, a lass.'

'A lass?' He stiffened, his eyes tight on her face. 'Why would I want to bring a lass home?'

'Well, you must meet a few.' She turned back to the cocoa and spooned sugar into the foaming liquid. 'And I know there are quite a few hereabouts who fancy you.'

'Are there? That's nice to know.' But the way he spoke indicated just the opposite.

'What about Jane Boulton or Annie Brice? They're both nice and –'

'Jenny . . .' He hitched himself off the table as he spoke, his big, lean body straight as he stood looking down at her. 'I don't want Jane Boulton or Annie Brice, all right?' Her hair was shining like a cloud of gold in the weak artificial light and the sight of it ran liquid in his veins as he took in the slim narrow back and slender waist. Hell . . . He almost groaned out loud but stopped himself just in time. He needed to pay a visit to Tinsley Street, and soon. He'd have gone there the night but the amount Frank had drunk, he'd never have got home by himself.

'Well, not them maybe, but there must be someone you like.' She put the mug on a small tray and reached for the tin of biscuits before turning, and then froze, the tin still in her hand, as she took in the expression on his face.

'There's no one.' His voice was thick but it was the hot intensity of his eyes that stopped her breath, but then he'd swung round in the next instant, walking to the door as he continued to speak. 'What you trying to do anyway? Marry me off?' His laugh was forced. 'It'll take more than a pretty face or a nice pair of legs to get me down to the altar, Jenny.'

As the door closed behind him Jenny's breath was expelled in a long and slow quivering sigh and she steadied herself against the hard wood of the cupboard, closing her eyes. She was mistaken. Of course she was mistaken. The biscuits almost slipped from her grasp as she sagged forward. She was, because to be anything else was . . . unthinkable.

CHAPTER NINE

'Jenny, sooner or later you are going to have to let me meet your family.' Peter's voice was soft but firm. 'It's been four weeks now and all this skulking about is getting on my nerves. I know how you feel about things, I do –' He held up his hand when she would have interrupted him. 'But don't you see that you're feeding this . . . obsession they've got about keeping you locked away just by behaving like this now? We aren't doing anything wrong and I want to be seen with you, that's not too much to ask, is it?'

'No, I know.' She looked up at him, his craggy face a mass of lines and shadows in the dimly lit and narrow terraced street.

'And you're on tenterhooks the whole time, you know you are. And look at that poor pair in front.' He gestured towards Connie and Mick, who had agreed to venture out on a walk in the bitingly cold December night to provide an alibi for Jenny, should David arrive at Connie's house and find she wasn't there. 'They wanted to go to the pictures to see that new film everyone's talking about, *Bonnie and Clyde*, and instead they're tramping the streets with their eyes fixed firmly in front so we can have a bit of privacy.' He grinned disarmingly. 'Do you think we could at least stop and have a drink somewhere? I can't feel my feet.'

'Peter, just be patient for another few days. If anyone should see us in a pub or at the pictures or something, David would hear of it, I know it. Let's just get Christmas over and I promise I'll tell them. I will.'

'If you don't I shall.' He stopped and pulled her close to him, his big black overcoat making him seem even bigger against her tiny fairness. 'You know how I feel about you, I can't carry on like this.' He kissed the top of her nose before tucking her hand under his arm as they continued walking again. 'It's a wonder I haven't run into David before now as it is. It can't last. And he's never going to get used to the idea of you having a boyfriend if he doesn't know, is he? You've got to face him with it and be strong, Jenny. What can he do after all?'

'I don't know.' She raised her face to his, her eyes troubled. 'That's the thing. You don't know him, Peter –'

'Exactly. And that is something I want remedied at the earliest opportunity. Whatever he is like, I'll get on with him, I promise you.' He looked down at her on his arm, holding her gaze as he lowered his head slowly and laid his lips gently on hers, the kiss deepening as he felt her response. 'I've got too much to lose not to, haven't I?'

'You won't lose me.' She smiled at him as her eyelids blinked rapidly. She was happy. She couldn't remember being so happy. 'Whether David takes to you or you to him will make no difference to us.'

'Do you mean that?' he asked softly, his breath a cloud of white in the icy air.

'Yes, yes, I mean it. I didn't ever imagine I could feel for anyone what I feel for you, Peter Knowles.'

'Nor I for you, Jenny Longbridge.' They laughed and clung together for a second until a voice in front of them broke the moment.

'All right, all right, enough of that, me bairns.' Mick grinned at them as they approached him and Connie. 'This old lady is feelin' tired so we're for home, all right? You comin'?'

'We better had.' Jenny looked at Peter pleadingly.

'And I won't come in, I'll leave you all on the corner. I've got a feeling David will call in tonight with your dad, Connie. I think he suspects something.'

'Well, *tell* him.' Connie's voice was impatient. 'You can't –'

'She's going to tell him, tell them all,' Peter cut in as his arm went protectively round Jenny's waist. 'After Christmas. Right, girl?' He smiled down at her, his gaze warm. 'So it'll be the Fifth of November several weeks too late, by all accounts?'

'I hope not but if we prepare for the worst . . .' Jenny's gaze moved to Connie's face. 'You look more than tired, Connie. You feeling all right?'

'No.' Connie shot a quick glance at Mick and then smiled. 'But it'll pass, all things do, don't they?'

'So they say.'

The four of them walked back together through the bitterly cold, long narrow streets but in spite of the silly banter between them all Jenny's eyes were drawn constantly to her cousin's face. There was something worrying her, she just knew it, but as yet Connie wouldn't confide in her, and she knew better than to try and force a confidence. Although Connie was the epitome of the young modern woman, free and open and without pretence, she had that other side that was pure Malley . . . But Mick wasn't himself either. Jenny's brow wrinkled as she bit her lip. She'd have to get her alone and ask her what was wrong whether her cousin liked it or not.

She left the others on the corner of Crown Street and even then her eyes were flickering to and fro while she said her goodbyes. 'Relax . . .' Peter's voice was a low growl. 'What is this fellow like anyway? Anyone would think he was Old Nick himself rather than your brother.' She smiled weakly but said nothing. He didn't know, he didn't understand, none of them did really. She wasn't even sure if she did herself.

Mrs Brown was still sitting with her grandmother when she popped her head round the sitting-room door a few minutes later, it being her grandfather's darts night, and she was just making the two old ladies a hot drink when her grandfather walked in. 'Would you like a drink?' she asked quietly as she prepared to carry in the mugs with the requisite plate of biscuits.

'No, no thanks, lass. Two pints of bitter are enough liquid the night. Your brother in yet?' She shook her head silently. 'And you had a nice evenin'? Round Connie's?' She looked at him sharply. There was something in his tone that led her to think he was saying more than the mere words indicated.

'I –' She looked full into his face now and suddenly felt ashamed she hadn't confided in him before. She should have. She knew she should have. She could trust her grandfather. 'I wasn't at Connie's all night. I went for a walk – Me . . . Me and Connie and her boyfriend and –' She stopped abruptly. 'His name's Peter,' she added lamely. 'Peter Knowles.'

He didn't question who she was talking about. He bent towards her, his face straight, and gestured towards the sitting room. 'Be careful. Be very careful, lass. You know what I mean?'

She bowed her head before looking at him again. 'I'm going to tell them, Grand-dad, but later, after Christmas. I – I want one Christmas without them knowing, without any trouble.'

'Aye, I can understand that, lass. And this Peter? You like him?'

She nodded vehemently. 'He's a teacher. He's just moved up here from London because his mother has remarried. His father's dead, and he doesn't get on with his step-father or the kids he brought with him. He thought it better to move clean away and use the fact that the house had become so crowded and he'd just been offered a job here as the excuse, rather than just move out of his mother's home, which might have hurt her feelings. He finds the whole lot of them hard to take, although he says that if she's happy with this new bloke that's all that matters in the long run, but he thought he could keep his opinions to himself more easily if he put a good few miles between them and him.'

'Aye, he's right 'n all. How old is this here teacher, then?'

'Twenty-four, twenty-five in February,' she said softly.

'An' he likes you? No, you needn't bother to answer that, daft question, it is. Of course the lad'll like you if he's got eyes in his head. So . . . that's how things are?' His gaze was quizzical.

'I should've told you before, Grand-dad.'

'Aye, you should.' He grinned at her now. 'I knew somethin' was up, you being round at Connie's nearly every night now, but I thought it was maybe 'cos you were still smartin' about the job. Then old Dickie Wrainwright said he'd seen you on the corner a few nights ago with a nice-lookin' lad.'

'He didn't tell Davie?'

'He's got more sense than that, lass, the man's a friend of mine. No, he didn't let on but someone will. You can't keep anythin' to yourself round here, you know that as well as me. You know you'll get some stick when you tell 'em?' His face straightened. 'Especially from the young 'un?'

'I know.' Her voice was quiet.

'An' this lad knows how things are?'

She nodded. 'He knows about Grandma and how Davie's got this thing about looking after me. I explained Davie doesn't hold with all this free and easy love that's talked about these days, how fixed in his ways he is, and that he worries about me.'

'Aye.' He'd got his own views about his grandson's morals but now was not the time to expound them.

'But –' She paused and looked down at the tray in her hands. 'I – I haven't said anything about before we moved here.'

'No reason why you should, lass. So, it'll be fireworks after Christmas, then?'

'That's what Peter said. I'd better take them their drinks, hadn't I? Else they'll be cold. Grand-dad?' She stopped just before she opened the kitchen door. 'You'll like him. I know you will.' She was unaware of the pleading note in her voice.

'If he's your choice I'll like him, lass.' George put an arm round the slim shoulders but the sound of the front door opening made him move away from her with a whispered warning. 'Just be careful for the time being, that's all I ask.'

Well, it was bound to have happened eventually. As George sat down on one of the kitchen chairs he heard Jenny and David talking for a moment in the hall before they both appeared to go in to see Mary. But how was his grandson going to take this? They had fought hard enough over the job. But this was something different, quite different. Now Mary might be reasonable, if he was a nice fella, and he was by all accounts. She'd like the fact he was a teacher and of an age to settle down, yes, she might be won over. But David? Never. His eyes narrowed as he made himself face the fact that there was something badly wrong with his grandson, something unnatural, disturbing. He'd seen it grow through the years, aye, he had, and he wasn't fooled by this so-called moral integrity David spouted in the house. He'd had women, he could see the knowledge in his grandson's eyes. He might not bring them to the house but he'd had them all right, but that didn't stop him wanting his sister. The thought kicked at his stomach and made him nauseous. *Damn it all*. He rubbed his hand over his face. And that 'un lying in there was the cause of all this, by, she was. From the moment the lad had took breath she'd instilled it into him.

He sat back in the chair and took a deep breath to combat the growing rage. But it was more than that, aye, he knew it deep down. There'd been something born in the lad, a perversion, a sickness, and right or wrong no one would ever convince him different but that it was all down to the man who had fathered the bairns. He swore softly, the words ugly in the quiet room. And his Jenny hadn't been willing. He knew in his guts she hadn't been willing, and the animal could still be here, in this very town.

He stood up as Jenny and David walked into the kitchen. 'Mrs Brown's gone and I've just settled Gran down if you want to say good night,' Jenny smiled at him.

'All right, lass, an' you're away to bed?'

'In a minute. I'll just set the things for morning.'

George and David didn't exchange a word, merely grim nods as George left the room, but once they were alone David made no effort to leave, seating himself on the top of the kitchen table as he watched her prepare some sandwiches and thick slabs of ginger cake before packing the bait tins and turning to the sink to wash her hands.

'You're spending a lot of time at Connie's these days.'

'Am I?' She kept her voice even. 'Well, there's no law against that, is there?' She didn't turn round but closed her eyes for a moment.

'Not that I know of.' She heard him move and the next moment he had taken up the tea towel and was drying the mugs and spoons at her side. 'You there again tonight?'

'Yes.' He couldn't know. He wouldn't be like this if he knew.

'You weren't there when I called in with Frank.'

'We went for a walk, me and Connie and Mick, and I left them on the corner of our street so they could have some time together.' Oh, she hated lying, she did. Perhaps she should tell him? But she couldn't . . . She knew how he would be. 'You didn't see them then, at Frank's?'

'Aye, I saw them,' he answered shortly.

'Why ask the road you know, then?'

'Because I don't trust our sweet little cousin, that's why. She's got something up her sleeve. I can tell from the way she looks at me.' There was an inflexion in his voice that chilled her.

'You're imagining it.' He hadn't seen Peter . . . She stopped her body sagging with relief. Peter couldn't have been with them, then, Connie must have realized her father was home. 'You've never liked her, have you? Not from when we first came here.'

'No, I haven't.' He had stopped rubbing the cloth over the crockery and now out of the corner of her eye she saw him raise his hand and then he was turning her face to his. 'An' I'll tell you something else, Jenny. If I find out you've been havin' me on I'll take it out on her hide, you understand me? So think on.'

She could feel her flesh draw back from his, although she made no movement, but the withdrawal was in her eyes and he sensed it, his eyes darkening with a combination of pain and anger. 'You wouldn't – You wouldn't hurt her –'

'I wouldn't think twice about it,' he said brutally. 'She's been aimin' to turn you against me from the day we first met, she knows it and I know it –'

'That's ridiculous –'

'The hell it is.'

She jerked her face out of his hold and turned away from him, opening the back door in one violent movement and then running to the lavatory and bolting the door behind her. Why did he act like this, why? She pulled the wooden top of the seat down and sat on it, swaying back and forth, her head pounding as memories swirled hot and fierce in her head. But that day seven years ago, she'd been young and frightened and sore and there hadn't been the smell of the Mulgatties' lavatory seeping into theirs, just the fresh clean air of the Kent countryside. Steve Baker. She shut her eyes tightly to stop her body remembering the feel of his hands and mouth on her flesh. Steve Baker . . . But it had been an accident, it had. He'd fallen whilst drunk and banged his head, they'd said. *They'd said.*

She shivered but the chill was inside her. She hadn't gone with the rest of the villagers to see Steve's body being brought out of the wood but David had, and when he'd come home that day there had been a quietness about him, almost a satisfaction, that had brought on the bout of sickness that had kept her in bed for a week. Perhaps it would have been better if she had gone with the others. Nothing could be worse than the images that stalked her night hours once she was asleep. She had started to have nightmares again, after years of being free of them. Since she had met Peter, Steve's face, torn and bloody, came to her night after night, grotesque and misshapen and vengeful. He was blaming her, blaming her for having his life snatched away . . .

Oh, she couldn't think like this. She opened her eyes and stared straight ahead as she fought for control. The past was gone, whatever had happened, and now she had the future to look forward to, and a future she had never dreamed was possible just a few weeks ago. She knew Peter would ask her to marry him, and she would say yes, like a shot. She nodded to herself. Whatever the consequences. They would face them together, *together*. And she had to find it within herself to stand up to David, and her grandmother, too. Their rule over her had to end. She knew it, she had known it even before she met Peter, but now it was imperative she acted on her knowledge. And she could do it. For the first time in her life she knew she could do it.

CHAPTER TEN

The run-up to Christmas was completed. It was Christmas Eve and Jenny was lying as wide awake as any child on that special night, but it was fear, not excitement, that had her in a stranglehold. Panic clawed at her throat as she thought about the Malleys' party the following day, an affair that had become something of a tradition, with friends and family automatically congregating in Frank and Martha's smart little house. She hadn't thought about Mick inviting Peter along, which was stupid, *stupid*, because after all, as Connie had pointed out, where else would he go? He'd got no family in this part of the country and he had been quite definite about staying in Sheffield, even though Mrs Anderson had been less than struck by his determination to stay in the house alone while she visited her sister's family in Glasgow for the holiday.

'You can't ask him not to come, Jenny.' Connie's voice and face had expressed her horror at her cousin's lack of enthusiasm after she had told her what Mick had done the day before, when they were alone in Connie's bright bedroom. 'He's all by himself, and at Christmas –'

'I wouldn't, you know I wouldn't. Of course he must come. It's just . . .'

'David.'

'Yes, David,' Jenny said flatly.

'But don't you see? It's probably better for him to see Peter here, with everyone about, for the first time. Even if he clicks on to the fact that you two are more than just good friends he won't make a scene in front of such a crowd, and you were going to tell him after Christmas anyway.'

'Yes, you're right.' Jenny managed a weak smile as she watched her cousin fiddling with her hair. 'As always.'

'I wouldn't say that.' There had been a trace of bitterness in Connie's voice. 'Certainly not at the moment.'

Jenny leant back against the upholstered headboard as her cousin turned round from the dressing table and plumped herself on the bed beside her. 'What's wrong, Connie?' she asked softly. 'Let me help.'

'No one can help.' And then her cousin had surprised her utterly by flinging herself against her, burying her face in her shoulder. 'I'm so frightened, Jen, I'm scared stiff.'

'Connie –'

'I'm pregnant.'

Jenny could say nothing, her mind seemed to have gone a complete blank, the more so since she had never seen her brash, confident cousin looking really frightened as she did now. But then the thought was uppermost that she should have known, she should have guessed. Both Connie and Mick had been so different over the last two or three weeks, but she had thought they were just having problems, and they were. One big gigantic problem. She'd known something like this would happen, she'd known it.

'When? How far gone are you?' she asked carefully.

'I've missed two periods now. The first time I put it down to that flu bug I had, I just couldn't believe –' Connie gulped deep in her throat as she raised her head, looking at Jenny with swimming eyes. 'But then last week there was nothing again and the last three mornings I've been sick. Oh, Jenny, what am I going to do?' she finished on a wail of desperation.

'What does Mick say?'

'He's – he's frightened too. On the one hand he says for me to have it and we'll get married and that, and then he's talking about . . . getting rid of it, you know. I just don't know what to do, Jen. I can't sleep, I can't eat and I feel so bad now, not just sick but tired. But – but I don't think I can get rid of it. That's murder, isn't it? Whatever way you look at it it's murder, and although I'm not a good Catholic like me mam I do believe there's some sort of judgement in the hereafter. What if it came and faced me –'

'Stop it, Connie.' Her flesh had gone cold. 'Stop thinking like that.'

'I can't, I can't. But then the thought of getting married now, at my age, well, that scares me to death too. And Mick's only an apprentice in the garage, it'll be another eighteen months, two years, before he earns anything, like. I just don't know what to do, and me Dad'll kill me . . . and Mick.'

'More likely Mick, your mam won't let him hurt you.'

'You don't know our dad like I do, Jen. There's things –' Connie stopped abruptly. 'I think me mam's had a time with him over the years, although she never says anything, but I've got eyes and ears and I've heard them rowing at times, quiet like. I think it's all to do with his possessiveness, the way he thinks about her. That's why she had to go out to work, I reckon, for her own sanity. And a bit of that feeling spills over to me, although I've never let him come the old soldier with what I can or can't do. But this – this is different. He'll go berserk. I've only seen him lose his temper once but it was scary, he wasn't like me dad. You know, when he found out that lad across the road had a pair of binoculars and he'd been looking in their bedroom window –'

'I remember.' The whole street would remember, no one could ever forget the sight of Frank kicking the big brawny nineteen-year-old, who was head and shoulders above him in stature, up and down the street until he'd been grovelling at Frank's feet in submission. 'But that was understandable, Connie, your dad reacting like that. Even that boy's parents said so. He's not going to hurt you, especially in your condition.'

'My condition . . .' The words were a whisper. 'I can't believe it, Jen, I really can't. How could we have been so stupid? Mick thought he'd been so careful.'

'Accidents happen.' Jenny took Connie's limp hands and squeezed them.

'I don't think me mam and dad'll see it that way. I was going to try and get hold of that pill, you know, the birth pill they brought out a couple of years ago? But Maggie works in the doctor's surgery and she says they won't just dish 'em out willy nilly. You have to be married or older and even then Doctor Mead don't like it. I suppose the simplest thing would be to go and see one of those women down Fen End way. I know Joan Watson went there when she got landed last year. They sorted her out but it cost a bit. But – but I don't think I could go through with it, although I can't see how I can have it either.'

'You can't go to Fen End, Connie, don't be daft. There's no question of that. What if something went wrong . . .' Her voice softened at Connie's white face. 'Well, you can't. You know you can't.' Fen End was a byword in the town.

'But I can't have it either, can I? Not round here. We're supposed to be more open and all that, but look how they treated Janie Wilson several doors up when she fell last year and said she was going to keep it by herself. It was back to the Dark Ages, me mam said. She even saw old Mrs Staples spit at her when she walked past, old crow. Things are slow to change here.'

'I know, I know.' Jenny shook her head slowly. 'But if you got married quick no one would know anyway, would they? Or they wouldn't be able to prove anything anyway. Babies come early sometimes.'

'Not that early.' Connie looked back at her, her eyes enormous in her white face. 'I mean, come on, Jen, you know me dad. He's like a ferret when he's got the smell of something. We don't get on at the best of times. When Mam let me choose all the things for this room when they did it up he nearly threw a blue fit, nothing was right. He didn't like my posters and the fact I wanted window blinds instead of curtains, I mean, who has curtains nowadays? They're just not in. And he wanted a flowered bedspread and all that rubbish, he hates this . . .' She indicated the bold geometric design on the brightly coloured bedspread and vivid lime-green walls. 'He's only just finished doing it too, he'd go barmy if I said I was going to move out.'

'Mick could come here –'

'Now you really are talking through your backside,' Connie said scathingly. 'The last time he saw Mick was when I let him come up here, when I thought me dad was out for the night with David. We were only listening to records, fortunately, but I burnt one of those joss-sticks they're selling down the market and he came roaring up here like a madman, saying the house smelt like a brothel, and then when he saw Mick . . .'

'I can imagine,' Jenny said dryly. At any other time she would have been helpless with laughter at the picture Connie had painted but this was too serious to raise a smile.

All that had been two days ago and she hadn't seen her cousin since, but she had thought about her constantly, along with the party. Something would happen, she just knew it. She snuggled further under the heaped blankets and hugged her hot-water bottle, drawing the warmth into her chilled flesh. The old terraced houses were freezing in the winter and unlike her cousin's this one had had little done to it to improve its original structure. Her grandfather seemed to have had little interest in the house ever since they had arrived back in Sheffield. They were one of the few families in the street not to have fitted carpets or at least a fridge. There had been ice inside the window this morning, the pipes would freeze again.

Oh, she had to stop thinking and get some sleep. Connie wouldn't do anything silly in spite of the Fen End talk. Mick wouldn't let her because whatever else he loved her: seeing them together she was sure of that. They'd work something out, they had to.

And Peter? He wouldn't stand for any more of this cloak-and-dagger stuff, he'd told her so plainly, so tomorrow was as good a time as any to come out in the open. The thought set her stomach churning again and she screwed her eyes up tightly as she fought the panic. As Connie was so fond of saying, this was the Swinging Sixties with couples living together all over the place and a new sexual freedom among the young that was sweeping all the old values before it. And all she wanted, *all* she wanted, was to be able to walk out in public with her first boyfriend. What was so terrible about that? Her stomach did a giant somersault in reply.

She didn't like this side of her when she thought about it, the side that could be frightened, intimidated, until she felt like a small hunted animal scurrying about in its own waste. She'd never felt like this before – before Steve Baker. Until then the world had been bright and beautiful like that old hymn they used to sing at the village Sunday school, 'All things bright and beautiful' . . . But the world wasn't bright and beautiful, or it hadn't been until she had met Peter. Peter . . . She went to sleep with his name on her lips.

'Enjoyin' yourself, lass?' Martha's voice was cheerful as she looked down on her niece and Peter sitting close together on the leather pouffe in the corner of the room as the talk and laughter ebbed and flowed above their heads. He was a nice lad, that Peter, reliable, and he'd got it in him to stand up to the lass's brother, which was more important.

She glanced across to David, who was standing just inside the door with a glass of beer in his hand, his eyes tight on his sister's face. He had been like that for a good hour now, you'd think there was no one else in the room but Peter and Jenny. Well, just let him try anything now, the big lout . . .

'This is very nice, Mrs Malley.' Peter had gone to rise as she had stopped in front of them but she had waved him down with her hand. 'It was very kind of you to find room for me in all this lot.' He glanced round the crowded room with a smile.

'Well, what's one more when the house is bursting at the seams, lad?' She laughed quietly. And bursting it was, what with her Sally's and Rosy's families, Bill not able to make it again, and Frank's relations from

Barnsley, besides a few of Connie's friends. But she didn't mind the house being over-full. It was when it was empty, and there was just her and Frank, that she couldn't stand it. She caught a glimpse of George talking to Connie across the room and as always her heart gave a little lurch at the sight of him before she brought her eyes sharply away. And there was something wrong with that girl of hers, she'd have to have a good talk with her once the festivities were over. She'd been drooping about the house for days now, and that wasn't like Connie.

'Any more turkey sandwiches goin', Martha, me girl?' One of Frank's relatives, a large florid man with wandering hands, caught her round the waist as she made to pass, his breath smelling strongly of whisky as he put his face close to hers.

'I'll cut some,' she said stiffly.

'And I'll help you.' She glanced up to see George in front of her, his face straight as he looked hard at the other man, who hesitated for a moment before letting go of her with a little huh of a laugh.

'You shouldn't have done that.' As they reached the relative quiet of the kitchen she turned to him, her face scarlet. 'It doesn't take much for that lot to talk.'

'There's nothin' to talk about, is there?'

'That's never stopped them before.' They faced each other for a moment without speaking until Martha wrenched her eyes away and turned to the remains of the turkey in a covered dish on the kitchen table. 'I – I'd better do the sandwiches.'

'Damn the sandwiches.' His voice was low and deep. 'How are you, Martha?' He took a step towards her and then stopped.

'How am I?' Her voice was too high and she bit her lip

before speaking again in a more moderate tone. 'I'm fine, I – I'm fine.' Her eyes were still cast down but her colour was high.

'Liar.' His voice was thick and deep and made her tremble.

'Georgie, stop this.' She swung to face him, her eyes desperate. 'Frank –'

'And damn him 'n all.' He didn't know what had got into him, he didn't really, but when he'd seen that fat swine put his hands on her he'd had a job not to leap across the room and grab him by the throat. 'Martha . . .' His voice was harsh now. 'How are things really? With him?'

She made a small movement with her head but her eyes didn't leave his face, seemingly held there with the force of his gaze and they remained absolutely still, staring at each other.

By, she was beautiful. The thud of his heart reverberated through his head and for a moment his legs felt weak. Close to like this, really looking at her for the first time in months, years, she didn't appear a day older than when they had first left the town sixteen years ago. Her face was smooth and unlined, her blond hair thick and luxuriant, only the faint trace of silver here and there gave lie to the impression that she was a young woman of thirty, thirty-one. His guts twisted and turned hot and he forced himself to speak again. 'Well? I need – I need to know.'

She could pretend. She could stop this now and tell him that everything was as it should be between her and Frank, that she was happy, fulfilled . . . But she didn't. 'I hate him, Georgie, God forgive me but I do,' she said quietly.

'Martha . . .' As his eyes moved to her mouth it was almost as though he had kissed her but when, in the next instant, the sound of the party swelled as the door opened she had turned to the table in one movement, her hand reaching for the carving knife to one side of the decimated bird.

'I wondered where you were.' Frank's black beady gaze moved from her stiffly bowed head to George, standing to one side of the table. 'Anythin' wrong?' he asked grimly.

'No, of course not.' Her voice was brittle and caused her husband's eyes to narrow further as he sucked air between his teeth. 'That Arthur wanted more sandwiches.'

'Did he?' The voice was quiet and controlled. 'Then you'd better give him some, hadn't you?'

'Frank –'

'Hadn't you?' As she nodded dully Frank walked across the room to a small low table in the corner on which a crate of beer bottles was standing. 'They want more beer. Take it in, George, would you?' There was no semblance of a request in the words. Both the tone and the manner in which Frank spoke made it perfectly clear he was giving an order that he expected to be obeyed, the superior talking to the subordinate, the boss to the employee.

'Now look here –'

'George?' Martha only spoke the one word but it brought her brother-in-law's blazing eyes to her white face, and after a tense moment, in which he caught and held her pleading gaze, George took a long shuddering breath and his eyes switched back to the man in front of him.

'We aren't at work now, Malley,' he said softly. 'If you want the beer taking in, take the damn stuff yourself.' And he held Frank's black malevolent gaze for a few seconds more before swinging round and walking quietly from the room.

'You slut –'

'*Don't!* Don't you dare start that now.' As Frank gripped her arm, bending it backwards behind her, Martha brought her other hand holding the carving knife to within an inch of his face. 'I'll mark you, I swear I'll mark you,' she hissed quietly. 'And you've got no right to call me that. Not in the past, not now, not ever. You know that, so don't come the old soldier with me, Frank Malley.'

'No? When you're givin' him what you deny me –'

'I'm not.' She shook her head at him, her eyes blazing. 'I'm not, I tell you.'

'I don't believe it.'

'That's up to you.' He had let go of her arm now, recognizing that in her rage she was quite capable of carrying out her threat to cut his face. 'But don't you ever ask yourself why? Why I don't want you to touch me? I don't care about a nice house, all the money you bring in, I just want – I just want things to be as they were at first. But now, the things you want to do –' She shut her eyes and shuddered. 'They're filthy, dirty –'

'I won't. I'll do it normal. Just give me one more chance, Martha.'

'I've given you chances.' Her voice was high-pitched now, almost a scream, and he glanced behind him before moving from her side and shutting the door quickly, leaning against it as he continued to look at her. 'Oh, heaven help me . . .' The arm holding the knife drooped but as he made to move towards her she brought it sharply upwards again. 'That last time, do you know what you did to me?' she said more quietly. 'I bled for days, days . . . I couldn't sit or stand. Well, I told you then an' I'm tellin' you now, you ever come near me again and I'll kill you, I will, Frank. I don't care where you go to get satisfaction but it won't be from me. I'm your wife, *your wife*. Not some common little whore that you've paid for your perversions.'

'*Shut up*.'

'Why? Because it's not done to talk about what happens in the dark? I can't believe your mentality at times, I can't. An' you talk about me carryin' on with someone else? I never want a man to touch me again in all of my life, that's what you've done for me, Frank Malley. You've no idea of the number of times I've thanked God, on bended knees, that our Connie was a girl. The thought that I might have given birth to something that would do the same to another woman as what you've done to me has made me sick to me stomach.'

'I've told you, *shut up*.' His eyes were blazing, his lips white. She knew how far she could push and she'd reached her limit, the white lines round his mouth told her that, but the thought of what she'd endured for so long was burning hot in her stomach like pure acid. The humiliation, the degradation, that she'd kept hidden for years until she'd told Father Michael one day at confession, when she'd reached the end of her tether. And what good had that done? It had earned her that last little episode some months ago when she had really wanted to kill him. Why? She stared at him across the expanse of the kitchen. Why would a man, a human being made in the likeness of the Almighty, want to do the things he craved? 'You'd better go back to them.' Her voice was strangely flat now that her rage and anger had died. It was the look on his face that had done it. That look of utter torment that seemed to come from the pit itself. But the time when it had affected her and made her feel pity and compassion had long since died. She had learnt the hard way that you didn't reach out a hand to a ferocious beast unless you were prepared to have it bitten off. And she wasn't. Not any more. 'I'll come in a minute.'

'Martha –'

'Just go.' She gestured savagely with the knife. 'I mean it.'

And he went, his head bowed and his hands slack but his eyes, had she seen them, were the eyes of a thwarted animal, narrowed and angry and dangerous.

'You two know each other then?' Jenny had seen David moving to their side but Peter's hand, pressed firmly on her arm, had prevented her leaving the room, although she had tried to rise twice. She despised her fear, it was degrading, but she couldn't help it.

'This is Peter –'

'I know his name.' His eyes were intent on her face.

'David –'

'I asked you if you knew him. Do you?' he asked softly.

'Yes, yes, she knows me.' Peter rose himself now and his face was on a level with David's when he next spoke.'We've known each other a few weeks as it happens.'

The grey eyes moved slowly from Jenny's face, very slowly, and when they held Peter's straight gaze they were bitter and full of hatred, the cheekbones shining white beneath them and the square hard jaw tight as he ignored Peter's outstretched hand. 'I see. Aye, now I see. Connie's little secret.' His laugh was bitter and devoid of amusement. 'Well, well, well . . .'

'Is there anything wrong?' Peter's hand had dropped back to his side and his face was tense but without fear as he stared at Jenny's brother. So this was David.

Yes, he could see how a big brawny fellow like this one could intimidate a little thing like Jenny, but he was damned if he'd do so any longer. There was something here he didn't like. He hadn't liked it before he'd met the man but he liked it a damn sight less now. It was the way he looked at her, it wasn't the way a man normally looked at his sister.

'Wrong? Well, you tell me. You're the teacher aren't you? Or is that a secret like everything else?'

'It isn't like that, Davie.' Jenny's cheeks were without colour as she stood to face her brother, her lips trembling and her eyes beseeching him to stop.

'Isn't it? What do you take me for?'

'David, you may not be aware of it but you are causing a scene.' Martha's voice was low and cool and as her nephew swung round at the sound of it he almost knocked the plate of sandwiches she was holding to the floor. 'This is a Christmas party and I want it kept civil. If you've got anything to say to Jenny could you do so in private, please.'

'The hell I –'

'David.' Mary had joined her sister in the silence that had fallen and now she placed a hand on her grandson's arm as his furious gaze moved from her sister to herself. 'David, listen to me. We'll sort this out later. Come and have a bite to eat, lad, you've been drinking too much without eating. C'mon.'

'You coming?' David turned to stare straight into Jenny's white face and when she made no reply it was an answer in itself, and he knew, as well as she did, that a choice had been made.

'David, please.' Some quick-witted soul had placed a record on the gramophone in the corner of the room and as the psychedelic strains of the Beatles' *Sergeant Pepper* album were heard, an embarrassed buzz of conversation rose with them, drowning Mary's voice to everyone but her grandson. Peter and Jenny had seated themselves on the pouffe again, Jenny's head turned into Peter's shoulder, and as David continued to stare down at them, Mary spoke again. 'David? This is not the way, you hearing me, lad? You want to make her more keen on him? 'Cos that's what this'll do.'

'It's that Connie.' She could barely hear his voice, so low it was. 'I knew she was up to somethin'.'

'Leave it for now, come and have something to eat.'

He allowed her to lead him away, but, having seated himself on the other side of the room, kept his gaze fixed on Jenny's drooping head. He began to drink heavily, his face dark and morose.

As time slipped by, Mary was aware of Frank watching Martha and George talking in the far corner of the room, their heads close together, and she found herself wishing with all her heart that she could seek the solace of the bottle along with her grandson.

And the night wasn't finished yet.

'Announcement! Announcement time everybody.' Connie's voice was high and shrill, which sounded like excitement to those but the most finely tuned ears, but as Jenny glanced up she knew what her cousin was about to do and her heart jerked and began to pound in her ears like an express train. Connie was following the same reasoning she had expounded to her just a few nights previously, that of *fait accompli*, assuming a very public declaration, right in the midst of family and friends, wouldn't be challenged by her parents. She and Mick had obviously decided to be married and she was glad about that, of course she was, but couldn't Connie see this might backfire in the worst possible way? Oh why hadn't her cousin *told* her what she was going to do?

'An' what's this?' Frank, like David, had been drinking both whisky and beer steadily for the last two hours, and now he lurched to his feet and stood, swaying gently as he faced his smiling daughter and her boyfriend. He had been hoping for the last half an hour that people would start to leave soon because he wanted, he *needed*, to get his wife alone. Quite what he was going to do once he'd accomplished that he wasn't sure, his mind didn't dwell on her naked warning in the kitchen, but he'd teach her a thing or two, by, he would that. Flirtin' with that fancy man of hers, shameless with it. And now here was Connie delaying things. She'd better have a good reason.

'This?' Connie laughed gaily, but the sound narrowed David's eyes as he sat watching the scene in front of him. He'd glanced once at Jenny when Connie had first stood and seen the widening of his sister's eyes and the apprehension on her face, and that, added to Connie's brightness and the awkwardness of that weedy little youth she hung about with, suddenly tipped him the notion of what this was all about. Never . . . He rubbed his hand across his mouth, placing his glass carefully on the floor. She'd not got caught. Not Miss Clever-clogs, little Miss Know-all. 'Mick and I just thought this was as good a time as any to let you all know that he's asked me to marry him and I've said yes.' He was right. *Dammit, he was right*.

'You what?' Frank's voice was fuddled as he peered at them both.

'Mick's asked me to marry him Dad.' Connie kept her eyes wide open, her face bright. She'd timed it just about right, he was drunk but not too drunk, and with her uncle Arthur here from Barnsley her dad wouldn't want to make a scene. He might rant and rave later but once he'd given his approval in front of this lot there'd be little he could do, and if the wedding happened a bit quick, so what? Lots of 'em did these days. 'Look.' She thrust out her hand on which glittered the small dress ring they'd bought on Dronfield Market a few days before. 'We told his mam and dad earlier and they're pleased.'

'Connie?' Martha had appeared at Frank's side. 'Why didn't you say anythin' before?' she asked, her voice low.

'We wanted to surprise you, make it special like on Christmas day.'

'Well, well, well.' Arthur's voice boomed out from Frank's side, the tone jovial. 'I married me own missus when she was a lass of sixteen and I was eighteen and we've done all right on it, haven't we, lass?' He turned to his wife, a thin stringy woman with tight hard lips and beady eyes who nodded primly, her face blank. 'So I say good luck to you both, aye, I do that.'

The fury was rising up in David like a red mist. She wasn't going to get away with it, was she, the brazen little liar? Couldn't they see? She was foolin' 'em all, like she'd fooled him for weeks while she'd pushed Jenny into that great oaf's arms. There was a string of swear-words in his mind and for a second the urge to spew them at the young girl in front of him was savage. But there were more ways to skin a cat than the obvious and he had to go carefully, she was Frank's daughter when all was said and done. Frank and Martha's. He looked at his aunt as she stood at her husband's side. And he'd like to bring her down from her lofty pedestal, she'd had it coming for years. Giving him the cold shoulder with that cool manner and holier-than-thou look when all the time she was like a bitch in heat . . . He knew, oh aye, he knew. They were all the same. All except Jenny. Jenny. He glanced across at his sister and his stomach clenched when he saw her face, soft and warm, as she gazed up at the man next to her. And he'd get his 'n all, but he'd have to go carefully, very carefully.

'You don't mind, Dad?' Connie seized the advantage Arthur had given her by putting her arms round her father's neck and hugging him briefly. 'We were going to ask you first but I got carried away, I'm sorry.' She stepped back a pace and dimpled up at him. 'What with the party and everything.'

'We'll talk later.' Martha took charge of the situation, her mouth smiling but her eyes tight on her daughter's face as she gestured with her head towards the two plates of turkey sandwiches she was holding. 'Now eat up everyone, there's hot mince pies to follow and a piece of me Christmas cake for them that want it.' She glanced round at the assembled company and then was caught by David's gaze.

'Who wouldn't want a piece of your Christmas cake, Aunt Martha?' David's voice was slurred, not enough to fuddle his words but enough to convince those round him that he was a little more than merry, that the looseness of his tongue was due solely to the amount of alcohol he had imbibed. 'If it's anything like the christening cake you made for Rosy's nipper last year it'll be fit for a king. Handsome, it was.' He smiled, his face cheerful as he looked straight at Connie. 'You remember your mam's cake, don't you? You'll have to ask her to make one for your bairn.'

'I –' Connie swallowed deeply and as Mick moved from behind her to her side she glanced at him once, quickly. She could pretend she hadn't caught the innuendo endo in David's barbed pleasantry, act as though he had merely expressed himself badly, which she knew he expected her to do. She also knew that having come this far he wouldn't let it drop. Somehow he knew, or he suspected. Whatever, he wanted his pound of flesh. She glanced across at Jenny and saw the other girl's eyes were wide with horror and disbelief. Yes, you might well look like that, she thought for a moment as bitterness rose in her throat. This is your precious David, the possessor of such high values and morals. Take a good look, Jenny, this is the *real* David. The dirty, conniving, cruel swine . . .

'Yes, I might well do that, David.' It was strange how everything in the room had taken on a clarity that was stark and vital, the silent, wide-eyed faces, the new three-piece and matching curtains that her mam was so proud of, even the smell of the liquor was sharp and distinct. She saw her half-sister, Rosy, put her hand to her mouth and shake her head silently, and others watching her were perplexed, unsure of what was really being said.

There was a dark indent between Frank's eyebrows as he stared first at Connie's white strained face before turning to David's smiling countenance which slowly straightened as though he had just realized the import of his words. 'I didn't mean . . .' David let his voice die away in an embarrassed laugh. 'I – Good heavens, girl, you aren't . . .'

'What? What's goin' on?' Frank shook his head as though to clear it from the dulling effects of the alcohol, blinking hard. 'What you sayin', David?'

'I'm not sayin' anythin', I seem to have said too much already. I didn't realize –' David stopped abruptly and lowered his gaze to the floor. 'I'm sorry, Connie, I had no idea.'

'You liar. You sanctimonious, *dirty* liar. How can you –'

'Connie!' Her father's bark had no effect on the young girl as she moved closer to David, stretching her neck, her eyes full of loathing.

'You disgust me, David Longbridge, do you know that? Disgust and revolt me as you would any decent human being who looks beneath the outward skin. You think I don't know what you're like? What you're really like? Well, I do, believe me I do, and there's worse things than having a baby.'

Frank, his face flooded with dark red colour that made his eyes seem as though they were popping out of his head, cut into her words, swinging her round to face him so violently she almost lost her footing. 'What you sayin' here? You've been landed? Is that it? I'll kill him –'

'Frank.' As Martha held on to her husband, who was ready to take a swipe at Mick, now partly shielding Connie's body with his own, she glared at David, who had gone rigid at Connie's attack. 'You! You've caused all this.'

'Me? Me, Aunt Martha? I wasn't the one who put a load in her belly. I wouldn't touch her with a barge pole.'

'You –'

'She's a tramp and I pity that dumb fool for getting himself caught, although if I was him I'd wonder if it was my bairn in there.'

'That's enough.' George stepped into the mêlée, shaking off Mary's restraining arm, his face black as thunder as he glared at his grandson. 'Don't you dare talk to your aunt Martha like that, me lad, or big as you are I'll flatten you, you hear me?'

'I don't think so.' David's voice was cool now and full of a biting contempt. 'Not you. But you could always try.'

'Oh, I'd try it, lad, make no mistake about that, but now is not the time or the place. You've done your work here the night, so just get on home.'

'And you, you get up to your room.' Frank cut over George's voice, his own shaking with murderous rage and his black eyes venomous as he stared at his daughter. 'It's not David who's at fault here tonight, not in my book.'

'Well, surprise, surprise.' Martha had let go of Frank as George had appeared at her side and now her face was rent with the bitterness of years as she swung on her husband. 'And why do you think the girl has turned out like she has? It's not her fault, none of this is her fault. If you'd been anythin' like a father to the lass she wouldn't be desperate for attention like she is. When did you last talk to her, *really* talk to her? I can tell you, never. You've never shown any real interest in her, your own flesh and blood, and she knows it, she's not a fool. But that one –' Her gaze was hostile as it moved to David. '*Him*. He can't do no wrong, can he? The sadistic young swine.'

'Oh, Peter . . .' Jenny felt as though she was going to faint from the dark emotion that had suddenly burst forth into the room. She could hardly believe what was happening in front of her, and it was David, David, who had caused all this. That intuition, which formed an integral part of her love for her brother, had told her the instant he had spoken that he had meant every word he had implied. He had set Connie up, cold-bloodedly and without mercy, and waited for the fall. How could he? How could he? 'Please, let's get out of here.'

'Don't you put this at my door.' The effect of his wife's words on Frank was electrifying, and for a moment Jenny, along with everyone else in the room, thought he was going to strike her, but as George stepped in front of Martha in much the same way Mick was standing in front of Connie, Frank seemed to get a hold on his temper. 'I'm tellin' you, don't you put this at my door. The little slut! I'll teach her a lesson she'll never forget.'

'That's enough.' As George was speaking, he gestured to those who remained in the room to leave. 'They've only done what many a young pair, and aye, those not so young, have done afore 'em.' He looked across at Mary, who was sitting as still as a statue on the settee, alone now as the rest of the company had departed. 'Get up. We're leavin'.' He made no move to leave Martha's side to help his wife rise and her eyes were deep pools of bitterness as David crossed the room to pull her to her feet. 'If I were you I'd go easy the night, Frank.'

'Well, you're not me, are you?' Frank spat the words in George's face. 'However much you'd like to be at times, eh? You think I don't know what goes on in that cesspit you call a mind?'

'Leave him, Georgie, he's not worth it.' Martha pushed George to one side and moved from behind his bulk to stand between the two men. '*Please*, leave it. An' you, Mick.' She turned to Connie's boyfriend whose face was as white as a sheet. 'I'll see to her, I promise. You get off home and we'll discuss this tomorrow.'

'Discuss it? It'll be me belt that does any discussin'.'

She ignored Frank, leading Connie and a clearly stunned Mick out of the room, George and David half carrying Mary as they followed, with Jenny and Peter making up the rear. 'Go on, lad, go on home. I won't let him lay a finger on her.'

'Mrs Longbridge?' Mick was speaking to Martha but with his eyes on Connie. 'My mam would let her stay with us, she's said so.'

'I'll be all right, Mick.' Standing on the first step of the stairs, Connie smiled shakily and then turned away. 'I'll kill him if he tries anything with me, I'm not frightened of him.' She turned again to face her mother. 'I'm not, you know, he's just a big loud-mouthed bully. He always has been.'

'All right, lass, all right. That's enough.'

'That's enough? That's all you're going to say to her?'

'*David.*' This time it was Jenny's voice that cut into the charged atmosphere in the crowded hall and her tone was bitter. 'Just shut up, will you.'

Once they were outside the icy air sliced their faces with its breath but it was a few seconds before anyone spoke, and then it was Jenny who broke the silence. 'I'll see you tomorrow, Peter.' David was holding his grandmother's arm one side with George now supporting his wife on the other side, but no one made any attempt to move. 'I'm sorry about this, it must seem awful to you.'

'Not at all.' Peter nodded to the three grim faces by his side before smiling down at Jenny's upturned face as though they were completely alone. She felt a dart of admiration for his coolness and at the same time her heart jerked and thudded as she thought of how David would respond to this refusal to be intimidated. 'These things happen in all families. Good night Mr and Mrs Longbridge, David . . .' He nodded politely at the others and then quite deliberately kissed her gently and swiftly on the mouth. 'Good night, love.' He indicated Mick, standing some distance away. 'I'd better see to him.'

'Good night.' She knew her cheeks were scarlet as she turned in one direction and Peter in the other to go their separate ways. Peter. Oh, Peter. She wished she was walking away with him instead of having to return to what she knew was about to come. But she would face it. She wouldn't weaken. The way David had behaved tonight, the sheer ruthlessness in his dealing with their cousin, had released something in her that had been bound for a good many years. She loved him, she would always love him, he was her brother after all and everything he'd ever done had been for her, but she couldn't continue with the life she had been leading for the last few years. The cord had to be cut. She wasn't so naïve that she didn't know why David had humiliated Connie in front of everyone that night, and it had nothing to do with his moral integrity or anything else. It was because of her. Because she had deceived him and Connie had helped her. And she had deceived him because she was frightened of him.

Her stomach was turning over as she followed the three down the frosty street, the dim glow from the cast-iron street lamps turning her hair into spun gold as David turned at the corner to look at her. 'You knew? You knew she'd got a bellyful?'

'We'll discuss this at home, David.' Mary's voice was as cold as the air they breathed.

'I told you, didn't I? That little slut isn't fit for Jenny to be runnin' around with. I told you –'

'*David.*'

No one spoke again until they reached the door of 14 Crown Street, and then Jenny came forward to take her grandmother's elbow as George left her to open the door, but Mary shrugged her touch away without glancing to left or right.

'Don't take out the night's happenings on the lass, I won't have it.' George had noticed his wife's gesture and his mouth was hard. 'If anyone is at fault it damn well ain't her.'

'Don't swear at me, George Longbridge.'

'I'm not swearing at you and don't be so bloody stupid, woman.'

They entered the house in a stiff silence that lasted until Mary was established in the easy chair by the window. 'I'll get your hot water bottle.' Jenny left the room without looking at her grandmother again and once in the kitchen leant against the stanchion of the door as she fought for control. She'd done nothing wrong, she hadn't. *She was nearly twenty-one years old.* The words were a scream in her mind. She'd probably used up over a quarter of her life already and she couldn't let the next quarter be like the first, she couldn't. She wanted to be married, have bairns, just be ordinary. That was all she wanted, to be ordinary. Because she'd always felt slightly different, set apart from the children she'd played with, the girls she'd gone to school with, and she'd never known why until Steve Baker had hissed that word at her. Bastard. She shut her eyes against the rawness of it. But it was a fact and she knew it and Davie felt it too, she knew he did, even though they'd never discussed it. And as usual the thought softened her heart towards her brother.

As though her mind had conjured him up David walked into the kitchen in the next instant, forcing her to move sharply from the door to avoid being bumped. 'I – I'm just getting the hot-water bottle.' She busied herself, putting the kettle on the stove but when he still didn't speak and the silence became painful, forced herself to turn slowly and face him. And as usual his eyes were waiting for her, but tonight there was none of the deep softness she associated with his gaze but a hard, hot blackness that caused her to clutch at her throat in protest. 'Don't look at me like that.'

'Don't look at you!' He almost spat the words in her face and, when they would have exploded into a shout, forced his tone lower through gritted teeth as he glanced back towards the sitting room. 'You can say that when you've been seeing that bloke for weeks now.'

'Yes, I've been seeing Peter, and what's wrong with that?' She drew herself up, pressing her buttocks against the side of the sink as she straightened herself. 'He's a nice man, a teacher –'

'A nice man? There aren't any nice men, don't you realize that yet? They all want one thing.'

'No, no, he doesn't, he hasn't tried.' She was gabbling in her panic to make him understand and heard herself with a burst of self-contempt. She didn't have to beg for his approval. The thought put ice in her voice and enabled her to confront him without flinching. 'I don't have to explain anything to you. I'm twenty years old, David, not a young child.'

It was the first time he could remember that she had spoken his name with such naked hostility and that hit him harder than this new defiance, although he didn't betray his feeling by gesture or word, his mouth hardening still more. 'Think again. Oh you think again, girl. I'm not havin' him touch you, you hear me? You end this now.'

'I won't.' She was as straight as a ramrod, her face white but two spots of bright colour burning high on her cheekbones. 'You've got no right to ask me.'

'I'm not askin', I'm tellin'.'

'You can't, you can't make me, and you'd like him if you'd only give him a chance. Connie –'

'Connie? Don't talk to me about her.'

'Stop this, David.' She felt she was being torn apart, feeling his hurt through the outward rage and condemnation and hating the fact that she was responsible for making him feel so bad, but knowing that if she weakened now it was the end of all her hopes and dreams for the future, her and Peter's future. And the way he had treated Connie, his callous, premeditated cruelty to the young girl, had shocked her far more than she had realized. It had confirmed something she had always suspected but never faced, that David was capable of being two quite separate people, and the knowledge was terrifying. 'And why did you have to do that to Connie tonight? Show her up in front of everyone?' she asked, following her train of thought. 'It was unnecessary and cruel.'

'Unnecessary and cruel?' There was a faintly incredulous note to his voice. 'Unnecessary and . . .' He shook his head as he stared at her, his eyes narrowed and his mouth straight. 'You think I did it on purpose? How was I to know she'd been took down?' He held out his hands appealingly. 'Now you tell me how?'

'You did know,' she said flatly.

'I didn't.' He continued to keep his eyes fixed on hers and there wasn't a flicker of unease in them, anything to make her doubt him but . . . she did. For the first time in her life she acknowledged she did. 'I swear I didn't know, Jen. I just opened me big mouth and spoke before I thought and she put the wrong idea to it, with things being as they are. Don't you believe me?'

'I – I don't know. She thought –'

'And because she thought I knew, you think so too? Now come on, Jen, think it out. She probably thought you'd told me.'

'No. No, she knows I wouldn't do that.'

It was the wrong thing to say and his voice was harsh as he bit back, all control gone.

'Oh, she knows that, does she? Well, good for her. Encourages you to have your little secrets on the side, does she?'

'David –'

'You tell him, Jen, you tell him to leave you alone.'

'No. No, I won't do that. I'm seeing Peter and I'm going to continue seeing him and Connie too if I want. You can't stop me.' She clenched her hands as she spoke. 'You can't.'

'Can't I?'

'You do anything, anything at all, and I'll hate you as long as I live.' She was breathing hard, her face a sickly white, but there was no doubt she meant what she said, and as David stared at her the bitterness in him began to boil over.

'You're putting them before me? That – that lout of a schoolteacher and that damn whore? *That disgusting, filthy whore?*' As a string of obscenities followed there was the hard crack of flesh against bone and then an absolute silence when the world and everything in it held its breath.

'Davie . . .' She was appalled at what she'd done, the print of her hand scarlet on one side of his face, but strangely he seemed almost unaware of the force of the blow, merely the reason that had prompted it.

'You are, aren't you. You're putting them before me. That dirty conniving little hussy back there and him, *him!* You've known him longer than a few weeks, haven't you? Have you been with him, then? Is that it?' His voice was low now, a hard hiss between clenched teeth, and as she stared into his dilated eyes the thought came to her that he was mad, that this affair had unhinged his mind, but at the same time she knew that that was one excuse she couldn't use for his behaviour. He wasn't mad, it was icy-cold, bitter sanity staring at her from those enraged eyes and all the more frightening because of it. He knew what he was doing and saying, and he'd known what he was doing and saying back at her aunt's house too.

'Just leave me alone.'

'The hell I will –'

'What's going on in here?' As George thrust open the door, his gaze moving from Jenny's white, frightened face to David's, Jenny seized the opportunity to escape, pushing past her grandfather with a tiny inarticulate cry and running down the hall before taking the stairs two at a time.

'You're mad, you know that, boy?' George had moved closer to David, pushing his face nearer and nearer until they were but an inch apart. 'Stark, staring mad.'

'You think so?' David hadn't moved, the big powerful width of his chest and shoulders a match for his grandfather's brawny build and the muscles of his arms bulging as he flexed them at his side. 'Because I want to make sure something like that other affair never happens again? Well, I care about her, I care about 'em both, me grandma and Jenny, which is more than can be said for you.'

'Don't talk to me about carin'.'

'Why? Why shouldn't I?' His voice was a low hiss but none the less deadly because of the quietness of the tone. 'Someone has to. You! You're nothin', a nowt.' As George raised his fist David's eyes narrowed, their greyness glowing red. 'Just try it, try it and I'll kill you. I'm not blind, you know, or daft. I know the way things've been with you and Martha, but you've never had the gumption to do owt about it.'

'You've been listening to too many stories, me lad.'

'Have I now? Well, maybe so but one thing can't be dressed up or changed about, can it? And that's the way your daughter turned out. An' you still don't know who she was whorin' for.'

'Get out.' George's voice was almost a whisper but throbbed with such enmity that it quivered in the air like a live thing. 'You can't talk about your own mam like that.'

'Oh aye, I can.' David took a step backwards but they both knew there was no deference or surrender in the motion. It was almost a squaring up of the adversary before the next attack, and his subsequent words bore this impression out. 'An' I'll tell you somethin' else while I'm on, an' that's there's no way I'd have stood by and let a bairn of mine make a monkey out of me like yours did. I'd have got to the bottom of it at the time, I'm tellin' you, and there'd have been murder done.'

'She was a good girl.'

'There's no such thing.' David's voice was thick and deep and the look in his eyes froze George's next words in his throat – he had never before seen such malignant viciousness on another human being's face. He was still reeling from the shock of it when David brushed past him and strode down the hall, ignoring his grandmother's voice calling his name as he made for the front door, banging it behind him with blazing savagery as he left.

'What's happened? Where's he gone? Where's Jenny?' As George walked dazedly into the hall Mary stood holding on to the edge of the door to her room, her face white and drawn and her lips blue. 'What did you say to him? –'

'Shut up.' The words were soft but the look that accompanied them was anything but. 'You ask me what *I* said to *him*? In all the years I've worked in steel I've never come across anythin' like that which you've spawned and I've met some right 'uns in my time. And he's a product of you, lass, aye, he is that. Our Jenny might have put breath in his body but his mind is somethin' you've got to be answerable for.'

'What are you talking about?' Mary stood swaying as she stared at her husband, her eyes stretched wide.

'You know what I'm talkin' about. You know, all right. And I only hope this God that you talk to can forgive you for what you've done, because I can't. No, by all that's holy, I can't.'

CHAPTER ELEVEN

David knew exactly where he was going when he left the house, and as he made for Tinsley Street he passed row after row of identical terraced houses with windows displaying scrawny Christmas trees festooned with tinsel and glass baubles. There was already a thick covering of frost on the ground that sparkled like tiny diamonds when the weak glow of the odd street lamp hit it, and the black sky above the town was punctured with a myriad of twinkling stars, but the man walking with such intent down below was blind and deaf to the natural beauty of the night.

His body needed easement. The hot ache that had been raging all evening as he had sat and watched that . . . scum with his thighs pressed close to her was like a physical pain now, gripping his innards and twisting his bowels until he couldn't think of anything else. And he needed to vent that pain on female flesh, savage it . . .

The streets were empty and deserted, it being past ten o'clock at night on Christmas day, but he heard the sound of merriment from the occasional house as he passed and it served to emphasize still more what he'd lost. But he hadn't lost her. Dammit, he wouldn't let that dirty swine come within a mile of her, he'd burn in hell first. What a Christmas day! He shook his head as he walked. He'd known something was up, he'd known for weeks, but he hadn't thought of that. Stupid really, but that job episode had blinded him, he'd thought she was still upset about that. And she'd barely glanced at the gold bracelet he'd given her that morning . . . What had this Peter given her? He knew what the scum would like to give her. He groaned out loud as his stomach clenched until he felt nauseous. But he'd see about him, aye, he would that, but carefully. He'd definitely have to go carefully.

But for now the main thing was to see to his needs. Hell, how he needed a woman, any of the ones on service would do tonight. The desire to bruise soft flesh, to see the weals on white skin as he inflicted his punishment was so strong he could taste it.

Tinsley Street was in a part of the town where it didn't do to wander after dark unless you were big and knew how to use your hands and your feet, but David had been visiting a particular house at the far end of the grimy, dirty street for four years now, having first ventured there just after his sixteenth birthday. He was well known, he was very well known and feared.

''Allo, ducks.' The woman who opened the door after he'd been knocking for some time was small and fat and greasy, a cigarette hanging from her slack lips and an old dressing gown pulled round her squat body. 'What you doin' here the night? Didn't expect to see you for a while.'

'Is Bett available?' He didn't bother to socialize, brushing past her into the squalid hall before moving into the large downstairs room in which a few sofas and chairs were scattered. Several women looked up as he entered, and they were all scantily clad with glasses of whisky or gin at their elbows. A television screen flickered in one corner of the room but the sound had been turned down and a gramophone next to the TV was blaring out an Otis Redding number at full pelt. There was a sweet, sickly smell to the room from the cigarettes one or two of the women were smoking and their eyes were slightly glazed, vacant almost, but overall the girls were good-looking although heavily made up.

He was greeted by name by one or two of the women to whom he gave a brief nod of his head, and the old woman who had answered the door, following him into the room, carried on their conversation as though she hadn't been interrupted. 'No, Bett's gone 'ome for the 'oliday, so's Milly and Vera, but one of these here'd be glad to oblige, eeh girls?' Several pairs of heavily mascara'd eyes looked up at the handsome, well-built young man standing in front of them and a stranger in their midst would have wondered why they didn't jump at the chance to 'oblige'. Surely it wasn't that often, it could be reasoned, that such a presentable male came their way? But the girls' eyes were wary, even nervous.

'You want your usual extras?' A big brunette on one side of the gramophone spoke after a long minute of absolute silence. 'You know only Bett and Vera stand for the rough stuff.'

'You'll be paid well. Double. It is Christmas day.' David smiled and it was just at that moment the door to the kitchen beyond the main room opened and a slight, blond-haired girl entered, less scantily clad and made up than the rest.

'Well, well, well, what do we have here?' David's eyes had narrowed but the smile was still in evidence and the girl's pretty, pert face brightened as he let his eyes run over her.

'This is Julie.' The big brunette stood up and moved across the room quickly with a brief nod of her head in the direction of the others, which could have been taken as a warning to them to get the other girl out of the way. 'She's new to the game, only just come down a week or two ago.'

'I haven't seen her.'

'No. No, well, you wouldn't, would you.' The brunette smiled as she took David's arm. 'You're with Bett usually.'

'And Bett isn't here.' He shook off the red-tipped fingers brusquely. 'But Julie is.'

'I said she's new to it.' The woman's voice was low now and she darted a look at the woman who had answered the door, who shrugged easily, her fat face bland.

'Up to her, ain't it?' The old woman turned to the pretty blonde and smiled, showing blackened teeth. 'You wanna service him, Julie? He likes the extras.'

'Does he?' Just for a moment the younger girl looked unsure but then her eyes went over David's big muscular body and handsome face and she smiled coquettishly, her eyes flicking to the brunette with a look that clearly spoke of triumph. 'All right.'

As David and the girl left the room the brunette walked over to the older woman, thrusting her face into the fat jowls. 'You shouldn't have let her go with him, Ma.'

'She's gotta learn, and she ain't so innocent that she didn't want to do you down.'

'You still shouldn't have let her go with him. *Him*. Of all people. You know what he's like. Bett's used to it and she has a job to manage that one, she's been black and blue at times.'

'Stop your moanin', Lil. I said, she's gotta learn.'

But later the next day, when they had to fetch the doctor to the house, Ma didn't say a word.

CHAPTER TWELVE

'You're making me nervous.' Peter grinned at Jenny as he lifted her up in his arms and swung her round before letting her feet touch the ground again, holding her pressed to him. 'If you've looked over your shoulder once you've done it ten times in the last hour, now just relax, will you, woman? What do you expect to see behind you anyway?'

She smiled weakly as she looked up into his tanned, very masculine face. It was the first Sunday of the new year and they had driven out to the countryside for the day in Peter's Morris Minor, making first for Howden Moors only to find large parts of the road blocked by fresh falls of snow which the wind was still whipping into icy drifts. They had retraced their route to Ewden village, stopping at a small pub en route for steak and kidney pie and chips and two half-pint bottles of pale ale before venturing for a walk along the frozen river bank, arm in arm. 'Nothing . . .' She wrinkled her nose at him. 'You'll just think I'm being silly.'

'My Jenny? Silly? Heaven forbid.' As his mouth covered hers his arms tightened for a moment before he raised his head to look down into her upturned face. 'You're so beautiful, so incredibly, breathtakingly beautiful, do you know that? I still can't believe you're bothering with a bloke like me.'

'Now it's you who's being silly.' She laughed at him, her cloud of silky blond curls drifting across her face in the wind and her skin fresh and glowing from the icy-cold air. 'I'm nothing special.'

'You are.' He pulled her against him again with a fierceness that took her breath away. 'And not only because of your looks. You're special right through. I've had girlfriends before, you know that, but I've never felt like this. Do you believe that?' The question was in earnest and she nodded slowly, her big grey eyes luminous as they stared into his. 'You're so sweet, Jenny, so untouched. All woman yet childlike too, I never thought women like you existed.'

'Peter –'

'I love you. It's only been a couple of months I know but I do love you, Jenny.'

'I love you too.' For the first time in their relationship it was she who strained up to kiss him, standing on tiptoe as she touched his mouth. 'I do.'

'Jenny, I want to tell you something, something I've never discussed with another human being.' He had held her away from him gently before tucking her arm through his and starting to walk along the hard compacted frozen bank again. 'I know I appear something of a big fellow to you, I've been to university, abroad, done and seen things that you can only guess at.' He turned and smiled down at her but there was a look in his eyes that prevented her from smiling back. 'I'm right, aren't I?'

She nodded quietly. What now? Please, please don't let there be anything to spoil this, she thought desperately. The last few days in the house had been hell on earth, with her grandmother maintaining a cold disapproving silence and Davie – *Davie* . . . Her mind couldn't think of her brother without wanting to scream her guilt and pain and confusion out loud. But she'd done nothing wrong, certainly nothing to cause the almost tangible black waves emanating from his stiff body. And the only thing that had kept her going, made her able to bear it all was this tall broad man at her side. She couldn't believe how much she loved him, the feeling was growing in leaps and bounds and it made her feel . . . vulnerable.

'Well, just listen to me a while, would you, love? Without saying anything? Because I'm not going to find this easy. As you know I came up here because my mother married again a short time ago, a man who's nearly ten years younger than her, incidentally, but that's by the by. He's not a bad bloke really, he was widowed just over two years ago and left with three young kids which can't have been easy for him –' He broke off abruptly and shook his head, his brow wrinkling as he frowned at himself. 'But I'm digressing. That's another thing you'll learn about me, I'm a great procrastinator.'

'I –' She hesitated. 'Just tell me before you say anything else. Is it about another woman? I mean –'

'No. Good heavens, no. I'm sorry Jenny, is that what you've been thinking?' He stopped and turned her towards him with his hands on her shoulders as he looked down into her eyes. 'Look, get one thing clear in that beautiful head of yours. I've had girlfriends. I slept with a couple at university because it was offered and I'm no angel. I wish I could say to you that you'd be the first but I won't lie about this or anything else in my life. But –' And here he took her face in his hands, cupping it gently between his fingers as he kissed the tip of her cold nose. 'But it wasn't anything meaningful, not to me and not to them. It was just the thing to do at the time. You know?'

'Not really.' She smiled shakily.

'Good.' He was perfectly serious now. 'Keep it that way, please, Miss Longbridge. Now, where was I?' They started walking again, arms linked, but both their faces staring ahead at the ice-bound world in front of them, the trees on either side of the bank bare and stark against the silver-grey sky. 'My mother married again and I couldn't be glad for her, I tell you straight, I couldn't, Jenny. Not because I've got any mother-fixation or anything like that, I hasten to add, but because she'd made my father's life a misery from when I was a toddler, and mine too for that matter. He was injured in the war, and they shipped him home when I was just fifteen months old, what was left of him, that is.' He screwed up his eyes against the memory. 'War is the very devil of a thing, Jenny, the very devil. He'd left England a young man of twenty-three with a wife and a baby son and he came back – he came back half a man, both legs gone and blinded in one eye.'

'Oh, Peter!'

'Here, here, it's all right.' He put out his hand and touched her cheek, his face tender. 'He was a brave man, brave and very loving, but from the day he came home, once he'd left the hospital, that is, because they kept him in there nearly twelve months, but from the day he came home she made it clear to him he was on sufferance. She did her duty, mind you, she was nurse and cook and everything else that was required of her but there was no softness, no real caring . . . Not even to me. She resented us, both of us, in different ways. I grew up very quickly and that's not good for anyone, any child should be allowed all the stages in its life. And then when I was fourteen he died. A piece of shrapnel they hadn't been able to dig out. It was very quick. I left the house in the morning and when I came home from school he'd gone. And she wasn't able to hide her gladness.'

Her mouth opened and closed again as she searched for something, anything to say to alleviate the pain which was deepening the craggy lines near his mouth still more.

'And something died in me that day. It's not too dramatic to say that. I found from that point on that I couldn't really feel like I'd felt before, care about people deep down inside . . . I can't explain it properly but looking back it's almost as though my feelings went into ice. I could put on a show, of course. I was popular at school, something of a Jack-the-lad if the truth be known, and once at university I found an environment that was tailor-made for me, fun and more fun with no commitments and no ties, but all good things come to an end, and after four years there I was, thrust back in the maternal bosom, so to speak. And then she met Martin. I thought I was doing all right till then, but when I saw her happy –' He stopped and shook his head, his breath white in the darkening afternoon. 'I realized – I realized I wasn't as nice a chap as I thought I was.' He turned and looked down at her, his eyes narrowed. 'The resentment and bitterness made it difficult to talk to her, to them both. And she was acting like a skittish schoolgirl in love for the first time, Martin this and Martin that, and all I could think of was the way she'd treated my father, the way she'd crucified him over and over again.'

'Why didn't she just leave him if she felt like that?' Jenny asked softly. 'I don't understand why she stayed.'

'Money mainly.' His voice was tight. 'My father was reasonably wealthy in a humble sort of way. The family had had their own haulage business before the war but they got bombed out, and once father came back in the condition he was in there was no point in resurrecting it as both his brothers had been killed in the war and they were unmarried. I think she married him in the first place because he was considered a catch for a girl like her. She came from the wrong side of town and had no social standing. Oh –' He turned away from her to stare out over the grey river. 'I don't know. What makes people do things anyway? We can none of us really know what goes on in another person's mind, can we? But she didn't love me, I don't even think she liked me very much. I am very like my father, both to look at and in our mannerisms and so on, and once he was home and I got to know him we got on too well for her to stomach. I'd made up my mind I'd never get married, never commit myself to a woman and be put in the position my father was. He trusted her, you see, and she let him down in the worst possible way.'

'I'm so sorry, Peter.' She shook her head helplessly. 'I really am.'

'Yes, I knew you would be. Anyone else would say that without really meaning it but you've got such a capacity for seeing other people's pain, haven't you? You need protecting from yourself, you know, and I intend to take that job on.'

'I'm not a saint –'

'I wouldn't want a saint. A saint couldn't have got under my skin from the first time I laid eyes on her and made me realize what a fool I was to think I was immune to love. I've never said this to a woman, Jenny, and I know I'll never say it again to anyone but you, whatever the future holds. I love you, I shall love you to the end of my days and beyond. I can't imagine a world without you in it, you *are* my world. You've transformed my life and I can't believe you could care for me, not me –'

'Oh, Peter.' She threw herself at him now and as he caught her, covering her face in a frenzy of kisses, he murmured her name over and over again. 'You don't know, you'll never know what you mean to me. I've felt so lonely. Oh, Jenny . . .'

They talked and kissed and hugged as they wandered along the bank until it was too dark to see a hand in front of them, and once back in the car Peter put his arm round her after swathing her in the tartan car rug until only her head and shoulders were visible. 'I'm going to look after you from now on,' he said softly, 'I promise you. I'll slay all the dragons and fight all the giants and – Oh, Jenny. I'll never let you down. We'll grow old together and see our children and our grand-children . . . and the girls will all have blond curls and grey eyes.'

'And the boys?'

He grimaced as he sat back in his seat and started the engine. 'Ah, the boys. Well, with my genes I can't do much about the boys. They'll probably all have big hooters and square chins.'

'That'll suit me.' She was so happy she felt drunk on it. Everything would work out at home. When they saw what Peter was really like, how much he loved her, they couldn't fail to love him too . . . could they? Davie, Davie, be glad for me, she prayed desperately. Give him a chance. Without the burden of having to watch out for me you can find someone, a nice girl.

'Now. Are we for home or shall we call in for a drink somewhere?' he asked quietly as he drove on carefully.

'Home. Or I should say, Connie's. I promised her we'd call round this evening, she's feeling so rotten at the moment.'

'Well, it can't be easy for her with a father like she's got. At least she'll be living with Mick's family once they're married and that'll be soon now. She'll be all right there, his mother is a nice woman . . .' There was a touch of wistfulness in his voice and for the first time she understood why. She'd make it up to him, she would. She'd be everything he needed, mother, wife, lover, friend.

'Jenny?' She realized he'd carried on talking and she hadn't heard a word.

'Sorry?'

'I asked you what was wrong earlier, out there.' He gestured towards the car window. 'You seemed nervous.'

'It's silly.' She pulled a face at her own weakness. 'I know it really but I just can't get rid of the feeling that we're being watched.' She glanced at his profile, willing him not to laugh.

'Watched?' He shook his head. 'Out there? In that weather?'

'I told you you'd think it was silly.' She pushed him as he grinned briefly at her. 'I suppose it's all the hassle and everything, it's unnerved me.'

'That's over now.' His voice was very deep. 'You hear me, Jenny? It's over. I just want to make you happy now.' He grimaced wryly. 'Would you just hear me? I still can't believe it's me talking like this, and I tell you, all the lads back in London would think I'm an alien from Mars. You've no idea what you've done to me, my Sheffield lass.'

'I would, 'cos I feel the same,' she said softly, her eyes moist.

They drove back slowly on ice-bound roads and she was conscious all the time that part of her was saying to make the most of each moment, to hold on to it and treasure it as though time was short. But it wasn't, it wasn't. The way he'd been speaking they were going to be together the rest of their lives. He hadn't actually said the word marriage but he'd talked about children, grandchildren. But she hadn't told him yet, about the circumstances of her birth. Would it make any difference to the way he felt? She glanced at him under her long dark lashes, at the hard square face and masculine profile and felt reassured. No. It wouldn't. She knew it wouldn't. And when she was thirteen, with Steve Baker? She shut her eyes and leant back in the seat as though she was dozing. She'd tell him about that, and the fact that her mam hadn't been married, but not yet. Not just yet. Perhaps when he asked her – *if* he asked her to marry him . . .

Connie was pathetically glad to see them when they arrived at the house, immediately drawing them both into the front room and shutting the door behind her before she spoke. 'Mam said we could stay in here if you came round, less chance of bumping into Dad that way.'

'Oh, Connie . . .' Jenny looked down at her as her cousin dropped into a chair. 'Things are no better, then? He's still mad?'

Connie shook her head silently. 'He's awful, awful. He's banned Mick from coming here at all even though we're getting married a few weeks from now. I don't understand him, I don't really. I mean, what good will that do, not letting me see him?' She looked from one to the other and they stared back without answering. 'He's said some wicked things, Jenny . . .' She suddenly started crying, a quiet, hopeless kind of weeping that brought Jenny's heart into her mouth. She'd never seen Connie like this in all the time she'd known her, so defeated and broken. As she hugged her cousin close, sitting on the arm of her chair and gathering her against her, she looked helplessly over Connie's head at Peter, who shook his own in reply. 'And something's happened between him and Mam.' Connie raised a tear-streaked face. 'You know they've never got on that well, but now – now it's just unbearable. Everything's unbearable. I know we shouldn't have done what we did but – Oh, Jenny . . .'

'Hush, hush . . .' Jenny stroked the shorn head as she spoke, her throat aching with pity. 'You're going to be out of it all in a few weeks, so just hang on in there. Mick's mam's lovely and you know you get on well with his dad and his sisters. Once you're round there everything will be all right, Connie.'

'I dread coming home every night from work and this weekend, it was a nightmare. He's gone mental, I'm sure he's gone mental.'

'He's just upset, that's all, it's natural in a father. He'll come round.'

'He won't, you know.' Connie took a deep breath as she began to dry her face on the big white handkerchief Peter handed to her. 'I'm telling you, he won't. You don't know him like I do, there's times . . .' She shook her head slowly. 'There's times when he isn't normal. He didn't used to be too bad but in the last few years it only takes one word and he's off like a rocket. It isn't only Mick he's banned from the house, you know.'

'Who . . . Not me? He hasn't banned me?'

'Course not you, Jenny, you can't do much wrong in me dad's eyes. The times he's held you up as an example to me would have made me hate you if you weren't so nice.' She managed a weak grin at her cousin's surprised face. 'And as for David . . . Well, I ask you. Does the sun shine out of his backside or not?'

'Connie . . .' They were all laughing now, Jenny and Peter as much with relief at hearing an echo of the old Connie as anything else.

'No, it's your grandfather, Jen. Me uncle George.'

'Grand-dad?' Jenny's eyes stretched wide with amazement. 'What on earth for? What's he done? He never comes round here anyway from one year to the next.'

'Well, that's what he said. Christmas day, when you'd all gone, we had a right do here. He got his belt off to me and Mam got between us and went for him and shouted to me to lock meself in my room, and I didn't need to be told twice, I can tell you. His face was red with rage, like it was going to burst. But I could still hear them, I should think the whole street could. Anyway, he was blaming me falling for the baby on me mam and she was blaming him. It was like me and Mick had had nothing to do with it.' It wasn't funny, but the way Connie was telling it made it so and Jenny had to bite her lip hard to prevent a smile. 'Then – then he started getting really nasty with me mam and he said –' She stopped abruptly and looked straight up at Jenny. 'He said Uncle George and her had been carrying on.'

'I don't think you ought to be repeating this, Connie.' Peter stood up, clearly uncomfortable now.

'How dare he?!' Jenny's voice was shrill with outrage and Connie flapped at her with her hand as she glanced nervously to the shut door.

'Keep your voice down, Jen. Me dad's upstairs getting ready for the darts match at the pub with your David and he's got lug holes like an elephant.'

'But Grand-dad . . . That's ridiculous, just plain ridiculous. What did Aunt Martha say?' Jenny asked angrily.

'She denied it, of course, and then there was a great barney that went on for hours, or it seemed like it at the time. Then they came up and it all went quiet but they still aren't speaking. He's not speaking to me either but that suits me. I don't care if he never speaks to me again in my life,' she added with great bitterness. 'I hate him.'

'Give it a few weeks and you'll be back to normal,' Peter said with forced brightness. 'You know what families are.'

'I know what this one's like, Peter,' Connie said grimly. 'And if it wasn't for me mam I'd be as queer as a nine-bob note by now. My dad's really strange at times, I'm not kidding. He acts one thing outside these four walls and another inside, and I'm blowed if I know which is the real him. Mind you, I can't stand either of them, so it makes no odds.'

Her cousin had certainly recovered her equilibrium, Jenny thought dryly, but she couldn't bring herself to smile at the sally, not with the accusation against her grandfather still fresh in her mind. Her uncle Frank was wicked, to turn on her grandfather like that just because he was mad at Connie. The two men had never liked each other but that was a thing apart, and if anyone should be upset it was her grandfather. Look how her uncle had turned Davie against him, and he had. She knew he had. And Davie wouldn't be like he was now if he hadn't had so much to do with their uncle. But to say that her grandfather was . . . with her aunt Martha! She turned to Peter now, her eyes dark with indignation. 'You don't believe what Uncle Frank said, do you?' she asked as she leant forward, appeal in every line of her body. 'About my grand-dad.'

He stared back at her without blinking and lied with a steady voice. 'Of course I don't, Jenny, you don't have to ask that, do you?' Believe it? It had been in every gesture the two of them had made, every effort to avoid looking at one another, to keep their bodies from touching, and then the way he had defended her when the rumpus had started! George had been into that fray like a shot. His eyes softened, as, reassured, Jenny turned back to her cousin. He'd take her out of all this as soon as he could, sooner if necessary. There were more undercurrents in these two families than in the rest of Sheffield put together. He'd thought his own home was bad enough but at least everything was out in the open there. Here – He gave a mental shake of his head. What with that brother of hers breathing fire and damnation and this Frank going off the deep end . . . What a crew! And there was Jenny, in the midst of it all, as innocent and fresh as they come. And she'd stay that way until he had a ring on her finger but . . . His gaze drifted over the sheen of her hair and the slim line of her body as she talked to her cousin. It would have to be a short courtship. A certain part of his anatomy seemed to have a life of its own these days.

When the door burst open in the next moment all three of them shot to their feet as though they were connected by a single wire, so savage were the sound and motion. Frank stood in the doorway, his face a turkey-red as his hard little eyes ran over them. 'Oh . . .' He seemed slightly taken aback. 'It's you, Jenny lass. I heard voices an' I wondered who was here.'

'I –' Her uncle's manner had been terrifying and Jenny gulped before trying again. 'I, we, came to see Connie for a few minutes if that's all right.'

'Course, lass, course. You know you're welcome here any day.' It was noticeable that the older man didn't acknowledge Peter's presence by so much as a blink of his eyes, and his daughter was clearly non-existent too.

Jenny felt, rather than saw, Peter stiffen on the other side of the room and opened her mouth to speak quickly before he said anything that might add to the painfully charged atmosphere, but Connie was there before her. 'You thought I'd got Mick in here, didn't you? Didn't you?' she asked softly, her voice low and trembling.

'Would that be so surprisin'?' It wasn't the actual words that sent a shiver down Jenny's spine but the look that accompanied them. As her uncle's gaze moved from her own face to that of his daughter it underwent a complete transformation that turned his black eyes stony, a malevolence in his face that seemed quite out of proportion with the crime Connie had committed. And then in the next instant it was gone as he turned back to her. 'I'm off out in a minute with David,' he said quietly, 'so I'll say goodnight, lass.'

She was quite unable to speak, nodding dumbly as he turned and left the room still without acknowledging Peter's presence.

'He can't bear it because I won't grovel at his feet and seek absolution.' Connie's expression was angry and hard as she looked at them both, and in that minute she resembled her father more than anyone else. 'The other three, Rosy and Bill and Sally, they all left home as soon as they could 'cos of him, you know. He used to scare 'em half to death, but he won't get the better of me. I mean it.' She shook her head now, the gesture defiant. 'Once I'm out of here I shan't come back. Me mam can come and visit us at Mick's till we get our own place, but there's no way I want any more truck with him. We've clashed all our lives and it can only get worse. Why me mam ever married him, I'll never know.'

'Well, you wouldn't be here now if she hadn't.' Peter was attempting to lighten the situation but as Jenny heard the sound of male voices in the hall outside she almost shut her eyes. Davie. That was all they needed. But her brother didn't come into the room and in a few moments they heard the sound of the front door slam and silence reigned.

'I think we'd better be going. I promised Granddad I'd sit with gran for a while so he could go to the club with Dickie Wrainwright.' It seemed to Jenny that Connie came back from a great distance and it was a few seconds before she responded.

'Yes, yes, that's fine. Thanks for coming, you too, Peter.'

'I'll just say goodbye to Aunt Martha.'

'She's lying down, got a bit of an upset tummy.'

'Oh, right . . .' She looked hard at Connie as they walked out into the hall. 'Connie, what is it? You look like you've seen a ghost. You feeling bad?'

'What?' Connie turned to her but her eyes were miles away.

'Are you feeling all right?'

Connie's mouth twisted in a semblance of a smile. 'I'm just thinking that I must be the dimmest female on God's earth, if you want to know, Jenny. The dimmest and the thickest. It was staring me in the face all this time and I never cottoned on. When I think – The *hypocrite*. The two-faced, snivelling –'

'Who? What?' Jenny turned to Peter but he shrugged his shoulders.

'Nothing. No, nothing. Forget it. I'll tell you another time.' Connie almost pushed them towards the front door.

'Tell me what?' She didn't like the expression on her cousin's face. It reminded her of the time she'd seen a young girl hit in the stomach with a football, when some of the lads were playing a game on the stretch of wasteland a few streets away.

'Nothing. I mean it, go on. Take her home, Peter.'

'Connie, there's something wrong, I know it. I don't like leaving you like this.'

'You're worse than me mam!' Connie's laugh was more natural now but the look on her face remained. 'Just go on home, will you? and I'll see you tomorrow. Call in the shop if you can and I'll slip you a few of those fresh eggs we have in on a Monday before they all go. OK?'

'But –'

'Jenny.' Peter took her arm, the pressure gentle but firm. 'It's time we were going.' He opened the front door before she had time to protest further and shut it behind them once they were in the deserted street. The biting cold made her snuggle up into his side, with his arm round her waist, but they had only gone a few steps, treading carefully on the frozen pavement, before she stopped and looked up into his face, her brow wrinkled.

'I don't like leaving her like that, Peter.'

'Like what?'

'Like . . . I don't know really, but in those last few minutes something was wrong.'

'There is something wrong, Jenny.' Peter tried to keep his amusement from showing in his voice. 'And in seven or eight months it'll be sleeping all day and yelling all night, or the other way round if they're lucky.'

'You know I don't mean that.' Her voice was flat.

'Look.' He turned her to face him, his hands on her shoulders as he stared down into her eyes, his craggy face soft and tender. 'Stop worrying about her. I know she's your cousin and the two of you are as close as sisters, closer maybe, but she's a grown woman in her own right, Jenny, and she's proved it the last few weeks. I know Frank Malley's sort, I've seen it before with some of the fathers I had to deal with in that school in London. They are right little Hitlers in their own home, can't bear to be crossed, and in his opinion she's crossed him in the worst possible way. He isn't thinking of Connie or his wife. The only thing that really concerns him at the moment is the loss of face he'll have to endure in his work place. But once she's out of his control she's free of all that, he can't touch her.'

'And in the meantime?' She shivered but it wasn't the outside temperature that caused the trickling chill down her spine. 'Did you see his face when he looked at her?'

'You're really worried?' She nodded dumbly and he pulled her against him fiercely, his mouth hot and sweet on hers before he raised his head. 'I love you, you know that? I've never met anyone with such a capacity for caring as you but I can see I'm going to have to protect you from yourself in the future, else we'll have all the lame dogs of the town on our doorstep. Now, how about if I have a discreet little word with Mick's mother? For some ridiculous reason she's got the idea I'm a good influence on her son, and being a teacher too . . .' He grinned with a touch of embarrassment. 'I'll put her in the picture but carefully, and suggest that it might be better all round if Connie moves in with them now. She can have Mick's room and he can come next door and share my room for a couple of weeks till it's legal.'

'What about your landlady? Won't she mind?' Jenny asked anxiously.

'No, not if I explain things. She's a bit of a Tartar but her heart's in the right place.'

'What you mean is, you've charmed her?' She tilted her head at him.

'Well, that too.' He grinned again and touched her face with his hand. 'Anyway, does this idea suit madam?' he asked mockingly.

'Oh, Peter . . .' For some reason she wanted to cry again. That feeling seemed to be paramount these days with the happiness that threatened to consume her, which was quite illogical when you came to think about it. But she'd never had anyone love her for herself like he did, and she loved him, oh, she did. She had never imagined loving anyone like she loved him, and it wasn't just for the life he had opened up to her. It was everything about him, the big solid thick-set body and hard craggy face that hid a heart that was gold, pure gold. 'I love you.' She smiled up at him but her smile was shaky. 'So much.'

'Of course you do.' He tucked her arm in his and started walking. 'I'm a very lovable person, I'd have you know.'

He didn't come in when they reached her door and she didn't press the point even though she'd made it clear David was out. 'Give the old people a few days to get used to the idea and then I'll make my presence known,' he whispered as they stood on the doorstep, his body enclosing her with its warmth.

'You don't have to worry about Grand-dad,' she said quickly. 'He's for you. He couldn't be more pleased, but Gran . . .' Her voice dwindled away and he smiled that slow smile, which, she was learning to recognize, meant he understood the situation perfectly.

'Come here.' His voice was very soft and very deep.

He kissed her thoroughly in spite of the fact that her grandmother's window overlooked the street, and when she stepped into the hall a few minutes later her cheeks were flushed and hot in spite of the bitter weather.

'Jenny?' George came out of the kitchen, where he'd been sitting reading the paper. 'I didn't expect you back so soon.'

'I told you I'd be back early so you could go with Dickie tonight,' she said a trifle breathlessly as she smoothed her hair.

'That's kind of you, lass.' He went back in the kitchen and re-emerged with his jacket and cap. 'Mrs Brown's with your gran so there's no need to dance attendance. Just make your presence known and then you could have an early night if you like, you look done in. I'll see to her when I come back, I shan't be late. Nice day?' He paused with his hand on the front door and she nodded smilingly. 'Well, I think the young fella is goin' to have to pay us a visit in the very near future, don't you? I've had a word with your gran,' he added, his voice very low now. 'Just pointed out a few relevant facts, like a teacher's salary isn't to be sneezed at and it's a nice reliable job, a few things like that, you know, so I think he might be gettin' an invite to Sunday tea some day soon. She's comin' round, lass, so just be firm, all right?' He grinned at her, his eyes soft.

'Thanks, Grand-dad.' She smiled up at him as she felt a surge of bitterness against her uncle Frank. How could he say things like that about her grandfather? Nasty, mean-mouthed little man. And there'd be all hell let loose if her grand-dad heard about it, she'd have to tell Davie to keep his mouth shut when she saw him.

Davie . . . Her mind returned to her brother once she'd said goodnight to her grandmother and was settled in bed with an open book in front of her and a mug of tea at her side. She couldn't quite fathom his attitude at the moment. On the surface he was controlled and quiet, although they had barely exchanged two words since the night of the party, but she felt almost as though his composure was worse than the rage he had displayed on Christmas day. There was a brooding quality about it, a dark stillness, as though he was waiting for something and it unnerved her to the point where she was constantly glancing over her shoulder. She shut her eyes tightly for a moment as she felt the fluttering of troubled nerves in her stomach. She had to pull herself together over this, she did really. She couldn't go on imagining he was beyond every corner. She'd almost blurted out her fears to Peter today, and he would think she was crazy. Perhaps she was. She opened her eyes and tried to concentrate on the book but the letters weaved and ducked beneath her eyes as her mind wavered.

She would have to tell Peter about Steve Baker and soon. She felt – Her eyes opened wider now as she faced her thoughts. She felt as though it would be a cleansing, a laying of this ghost that haunted her when she was at her happiest. The nightmares had been so vivid the last week or so that it had got to the point where she was putting off going to sleep until she was dropping with exhaustion. And she'd tell him it all. Even – even the way she had found out about her parentage. Who could her father have been? Why hadn't he looked after her mother?

She let her mind drift off where it would now as she lay, her mind dull with tiredness, in the comforting warmth of the soft bed. She'd gone through a stage just after the attack when that thought had tormented her almost as much as the incident that had caused it. It hadn't helped that Davie wouldn't discuss it either, she'd needed someone to share it with and she couldn't broach the subject with her grandparents, she just couldn't. Had her mother loved him? She shook her head wearily. She'd never know, would she? Never know whose blood ran through her veins, where she came from. It was a disturbing thought and one that was not new to her. It made her feel . . . rootless.

As her eyelids grew heavier the book slipped from her fingers and she slept, half propped up against the pillows, the tea growing cold by the side of the bed. But it was a troubled sleep, populated with veiled images and dark shadows that were an ever-constant reminder of the past, and once again she was in that clearing, a sun-filled dell with a carpet of daisies and bluebells and the whisper of trees overhead. She should have felt happy, it was beautiful, beautiful, but there was something – something lurking just beyond the range of her vision and she couldn't see . . . And then the air thickened, changed in an instant to a dull grey mist that sent fingers snaking towards her until she couldn't breathe, and then he was there, Steve Baker, his face mutilated and bloody and his mouth fixed in a grinning death-mask. But his eyes should have been blue, not grey, there was something wrong. Something . . . She came out of the dream to the feel of a hand shaking her none too gently and the smell of beer-thickened breath on her face as she opened her eyes in the semi-gloom.

'Wake up. Do you hear me, Jen? Wake up.' David's voice was harsh.

'What – what's the matter?' As her eyes opened wide she saw David bending over the bed still in his overcoat and even in the semi-darkness the thin light from the small bedside lamp she had left switched on showed his face to be contorted with rage. 'Davie? What is it?' she asked, dazed, as she struggled to wake fully.

'Do you know what he's done? Do you?' It was a savage hiss, his voice was low but shaking with fury.

'What who's done?' She shook his hand off her arm, pulling the candlewick bedspread up round her shoulders as she sat upright in the bed. 'I don't know what you're talking about.'

'That fancy man of yours.' There was a stark violence in his face that should have intimidated her but didn't. Instead she felt a rage that was new to her beginning to bubble in her chest. He thought he could just barge in here, wake her up and then yell and shout – But he wasn't yelling or shouting, was he? Nothing so open. And she liked that still less.

'I presume you're talking about Peter?' It was clear both her tone of voice and the icy manner in which she spoke surprised him because he straightened and took a step back before he spoke again.

''Course I'm damn well talkin' about him, you haven't got more of 'em hidden away, have you?'

'Davie, it's gone midnight. If you've got something to say, then say it and go to your own room. I want to go to sleep.' Again she had surprised him but now his eyes narrowed into jet-black slits and his stance was threatening as he lowered his head into his neck.

'Oh, I've got somethin' to say all right, and it's just this. You see anythin' of that scum again and I'll break his back. Do you hear me, Jen? *I forbid you to see him*. What he's done the night won't be forgotten in a hurry, I'm tellin' you.'

'You're not *telling* me anything!' She knew her voice had risen in spite of her efforts to keep it down. 'You're just talking at me like you always do. What is Peter supposed to have done that's so terrible? He was with me tonight –'

'I know that. An' you were round Connie's, weren't you? havin' a nice little chat about this and that.' He ground his teeth in his rage and as she saw her grandfather hurry into the room, pulling his dressing gown over his pyjamas, she felt a deep thankfulness that she wasn't alone with her brother. 'And as for her! That two-faced, stinkin' little slut! When I think of all the trouble she's caused one way or another –' He stopped as he became aware of his grandfather.

'What's goin' on? You'll have the whole street awake at this rate.' George took hold of his grandson's arm only to have it shaken away so violently he almost lost his footing on the shiny hard surface of the linoleum as his feet slipped from under him. 'Here! That's enough of that, lad. What's up now?'

'Ask her. Ask her what that pious, self-satisfied bit of scum she's hanging around with has done. Go on, *ask her*.'

'All right, all right.' They could hear Mary shouting from downstairs but not one of them acknowledged the sound. 'You know what this is all about, lass?' he asked her quietly.

'No.'

'You don't? Then I'll tell you. Mr High-and-Mighty Knowles, him that's as pure as the driven snow, told Frank's daughter that she was already on the way when her mam and dad got married.'

'You liar.' Jenny shot up in bed now, her face scarlet as she glared at her brother. 'You dirty, wicked liar. Peter said no such thing! I was there, I was with them and he said no such thing.'

'I'm tellin' you –'

'Just a minute, just a minute.' George didn't make the mistake of touching David again but moved round the side of the bed beside Jenny to face his grandson. 'What exactly did Connie say?' he asked tightly. '*Exactly?*'

'What's it matter? That smooth-talkin' galoot –'

'He's not! You shut up, you! He's worth ten, twenty of you, David Longbridge. You make me sick –'

'*I said, hold on!*' George rarely raised his voice, which made the effect of his roar all the more dramatic. 'Now you.' He turned to his grandson. 'You tell me exactly what was said without any of your embroiderin'. And you,' He turned his gaze to Jenny, 'Keep quiet a minute.'

The glance that David levelled on his grandfather would have melted steel but the older man met it without flinching, his back straight and his eyes steady. 'Well? Them's serious accusations you've made the night, lad, now let's see if you can back 'em up.'

'Back 'em up? I can back 'em up, all right.'

'Then let's hear it.' George kept his eyes on him. 'Now.'

'When Frank and I got home to his place tonight Connie was sittin' waitin' for him in a right tear, I can tell you. She didn't let him get through the back door afore she started, I could hear it all.'

'Where were you?' George asked, gesturing at Jenny to keep quiet with the flat of his hand as she reared up again.

'In the lav. I heard her start shoutin' and then screaming like a maniac. By! I'd have knocked her from here to kingdom come if she was mine.' He shook his head in disgust, his face contemptuous.

'And? –'

'She said she'd got hold of her birth certificate tonight and their marriage certificate 'n all after that nancy-boy had told her –'

'Told?' George put out a hand. 'Wait a minute. You're sayin' to me that the lass said to her dad young Peter had *told* her they weren't married when Martha fell for her?'

'Near as dammit.'

'Well, let's hear the dammit,' George said softly. 'What *exactly* did the young lass say? Word for word.'

'I remember.' Jenny broke into the conversation now, her brow wrinkled as she looked first at her grandfather and then to David's glowering face. 'I remember what Peter said and it wasn't like Davie's saying, it wasn't. Connie was moaning about her dad and she said she didn't know why Aunt Martha had married him and Peter said – He said she wouldn't be here now if they hadn't. That's all he said.' She looked straight at David. 'I swear that's all. How could he have said anything else when he didn't know?'

'Well, it was enough to set the ball rollin',' David said grimly. 'An' he's got a lot to answer for.'

'Don't be so stupid.' She glared at him, her voice tight.

'Stupid, is it? Well, because of that smart so-and-so there was near murder done, I'm tellin' you.'

'It seems like you're tellin' us an awful lot, lad, and not all of it gospel from what I can make out.'

'And that's it?' David swung on his grandfather so savagely Jenny thought he was going to hit him for a moment, and as George stumbled back a step it was clear he'd thought the same. 'You're takin' his side when he's caused Frank to half-murder the slut, is that what you're tellin' me?'

'He's hurt Connie?' Jenny was out of bed now, careless of the fact she was in her nightie, pulling on her skirt over her night attire and then reaching for her jumper. 'What's he done?'

'Hold your horses –'

'Grand-dad?' She shook off George's restraining arm, her face as white as a sheet. 'You know what he's like, he's capable of anything. I have to go to her.'

'It's the middle of the night, lass –'

'I don't care.' She pulled her jumper over her head. *Oh, Connie . . .*

'She's not there anyway.' David had said nothing as they talked, his eyes fixed on Jenny as she'd dressed, but now he walked across the room to lean against the wall. After crossing his arms on his broad chest he surveyed them both through narrowed eyes, his blond hair gleaming like a halo in the dim light.

'What do you mean, she's not there?' It was George who asked the question. There had been a darkness, a satisfaction in her brother's face that had dried up Jenny's voice. 'Where is she, then? An' none of your smart answers either.'

David shrugged slowly. 'I don't know and I don't care, in the gutter where she belongs if there's any justice.'

'*David* –'

'I don't know, I'm tellin' you. There was one hell of a row and when she started screamin' Frank took off his belt and started walloping her. She deserved it.' His voice was without expression. 'She fell and started crawlin' out into the backyard and he followed her out there and then Martha came down –'

'*Martha?*' George took a step or two towards his grandson.

'Aye, Martha.' David's heavy-lidded gaze moved to his grandfather's face from where it had been fixed on Jenny's.

'An' you stood and watched all this? You didn't try to help the lass?' George asked grimly.

'Me?' David levered himself off the wall and there was a wealth of contempt in his voice and face as he looked across at his grandfather. 'She got everythin' she deserved.'

'And you don't know where she is?' Jenny asked flatly.

He shrugged again. 'The screamin' Connie and Martha were doin' brought the neighbours out and that copper that lives at the back of 'em got involved. Hauled Frank inside and read him the Riot Act. I wouldn't be surprised if that bloke of yours has landed him a stretch inside –'

'I couldn't care less whether he has or not,' Jenny said bitterly. 'No, I do care, I hope he has. I hope he's put away for a good long time. I hope he rots –'

'All right, all right, lass.' George was feeling sick. 'Obviously one of the neighbours took Connie in. What about Martha? Was she all right?' he now asked David.

David considered his grandfather for a full thirty seconds before he replied and then his lip curled away from his teeth in a contemptuous snarl. 'Aye. She came back in after a time and the copper cleared me and everyone else out. I waited around some, in case he came out with Frank, but he didn't and it was fair freezing me lugs off so I came home. That little slut –' His eyes, full of hate, looked inwards. 'She set Frank up, that's what she did.'

'Because she found out about her beginnings?' Jenny protested angrily.

'A birth certificate's no proof. She could've been early –'

'Did Frank deny it?' George stared hard at David. 'Did he? Course he didn't, lad, and you know damn well why, and to my mind the lass wouldn't have reacted like that if he hadn't been the way he's been about her and Mick fallin'. Now just think on.'

'She said he was a hypocrite.' Jenny was talking as if to herself. 'Just before we left tonight she said he was a hypocrite but we didn't know who she was talking about. I thought she seemed funny . . . I should never have left. Grand-dad –' She caught hold of his arm now. 'I should never have gone. I should have stayed and found out what was wrong.'

'Now don't blame yourself, lass. All this started seventeen years ago when Frank took her mam down and he was of an age where he knew what he was doing. If anyone's at fault it isn't the lass or you –'

'I don't believe I'm hearin' this.' David's voice was shaking with the force of his feelings as he glared at them both. 'That dirty little upstart you've taken up with goes out of his way to set Connie against her own flesh and blood and accordin' to you he's still whiter than white. An' you –' He turned to his grandfather with a snarl. 'You talk about Frank objectin' to his daughter behaving like a slut as though the man should stand by and see her wallow in her own filth. It's not Frank that's the hypocrite from where I'm standin' –'

'That's enough.'

'Enough?' The spittle sprayed from his lips but as he made a move towards the older man Jenny threw herself in front of her brother, gripping the lapels of his coat with her fingers as she pleaded with him.

'Davie, Davie please, stop this. Grand-dad's not at fault. You're making everything worse, can't you see? Please, Davie . . .'

The touch of her had frozen all movement in his body and he stood glaring above her head at his grandfather for a long minute before his gaze moved to her face, lifted up to his. He shuddered, shutting his eyes tight for one moment before raising his hands and moving her gently away from him as he stepped back a pace. 'He's no good, Jen. This bloke of yours, I'm tellin' you, he's no good. He's just like the rest of 'em –'

'But you don't know him. Please, get to know him, Davie, give him a chance,' she pleaded desperately. 'Please?'

Get to know him? He'd rather walk through coals of fire than have any truck with that mealy-mouthed, white-livered nancy–boy. When he thought about him touching her, putting his hands on her flesh – He wasn't fit to be dust under her feet. He thought she'd have found out by now, known what the scum was after, but perhaps – perhaps she liked it? Maybe she was like the whore who birthed them? *No. Not his Jenny*. She was different to all the rest. Set apart. But he'd have to do something soon, he would that because this fire inside that always accompanied thoughts of them together wasn't to be borne.

'Davie?' Her voice brought him back and his eyes focused on her face. 'Will you? Will you talk to him? Please.'

'Talk to him?' He repeated her words almost vacantly. 'Aye, I'll talk to him.'

'Oh thank you, thank you . . .' He knew her intention to fling herself on him and he also knew how much he could take whether his grandfather was in the room or not and he moved in the same instant towards the open door.

'I'd better see to her.' He flicked his head towards the sound of Mary's voice, rising in increasing volume from downstairs. 'You comin'?' He spoke directly to George now, whose eyes hadn't left his grandson's face in the last few minutes.

'Aye.' George followed David out of the room, pausing in the doorway to nod at Jenny as she came towards him. 'You stay here, lass, we'll see to your grandma. And, Jenny? Move that chair and put it under the knob of the door till I can get a lock fitted the morrow.'

'What?'

'Just do it, lass, will you?'

CHAPTER THIRTEEN

Martha sipped slowly at her tea, her eyes fixed on her husband while he sat stiffly regarding the young policeman who had just put down his cup. 'You understand me, Frank? You understand what I'm saying? If Connie wants to press for assault you could go down the line for this lot. What possessed you, man? What on earth possessed you to lose control like that? Whatever the lass's done it didn't merit that sort of hammering in her condition –'

'And you ask me what she's done? In the same breath as sayin' she's expectin'? The little –'

'Now look. By rights I should take you along to the station until the lass decides whether she's going to take it further, so just think on. If every father in your situation reacted like you've done tonight the cells would be full and you know it. I know at least three or four of her class-mates who are living in sin in this new phase of things. Not that I agree with it, mind.' He lifted his hand against Frank's exclamation of protest. 'But there it is, it's a fact. They are all half-stupid, to my way of thinking, with this pop craze and the like, but I can tell you it's a sight more worrying up London way. This marijuana was bad enough but they're popping pills like nobody's business now and they don't wait for the rock concerts anymore either. So . . .' He rose now, his gaze moving briefly to Martha before returning to Frank's glowering face. 'Just be thankful it's only a bairn. There's worse, Frank, much worse, and not so far from home either.'

'That's easy for you to say.'

'Aye, maybe.' The young man narrowed his eyes

against the resentment in Frank's voice. 'But I've got three young 'uns of my own and they're getting older every day. Now. I'll have to check on the lass before we can call it a night. You say she's at Mrs Henderson's, Martha?'

'She was.' Martha glanced briefly at her husband and then away again. 'But I understood Mr Henderson to say she wanted to go round to Mick's house, her lad, you know. He was going to take her round in his car once they'd checked if it was all right. She was in a state,' she finished bitterly.

'Well, I need to talk to her.'

'Yes, of course.' As the policeman moved towards the back door Martha followed him quickly. 'And thank you, John, thank you for coming over,' she said quietly. 'It brought him to his senses.'

'If Connie doesn't want to press charges against her father we can keep this unofficial, but if she does . . .' He eyed Frank, who was staring down at his hands, flat on the kitchen table, as he spoke. 'If she does I'll be back later and it'll be with the hat on, you understand? Now, what's the address of her young man?'

There was complete silence in the kitchen once the policeman had left but the stillness was electrifying. Martha walked slowly across to the table, pulling her dressing gown more closely around her before gathering up the three mugs and taking them over to the sink where she doused them under the hot tap.

'You satisfied now? Now she's brought the family this low?'

'Me?' Martha swung round so sharply her hand caught one of the mugs, sending it spinning on to the floor where it smashed in a hundred pieces. 'You're talking to me?'

'Who else would I be talkin' to? She's your daughter, she's always been more your daughter than mine.'

'Don't you blame this on me or Connie or anyone else but yourself,' Martha hissed savagely as she moved to stand almost in front of her husband. 'You've been preachin' at her for days, making her feel lower than a worm. How do you expect her to feel when she finds out the truth. And it was bound to come up one day, you know it was, it's there for all to see on her birth certificate! What can't talk can't lie. But she wouldn't have thought anything about it, she wouldn't have cared, but for the fact of you sayin' one thing and doing another. Hypocrite was right.'

'Shut up.'

'No, I won't. If you'd been halfway to normal when she told us about her and Mick all this could have been averted, but no! You had to come the holy Joe and carry on until the lass was half-mad. I'm not surprised she snapped, but for you to go for her like that! You could've killed her, Frank. When I came down and saw you hitting her like that, and that – that perverted animal standing there watching you and enjoying it –'

'*Shut your mouth, woman* –'

'He was, I'm telling you he was. The look on his face as that belt was hitting her – I couldn't believe it. He's not normal! You're not normal! No wonder the two of you are so thick. If you thought half as much of Connie as you did of that sadistic young swine –'

'I'm tellin' you, Martha, shut your mouth.'

'Why? Because I'm daring to criticize David? You can half-kill our daughter while he treats it as some sort of side-show, and you tell me I'm the one who's got to keep quiet? I'm sick of seeing him round here, do you hear me? I'm sick of it. And what you did tonight was unforgivable.' She turned her body in one sharp movement and walked out of the room, hearing the scrape of his chair as he followed her with a sick feeling in the pit of her stomach. She loathed him, she *loathed* him, but with Connie gone there was nothing more holding her to this house and him, nothing. She'd walk out with nothing too if that's what it took, and be glad to do it.

He was right behind her as they mounted the stairs and caught her arm just as she was about to enter the bedroom, swinging her round so violently her head snapped back and her thick blond hair fell across her face. 'Don't walk out on me like that.'

'I didn't –'

'An' while we're having a few home-truths I'd say Connie is actin' like she's been shown,' he said thickly.

'What?' She tried to jerk her arm out of his grasp but his fingers merely tightened on her flesh until the knuckles gleamed white. He wanted her to gasp in pain, to plead, it was his usual way, but tonight she'd rather die first. 'Well, it takes two and if I remember rightly you were the one who wouldn't leave me alone.'

'I'm not talkin' about us.' He pushed her into the bedroom, his small eyes glittering. 'I'm talkin' about you and that great lump of nothin' that's married to your sister. You think I've been blind all these years, that I don't know what the pair of you've been up to?'

'You're crazy, George has never laid a hand on me.'

'Only because he hasn't had the guts to do what his mind does every time he sets eyes on you.' He pushed her hard now as he let go of her and she fell over a chair at the side of the bed as he had intended she should, her hip catching the corner of the seat with a thud that made her face whiten, but she still made no noise. 'I know what you feel about that great lumberin' lout, I've always known and that's what's been eatin' me from the day we were wed. You've never given me a chance, have you? Have you?' he spat furiously.

'Yes, I did, you know I did, and it was all right at first until you wanted –' She stopped and then shook her head, sickened to think about his practices, let alone voice them.

'No, no, it was you. Flauntin' yourself in front of me even before Bill died. You knew how I felt about you and you liked it, I could see it in your eyes. Fun, was it? To have one man pantin' after you while you took your pleasure with another? When I think what you've driven me to do, and then you whine about the boy –' He stopped abruptly.

'What I've driven you to do?' She stared up at him, making no attempt to move from the floor. What was he on about? There was something here she didn't understand, something her mind was trying to tell her but she couldn't grasp it. 'I haven't –'

'Get up.' She knew that look on his face and now sheer dread made her weak, her bowels turning to water.

'No. No, Frank. Please –'

'Get up.' As he moved towards her she cowered back against the side of the bed, her eyes dilated with fear. 'I only want it natural, I promise you I'll only do it natural –'

'No!'

'I need you, Martha, I've got to have you, you know that. I can't live without you.' As he pulled her up from the floor she knew better than to try to struggle. It hurt much more if she struggled and that inflamed the lust that took him over every time he laid a finger on her still more. 'You know I'd kill you if you ever tried to go to him, I'd kill you both.' He was stripping the clothes from her body as he talked with a savagery that brought his finger-nails into searing contact with her flesh and, in spite of her knowledge, as he turned her over on the bed she began to twist and turn but then the pain hit her, that pain that seemed as though it was tearing her apart, and all she could do was pray it would soon be finished.

'Martha? Martha, I'm sorry.' He was crying, but he always cried when it was over and that disgusted her still more, bringing the nausea burning hot in her mouth. She rose painfully from the bed and stood for a moment to steady herself before walking from the room, pausing for a moment to look back at him, undone and repellent, on the bed.

'I'm not surprised you're the way you are with David.' Her voice was bitter and cold. 'You're two of a kind, I've always known it. He should've been related to you rather than me. But I tell you this, Frank Malley, and I mean it. You ever lay a hand on me again, ever, and I'll leave you. I'll go so far away you'll never find me, I swear it. And before I go I'll broadcast to all and sundry exactly what you are under that façade of the big I am. You hear me?' He didn't reply, lying motionless and exposed on the stained sheets as she shut the door behind her.

CHAPTER FOURTEEN

'Enjoying yourself?' How could she do anything else when she was with him? Jenny thought with a burst of happiness so blinding she wanted to leap at Peter then and there. Had anyone ever loved someone else like she loved him? She doubted it. They couldn't have. 'There'll be another fast number in a minute and I don't think I'm up to it. How about a last drink?' he asked hopefully.

'If you like, you poor old man.' She giggled at the face he made.

'Come on, one drink, and then I'd better walk you home. If I'm coming to Sunday tea I'd better not blot my copy-book beforehand, had I?' he asked, smiling now as he drew her into his side.

Once seated at the side of the floor in the big dance hall they watched the gyrating crowd as the disco lights flashed a kaleidoscope of moving colours over the sound of the Rolling Stones record on the turn-table. 'Happy?' She couldn't hear the rest of what he said and wrinkled her brow at him. 'I said, are you happy about Sunday, about me coming to meet them all? Oh look, let's get out of here, I can't hear myself think.'

Outside, the cold February night gave the air a rawness that was chilling after the excessive heat of the building they had just left but she was hardly aware of it, tucked in the shelter of his body with his arm tight round her, as they began to walk to the bus-stop. But even his broadness, the comfortable bulk of him, couldn't banish the niggling unease she had been feel-ing all night. It was ridiculous. She knew it was ridiculous but this feeling that they were being watched was especially strong today. It wasn't so bad when they went out in his car but on the nights like this one, when he knew he was going to drink a few beers and left the car outside his lodgings, she always felt as though unseen eyes were boring into the small of her back. She had ceased to glance behind her, though. Peter didn't like it, he somehow seemed to take it as a reflection on his masculinity, but she wished, she *wished* they were safely home.

'On Sunday? Do you think there'll be any chance of getting your grandfather alone for a few minutes?'

'Grand-dad?' She looked up into his face in surprise. 'What for?'

'I want to ask him if he's happy for me to marry his grand-daughter, if she'll have me, that is.' He pulled her into a shop doorway opposite the bus-stop as he spoke and positioned her in front of him, his arms tight round her waist. 'Will she?'

'I –' The moment had come, the moment she had been hoping for, longing for, had anticipated a hundred and one times in the darkness of her bed at night as she hugged the vision of what it would mean to be joined to him in name and body, and now it was actually here the sheer wonder of it caused a constriction in her throat that made speech impossible. This strong, gentle, kind and educated man, this natural gentleman who could be funny and wise and was handsome, so handsome, at least to her, actually wanted her for his wife. He had transformed her life in the last few months in a way that would make her eternally grateful. It wasn't too extreme to say she felt reborn. And it wasn't going to end. He wanted her. He really wanted her.

'I love you, Jenny, but you know that.' He cupped

her cold face in his hands as his piercing blue eyes held hers. 'You are everything any man could want in a woman, beautiful inside and out. You've done things for me you could never imagine and I can't find words to tell you. When my father died something happened inside me I can't explain. I'd always imagined in the years before his death that once I could leave school I'd get a job and rent a place somewhere for the two of us, make up to him for all the years of humiliation and suffering he'd endured at my mother's hands. I didn't care so much that she hadn't got time for me but the way she treated him used to tie me up in knots so I couldn't sleep at night. He used to cry, Jenny, when he thought he was alone and no one could hear him.' His fingers tensed for a moment on the smooth softness of her skin before relaxing again. 'And when he went and she had won it was too late. I hadn't told him I loved him enough, I hadn't spent enough time with him –' He broke off, controlling his voice with an effort. 'And I wasn't there when he died. He left this world without anyone to hold his hand, to tell him they loved him, that he mattered.'

'Oh, Peter . . .' She didn't know what to say to him but her face was expressive and his hand was shaking as he touched her cheek.

'And I was bitter. I was so, so bitter, Jenny. I tried to conceal it from the world and myself in a million different ways. Peter, the great joker. Peter, Jack-the-lad. I played around, I did things that I'm deeply ashamed of now. You wouldn't have liked me in those days –'

'I would.' She looked straight into his face, her eyes soft. 'I know I would.'

'And when I came down here I was so mad with everything, God, the world, myself. To see her settled and happy, enjoying life, it was so unfair. And then I met you. *Then I met you.*' He took a deep long breath. 'You know, I can't imagine a life in which you don't feature now. You're everything to me, Jenny, everything. Sun, moon and stars. I want to love you, to have children with you, to grow old with you. I want us to laugh together and cry together –' He shook his head as though in bewilderment. 'You opened up a door in my head, Jenny, as well as my heart, made me face the guilt and the remorse. I can't alter what she did but I can make a life for myself because that's what he would have wanted, I see it now. He would have wanted grandchildren, a grandson to carry on the Knowles name, he was old-fashioned that way. So . . . will you marry me?'

She nodded, but when he would have taken her into his arms her hands pressed against the hard wall of his chest. 'Peter, first – first I've got to tell you something.'

He listened quietly as she told him about her mother and even more quietly as she related the incident that had driven them back to the steelworks of Sheffield, and it wasn't until she finished and, her eyes dropping to the floor now, asked if he still wanted to marry her that he reacted. And as he cradled her in his arms, kissing her over and over again in an agony of love, neither of them saw the dark shadow on the other side of the road as it gazed across at them with a malevolence that was chilling, the dark grey eyes alive with hate and maddened jealousy. It would have been so much better if they had.

When, on Sunday afternoon, Jenny found herself pacing the kitchen and hall, her nerves as taut as piano wire, even Mary was forced to relent. 'For crying out loud, lass, there'll be no lino left in that hall if you don't calm yourself,' she called as Jenny passed the open front-room door for the umpteenth time in five minutes. 'Now come in here with me, lass, and let's wait for him together.' Jenny glanced back towards the kitchen and saw her grandfather raise his eyebrows in an expression of wry amusement as he nodded towards the sitting-room door where her grandmother was sitting in the chair by the window.

'Oh, Gran . . .' Jenny couldn't keep the trepidation out of her voice. What would he think of her home? Her grandparents? She bit on her lower lip nervously. Their place wasn't like Connie's, all smart and modern inside with light paintwork and fitted carpets, but – but he wasn't like that. Snobby. He wasn't. If only her grandmother was halfway nice to him it'd be all right. 'You'll like him, Gran.' Her eyes were enormous as she seated herself on the arm of her grandmother's chair. 'I know you will.'

'All right, lass, all right.' Mary's voice was brusque but her eyes were soft as they surveyed Jenny's anxious flushed face. 'If he's your choice there can't be too much wrong with the lad. Now, is everything done? You've got the table set? You bring him in here to me first so I can get a good look at him and we'll go through to the kitchen later and – and it'll be all right, lass.' As Jenny's arms went out to hug her, Mary's voice was cut off with the emotion that filled her throat.

She couldn't bear to be at odds with this lass of hers, and like George had said last night when he had sat and talked to her, or talked *at* her, she corrected grimly, if she didn't reach out and do something to heal the rift between her and her grand-daughter soon, she would lose her completely. She just hoped George was right when he said the lad's intentions were honest because it would be obvious to a blind man that their lass was fair barmy about him, and nothing David had said so far had given her any peace of mind about the situation. Still . . . She smiled at Jenny now as the younger woman stood up. Perhaps David wasn't the best person to take heed of in all of this. And this Peter was a school-teacher, when all was said and done, an educated sort.

When the doorbell rang in the next second Jenny's hand went to her throat and her grandmother tut-tutted deep in her chest. 'Don't keep him waitin' on the doorstep, lass, in this weather.'

The next half hour passed by with relative smoothness, mainly due to George and Peter keeping the conversation flowing in a manner that seemed perfectly natural. Jenny could see her grandmother was warming to Peter as he treated her with a courtesy that was entirely devoid of obsequiousness, even though she asked one or two pertinent questions that made Jenny cringe inside. And when Mary suggested they walk through to the kitchen it was Peter's arm she took, which earned another wry glance from her grandfather in the background.

'Where's David?' As Peter and George settled Mary at the table Jenny looked straight at her grandmother. 'I told him we were having tea at half past four. Peter's promised to take Connie and Mick and Mick's parents to see Father McLeary after mass tonight to settle the details about the wedding. Mick's mam's legs are bad again, she's having her veins done in a few days, and Peter didn't want her messing about with buses. Where is he?'

'Give the lad a minute, it's only just touchin' half four.'

'I'm not waiting long, Gran. He knew what time I said.'

'Mr Longbridge?' Peter spoke into the awkward silence that had briefly fallen. 'I wonder if I could have a word with you while we wait for David?'

'A word?' George looked startled for a moment and then rose quickly, indicating the empty room at the end of the narrow hall with a wave of his hand. 'Come on then, lad.'

'Well?' As soon as the kitchen door had shut behind them Mary leant across the table, her thin body straining towards Jenny, whose cheeks had gone scarlet. 'Is that what I think?'

'He – he's going to ask your blessing for us to get married.'

'Aye, I didn't think he was askin' for another cup of tea. Well, at least the lad has got the gumption to do it right. And if I, we, said no? What'd be your reaction to that, lass?'

Jenny raised her eyes from the tablecloth and looked her grandmother straight in the face. 'I'd marry him anyway.'

'I thought as much.'

'But I'd rather you were happy about it. It's – it's important to me, to have your approval.'

'Aye.' Her grandmother's voice was softer now. 'Well, I can't speak for your grand-dad, lass, but as far as I'm concerned you could go a lot farther and do a lot worse than that lad in there.'

'Oh, Grandma –' For the second time that day Mary felt her grand-daughter's young body pressed against hers as Jenny came round the table and put her arm round her shoulders. 'You'll love him, when you get to know him you'll love him. And he hasn't had much of a life so far, not really, not in the things that matter, but once we're married . . . And I can come and see you most afternoons, you won't be alone –'

'One thing at a time, lass, one thing at a time.'

They were sitting drinking another cup of tea when the two men returned, and George's eyes went immediately to his wife as he entered the room. 'You know what Peter was askin'?' She nodded slowly. 'And?'

'They'll be wanting to put their name down at the council once they know what school Peter's working in permanent, like.'

'Aye.' George nodded, his face relaxing.

'Oh, there'll be no need for that, Mrs Longbridge.' Peter took his chair, his eyes moving, seemingly with an effort, from Jenny's face. 'When my father died I came into a bit of money, enough to set us up in our own place anyway.'

'Really . . .' Mary tried for nonchalance but it didn't quite come off. 'Well, if you can start off married life with a clean slate it's all to the good, lad, and Jenny's a good little housekeeper. One thing I've taught her is to look after the pennies so's the pounds look after themselves.'

'She's taught her a few more tricks, lad, but no doubt you'll find out about them yourself.' It was the startled look on Peter's face before he remembered to smile politely that set Jenny off shaking, and once started she found, through a combination of nerves and happiness, that she couldn't control her mirth. And then her grandfather was laughing, followed by Peter, and, wonders of wonders, even her grandma was spluttering in a way Jenny hadn't seen her do for years. And it was like this, clustered around the laden table with their eyes wet with laughter, that David found them.

'Davie . . .' Jenny jumped up as her brother surveyed them all through expressionless grey eyes from the doorway. 'We haven't started yet, come and sit down.'

He ignored her, his cold glance moving from one smiling face to another until it settled on Peter's, but even then there was no emotion in the blank façade.

'Somethin' funny?' Peter returned the look, his face straightening, but before he could speak George had stood up, indicating Jenny and Peter with an expansive wave of his hand.

'Not really, lad, just somethin' I said, but we've got somethin' to celebrate the night. Peter and Jenny are goin' to be wed. What you think about that, then, eh?'

'Wed?' The one word was like his face, cold and expressionless, but it set off a number of different reactions in the four round the table. Jenny felt that sick pain that squeezed her insides to melted jelly rise up and puncture the bubble of happiness that had held her. She had wanted, she *needed*, Davie to be happy for her. The others wouldn't understand, they couldn't, but he was part of her, he always had been. She wanted him to be understanding, glad that Peter had proved he really cared for her and wasn't stringing her along as he'd always maintained. She'd expected – What had she expected? In this instant she didn't know. All she did know was that the old familiar feeling which was a mixture of bewilderment, panic and fear that formed part of her relationship with her brother was threaded through with another new emotion, bitterness, and it showed in her eyes as she stared at him.

'Yes, wed.' When Mary addressed her grandson she kept her voice flat and steady, willing his eyes to turn to hers. It had been hard over the last few weeks to accept she'd done her lass a great harm, albeit unknowingly. Whatever the obsession that made up a large part of David's thinking regarding his sister, she'd added to it. Aye, she had. And now – now the time had come to let the lass go into another's hands, and if she were honest she couldn't have picked better if she'd chosen the lad herself, but David wasn't inclined to see it that way. So he'd have to be told. It was the only way. 'You goin' to offer your congratulations, lad?' The unblinking eyes were on her momentarily but it was long enough for her to bring her hand to her throat and strangle any further words she might have uttered.

'*David?*' David didn't respond to his grandfather's warning, he didn't even acknowledge his presence, but simply turned in the doorway and left as noiselessly as he had come and somehow the quietness of his departure was more ominous than any verbal abuse.

'I'm sorry, lad.' George looked straight into Peter's face, which was dark with controlled anger. 'He's a rum 'un, no mistake.' Rum 'un? He was that and a few more things besides. He'd like to get hold of that young whipper-snapper and give him a good kick up the backside, although right at this moment the thing needed playing down. But there was something wrong with that lad. Something seriously wrong . . .

'It's all right, Mr Longbridge.' Like George, Peter recognized the need to make light of a situation that was all too clear to him now. When David had held his gaze in that malevolent grip, he had identified, for one jagged second as the mask had slipped, the tortured feeling that had put a red glow in the back of those narrowed grey eyes, and it had been jealousy. Devilish and malignant and as black as hell itself. Did she know? Did she know how her brother regarded her? He raked his hair back with his hand as his eyes moved to Jenny's pale face and the answer was there in the wide clear grey eyes and tremulous mouth. No. No, she didn't. She might suspect all was not as it should be, feel uneasy and disturbed by David's compulsive need to dominate every aspect of her life, but that was all. And he prayed it would remain so. He had to take her out of this, even if it meant getting a special licence to do it. Every second she was under the same roof as that pervert was too long. *Dammit!* He forced his face to betray none of his thoughts. You heard about these things, read about them in the papers but to be actually confronted by such warped, aberrant depravity made him feel sick. She was his *sister*, for crying out loud, his twin sister.

'Peter?' Jenny moved round the table and as she reached his side he stood up and caught her hand, drawing her gently into him. 'I'm sorry . . .'

'You have no need to say that.' His voice was low but firm and now he included her grandparents in their conversation, raising his head and glancing at them both in turn. 'Has she?'

'No, no she hasn't, lad. If anyone's to blame it's the wife and meself, we've given David too much rope –'

'You mean I have.'

'I said us both, Mary. I've got eyes in me head and a tongue in me mouth, haven't I? I shouldn't have let you spoil the lad, I should've stepped in years ago and put the young blighter in his place.'

'It won't make any difference to our plans, Mr Longbridge.' Peter brought George's and Mary's eyes to him when he spoke again, his tone courteous but unwavering as he faced the older couple. 'I intend to marry Jenny as soon as I can. We are both of an age where we know exactly what we're doing and as far as I can see there is no need to wait. If necessary we can rent a place while we look for something more permanent.'

'Peter?' Jenny's voice was high with surprise at the turn the conversation was taking.

'I think David will come round to the idea once we're actually married, Jenny,' Peter said steadily, 'although I'd say from the way he was tonight there's not much chance of him doing so beforehand.' Come round? He'd never come round. If the power of thought could kill he'd be six foot under at this very minute. 'And the schools are much more likely to look favourably at a job application if the candidate is married. It makes for a more dependable, steady teacher in their opinion. Single men are more likely to move on, statistically.'

'Makes sense to me. What do you say, Mary?' George looked hard at his wife as he spoke. He'd push these two to get wed by himself if he had to, but it'd be a darn sight easier if that one was with him.

Mary made a small noise in her throat before she spoke and then her voice was shaky. She too had seen something dark in David's eyes and it had disturbed her far more than she would admit. 'If it's what Jenny wants.'

Peter looked down at her, his tanned rugged face soft and his eyes warm. 'Is it? What you want?'

'You know it is.' She fell against him as her eyes misted.

'Then that's settled.' George cleared his throat loudly and at some length before gesturing to the table groaning with food. 'Now I suggest we get busy on that lot 'cos I for one am fair starvin'. In honour of your presence this afternoon we only had a bite of somethin' at dinner-time. Your intended has been runnin' around like a chicken with its head cut off all day.'

'Grand-dad.'

But in spite of the combined effort of George and Peter to make the tea-party a happy affair the atmosphere was strained in a way that it hadn't been before David's entrance. Both the women found their thoughts returning to him time and time again, Mary's with a heavy dose of guilt that made the food like sawdust in her mouth and Jenny's with a pain that constricted her throat and put an ache in her chest. Why did he have to be like this? Why? If he didn't like Peter he could at least be civil. She was sick of him, she was. He was an ignorant pig and she'd tell him so when she saw him next but . . . but she loved him too. Oh, she could kill him for all the trouble he caused but one thing she was determined on, she would marry Peter as soon as he wanted her to. David wasn't going to spoil this for her with his rages and his sulks. There were times when she thought she knew him better than he knew himself and others when he was like a closed book, and the latter were becoming more and more frequent these days. The dark little question mark that surfaced when she thought like this made its appearance and she pushed it back into the recesses of her mind without examining it in the light of day. He loved her. She was his sister. That was all. And she'd make him be glad for her.

'We're gonna have more snow the night, David.' As one of his co-workers at the factory hailed him from across the other side of the road David raised a hand in greeting but said nothing.

Marriage? That slimy stinkin' scum thought he was

goin' to marry her? Put his filthy hands on her, lie with her and touch her skin? That smooth, satiny-soft skin – There was a screaming in his head that actually pained him. And the old 'uns, they were encouraging it, damn them. He'd expected nothing more from his grandfather. His lip curled away from his teeth at the thought of the old man he despised so much. But his grandmother? What had come over her? She'd been his ally, the only one who saw things like he did, the only one who could understand how it was, that they couldn't touch her. None of them must be allowed to touch her. There wasn't one who was worthy to be dust under her feet. Well, he'd always known what he intended to do, hadn't he? But now it would have to be brought forward, before – Again the screaming was so loud it caused his eyes to wrinkle against it as the blood pounded through his ears. The rage in him was like a live thing, he could feel it eating his insides . . .

He turned into a greasy dark alley that ran between two rows of mean little backyards and was used as a general dumping ground by all and sundry, and after walking part of the way down stood for a minute, breathing hard. The late afternoon was grey and dark with tiny particles of ice in the slow drizzle that was falling but David was oblivious to the raw air as he balled his fists against the heat inside him. He needed to get down to Tinsley Street, to take this rage out on Bett's hide . . . He shut his eyes tight and sucked in breath through clenched teeth. The nerve of that filth, thinking that he would be allowed to lie with her, to have her. He'd seen his hands all over her, their faces pressed together, but he also knew that as yet Jenny was untouched. He'd been with too many women not to know when they were broken in . . .

As he began to curse, swearing his venom into the

silence around him, the screaming in his head had to have release and he drove his fists time and time again into the solid brick wall against which he had been leaning, taking the pain into him, revelling in its ferocity as the wall became red with blood from his lacerated hands and the flesh hung in raw strips from his bruised, bleeding knuckles.

CHAPTER FIFTEEN

'I've always fancied myself as something of a secret service agent. No, no listen –'

'You daft thing . . .' Jenny was laughing as she pushed him with the flat of her hand in his chest. It was the Saturday evening after the somewhat disastrous Sunday tea and as Jenny and Peter left the bright lights of the cinema and stepped into the dark night, large fat snowflakes were beginning to fall from a laden sky.

'I think I'd make a very good James Bond.' Peter's voice was full of mocking indignation. 'I'd have handled that Doctor No with no trouble. Haven't you noticed the look of Sean Connery in your intended?'

'No, I haven't, actually.' Jenny giggled as he struck a pose with an imaginary gun. 'Anyway, doesn't he always leave his women? I'd prefer you as Peter Knowles, husband, than some tough guy who's always nipping off here, there and everywhere.'

'There's no adventure in you, woman, that's what it is.' He pulled her into his side just as a load of youths pushed past them in the icy street, jeering and catcalling a crowd of leather-clad bikers across the other side of the road.

'Not more trouble.' Jenny looked up into Peter's face anxiously as he kept her protected with his body until they had passed. 'There were several incidents in the town today with Mods and Rockers, you know. Grand-dad said the police carted a good few of them off to the police station in the end, and they'd got bicycle chains and knuckledusters and flick knives –'

'That load that just passed us were the same ones

that were causing all the noise in the pictures, I think.' Peter shook his head as they watched the procession down the street, each side giving a good deal of verbal abuse but keeping strictly to their own boundaries. 'Most of them are just kids, really, in fact I recognized a couple of them from the college.'

'They might be just kids but with the sort of weapons they're armed with –'

'Don't worry.' As the sound of the insults and shouts died away Peter bent his face towards hers, kissing her long and hard before raising his head again. 'It's mostly bravado. There was the same sort of thing with the Teddy boys a few years ago and that died down. It's just a craze. Anyway, you're safe with me, I told you, James Bond has got nothing on me.'

'You wish.' She pushed against him and they laughed before walking slowly down the street, which was already turning a Christmas-card white.

'We're lucky, Jenny, we're so, so lucky.'

'Are we indeed, and why?'

'Because many people go through a whole lifetime and never meet anyone they can love like we love each other. With my parents being the way they were I used to look at people a lot, relations and friends and so on, and it's amazing what you see if you really look. People marry for all sorts of reasons, companionship, social status, because they feel the need for a family, but very few feel the way about each other that we do.'

'You're just an old cynic –'

'No, I mean it.' He stopped again and drew her round to face him, his expression serious. 'I had one aunt and uncle who really cared about each other, Aunt Mabel and Uncle Jim. They were queer old birds, living in a big house in Hastings with an absolute menagerie of assorted animals, all waifs and strays they'd taken in off the street. The rest of the family used to think they were bonkers but I loved spending my holidays with them when I could. They had something . . . special. I don't think they could have children, I remember hearing some talk about it once, but the way they loved each other –' He shook his head, his eyes far away.

'What happened to them?'

'Aunt Mabel died of a heart attack. She was a good age, I think, eighty odd, and he –'

'What?' She peered up into his face as he hesitated.

'Well, he killed himself. I don't think he could face life without her. He apparently put all the animals to sleep with some stuff he'd bought and they found him in the kitchen. He'd put his head in the gas oven –'

'Oh, Peter.' The chill that wound down her spine made her shiver and he pulled her close, his arms fierce.

'Don't look like that. They'd had sixty or more years together, Jenny, and more happiness than anyone could imagine. And now it's our turn.'

'I hope so.' She wished he hadn't linked them with his aunt and uncle nevertheless.

There was an escalation of noise in front of them again and they saw one or two youths run into the middle of the road swinging chains above their heads, and then more followed, chanting some rhyme over and over as they careered about slipping and sliding on the light layer of snow covering the icy ground.

'I think we'll get you home the back way,' Peter said calmly. 'All right?'

She nodded hesitantly. It made sense to avoid obvious trouble but somehow the youths shouting and tearing around in front of them frightened her less than the murky alleys and ill-lit streets that led off the main thoroughfare. The feeling was strong on her tonight, it had been all week, that told her they were being watched by hostile eyes, and in spite of the fact that she knew it annoyed Peter she found herself glancing back several times on the way home.

'The sooner I get you into my bed the better.' They had reached Jenny's doorstep and Peter took her into his arms as he laughed down into her wide eyes. 'There's nothing like married life to take away nerves, you know. Best cure for the vapours I know of.'

'I haven't got the vapours.' She tried to be indignant but it was hard with his eyes warm on her face.

'Well, it'll do for an excuse till I think of something better. Now I want you to go indoors and make yourself a nice fortifying cup of cocoa and dream of me until I can provide something more substantial than dreams. Speaking of which . . .' He eyed her smilingly. 'I've had a little word at the town hall and we can set the date fairly soon if you like.'

'How soon?'

'Six weeks soon unless you want a white wedding with all the trimmings. I don't want to do you out of that if you want –'

'All I want is you.' She looked up at him with a wealth of love in her eyes and he grinned back, something in his gaze making her blush suddenly.

'My sentiments entirely, but then you know that.' His kisses were different tonight, more urgent, and she found herself answering them with a passion that matched his until by the time they drew apart, as one of the neighbours further down the street passed by with a cheery goodnight, both of them were shaking but it wasn't the chill of the night that had affected their limbs.

'Correction. Four weeks.' He smiled at her but his hand wasn't quite steady as he touched her face in farewell. 'I've never wanted anyone like I want you, Jenny. I still can't believe my luck.'

'My sentiments entirely, but then you know that.' As she repeated his words with a cheeky little grin he laughed out loud, brushing the soft flakes of snow from the top of her head with a loving hand.

'You're turning into a snowman. Get yourself inside, wench.'

'Yes, kind sir, thank you, kind sir.'

He turned to walk back to his lodgings the way they had come but on an impulse she couldn't explain she called after him. 'Peter?'

'Yes?' He turned, big and broad and oh so dear in the dark street.

'Don't go that way. Go the main way, down Turner Street and up past MacKay's.'

'That's another ten minutes walking, Jenny.' He eyed her with a shake of his head. 'Don't tell me, you're convinced the spooks are out again tonight?'

'Please, Peter.' She walked the few steps to his side now and stared up at him imploringly. 'Go the lighted way. For me. I can't help the way I feel at the moment. It'll pass, I'm sure it'll pass, but just do it for me.'

'How can I say no?' He ruffled her blond curls and put his arm round her, walking her back to the door-step before carrying on up the street. 'I'll see you tomorrow, love. Same time, same place.' The last few words were said in a mock Humphrey Bogart accent and her laughter followed him.

'Bye . . .' She watched him until he turned the corner and then had the crazy impulse to run after him, run after him and hold him tight and never let him go. You *are* suffering from the vapours, girl. But the admonishment didn't take away the feeling that something cataclysmic was about to happen and she found herself standing there, in the deserted street, for another full minute before she could bring herself to delve into her handbag for her key.

Turner Street was exceptionally well-lighted for the somewhat run-down part of Sheffield it was situated in, and Peter was smiling to himself as he strode down the pavement already a half-inch deep in powdery snow. Quite when the feeling of well-being left him to be replaced by a distinct sense of unease, he wasn't sure, but when he caught himself looking over his shoulder in much the same way Jenny was wont to do he gave himself a mental slap on the hand. It was one thing for a little scrap like Jenny to be nervous but a great hulking man like him? He shook his head in self-disgust. Come on, Peter, my lad, enough of that.

When he reached the top of Turner Street there was a large lighted expanse of road bordering MacKay's scrap-yard. This was always kept lit as bright as day since old man MacKay had been broken into three nights on the trot a few months ago, and he walked swiftly past, his footsteps making no sound on the snowy ground. He had just reached the main road on which he and Jenny had found themselves some minutes earlier when an impulse he couldn't explain made him turn again, looking back the way he had come, and there, silhouetted against the glaring light, he saw the figure of a man advancing slowly, head bent and shoulders hunched.

'So what?' He found he was talking to himself as he continued along the street. 'Pull yourself together. It's that girl of yours, she's put the wind up you, that's all.' He had been walking steadily for five minutes when he approached the slight curve in the road beyond which the cinema and a few shops were situated, some two or three hundred yards in front, and in the same instant these came into view the source of the distant sounds he had been hearing for some minutes identified itself and he saw several members of the rival gangs fighting in the middle of the street, the odd car that was about swerving to avoid the youths with a loud blaring of its horn.

'Great, just great.' He came to a standstill and stood, hesitating for some moments, just as the footsteps that had been following him since Mackay's joined him.

'Damn fools.' The tall, heavily set man was scathing as he gestured towards the rumpus in the distance. 'They'll have the law here soon. A good spell of national service wouldn't hurt louts like that, I'm tellin' you.'

'No . . .' Peter nodded his head in agreement.

'You'd be better avoiding 'em, though, lad. Right nasty bits of work some of 'em if they're the same lot that caused all the trouble in the town centre earlier. One lad's in hospital, I'm told. Where you makin' for anyway?'

'Worral Road, I'm in lodgings there.'

'Oh aye, I know it. Well, your best bet is to go back along this street to the end of Mackay's –'

'I've just come from there.' Peter found he was annoyed, with himself for being spooked by this perfectly normal man who was now trying to be so helpful, with the group of thugs in front of him who had twice deterred him from going where he wanted to go and with the fact that he had been persuaded to come back by this route in the first place. If he'd have gone the short way, through the back streets, he'd have been home a good five minutes ago. *Dammit*.

'Well, it's up to you, lad, but I think I'll go back a way and cut down by MacKay's. Looks like it could be nasty down there.'

'I think they're too interested in each other to bother about anyone else.'

The man shrugged, flicking up his coat collar as he prepared to face the driving snow. 'Up to you lad, up to you. You're young anyway, not some old codger like me.'

Peter watched him walk away, bent almost double into what were fast becoming blizzard conditions, and then turned back to survey the fray in front of him. All he wanted at this moment of time was a hot drink and a warm bed and he was blowed if he was going to put another fifteen minutes on a journey that should have only taken him five in the first place. He spotted what looked like a large piece of wood just in front of him, lying in the gutter, and as he bent and brushed the snow from it found himself looking at what was almost a cosh, the smooth wood hard and strong. That'd do. If there was any trouble he could swing that around a bit and probably deter them, not that he thought they would bother with him anyway. From the lights going on in neighbouring streets it was clear that the police would be here soon and they would scarper like rabbits.

Tucking the wood in his deep coat pocket with the end protruding some six inches he began to walk along the street and the nearer he got to the fracas, the more reassured he became that it was a big to-do about nothing. Two boys were left fighting now, cheered on lustily by their respective cronies, but even from some distance away he could see that the two in the firing-line were more interested in finishing the brawl with a modicum of self-respect than scoring points. Some seconds before he reached them they drew apart, warning each other loudly of the dire consequences each was facing in continuing the fight, and he had passed them in the next instant, walking steadily and quietly and feeling slightly ridiculous about the length of wood in his pocket.

He'd covered some twenty-five yards when the sound of the police siren first met his ears, and in the same instant a shadow in the black shop doorway he was passing moved behind him and the ugly-looking blade of a vicious knife glinted for a second in the light from the street lamp.

It was the thud of metal entering his body that registered before the blindingly savage pain, the force of the blow sending him to his knees, but even as he tried to turn the knife drove into his body again almost to the hilt, slicing a path from his neck to the small of his back as it tore away at his flesh. The world exploded into vivid flashing spikes of colour against his closed eyelids and as he forced them open through the piercing agony, he saw the snow was splashed with red, trickling rivulets of bright red. 'Jenny . . .' He died with her name on his lips, the life leaving his body in a long slow gasp of disbelief.

'Miss Longbridge? Miss Jenny Longbridge?'

'Yes?' Jenny stared at the two policemen on the doorstep as her heart jumped into her mouth. She had been awake most of the night, only drifting off into a light doze as dawn made its stealthy way across the window. She had heard her grandfather arrive home from his evening with Dickie Wrainwright, and then later David, but still she hadn't been able to sleep, and the first knock at the door this morning had brought her wide awake and sitting upright, even though it was still only six o'clock.

'May we come in?'

'I – I don't know. What – I mean –'

'I think it would be better if we spoke inside, lass.' The older of the two men smiled at her but it wasn't a real smile. 'And perhaps you'd wake your grandfather? I understand you live with your grandparents at this address?'

'I –' She took a deep breath and pulled her dressing gown more tightly round her. The snow was inches thick and the two men were obviously freezing. 'Yes, come in. Of course you must come in. It's just that you took me by surprise . . .' She backed from the doorway as she spoke and they followed her into the house, the younger policeman shutting the front door carefully behind him. He hated this side of the job, and the lass looked even younger than he'd expected although the landlady had said she was nigh on twenty-one. And a beauty. What a beauty. But that wouldn't make it any easier for her to hear what she was going to hear.

'I – Do you mind coming into the kitchen? My grandmother's got a bad heart and can't manage stairs so she has the front room.' Jenny had to force the words past the constriction in her throat.

'Fine by us, lass, and perhaps you'd like to go and fetch your grandfather?'

'But what? – What's this about? I mean –'

'Just fetch your grandfather, there's a good girl.'

She scurried out of the kitchen, having asked them to sit down, and heard her grandmother call her name as she passed her door. 'Jenny? What is it?'

She glanced up the stairs and then opened the door

quickly, her face as white as a sheet. 'Gran, there's two policemen here. They want Grand-dad.'

'George?' Mary's voice was high. 'Why? What's he done?'

'I don't know, I'd better get him.'

'Saints alive. What next, what next? . . .' Jenny left her grandmother muttering to herself as she reached for her crocheted bed jacket and flew up the narrow stairs, knocking on her grandfather's door frantically as she called his name, her voice shrill.

'What on earth? What is it, lass?' George flung open the door and stood blinking on the threshold, having obviously been woken from a deep sleep. 'What's the matter?'

'There's two policemen downstairs, they want to speak to you.' She was sick with fear now, it was clutching her throat and turning her stomach into hot lava. 'Oh Grand-dad –'

'Hold on, lass, hold on. Two coppers, you say?'

'Yes, and they want you. Oh Grand-dad, I'm frightened. What if it's anything to do with Peter? I've had this feeling and the policeman was smiling at me –'

'Well, if he was smiling I wouldn't say there's much wrong –'

'It wasn't like that.' She was following him down the stairs now and it wasn't until later, much later, that she thought about the fact that David hadn't emerged from his room in spite of all the noise . . .

'Mr Longbridge?' There was no vestige of a smile on the policeman's face as he looked at the elderly man and young girl in front of him. Hell, what a job, what a job. Why did he do it? Times like this made him wonder. 'Good morning, sir.'

'Good mornin'.' George glanced from one face to

the other and motioned for them to be seated again. 'I understand you want to talk to me?'

'In a way, sir. We've got some bad news for your grand-daughter here and we felt you should be present. There's been an accident –'

'Peter?' Jenny sank into a chair as her legs gave way. 'What's happened? Where is he –'

'I'm afraid it's serious, Miss Longbridge.' And then she knew, before they went on to explain about Peter being caught up in the gang violence that had exploded the night before, an innocent victim who happened to be in the wrong place at the wrong time. She was quite numb as they spoke, hearing their voices, seeing their lips move but unable to respond by even the flicker of an eyelash to what was being said.

George had risen immediately to put his arm round her shoulders but she couldn't even feel his touch, she was just aware of the policeman's face as he talked and talked . . .

'Did you get the one that did it?' George's voice was unnaturally quiet.

'Not yet, but we will, rest assured on that. The others know who it is, they must do, but as yet they're protecting their own. It'll be different in a few hours. A prison cell has a way of breaking these big boys down to size.'

'How? – What was it . . .' Her voice trailed off as she held the older man's eyes and there was a wealth of compassion in the worldy face when he looked at her, her face ashen and her eyes dilated and black with shock.

'I think it would be better to go into that later –'

'*How did he die?*'

'He was stabbed, lass, in the back.' The long drawn-out moan came from the depth of her, from that place only Peter had touched. It rose up and up, spiralling out of her throat and mouth in an inhuman sound that brought Mary tottering from the front room and the younger of the policemen running for the doctor when it became clear the paroxysm was out of control. *She'd lost him*. She wouldn't ever see his face again, be able to hold him, tell him she was going to make the past all right. He'd gone, dying in agony, a violent death, and as with his father there'd been no one to hold his hand, to comfort him, love him. She couldn't bear it. She couldn't bear this pain. She wanted to die. She *would* die . . . She wouldn't be left alone again, she would follow him somehow. She loved him, oh, she loved him. How was she going to manage without him? *Peter*.

The doctor gave her an injection when he came and when she awoke eight hours later and started screaming again he came back and gave her another, and this time a full twenty-four hours elapsed before she opened her eyes. When she did it was to a room filled with the grey light of late afternoon and she found she was in her own bed, with her grandfather sitting in a chair by her side, his eyes fixed on her face. 'Hallo, lass.' He reached out a hand and took hers, which was lying limply on the counterpane. 'How you feelin'?'

When, in answer, the tears began to stream down her face he lifted her up and held her pressed against him, stroking her hair as he murmured words of comfort that, he knew, were no comfort at all. She cried for a long time and when at last she became quiet she felt as if she had left all traces of her youth behind. She was old now and she would always be old, always carry the weight of his death in that secret place in her heart that was wholly his. The Knowles name was finished. There would be no grandchildren playing in the sunshine, no grandson that his father could see through Peter's eyes. The dream was dead. He was dead. And oh, how she wished she were dead too.

It was the morning of the next day, a Tuesday, and George had taken that day, like the previous one, off work. His mind was a little easier about Jenny now that she was quiet, but only fractionally so. He still felt he dare not leave her alone, but the other thing that was pressing down on him, causing him to wrinkle his eyes against it a hundred times a day, was the dark suspicion in his mind. He'd told himself it was insane, mad, that the police were convinced it was one of these rival gangs that was responsible for the lad's death, and after all they should know, they were the experts, but still . . . Still he had a sense of having been there before years ago. Seven years ago to be exact. *No*. He shook his head as he mashed the tea and set the patchwork quilted tea-cosy on the teapot before sitting down heavily at the kitchen table. He was imagining things. True, he and his grandson didn't get on but that was no reason to put the blame at his door. He wouldn't, couldn't, have hurt his sister like that. He rubbed his hand across his face as he realized he hadn't dismissed the possibility of David being capable of such an act, merely that in this instance it was impossible, with him loving Jenny like he did. But how could he be sure of that? Damn it all, how could he be sure?

He poured the tea and took Mary's in to her. David had left the house an hour previously to go to work and they had exchanged the barest of words before he'd left, not that that was unusual. What was unusual, however, was that the lad hadn't spent two minutes alone with his grandmother since the morning the police had called. Now why was that? He asked Mary precisely that as he set the cup down on her bedside table.

'I don't know.' Mary shrugged her thin shoulders as she reached for the tea. 'He's not obliged to come in here, is he? He's a life of his own.'

'He's got a life of his own all right.' George looked hard at his wife. 'There's more to that lad than meets the eye, I'm tellin' you, Mary. One or two of the men at the works have dropped the odd hint about how he spends his leisure hours, and it's not all darts and beer with Malley either.'

'What do you mean?' Mary bristled immediately. 'What have they been saying?'

'He's been seen, Mary, in, shall we say . . . less than respectable districts?'

'And you let them get away with that, sayin' things like that about your own grandson? He's a fine-lookin' lad, he'd have no need to pay for it, if that's what you're insinuating. Saints alive, but you take the biscuit, you do that, George Longbridge. Any other grandfather would have been in there defending his own with all he had –'

'Any other grandfather wouldn't have had to.'

'You know how our David feels about all that sort of thing, now then, hasn't he always made it plain? They're just jealous, there's not one among them that looks like he does –'

'For crying out loud, Mary, *face facts.*' He was almost shouting now and lowered his voice quickly with a glance towards the stairs through the open door. 'They're grown men, they're not likely to have the time or the inclination to worry about what our David does or what he looks like. They just mentioned in passin' that he'd been seen, that's all, and they aren't the types to think any the less of him for it, it wasn't said like that. They had to be there to see him, didn't they? Which makes it all the more credible in my opinion. Haven't you ever wondered why he hasn't brought a lass home here? Haven't you?'

'What are you saying exactly, George?' Mary's voice was very quiet now, flat and even. The days of 'Georgie' had long gone.

'I don't know. Damn me if I don't know.' He shook his big head slowly. 'But I don't feel right about all this lot, I tell you straight. An' they still haven't found the lad that did for Peter. Them in custody are protestin' they don't know nothin' about a big knife. Bicycle chains, the odd flick knife maybe, but nothin' that could have produced the injuries that lad took. His back was ripped open from end to end –'

'George.'

'I'm sorry, Mary, I'm sorry. But it was a frenzied attack, the police said it themselves, they'd never seen anythin' like it.'

'And you think our grandson could do something like that?'

'No, no I'm not accusin' the lad, course I'm not. Damn it all, I can't think straight at the moment with that one lyin' up there lookin' like death –' His voice broke and Mary's was softer when she spoke again.

'I know, I know. Look, why don't we try and get her up today, you know what the doctor said. Take her round to see Connie, that'd do her good. The lass's got the week off to look after Mick's lot while his mam is in having her legs done. Jenny needs someone her own age to talk to, and Connie knew Peter first after all.'

'Aye. Aye, I might just do that. I could leave her

there a while with Connie and then call back for her so you aren't alone –'

'Don't be daft, man. The state she's in she might just slip out and say she's comin' home, but I don't know if she'd even find her way with her mind like it is –'

'I'll get Mrs Brown in then –'

'I'd rather you didn't, George, really. She's one for goin' on and on at the best of times and I couldn't take it right now, not with the thought of that lad lyin' in the mortuary on a cold slab.' She pressed her hand to her eyes for a minute but when George would have reached out to her shook her head quickly. 'I'm all right, I'm all right. But he was a nice lad, wasn't he? He didn't deserve what he got.'

'No lass, you're right there.'

They stared at each other for a long moment before Mary dropped her eyes to the cup in her hand. 'Go and see if the lass is awake and suggest you pay Connie a visit. Insist if she doesn't want to go, it'll do her good and she's not in a fit state to know her own mind for the minute.'

'I don't know about that, Mary, I think she knows her own mind all right, perhaps for the first time in her life, if the truth be known. She won't be so malleable after this, so you'd better prepare yourself for a change, the lad 'n all. I've a feelin' she won't sit under what he dishes out any more.'

Mary's face tightened and she turned away from him, her lips pursed in a grim line, but it wasn't his wife George was thinking of as he climbed the stairs a moment or two later with a cup of tea in his hand, nor his grand-daughter, although his heart was rent with pity for her. It was Martha who occupied his thoughts as he reached the landing and walked slowly towards

Jenny's door. From the time that policeman had first opened his mouth till now he had seemed unable to think of anything else for more than a few minutes. He rubbed his hand across his face and shook his head. Barmy it might be but somehow that lad's sudden death had brought a lot of things into perspective. They were on this earth once, and then . . . Well, who knew? Mary would have him believe there was a heaven and a hell. His eyes narrowed as he paused outside Jenny's door. An' there might be, there might at that, but he was of the mind that it was heaven or hell right here, in the nitty-gritty, so to speak, and once you were dead you were dead. Well, he'd lived in hell, for years he'd lived in hell, and he wouldn't be surprised if Martha knew even more than him about that place. The surge of feeling in his chest made his face redden for a moment and Frank Malley's face was there against his closed eyelids. What he'd like to do to that fella, no one knew . . . And time was short. If nothing else, the last few days had shown him time was short. So what was he going to do about it? He shook his head again, took a deep breath, put a smile on his face and opened the bedroom door.

'Yes, I'd like to see Connie.' Jenny raised dark haunted eyes to George as she took the cup of tea from his hand, and he had to stop himself visibly flinching at the look on his grand-daughter's face. If he could get hold of the scum that had done for Peter there'd be no need of a court, that was for sure. Just two minutes would do. There was a sick fear in him that somehow the perpetrator of the crime would slip out of the law's net, he'd seen it happen before, more than once. People got away with things, and no one knew that better than him. He bit down the twisting pain, as fresh as when it had first gripped him twenty-one years ago when he had heard his lass, his beautiful, innocent lass, had been took down. He'd combed the streets for a time, asking, asking, until he knew he'd made himself a laughing stock in some quarters but he hadn't cared. He still didn't. He'd find out one day. He knew deep inside he'd find out one day. You couldn't want something as badly as he wanted this and not get it if there was even a shred of justice in the world.

'We'll go after you've had a bite of breakfast, lass. You've got to eat somethin'.'

Jenny nodded dully. She didn't care whether she ate or not, she didn't care about anything any more.

Once Mary heard the front door close behind her husband and her grand-daughter she lay back against the pillows for a while, facing what she had to do. She didn't know how she was going to accomplish it, she just knew it had to be done if she was ever going to know a moment's peace again. And if the worst was proved? . . . She shook her head. She'd cross that bridge when she came to it like a lot more she'd crossed through the years. She owed it to the lass to do this, whatever it took out of her physically or mentally. She'd heard the lad come in that night and it'd been late, very late, and for the first time since they had been here he hadn't come in to see if she was all right before going upstairs. She'd wondered then, aye she had, but when she heard about Peter . . . She shut her eyes tight, then opened them very wide and climbed carefully out of bed.

God would help her in this. He would. He knew her heart, knew her soul was sick with remorse for what she'd done the last few years. She hadn't been right with Him since that terrible day seven years ago when her mind had been filled with hate for young Steve Baker. He'd been squeezed out of her thinking, consciously, she knew that now, because there'd been no place for Him in the turmoil of fear and horror that had taken her over from that day. The compulsive need to control every minute, every second of Jenny's days, to aid and abet David in every ploy, every manoeuvre he thought up to command and restrain his sister, had been paramount, stifling every other thing in her mind. But she'd made her peace with Him now, for the first time in years she felt sane again, washed clean, and tonight she'd talk to her husband and ask his forgiveness too. But the thought of that fine young man lying there – She cut off her thoughts abruptly. She couldn't think of Peter now, not now. Later perhaps.

She reached for the heavy quilted dressing gown lying over the back of the chair near the bed and forced herself to breathe steadily, in spite of the jumping of her heart. It'd be all right. She was imagining things, of course she was, but she had to do it nevertheless, especially after that last talk with George.

She opened the door quietly and peered into the empty hall before taking a couple of steps to the bottom of the stairs. She glanced up the steep climb and felt a moment's panic at the thought that she wouldn't be able to do it. 'Steady, girl, steady.' She had only herself to blame for this. That young doctor, the new one, he'd laid it on the line to her. 'You've made an invalid of yourself too long, Mrs Longbridge.' How she'd hated him for that. 'Lying in bed and being waited on for years has weakened your heart to an extent that was never necessary. The initial damage of your first heart attack could have been overcome if you had lived as near a normal life as you could . . .'

Well. She hadn't. And both David and herself knew why. It had been a way to keep Jenny within the confines of their authority, may God forgive her.

Halfway up the stairs she had to sit down for some minutes, the constriction to her breathing severe, but eventually she was standing on the narrow landing and looking towards David's door at the far end. It had to be now. She had to follow this through. She'd never have another opportunity like this again.

The room, when she opened the door, was neat and tidy if Spartan. The bed was made, pyjamas neatly folded on the pillow like she'd taught him to do since a boy, and at the sight her heart swelled. Davie, oh Davie, please don't let it be true. He was her grandson, her support, her darling . . . She stood for a moment swaying in the doorway and then sank down on the hard chair just inside the room, taking a few long deep breaths that couldn't ease the cramping ache in her chest. What had she come to, doing this? She should go back downstairs now and put it out of her mind. It was bad, she was bad, to think like this of a lad who had shown only love and succour to her through the years. Where would she have been without his comfort and loyalty? She almost left then, almost, but then the memory of his face that evening when Jenny and Peter had announced their plans came sharply into her mind, the narrowed grey eyes burning into hers for one moment with something akin to devilishness in their maddened gaze. He hadn't been her Davie then, he had been someone she didn't recognize, someone who had put the fear of God into her . . .

The solid wood wardrobe wasn't locked and when she opened it the clothes were hung methodically, the shelves to one side of the hanging space full of neatly folded underwear with three pairs of clean shoes on the bottom shelf. Everything was visible to the naked eye, shipshape and Bristol fashion. She found herself expelling her breath in a great sigh, unaware she had been holding it till that moment.

The bed was narrow and high and the space underneath it devoid of dust or anything else except a shiny, and obviously never used, chamber-pot. There were two suitcases on top of the wardrobe and after checking the rest of the room Mary's eyes returned to them. If she stood on the chair . . . Once on the bed the suitcases, like the rest of the room, revealed nothing, not even the layer of dust she had expected. She sat for a moment, a great well of thankfulness in her heart, before she returned them to their home. She'd been wrong. Thank God she'd been wrong . . .

The sash-window was partly open, the curtains moving now and again in the cold breeze, and it was as she rose to leave that the slight noise that had been present since she had entered the room but hadn't registered as such on her consciousness, prompted her to turn round. What was it? She paused, her head on one side. It sounded like a flapping and yet it wasn't the curtains . . . Strange. She walked back into the middle of the room, standing on the edge of the rug that bordered the bed, and listened again, more intently this time, as she tried to trace the source of the flutter. It sounded, it sounded almost like the noise a bird's wings would make if it was trapped somewhere, and then her eyes moved to the small narrow fireplace which was never used and had an ornamental firescreen standing in front of it. There wasn't a bird trapped up the chimney, was there? Oh, she hoped not, she couldn't stand fluttering things at the best of times, a butterfly sent her frantic, but she couldn't just leave it. But surely it would have fallen right down to the floor? There was a three-inch gap between the edge of the fireplace and the fire-screen due to the small marble hearth that jutted out, plenty of room for a bird to escape, should it have been unfortunate enough to lose its footing and fall.

Warily now, she approached the fireplace, her hand on her chest, and carefully moved the small fire-screen to one side. It was definitely coming from here. She bent over, steadying herself on the small surround of tiles, but could see nothing. Dare she put her hand up? She shut her eyes tightly. It was only a bird and likely half-mad with fear. The most it could do was peck her. She inched a tentative hand into the hole and almost immediately felt the source of the flapping, but it was no bird. There appeared to be some material wedged just inside the chimney. She pulled it but it was stuck fast so she lowered herself to the floor, pulling again once she was stable, and then she felt as though her heart had actually stopped when a thick bundle of blood-stained clothing fell, along with a good deal of soot, into the space in front of her. It had been a shirt sleeve that had worked slightly loose and hung down causing the flapping noise, a shirt sleeve that was stiff and red and caked with dried blood. She picked up the other clothing, a pair of thick working trousers and a jacket, and they, like the shirt, were confirmation of that which she most feared.

Davie? Davie, what have you done? As her heart began to jerk and pound she addressed it out loud, her voice harsh. 'None of that, none of that. I'm all right. *I am all right.*' She shut her eyes for some minutes and the pain which had been a solid band round her chest, began to recede and became a dull ache. Lord Jesus, what has he done? She clasped her hands together as she prayed. What has he done? Her Davie, her sweet boy. It wasn't possible . . . She'd never intended – The Lord knew she had never intended for this feeling he had for Jenny to get to such proportions. Oh, God . . . She opened her eyes now and stared up at the ceiling. Help me. Help me to do the right thing because I can't betray him and yet I must.

As though in a stupor she thrust her hand once more up the chimney and there was a package, an object wrapped in something rough. She pulled it and again there was a shower of soot as it dislodged, and she saw it was a bulky parcel wrapped in sacking and tied with a piece of old string. Give me strength, give me strength, Lord. Her stiff fingers struggled with the string and then she sank back on her heels as she gazed with fascinated horror at the knife in front of her. The savage, eight-inch sawback blade still held traces of dried blood on its jagged edge which was honed to tear the maximum amount of skin on its exit from live flesh, and the memory of the description of the wounds Peter had suffered made her sway now on her heels as she began to whimper like an animal in a trap. No, no . . . Not her lad. To do something like this he would have to be a fiend from hell itself, bestial, insane. It couldn't be true, it couldn't. How long she sat there, rocking gently back and forth as her mind absorbed what she was seeing she didn't know, but when a sudden sound from the doorway brought her head swinging round she jerked back so quickly she went sprawling at David's feet.

'What are you doing?' His voice was flat, with a strange singsong monotone that sent her scrambling across the room on her hands and knees in a blind panic, only to stop as she reached the door which he had closed behind him. 'Why are you in my room?'

'I –' She pulled herself into a sitting position, trying

to ignore the pain that was gripping her chest, her throat and her arm in a stranglehold 'My tablets – Please –'

'You shouldn't be up here. You know you shouldn't be up here, Grandmother.' He had never called her Grandmother before, always Gran or Grandma, but then he'd never looked at her like he was now, his teeth bared in a snarl and his eyes blazing with a ferocious rage.

'Davie –'

'You've been pryin' haven't you? Sneakin' around like a big black spider? I knew you were for him from that Sunday, dribblin' all over him like a –' There followed a spate of swear-words that made her close her eyes against their foulness. Oh God, help me. This was her grandson . . . 'An' you would have let him touch her, lay his filthy hands all over her –'

'Davie –' She gasped his name. 'He loved her, don't you understand? He loved her, he wanted to marry her –'

He almost leapt across the room, saliva spurting from his lips as he called her every filthy name he could think of before yanking the door open and pushing her out on to the landing with the side of his foot.

'David . . .' She had to get to her pills, she had to. As she crawled along the landing she was aware of him behind her, watching her progress, glorying in her pain, and even though she knew what he was planning to do there was no preventing it. As she reached the top of the stairs she waited for his foot in her back, and when it came she allowed herself to fall without trying to save herself. God knew, He knew, and He wouldn't be mocked. She could leave his judgement to the Almighty now, it was better this way, and she was glad to be leaving this world, glad . . .

She was dead before she even hit the bottom of the stairs.

Chapter Sixteen

'Hallo, Connie.'

'Jenny. Oh, Jenny lass, come in, come in.' As her cousin pulled her into the hall of Mick's home she hugged her tight, the tears beginning to stream down her face, and with them something unlocked in Jenny's throat and she clung on to Connie as though she was drowning, her misery erupting in a loud wail.

'What . . .?' Martha, who had rushed out of the kitchen at the far end of the hall, stopped dead, her gaze moving from the two girls locked together to George standing just behind them, his face scarlet with embarrassment.

'Martha . . .' Her name was slow and deep. 'I didn't know – I wasn't told you were here –'

'I'm helping Connie out with the bairns and such while Mick's mam's in hospital. She's still not feelin' well herself some mornings.' She had moved to Jenny's side as she spoke and now pushed both girls into the room opposite. 'Sit down, sit down, lass, and I'll make some tea.'

'I –' Jenny tried to speak but shook her head helplessly. 'I didn't – I'm sorry.'

'It's us that are sorry, lass, heart sorry.' Martha pushed her daughter and Jenny down on to the well-worn settee that took up most of one dingy wall and beckoned to George with a nod of her head. 'Leave them to have a chat, it'll do your Jenny good to let it all out.' She walked briskly through to the kitchen.

'I thought she'd done that, she went –' He shook his head, the memory of Jenny's screaming still fierce in his mind. 'She went mad for a time.'

'Wouldn't you?'

'Aye, you're right.'

'She'll need to talk it out many times, many times before this lot is over, Georgie.'

'Aye.' The sound of his name on her lips, the old familiar 'Georgie' he heard so infrequently these days, brought physical pain to his breast.

'Do they know who did it yet? Have they got anyone?' Martha was filling the kettle as she spoke, her movements tight and busy as she kept her back towards him.

'No.'

'It'll be better when they catch him.' He made no reply and she fiddled with a biscuit tin to the side of the draining board before speaking again, still without turning to face him. 'How has Mary took it –'

'Martha. Look at me.' His voice was thick.

'Georgie –'

'I said, look at me.' The words came from deep within his throat and, when she turned, her hand was to her mouth, her eyes wide. 'I've wanted to see you for days, I haven't been able to think of much else. There was that bairn cryin' her heart out and all I wanted was to see you –'

'Don't. Please, Georgie, don't.'

'I've got to. Don't you see, I've got to –'

'No. No, I don't see.' She turned from him now and her voice was high. 'You've got a wife and I've got a husband.'

'He's no husband to you –'

'It's legal –'

'I couldn't care less about it bein' legal. He's not your husband in my eyes, never will be. He's less than the dust under your feet and you know it. You should never have married him, Martha.'

'*You think I don't know that?*' Her voice was harsh as she swung to face him but when she saw the pain twisting his features her expression altered, softened. 'Don't, Georgie, please. I can't stand it.'

'I love you. I've always loved you, lass. In the beginnin' I told meself it was because you were Mary's kid sister. You were only twelve when I was courtin' her and I told meself no man loves a bairn of twelve, even one as beautiful as you. But – But it got worse. I should never have married her –'

'But you loved her too,' she said flatly. 'You know you did.'

'Aye, I did once, in a way. Yes I did.' He nodded slowly. 'But not like I loved you. With Mary it was easy, ordinary-like, on an even keel, but the feelin' I had for you I can't explain. It's – It's like all the good things of me life rolled into one. I'm no good with words, Martha, never have been, but I love you more than life itself. Always have, always will. I worship you.'

She turned away now, tears seeping from her closed eyelids as she held up her hand, the palm raised in protest. 'Don't, Georgie, you don't know what you're sayin'. I'm not the young bairn you once knew or the woman that was married to Bill. I've changed, deep inside I've changed. I feel dirty –'

'*No*. Not 'cos of him. It doesn't matter about him.' How could he say that? he asked himself in amazement as he heard the words. The last seven years, and before, he'd been eaten up with the thought of her lying with him and now he was saying it didn't matter. But it didn't. Not now. Not when she was here in front of him and he was laying his heart bare. 'Our Jenny, our first Jenny, she was you all over again,' he said softly as she kept her head bent. 'I used to look at her as she was growin' and she was the image of you. Oh, the folks who used to comment on it, and every time they did a knife turned in me heart because I knew you should've been her mam.'

'Why are you saying all this now?' She raised liquid eyes to his. 'It's only going to make everything ten times as hard and you know it. It's not fair –'

'I want you to come away with me. No, no, listen.' As she made to leave the kitchen he pulled her back and then let go of her immediately as she crumpled in his hold, sinking down on to a chair, her head in her hands. 'This affair with the lad, with Peter, it's made me face things I've been hidin' from for years. I don't know how long I've got left, Martha, fifteen, perhaps twenty years if I'm lucky, but I know if I don't reach out and grab for what I want now I'll never have the chance again.'

'You mean me?'

'Aye, I do. You're the only thing in me life I've ever really wanted.'

'You don't mean it, you're talkin' wild –'

'I might be talkin' wild, lass, but I do mean it, every last word. We could go away, right away somewhere where we'd be left alone.'

'We couldn't, you know we couldn't. There's the bairns and Mary and – and Frank.'

'The bairns are grown, all of 'em. An' Mary – well, we haven't been man and wife for years, you know that. We don't even like each other any more. She'd have the house and David would look after her, they're as close as the cheeks of me backside, lass, always have been, always will be. The last twenty years there's been nothin' but the twins as far as she's concerned, she wouldn't even notice I'd gone.'

'Don't be bitter, Georgie –'

'Then say you'll come with me.'

'And Frank? You think he'd just sit back and say, here she is George, have her. Do you? *Do you?* 'Cos I can tell you he wouldn't. You've no idea of the man he really is, Georgie, no one has. He – he isn't normal. I didn't realize till we were married, and it was too late then with our Connie on the way. That's when things changed, when he thought he'd got me where he wanted me.'

'We could get right away –'

'He'd find us,' she said dully, her head bent.

'Then I'd deal with him. The bairns wouldn't blame you, none of 'em like him, do they? Especially his own daughter.'

'I don't know why we're even discussing this, it's impossible –'

'No, lass, no, it isn't. It's ours for the takin' if we want it bad enough and I know I do. The question is, do you?'

'Georgie –'

'Do you?' he asked quietly, his voice soft and thick.

'I –' She raised her head and in the next moment he had dropped down to crouch at her side, his large head, still with a mass of coarse, springy hair, mostly grey now, on a level with hers.

'Do you, Martha?' he asked again.

'You know I do.'

'Martha. Martha, Martha . . .' He pulled her up with him and as she fell against him he moved her into him so fiercely it was as if their bodies were already merging. The kiss was hot and sweet and urgent but then, as they heard the front-room door open, she jerked out of his hold, moving across to the gas stove and taking the boiling kettle from the hob.

'I'd better make the tea.'

'Martha –'

'Please, Georgie, leave it for the moment? I can't –'

Her words were cut off as Connie opened the kitchen door, her eyes pink-rimmed and her stomach already showing a slight bulge under the loose blouse she was wearing. 'And where's that tea, Mam?' she asked with a weak smile.

'It's coming, hold your horses.' Martha walked across the room and carefully shut the door before taking her daughter in her arms for a brief moment. 'How's Jenny?'

'Awful.' Connie shook her head slowly. 'Really awful but what can you expect? If I can't believe what's happened it must be a hundred times worse for Jenny. Peter, of all people. He was such a love, Mam.'

'Yes, yes, I know he was.' Martha raised her daughter's chin with a gentle hand. 'But terrible though it is, life must go on and I don't want you making yourself ill, that'll help no one, lass.' She turned, placing the tea pot and four cups and saucers on a tray before reaching for the tin of biscuits. 'You are back at work next week once Mick's mam's home, aren't you? Is there any chance of Jenny having that part-time job, now that the other girl has left?'

'She's left?' George glanced at Connie. This could be a way to get Jenny out of the house, and it was imperative she was out of there and soon. Left alone to brood all day with just Mary for company was no good.

'Yes. Mr Slater caught her helping herself to some bits so that was that. He hadn't got anyone last Friday but he could have by now. Do you want me to ask?'

'Aye, aye, I do, lass. That sounds just what Jenny needs and I know you'd keep an eye on her.'

'Well I'll perhaps pop down a bit later if you could hold the fort, Mam?' She glanced at Martha who nodded quickly. 'If I leave it till I'm back on Monday, ten to one it'll be gone 'cos he's keen to get someone as soon as he can. Although Mrs Slater's helping out again a bit now the bairn's arrived he doesn't like it, he worries about her.'

'An' you, lass? How're you feelin' now?' George asked softly.

'Better.' Connie shrugged with another quick glance at her mother. 'I miss me mam but I like it here, Mick's mam's nice enough and the kids and his dad are a laugh. Mind you –' Her voice became bitter. 'Anywhere away from me dad is heaven on earth. How Mam stands him –'

'Connie.' Martha's voice was a low warning to her daughter.

'I mean it, Mam. Since I've been here lots of little things I used to ignore keep on at me. I don't know how you've put up with him –'

'*Connie!*'

'Mam! You don't owe him nothing!' Connie's voice was a bawl now, matching her mother's. 'If it wasn't for you I'd have had him up before the magistrate quicker'n you could say Jack Robinson. If you hadn't come down that night he'd have lost me the baby, you know he would. As it was I was black and blue, I was, Uncle George.' She turned to George, her cheeks fiery. 'It was all I could do to stop Mick's dad and Mick going down there to sort him out and he's scarred me back with the buckle of his belt –'

'You should've let them go, lass. I only wish they'd have knocked on my door on the way.'

'It would only have made it harder for Mam in the long run, and at least I'm out of it now. He's never liked me, you know.' She turned to her mother with a faint note of amazement in her voice. 'But I didn't realize until that night he half-killed me. But he hasn't. He's only ever wanted you, everyone else is just another irritation to him.'

'Connie.' Martha bowed her head now but she couldn't find it in her heart to remonstrate with her daughter for speaking what was only the truth after all. She had always known her husband hadn't liked his only natural offspring. She could even remember the look on his face at the hospital when he came in to see her after being told it was a girl. He'd wanted a son, desperately. But she was glad he hadn't had one. Even with all this trouble they were in now she was glad, overwhelmingly glad.

'You think Gran would be able to manage?'

They were walking back towards Crown Street now and Jenny's voice was dull as she spoke.

'Of course she would, lass. There's old Ethel, and it's not like it's every day. You need to do something, you understand that, don't you?' he asked quietly, his eyes on her white face.

'I suppose so.'

'And if this falls through, then you get something else, now then. Promise me?' He tightened his arm round her slender shoulders.

'I'll be twenty-one in a couple of weeks' time, Grand-dad.'

George glanced at her quickly before returning his gaze straight ahead. Damn it all, what could he say to her? Peter had told him a few days ago that they were going to get engaged on her birthday come hell or high water and he'd already seen to things so it would be the shortest engagement on record. Well, hell had come, high water too, and he was going to have his work cut out to make sure his lass didn't drown in it.

'Jenny –'

'It's all right, Grand-dad, I'm not going to do anything silly.' She turned and took his arm and they both came to a standstill in the grey drizzle that was falling over the endless rows of mean terraced streets. 'I won't say I haven't thought about it because I did at first, but –' She paused and gulped deep in her throat but she didn't cry. 'Peter wouldn't want me to do that. He'd think it was the coward's way out and he'd be right.'

George put his hands on her shoulders, looking down into her eyes which were filled with an agony that caused a physical pain in his chest. 'Aye, he would, lass, you're right,' he said flatly.

'But Grand-dad?' Now, in spite of all her efforts, her eyes were swimming. 'Do you think it was me? That Peter dying was because of me?'

'Jenny.' He took a deep breath, aware he had to be careful, very careful, for in the heart of him, hadn't he been thinking exactly along the same lines? But she couldn't be meaning what he assumed she was meaning, not with her feeling for her brother the way it was. 'What are you sayin', lass?'

'I don't know.' She shook her head miserably as she clutched on to his rough jacket. 'It just seems so strange. First there was –' She paused and then forced herself to speak the name. 'First there was Steve Baker. He wanted me. Oh I know he went mad and everything but he said he wanted to marry me, that he loved me –'

'That wasn't love, lass.'

'Well, whatever, he wanted me nevertheless. And then Peter –' The tears were streaming down her face now and George felt highly embarrassed as a young woman passed them, her eyes lingering on Jenny's face before she continued on her way. 'And they both died, and not normal dying, Grand-dad, violent, horrible deaths. Do you think I'm jinxed?'

'Jinxed?' He didn't know whether to be pleased or otherwise about the interpretation she'd put on events. If she'd asked him outright if he thought there was a chance David was involved, what on earth would he have said? 'Jinxed? Of course not, lass. Whoever's been fillin' your mind with such rubbish?'

'Then you think Steve's death was an accident?'

'Of course it was.' His voice sounded too hearty, jolly, and he moderated the tone before he spoke again. 'Of course it was, Jenny, what else could it have been?'

'And you think Peter was murdered by one of these Mods and Rockers lads? Not . . . anyone else?'

So he had been right. There was a grain of suspicion there whether she liked it or not, and knowing what he knew about Steve Baker's death, was it unnatural she was wondering? Darn it all . . . He continued looking steadily into her eyes. Should he tell her what he thought? What he *really* thought? But he had no proof and what good would it do her if he spoke out now? And there was always the chance Mary was right, that their grandson had had no hand in this second killing, although as for the first . . . He narrowed his eyes against the rain. He would never believe David's version, told to him that night seven years ago as they had walked home, that he had been chasing the lad and Steve had slipped and fallen, hitting his head on a convenient boulder. No. He'd never believe that. But he'd missed his chance for speaking out then and he couldn't assuage the guilt he still felt by pointing a finger at David now when he had nothing to go on but a gut feeling. But he'd have another talk with Mary tonight, a talk that was coming seven years too late most likely. Find out what had really transpired between David and Steve that night, because his wife knew. Aye. He'd bet his life she knew.

'I don't know who killed him, Jenny, but the coppers aren't fools and they'll find who's responsible.' It was the best he could do. 'Now come on, lass, let's get you home and in the warm and we'll have a bite of dinner with your gran.'

They'll find who's responsible. They'll find who's responsible. Her grandfather's words were beating a rhythm in Jenny's tired brain as they walked home in what had now become a steady downpour. She hoped they would. Oh, how she hoped they would. Perhaps then this terrible feeling inside her would begin to ease a little, if it didn't, she felt she would go mad. All she could see on the screen of her mind was Peter walking away from her that night, tall and big and so, so solid, and then it would turn to him falling, perhaps with a scream of agony as the hard metal pierced his body, his vital organs, or perhaps all he had been able to utter was a gurgle of horror as his mouth had filled with the taste of his own blood? Stop it. *Stop it now.* But she couldn't, she couldn't. And if it was her fault? If she had some sort of a curse on her that brought violent death to anyone she was fond of? She almost missed her footing but immediately her grandfather's hand was there to steady her. Then terrible, horrific though that was, she would accept it and conduct her life accordingly, because it would be preferable to that other unmentionable thought that was haunting her day and night, the thought she had been unable to voice even to her grandfather.

Oh Peter . . . She wouldn't have thought it was

possible to feel like she was feeling now and still move and speak and communicate as though she was just like everyone else. She remembered little Mrs Finchley, a young widow in the street next to theirs, when her only child had been killed by a drunk driver mounting the pavement outside their home. She had been admired at first for her calm composure through the funeral and the next few weeks, although there had been one or two whispers that it wasn't normal, that she couldn't have much feeling to come to terms with such a tragedy the way she had. She had spoken to her one morning when Mrs Finchley was scrubbing her step, about four weeks after the child had died. They had had a polite, somewhat stilted, conversation, and she had gone on her way faintly perplexed at the control of the woman, but then a few days later Mrs Finchley had gone missing and they had found her stretched out on the child's grave at the cemetery, her mind completely gone . . .

'Here we are, lass.' She came out of the maelstrom of her thoughts to find they were home. 'Now, afore we go in let me make one thing plain. I want you to take that job or if not that one, then one like it. All right?'

She nodded dully. Her grandfather was trying to be kind, she knew he was, but he didn't really think a job was going to make any difference to this torment, did he? She glanced up at the house a moment before her grandfather unlocked the front door. She hated this house, this street, this whole town. She hated and loathed and detested it. Its greyness, its hardness, the endless monotony that imperceptibly ground lives and hopes and dreams into dust. And yet a few days ago she'd been perfectly happy to consider making her life here, working and living and perhaps even dying without ever moving elsewhere. But not now. As soon as she could she would escape. Where to, she didn't know and it didn't really matter. Anywhere was preferable to here. And she would go with or without her grandmother's blessing and yes, David's too. It was only now, as the door of the cage her grandmother had built around her was about to close again, that she knew just how near she had been to breaking point before Peter had come into her life. Peter. *Peter*.

She was still speaking his name in her mind as she followed her grandfather into the house only to cannon into his back when he came to an abrupt halt just inside the doorway.

'No. By all that's holy, no.'

'What is it?' As she peered round the side of him she brought her hand tight across her mouth, suppressing the high piercing scream that was filling her mind. She was frightened to make a sound like that again, frightened she wouldn't be able to stop like before. 'Is she . . .' She watched as her grandfather bent over the twisted broken form at the bottom of the stairs but she knew the answer to her question before he straightened himself. It was the unnatural way the head was lying, her grandmother's neck must be broken.

'I'm going to have to sit down . . .' As she watched her grandfather slump to the floor she realized he was suffering from shock, but curiously she felt no such weakness when she looked at her grandmother. What she did feel was . . . envy. She caught herself sharply as she acknowledged the thought in her head but it was there nevertheless. It was the look on her grandmother's face, an expression that was all out of order with the macabre tangle of limbs and contorted neck and back. It was one of peace, of tranquillity almost . . .

She bent down and stared into the face, and for the first time in years felt a rush of warmth and love for the woman who had controlled her life so ruthlessly. She looked younger too, like the woman of her childhood, who had bathed bloody knees and washed small dirty faces before chiding them to come to the tea table for plates of home-made bread and buttered scones.

'Gran . . .' She reached out a hand to straighten the head and then withdrew it as her courage failed her. What had she been doing? What on earth had she been doing? It was clear she had tried to climb the stairs and probably fallen in the attempt, but why? What had prompted such foolishness? She ought to cry, she had shed enough tears over Peter after all, but . . . She couldn't. Did that mean she'd finally snapped? 'C'mon, Grand-dad.' She knelt down at his side. 'You can't stay here.'

'I can't believe it, lass . . .' His voice was trembling and he shook his head as she put her arm round his shoulders. 'I can't believe it. First Peter and now this, what's happening to us?'

'It's all right, Grand-dad, it's all right.' She didn't know why she wasn't going to pieces but she was thankful for it. 'Come through to the kitchen for a minute, I'll get you some brandy or something –'

'I left her there in bed this mornin'.' He was speaking as though she was a stranger he was having to explain things to. 'What was she doing out here by herself? Damn it all . . .' He glanced again at the body of his wife. 'What was she doing? She knew I'd be home. I've always come home, haven't I?'

'Of course you have.'

'Then why? You think she was tryin' to get upstairs?'

'It looks like it. Grand-dad, try and get up and go and sit in the kitchen and I'll get you something.'

'Oh, Mary . . .' George shut his eyes tight. While he had been holding her sister, telling Martha he loved her, that he'd always loved her, his wife had died. She was dead, *dead* . . . She'd known, somehow she'd known . . .

'Come on.' They had just reached the kitchen when the front door, which had been slightly ajar, opened fully.

'*Gran?*' David's voice was thunderous.

'Oh hell, go to him quick, lass.' George closed his eyes as he sank down on to a chair. What was the lad doing home at this time of the day? He would come in now, to see his grandmother in that state! Whatever else, the lad loved Mary, he had to give him that. If David had had a fraction of the feeling for him that he had had for Mary they'd have got on like a house on fire.

'What's happened? Gran? . . .' He could hear the murmur of their voices in the hall and then David's sobbing but for the life of him he couldn't move. He couldn't believe she'd gone. All these years, all these long years and she'd gone like that . . . He ought to be feeling relief that the years of bondage, aye, of hell on earth, were over but he didn't. He felt sick inside, sick and empty and full of a feeling that was tearing his guts out. Mary, Mary . . . They had loved and laughed and, aye, cried together in the early years. Oh aye they had cried. What had happened to them? Why had it all gone sour? She'd loved him and the bairns, they couldn't have had a better wife and mother, and when their David had drowned . . . He gripped his throat as the memory of his first-born, his loving, warm-natured, precious son, burnt hot and fierce. They had clung together then like never before. She'd loved too much, that had been her fault. He pressed his hand to his eyes in an effort to stop his thoughts but still they churned on.

Aye, if anything was to blame it was that. When their Jenny had gone too all that love had been poured into the twins to such an extent it had warped and bent back upon itself, touching all their lives in one way or another. And now she was gone. And what had he been doing while she died like that? He'd been following through on the thing that had tormented her for years. And it had. He knew it had. He was no fool. *No fool?* The bile was bitter in his mouth. He was the biggest fool on God's earth. *Dammit*. Damn it all . . . Why had she tried to get up the stairs in the first place? Why hadn't she waited for him and the lass to come home? It could only have happened minutes ago.

David said exactly the same thing a few moments later when Jenny seated him at the table as though he was an old man. 'Why?' He looked straight at George, his smoky grey eyes pained and tragic. 'Why did she want to go upstairs? Do you think she'd done it before?'

'Gone upstairs?' George and Jenny stared at him in surprise.

'Well, it can't have been just this one time, can it?' David put his hand over his face as though overcome with grief. 'Perhaps she had tried it before, I don't know. That new doctor had told her she should try some exercise, perhaps that's what she was doing.'

'He told her she was supposed to try and walk a little each day, not mount a flight of stairs that must have appeared like Mount Olympus to her,' George said tersely.

'I know that, but you don't know how she thought

about things, lying in that front room day after day, month after month. It was no life was it?'

'I know that, David.' Was he doing it on purpose, adding coals of fire to the guilt that was already burning him up inside? But the lad had loved her, he had to remember that, and all things considered, he was taking this very well. He had the strangest desire, at this moment of time, to hold Mary's body tight in his arms and cry and cry and cry, and he brushed the notion aside savagely as he stood up. 'We need to move her, lad, get her on to her bed.'

'Shouldn't you? –' Jenny stopped as both men turned to her. 'I mean, I thought you should leave people until a doctor has seen them or something.'

'No doctor can help her now and I'm not leavin' her lying like that,' George said heavily. 'You nip down to the surgery and tell 'em what's happened while we make her decent.'

'Shall I tell Aunt Martha too?'

'*No.*' It was clear the harsh tone had shocked them both and he drew in a long shivering breath before he spoke again, moderating his voice as best he could. 'No, don't do that, lass. Let's get things sorted properly first. Just go and get hold of the doctor.' He leant hard on the big kitchen table for a moment and then forced himself to turn to David who was watching him through narrowed eyes. 'All right, lad?'

David lowered his head slightly and his eyes flickered downwards. 'I think Jenny might be right, perhaps she shouldn't be moved –'

'I've told you, I'm not leaving her there. Now I can do it with or without your help –'

'Don't be stupid.'

'Come on, then.' George's voice was very low now and very quiet.

Jenny walked in front of them when they moved into the hall, one hand pressed tightly over her mouth as she passed the body of her grandmother but still she didn't want to cry and it frightened her. Somehow she didn't seem to be feeling anything at all at the moment and in the face of her grandfather's grief, and David's too, it seemed even more unnatural.

She opened the door and stepped quickly into the street. It had stopped raining but the air was thick and cold and damp and she half-ran, half-walked on the greasy pavements to the surgery some short distance away, her mind numb and her eyes blank. She stopped outside the large, double-fronted terraced house and stood there for a full minute before she opened the door and walked into the small lobby, opening the glass door that led into the reception area with her heart beating as though she had run for miles. It was empty. Surgery must have finished a good twenty minutes since, but she could hear the sound of voices in the back room and rang the little brass bell on the side of the desk.

'Can I help you? Oh, Miss Longbridge, good morning.' Miss Hunter, who had been with Doctor Mead as long as Jenny could remember, looked faintly embarrassed as she saw her standing there. 'I – I'm so sorry about your young man. Do you need to see the doctor?'

'No, well, yes. What I mean is, it's not for me.' She was stammering now but as Doctor Mead came through she found her tongue. 'It's my grandmother, Doctor, she's had an accident.'

'An accident?' He stared at her in surprise. 'What sort of an accident?'

'Could you come?' She really couldn't go into details. Suddenly she was feeling very strange, and when in the next moment Doctor Mead moved swiftly round the desk and sat her down on a hard wooden chair, forcing her head down between her knees, she realized she had been a second from fainting. A glass of water was placed in her hand when she raised her swimming head and then Doctor Mead was joined by Doctor Penn who knelt down in front of her, his young face concerned.

'She isn't . . .?'

She nodded slowly. 'It looks as though she fell down the stairs.' She found she was beginning to shiver and clenched her hands tight.

Now both men straightened and glanced at each other before Doctor Mead gestured towards the door. 'I'll take you back in my car, Jenny. You should have sent someone to get us, lass, you're not well.'

'Do you want me to come?' Doctor Penn's voice was flat.

'Might be as well.' Doctor Mead nodded to his partner and then spoke to Miss Hunter, who had been hovering anxiously in the background. 'James will continue with the home visits from there but I'll call back here. Shouldn't be more than half an hour.'

They were back at the house within a minute in Doctor Mead's little Morris Minor and it was so similar to Peter's car that Jenny had to concentrate with fierce determination on the view out of the window to avoid breaking down.

Once in the house both doctors stared in silence at the covered shape stretched out on the wide iron bed in the curtained front room. 'What happened?' Doctor Mead turned to George after a long moment. 'What the hell happened, George?'

Jenny saw Doctor Penn dart a quick glance at his associate at the tone of voice and mode of address but he said nothing, moving towards the figure on the bed and folding back the coverlet. Her grandmother's head was lying at an acute angle and one leg was twisted grotesquely to the side but the expression on the still white face was the same and it was to that that Jenny's gaze was drawn as the men began to talk. It was almost as though – as though something had bathed her soul, if not her body, in a beauty that was unimaginable. And she hoped that was true. She shut her eyes tightly. She hadn't seen Peter after he had died, her grandfather had gone with the police and identified the body, dealing with the formalities, and the post mortem was scheduled for the day after tomorrow. She sucked in a few deep gasps of air at the thought of it. She couldn't bear the thought of what they would have to do to him. She wanted him left alone now, his poor body had been mutilated enough. How had *his* face looked? She opened her eyes wide as she nipped her lip and forced herself to remain still. She hadn't the courage to ask her grandfather because she would know if he lied. Had Peter had a faith like her grandmother? She didn't know. There was so much she didn't know.

'Come on, come and have a cup of tea.' David's hand on her arm brought her eyes to him and she allowed him to lead her from the room and into the kitchen where the kettle was boiling. 'I'll do it.' He pushed her into a chair and then made a pot of tea, pouring five cups as the others joined them in the kitchen. After handing everyone theirs he came to stand at the back of her, his hand resting lightly on her shoulder in unspoken love and support.

How could she have thought for a minute he had anything to do with Peter's death? she asked herself wretchedly. He had been awkward and hostile about her relationship with him but since his death he hadn't stopped telling her how heavily that weighed on him, how sorry he was, how he regretted behaving so badly. And look at him now. She knew he was being strong for her and even her grandfather, although the two of them didn't get on. He had adored her grandmother, this must be more difficult for him than anyone.

'Davie?' She turned her head to him and immediately his eyes were warm and soft on her face. 'Are you all right?'

He nodded slowly, putting his hand to her cheek for a moment before straightening again. 'Don't worry about me, Jen, don't worry about anythin'. I'll look after you, I promise.'

She stared up into his face and then lowered her head slightly, her long lashes shadowing her eyes. He meant to be kind, she knew he meant to be kind, so why couldn't she respond to him like she would have in the past? Why did her antennae react so violently to him these days, her flesh creep when he touched her like now? She was wicked, wicked, for the thoughts in her head. He was her brother, for goodness' sake, her brother. It was her that was the jinx on those around her. First Steve Baker, then Peter and now her grandmother. All violent deaths of one kind or another . . . Oh, she had to stop her mind from thinking, she had to have some peace. She would take one of those sleeping tablets Doctor Mead had left tonight. If she could just have a few hours' oblivion she would be able to cope. She would have to.

As David stared down at her bent head the intensity of his emotion was almost causing him to laugh or shout with the fierce joy that was filling him. She was his again and he was safe. He had taken everything from upstairs, he'd been meticulous this time and no one would find it, weighted down as it was with several bricks. No, the river would keep his secret and all he had to do was keep his mouth shut and play the part of the grieving grandson. And she had deserved what she'd got. By, that she had. When he thought of her snooping up there, trying to catch him out – But he'd been too clever for her, hadn't he, in spite of all her conniving. What would have happened if he hadn't forgotten his bait tin this morning? He screwed up his eyes and then turned to the doctors as they spoke to him, asking him one or two questions. They would think she was just a silly old woman who had gone upstairs on a whim, that was all. Because he was too clever for them, he was too clever for all of them, and now he had Jenny back where no one could touch her, lay a finger on her, she was his again. *She was his*. He sucked the words into him, savouring them in the dark recesses of his mind.

CHAPTER SEVENTEEN

It isn't stopping to rain, Jenny thought as she peered through the solid sheet of water outside the massive black umbrella her grandfather was holding over them both, and she knew it was only her grandfather's tight grip on her arm that was keeping her upright. The numbness that had gripped her since the day of her grandmother's death had given way to an aching sense of loss heavily riddled with guilt, but even that was bearable, compared to the biting, searing pain she felt for Peter. And *his* funeral would be in five days' time. How would she be able to stand it? She almost moaned out loud but then forced herself to concentrate on the words the priest was saying over Mary's grave, his voice heavy and sonorous.

She wished she could believe like some of these people here, and there were a lot of them, an amazing number. Her grandmother would have been pleased . . . Her thoughts brought to mind the conversation she had had with her grandfather the night before and she glanced at him now as he stared straight ahead, his eyes fixed on the priest.

They had been sitting in the kitchen despite the fact that the front room was now cleared and could be used as a sitting room again, and she had on impulse reached across and taken his hand, her voice soft. 'What do you believe about the hereafter, Grand-dad, really?' she had asked him quietly.

'Believe, lass?' He had raised his head almost wearily and she had been shocked at the expression in his eyes before it was veiled.

He had looked – How had he looked? She wrinkled

her brow now as she tried to find words to describe her thoughts. Wretched, bitter, sad, angry? And yet none of those really described the dark emotion she had seen for those few seconds.

'A few days ago I would have told you I don't believe in nothin', lass.' He hadn't looked at her as he had spoken.

'And now?'

'Now?' He had shut his eyes for a long moment and then opened them again as he shook his head. 'I don't rightly know, Jenny. It's a strange thing but since your gran has been gone I've felt – I've felt her near somehow, her spirit I suppose you'd call it, I dunno. But something's been on at me, promptin' me, like, all the time. I still can't work out what she was a-doin' of trying to get up them stairs, I'd feel better if I could get to the bottom of that.' He twisted restlessly in his seat.

'Perhaps it was like Davie said, an impulse or something?'

'Perhaps.'

'But you don't think so?' she asked quietly.

'I don't know what to think, lass, but I wish I'd been here, I do that.' His tone was bitter now.

'It wasn't your fault –'

'Oh, lass, lass . . .' He had shaken his great head as he looked at her and the guilt she felt about her past thoughts concerning her grandmother was mirrored in his eyes. It was strange, of the three of them it was David who was bearing up the best, putting a brave face on things when he must be feeling awful inside. But then Davie never showed his feelings, he never had. Not really.

'If you hadn't come to Connie's with me you would have been with her, wouldn't you, and Peter – If I hadn't insisted he went home the other way that night he'd still be alive.'

'You don't know that, Jenny.' He turned quickly as she spoke, her voice small and flat. 'Now then, lass.'

'I do. I'd had a feeling for days that something was going to happen, I shouldn't have let him walk home by himself –'

'Now be rational, lass, be rational. He was a grown man of twenty-five or so, not some schoolboy in short trousers. You could hardly hold his hand every second of the day and night.'

'Oh, Grand-dad, I can't believe he's dead. I miss him so . . .' They had cried together then, she remembered, but as she glanced up at her grandfather again his eyes were completely dry, his face expressionless. He'd been like that all day. She remembered the church service and his face when her Aunt Martha and Uncle Frank had come up to speak with him beforehand.

'I'm so sorry, Georgie.' As her aunt had touched his arm with her gloved hand he had remained quite still for a moment before moving his head slightly to look down at her without speaking. They had remained like that for some thirty seconds, and then her aunt had taken a step backwards, her eyes enormous in her white face under its black hat, and she had pressed a lace handkerchief to her lips for a second and shaken her head. 'You mustn't blame yourself in any way,' she had said softly. 'You've done all you could for years. No one could have had a better husband.'

'Couldn't they?'

'No. No, I don't think so.' Her aunt's voice had lost its softness then. 'It's been a difficult time for all of you with Mary's heart the way it was.'

'Aye.' His gaze had moved briefly to Frank, who had nodded curtly.

'We shan't stay long after, George, back at the house. Meanin' no disrespect but I'm sure you'll have a houseful.'

'No doubt.' Her grandfather's voice was stiff.

'She had a lot of friends.' Frank glanced round the small church, which was jam-packed. 'But I've always said to Martha that her sister was a saint, haven't I, lass?' The small beady black eyes were fixed on George's tight face and after a moment, when his wife made no reply, Frank continued with a little jerk of his head. 'What that poor woman has had to put up with, no one knows . . . With her illness, like.'

'Frank –' The small man didn't appear to hear his wife's voice as the gimlet eyes watched their prey.

'But now she's free of it all. That must be a great comfort to you, George. Aye, a great comfort.'

'Do you ever say what you really mean?'

Frank blinked rapidly a few times and Jenny herself was startled by her grandfather's words, although the tone in which they had been spoken was as flat and expressionless as his face.

And then Martha took her husband's arm, her face as white as lint and her voice low. 'If you don't sit down, I am leaving here, Frank,' she warned quietly. 'This very minute. And I'll leave you to explain why.'

'I'd listen to your wife, Malley.' There was expression in George's voice now and Frank Malley shrank from the force of it.

'I – Well, really! Let go of my arm, woman!' As Frank had stalked off like a small enraged cockerel Martha had turned to George, holding his glance for one long moment before turning away with her hand to her mouth.

'Grand-dad?' Jenny had watched them go before she turned to him.

'He's poison, Jenny, pure unadulterated poison. Now I'm no better than I should be and no one knows that better'n me, but Malley is something apart from the rest of us. He's taken your brother from me and he'd take you if he got the chance –'

'Never.' Jenny looked up into his face. 'Never in a thousand years, I promise you.' And then they had both become quiet, their hands joined.

That strange feeling was coming over her again. She forced herself to stand upright and glanced across to the opposite side of the grave, where Connie was standing with Mick and his parents clustered round her. Frank hadn't acknowledged his daughter's presence by so much as the flicker of an eyelash and she knew Connie was upset by her father's behaviour, although she would rather have died than admit it. She was showing a bit now . . . Jenny's gaze lingered on her cousin's thickening figure and a stab of envy shot through her with such fierceness she gasped. She would give anything, anything, to be standing where Connie was now, in spite of the fact she was pregnant and unmarried.

As the priest finished speaking he gestured towards George who moved a few steps forward and, bending, lifted a few clods of earth that he dropped slowly on to the coffin lying deep in the ground. The sound of the earth hitting the wood echoed in Jenny's mind like a slow tolling bell for several seconds after the noise had finished, and she shuddered helplessly. 'It's all right, it's nearly over.' David moved to her side from where he had been standing just behind her and took her arm in a firm grip, smiling briefly into her eyes. She leant against him for a moment, glad of his strength and amazed again at his composure, but when his hand tightened on her arm she knew that strange disquiet again and let her arm drop by her side as she straightened, her body stiff now.

Did she know how beautiful she looked? David forced his face to betray none of what he was feeling. Even dressed all in black with a great hat covering that glorious hair she was beautiful. All the other women looked like an assembly of black crows, hideous . . . And as for that slut across there – His gaze licked contemptuously up and down Connie and as his cousin raised her head for a brief moment, her glance seemingly drawn by the power of his, her face flamed at the derision and mockery in his before she lowered her eyes to the ground. And her mother was no better. He knew all about her mother, aye he did. Bett and her motley crew were more honest than that one. At least he knew where he stood with them, a few pounds and they'd put up with near anything, but she'd led Frank one hell of a dance in her time. He watched Martha now as, the service finished, she moved to her daughter's side, leaving Frank standing where he was. He'd been too easy with her, he should have brought her to heel sooner.

'I'm going to have a word with Connie,' Jenny said quietly.

'I'd rather you didn't.' He took hold of her arm as she made to move away.

'David.' She shrugged off his hand, her face indignant, and turned to him, her voice a low hiss. 'What's the matter with you? I want to see Connie.'

'Look at her.' His voice was scathing. 'She's got no shame, standing there in that condition –'

'You're being ridiculous.' Her tone was cool now, icy even, and it brought his eyes snapping to her face, which showed a mixture of surprise and anger. 'They are getting married in a few days' time –'

'And that makes it all right? Behaving like a bitch in heat?'

'I'm not discussing Connie with you, David, and although this is probably not the time or the place, let me make one thing perfectly clear. In a week or two we will be twenty-one years old, and as far as I'm concerned I am a grown woman who is quite capable of running her own life.'

He bit back the hot words that were hovering on his tongue and forced a conciliatory smile to his face. He could afford to be generous, he had nothing to lose and everything to gain. 'I'm sorry, Jenny, I'm just upset. Gran, you know . . .'

'Oh, I'm sorry, too, Davie.' She was quick to mollify him and he had to keep the satisfaction from showing on his face. He could handle her, he'd always been able to handle her, and now that scum was out of the way it'd be like the old days again.

'Go on, then, go and have your word.' He smiled at her but she didn't return it and his eyes narrowed on her back as she walked across towards Connie. He watched her for some minutes but she didn't turn round, and after a few more minutes he walked slowly to where Frank was standing, apart from the rest of the mourners.

'Look at that little tramp.' Frank turned to him, his eyes murderous as they left Connie. 'I know she's me own, David, but she's chalk to cheese compared with Jenny.'

'I know.' He always found Frank's company satisfying, uplifting. He was the one person who really understood him. He wished they were related by blood, he always had done.

'Flauntin' herself –' Frank took a deep breath and then forced himself to calm down. 'How you bearin' up, lad? I know you were close to the old lady.'

'At one time.' David smiled down into his uncle's face. 'Not so much lately.'

'No? Well, it's still hard on you but I'm glad you aren't one for wearing your heart on your sleeve. I can't abide that in a man. Your grandfather's puttin' on a show, ain't he?'

They both turned now to watch George for a moment and then David gave a huh of a laugh deep in his throat. 'Goin' for the Oscar.'

'Aye, I'd noticed. Makes you sick, don't it? But he's always been the same. All wind and water. I got his measure years ago, lad, long afore you were born . . .'

They continued to talk, standing remote and apart from the rest of the funeral crowd, who had gathered in large groups before leaving the cemetery, and Martha glanced across at them, her eyes bitter, as Connie and Mick's family began to leave. United as always . . . Her eyes narrowed on the two men, different in stature but similar in stance, their bearing arrogant and contemptuous and more alike than ever in the funeral garb of unrelieved black. How she hated them both, *she did*. She loathed and detested the pair of them. She shut her eyes tightly for a moment as her emotion threatened to overwhelm her. She shouldn't be thinking like this at a funeral of all places, and her own sister's at that. But it had been a welcome release for Mary after all those years of lying in that one room. It would have driven her mad. At least she still had her health, she had that to be grateful for.

Her gaze was drawn to George now as he swung round to leave, his cronies round him, and she knew he was aware of her standing across the way, but he didn't look in her direction once. Men were cruel, aye they were, the lot of them. He was blaming her for it all, she could read it in the blankness of his face and the coldness of his eyes. He'd been the one to speak out, to force the issue but now – She breathed in as the feeling in her throat constricted her windpipe. Well, she'd managed without him so far and she was blowed if she wanted him now. He could rot in hell for all she cared. But her eyes still followed the big broad body as it left the cemetery and her face was wet with more than the rain when she turned away. Damn him. *Damn them all.*

There were only a few mourners gathered round the grave now, the rain had forced most to beat a hasty retreat, but still Frank and David were talking. She could have gone with Connie and the rest of them but he'd have gone mad . . . Did she care that he would have gone mad? Not really. She didn't care about anything, perhaps she never would again. At least he hadn't come near her since she'd moved into Connie's old room but he'd found a number of new ways to torment her. Still, she could put up with his viciousness and his jibes and anything else he cared to invent as long as he kept his body away from hers. The thought of him anywhere near her now made her feel physically sick, and strangely David made her flesh creep in exactly the same way. She looked at them again and then froze, her mouth half-open and her heart pounding.

No, no it wasn't possible. She put her hand to her mouth and bit on the fingers of her glove, tearing the end of one to shreds. 'You're imagining it . . .' Her whisper was lost in the rain and wind but as her eyes were drawn again to the two men it was as though a veil had been lifted from her eyes and she saw, *she saw . . .*

'No . . .' Her voice was a whimper now and she stumbled across to lean on the trunk of a silver birch, still peering over the rows of headstones and neat pathways at the two men. Snatches of conversation came back to her down the years and her flesh chilled. Even George had said it, that last morning in her kitchen. 'Our Jenny, our first Jenny, she was you all over again. I used to look at her as she was growing and she was the image of you –' *No*. The scream was high in her head. How many times had Frank told her he had always wanted her, burnt up inside for her, from the first moment he'd laid eyes on her . . . But she'd been married to Bill and out of his reach, and she had made sure he knew it.

And then, when Bill had been killed in the war, he had been round within weeks, badgering her, keeping on and on until she had been forced to be short with him, to make it perfectly clear there was no chance of anything happening between them. She could remember the look on his face even now, that day she had spelt it out. He had been furious, his eyes hot and angry and his mouth a white line in the tightness of his face. He had flung George's name at her even then and she had denied it and kept on denying it but . . . *But he had had his revenge by taking down young Jenny*.

She let her umbrella drop by her side, her hands limp as her eyes stared ahead. Why? What had possessed a man, a fully grown man, to take down a young bairn of barely fifteen who hadn't known what it was all about? Had it been because her niece was so like her? Because it satisfied this obsession he had always had about her to have her double if he couldn't have have the real thing? Or had it been simply revenge on

George for what he had imagined was between them? But a young lass, a young, innocent bairn . . .

And that's why Jenny would never say who it was. 'Oh Mary, Mary . . .' Suddenly she longed for her sister with a fierceness that surprised her. All these years, all these years and the answer had been right under their noses. He must have raped her, lain in wait for her somewhere . . . She hugged herself tightly round her waist, feeling sick. And the lass had known that the family's very livelihood was in Frank's scheming hands. She could imagine how Frank had played on her niece's innocence, threatened her, manipulating her fear. He was good at that, was Frank, playing on fear. She should know.

What should she do? What *could* she do? She wiped her hand across her face as the rain poured down on her uncovered head. She was wet through now but quite unaware of it. If she said anything . . . She shut her eyes at the thought. There would be murder done, oh yes, quite literally. George was more than capable of it. And she still didn't know for sure, not really. But then, when she opened her eyes and saw the two men walking towards her through the sheet of rain she shrank back against the trunk of the tree as though it could offer some protection. Like father, like son . . . There was some knowledge that wasn't to be borne.

PART THREE

The Reckoning

1979

Chapter Eighteen

It was a beautiful room. Jenny sat down with her cup of tea and as she did so often glanced round the large, high-ceilinged lounge which was filled with light from the bright January afternoon. The colour of the walls exactly matched the thick, silver-grey carpet and the long gold drapes at the full-length window and dull rose-pink and gold suite were both beautiful and functional. Beyond the big wide window a balcony of considerable size was a blaze of colour in the summer from the many pots of flowers and scented plants Jenny placed out there and even now, in January, the miniature evergreen shrubs and ivy gave the room a pleasant alfresco feel. Yes, she loved this room. It wasn't too extreme to say it had saved her sanity. She shut her eyes and leant back against the upholstered chair. The rest of the flat was quite small, one bedroom with an *en suite* bathroom and a small kitchen and breakfast room that she rarely used at all in the summer months, preferring the balcony if the weather permitted. But this room had sold the flat to her the moment the estate agent had opened the door from the small square hall. And it was all thanks to Peter. Peter . . .

She opened her eyes and finished her tea before placing the cup on the small polished table at her side. It was over ten years since he had died. She could hardly believe it when she measured the time in days and weeks, but the memory of those few months with him was tightly locked in the storehouse of her mind. And when, after his funeral, she had discovered he had made a new will shortly before his death leaving all his worldly wealth to her she had been both touched and tearful, and then utterly astounded when the solicitor had revealed exactly what that meant. Six thousand pounds . . . She shut her eyes again, the light breeze from the open window taking the edge off the hot-house central heating. Enough to buy this top-floor flat in a converted house some miles from Crown Street but seemingly in a different world. The house was situated on a gracious avenue overlooking a neat and well-maintained public park, beyond which a small area of wild woodland mirrored the changing seasons in its massive oaks, copper beeches and other trees. And she loved it. Oh, how she loved her home. She had had it redecorated from top to bottom and then spent a small fortune on furnishings, the rest of the money being deposited in a bank account for future use.

What would she have done without this sanctuary? She didn't know. Gone mad most likely. The twitter of bird-song from the park and the sound of children at play, their voices muted and distant, began to lull her into a light doze and she came to with a sudden jerk, rising abruptly. This wouldn't do. She had tea to see to and her grandfather would be here shortly. As though the thought of him had conjured up his presence the buzzer rang stridently in her hall. 'Yes?' She spoke into the small mouthpiece.

'It's me, lass.'

'Grand-dad?'

'Aye. Who you expectin'? The queen mother?'

'I'm just coming.' She smiled to herself as she ran down the stairs to the hall. The bottom of the house consisted of two smaller flats, the occupants of which shared the small square of paved garden, part of the original garden having been taken in extending the living space, but she preferred her elevated position which ensured privacy, and the balcony was enough garden for her.

'I wish you'd let me get a key cut for this door and my flat,' she said quietly as she smiled up at the dour-faced individual in front of her. 'I don't like you having to knock –'

'Don't start that again.' George softened the words with a smile as he touched her face briefly with his hand. 'You don't want to give no one a key to your place, lass, no one. It doesn't do.'

'I've got a key to yours –'

'That's different.' If she gave him a key David would demand one like a shot. He had been angling for just that the whole ten years she'd been here, George thought as he climbed the stairs after the trim figure of his grand-daughter. He'd had enough difficulty in getting Jenny established in here in the first place, with her wanting to look after him and so on. Look after him! He shook his head but his eyes were soft as he entered Jenny's home. He could look after himself all right and so could the other one. Aye. However much he liked to play on his sister's heartstrings. And at least he could sleep at nights knowing Jenny was safe in this place. By, she got more bonny every time he saw her. As his grand-daughter turned to face him he caught his breath at her beauty.

'I can't see it's different.' Jenny returned to the attack once her grandfather was seated facing the balcony, his favourite position, with a cup of tea at his side. 'You know you love to come and sit here and watch the kids play and what have you. You could pop round whenever you liked if you had a key, when I was at work and –'

'Leave it, lass.' George patted the hand that was resting on the back of his chair, twisting round to look up at her. 'You're a good girl but I don't want you to give anyone a key, *ever*. You promise me again.'

She nodded slowly, the bright light dying a little in her face. 'You know I wouldn't.' She knew whom he meant but she had no intention of letting David have free access to her home. She never put a name to the feeling she experienced in her brother's company but nevertheless she was alone with him as little as possible. In the early days he had called round every evening without fail until she had made it clear it had to stop. She had cried for a week after that, her equilibrium still delicate and bruised from all she had gone through in the preceding year, but she had stuck to her guns knowing her very sanity depended on it. She couldn't go back to being a young girl again, that was the way she had explained her reluctance to be in David's presence for long to herself. She needed to find herself, to grow, and she had, acquiring a poise and composure in the last few years that she kept wrapped tightly round her like a cloak protecting her from . . . everyone.

'An' what culinary delight have you prepared for your old grand-dad tonight?' George asked with a heavy attempt at being jocular. 'Somethin' to titillate these decaying taste-buds?'

'Oh, you . . .' Jenny pushed at him with the flat of her hand as her smile returned. 'I'm a career woman, remember, no time to slave over a hot stove even if it is my half-day. Steak and kidney pie all right, with mash and peas?'

'Meal fit for a king.' He followed her into the kitchen after finishing his tea and stood watching her as she placed the pastry on the pie before slipping it into the oven. 'How's the job going?'

'Same as ever.'

'Slater must be doin' well for himself, opening them other two shops as well as yourn. He got manageresses in them too?'

'No.' Jenny began to peel the potatoes as she spoke. 'I manage the Slater Yard one and he does the bookies in Baxter Street, and he has his brother in Mercer's Row.'

'He's got on, I remember him as a nipper with a runny nose and holes in his trousers where his backside showed.'

'He saw the way things were going with these new supermarkets and such and moved in quick when the other shops went up for sale,' Jenny said quietly, 'took a chance. With turning the other two shops into a fish-and-chip shop and a bookies it means we're the only corner shop for miles now so he's won all round. He must be worth a fortune. Still, good luck to him. He treats me all right.'

'Aye. Well, it's not everyone who can get a good-looking young lass to work the hours you do without complaining. He knows which side his bread's buttered. You never think about doin' anythin' else?'

Jenny shook her head slowly. 'Not really, not yet. Perhaps I'll travel a bit one day.' She didn't like to think about the future at any length. For the first few years after Peter had died it had been enough to be in this beautiful home, this refuge, this precious sanctuary, and lick her mental and spiritual wounds in peace. Her grandmother's sudden death following so closely after Peter's horrific murder had traumatized her more than she had realized, and with her job and her home she had had more than enough to cope with day by day without thinking ahead. And then, the last two or three years, she had begun to be beset by the desire for more. More of what she didn't quite know, just more.

Perhaps it was the children she watched playing so often, or the feeling of loneliness that was more pronounced these days, or – oh, whatever . . . The thought of travel interested her, the world seemed to have opened up in the few years since the Apollo moon-landing. What would Peter have thought of Neil Armstrong's first step on the moon? He'd been so interested in all that. She cut her thoughts abruptly. Anyway, she didn't want to travel by herself and her grandfather needed her for the time being. Anything else was speculation.

'Jenny –' Her grandfather hesitated as he searched for the right words. 'You want to get out a bit more, see a bit of life –'

'I see enough life.' She turned from putting the pan of potatoes on the neat little stove and smiled whimsically. 'Believe me, Grand-dad, the life I see is no one's business.'

'I don't mean the argy-bargy of Slater's shop with the sorts that come in there,' George said with a touch of irritability. 'I mean –' He stopped, rubbing the end of his large nose with his hand. 'Life,' he finished awkwardly.

'I know what you mean, Grand-dad.' She moved across and stood in front of him, her eyes soft but her face straight. 'And *you* know how I feel about that side of things. I'm content as I am. I have a lovely home, a good job and you,' she finished on a lighter note. 'Who could ask for more?'

'It's not natural to live alone, lass, not at your age and lookin' like you do –'

'Looking like I do?' There was more than a shred of bitterness in Jenny's voice. 'Sometimes I think all the troubles in my life have happened because of the way I look. I wish I was plain, ugly even, anything –'

'Now, lass, that's just plain daft an' you know it. The way you look hasn't made a scrap of difference to things, it's just that life has a way of kickin' you in the teeth when its goin' its smoothest, an' that happens to everyone.'

'Perhaps.' She smiled now but it was forced.

'I'd like to see you settled, lass, you know that,' George said softly. 'Perhaps a great-grandchild or two? An' there's been more than one interested.'

'I am settled, Grand-dad, really.' She shrugged casually as she turned away, determined to lighten what had suddenly become a heavy conversation. 'And as for great-grandchildren, who knows? With the birth of that test-tube baby last year perhaps we won't need men soon anyway.' Both the tone in which she spoke and the look on her face told George his grand-daughter had said all she was going to say on the subject and he knew better than to pursue it further. Still, it was a shame, a crying shame, he thought as Jenny began to relate an amusing incident that had happened in the shop earlier. He had nothing against women remaining single if that's what they wanted, but his lass was made to be a wife and a mother, he knew it, added to which he would never feel really at peace until she was settled and secure with someone to look after her and keep that other one at bay. His eyes narrowed as he thought of his grandson. He knew David was round here on any excuse and it made him sweat at night, aye it did.

'Grand-dad?'

He came to with a jolt and realized Jenny was waiting for an answer to something she'd said. 'I'm sorry, lass, day-dreaming. Still, what can you expect from an old man?'

'Old man, my foot.' Jenny laughed out loud as she

flapped her hand at him. 'You're seventy years young. I just wondered if you'd thought any more about moving? That house is too big for you and David now and those flats in Raymond Street are –'

'Monstrosities,' George said scathingly as he raised his eyebrows in disgust. 'The day I can't manage in me own home is the day I shall kick the bucket, lass. I've no intention of moving, you know that.'

'David would like it.'

Aye. Aye, he knew David would like it. Raymond Street was a stone's throw from here instead of a ten-minute bus ride. Of course David would like it. 'That's as may be,' he said quietly, 'but I've got me pals about me there, lass, an' it's where I'm comfortable. You know what I mean?'

Jenny nodded. 'Yes,' she said softly. 'I know what you mean.'

They ate their meal in the lounge from trays on their laps and afterwards Jenny washed up while George enjoyed his pipe as he observed the comings and goings in the park opposite. She stood for a moment watching him, the thin spiral of smoke from his pipe wafting into the air, before taking the tray of coffee in. Was that how she was going to end her days? Sitting in this room, watching the lives of others? An old maid? Shrivelled and unproductive? She placed the tray slowly on the coffee table and as she straightened she saw her grandfather's eyes were tight on her face. 'David's round here the morrow, then?'

She shrugged lightly. 'Probably. I'm not sure. That's what the postcard said anyway. They get back about lunch-time, don't they?'

'So I understand. Why a load of fellas would want to go to Blackpool for a week at this time of the year is beyond me. They'll have spent all their time in the pub anyway.'

'Go on with you, you'd have jumped at it when you were young,' she chided him gently as she poured the coffee.

'Perhaps when I was young but they aren't all young, are they?' He jerked his head, his voice aggressive although she knew it wasn't directed against her. 'I can understand the young 'uns enjoying a week away on any excuse, but Malley? He's a good twenty years older than any of the others, 'tain't natural. Now then, I ask you, is it?'

She hesitated for a moment and took a sip of her coffee before replying. No, she didn't think it was natural but it wouldn't do to add fuel to the fire where her grandfather and Frank Malley were concerned. Personally she thought very little about her uncle could be termed natural. He appeared to loathe his only daughter more and more as the years went on, bitterly resenting the fact that Connie and Mick were happily married and doing well, and as far as she was aware he had never even acknowledged the existence of his three grandchildren. And her aunt Martha – from the little Connie told her about her mother's life with that man it was a wonder she hadn't left him before now. She couldn't understand that really, why her aunt hadn't left such an unpleasant individual. She clearly had no time for him. Strange . . . People were strange.

'Well? You think it's normal for a man of that age to want nothin' but David's company?' George said brusquely now.

'Of course not.' She raised her head and saw her grandfather's face held the hard, cold look that always accompanied any conversation about her uncle and

David. 'I couldn't, could I? But – but if it suits them? . . .' She let her voice trail away as her grandfather snorted deep in his throat. 'And anyway, it certainly suits Aunt Martha. Connie says she's a different person when Frank's not around.'

'Does she?' His voice was flat and they sat in silence for a minute before he leant across and tapped her cheek lightly. 'Sorry, lass, I wasn't getting at you.'

'I know.' Her voice was soft now. 'Grand-dad?'

'Aye, lass?'

'Why do you think Aunt Martha stays with him, with Frank? Connie says she's not happy but as far as I can see there's nothing to keep her from going.'

His gaze sharpened on her face for a good thirty seconds as though searching for something in her words and when she stared back at him, her eyes wide and clear, he shook his head slowly, relaxing back in his seat. 'I don't know, lass. Why does anyone do anythin'? You can live with a person for years and not really know them, so how can we ever think we know what makes another person's mind tick? She must have her reasons.'

'Connie thinks she's frightened of him, of what he might do to her if she left.'

George shut his eyes for a moment as he lowered his head. He couldn't stand this, he couldn't. How had this conversation started anyway? The lass was heaping coals of fire on his head without knowing it. He didn't think there was a day that had passed in the last eleven years his bowels hadn't turned to water at the thought of what he'd done to Martha, speaking out and then coming the old soldier like he had but – But he couldn't be any different. Heaven help him, he'd tried to work it through in his mind, tell himself he was a fool not to reach out and take her, if she'd have him after the way he'd cold-shouldered her at the funeral and such, but – It was no good. Something had changed. It had changed the moment he had walked through the front door and seen Mary lying broken and still at the bottom of the stairs. He rubbed his mouth with his hand as he pushed the picture away in his mind, rising abruptly. 'I shall have to be goin', lass.' He softened the words with a smile as Jenny rose too, her eyes anxious. 'Old Dickie's goin' fast and I promised I'd call on his daughter and spend a few minutes with him the night.'

'Oh, I'm sorry, Grand-dad. Poor old Mr Wrainwright.' She always gave him his full title as she had done as a little girl. 'I didn't know.'

'Aye, well, he's had a good innings and he'd be the first to say it. His Mabel is a good lass, havin' him there. Can't be easy for her, what with the nurses coming in and out all day. Anyway, I'll be off then, lass, an' thanks for the dinner. I'll likely pop round and let you know how old Dickie is tomorrow night.'

'All right.' Her face was thoughtful as she followed her grandfather to the door. She knew why he intended to be here when she got home from work tomorrow night and it was nothing to do with Dickie Wrainwright. There was a strange feeling in her now. Part of her wanted to tell her grandfather that she could look after herself where David was concerned, that the days of intimidation and mastery were over, but on the other hand . . . The little shiver that snaked down her spine told her she would be glad of her grandfather's presence. But it was stupid, stupid. She was a grown woman and had been her own mistress for over ten years, she could more than look after herself. Nevertheless she said nothing beyond a brief goodbye when her grandfather left, and as she closed the front door and stood for a moment in the small light hall she found her hands were clenched by her side. She had enjoyed this week when David was away. She blinked her eyes rapidly as she faced the thought. More than enjoyed it. She had felt light, easy, free . . .

Oh, it was ridiculous thinking like this. She gave herself a little shake, her brow wrinkled with irritation at herself, before walking through to the lounge and switching on the large standard lamp to one side of the sofa to banish the shadows. It was her grandfather with all his talk of the future, wanting her settled . . . She knew what that meant. You could substitute the word married for settled and that'd be about it. She sighed deeply as she carried the tray through to the kitchen. She had faced and accepted the fact she would never be married years ago, and she wished he would do the same. When Peter had died like that . . . well, it had just seemed as though God, fate, call it what you will was trying to tell her something. She didn't seem to bring much luck to those who loved her and the thought wouldn't leave her whatever her grandfather might say. There was no way she was going to risk getting close to someone again. Anyway, she was happy. She was. She walked back through to the lounge and glanced round the lovely room again as her eyes narrowed determinedly. *She was*, and fortunate too. She didn't question the fact that she had to tell herself this more and more of late.

As Jenny expected her grandfather was waiting outside when she arrived home the next evening, her arms full of shopping. 'Here, lass. I could've met you and helped you with that. You should've said.'

'I didn't know.' She smiled briefly as she handed the two bags to him and searched for her key-ring.

'Mr Slater said there were a few things needed clearing in the cold-meat section and then he gave me a loaf and a couple of other items as well.'

'Did he?' Her grandfather eyed her with a glance full of meaning. 'You watch him then, he might be wanting payment in kind.'

'Grand-dad –' She stopped abruptly as she caught the twinkle in his eyes. 'Oh you . . .' She put out her hand and pressed one of his, the skin thin and spotted with age, and managed a weak smile. She found it hard to respond to jokes like that and it annoyed her because she knew she was being over-sensitive. It was just that if David had been here he might have thought – Her line of reasoning was broken as the object of her thoughts rounded the corner in the distance. 'Here's David.' Her voice was flat.

Her grandfather turned and watched the tall, broad figure walking swiftly up the street with narrowed eyes. It hadn't taken him long, had it? He'd heard from one of the lads they'd only got back an hour ago. He'd barely have had time to drop his suitcase at home before he hightailed it round here.

'Jenny.' As David reached them he glanced briefly at his grandfather with a curt nod and then turned to Jenny, who had just opened the front door and was waiting for him, a careful smile on her face. 'Did you get my postcard?' he asked softly.

'Yes.' She gestured for him to walk through the open door but he didn't move, his eyes all over her face in that way she didn't like. George moved in front of David, breaking his line of vision, and as the three of them walked up the stairs to the flat with Jenny in front and David making up the rear, George could feel his grandson's eyes in the small of his back and the sensation wasn't pleasant. David'd be miffed 'cos he was here when he thought he'd have his sister alone, George thought grimly, and miffed he could be. He hoped to high heaven his suspicions regarding his grandson's feelings about his sister were groundless but he was too long in the tooth to live in a bairn's fantasy-land. All he could do was be here when he knew David was going to be around, the other times he could do nothing about. He felt tired suddenly, tired and weary and worn out. He'd lived too long, that's what it was.

Something of his thoughts must have shown in his face because, as they entered the flat and Jenny turned, her eyes fastened on his. 'Grand-dad? Are you all right?' she asked quietly, gesturing for David to walk through into the lounge beyond. 'You don't look well.'

'He looks all right to me.' David's voice held a touch of impatience but there was something else mixed with it, something that brought George's chin up and his neck stretching.

Aye, you'd like me to pop off, wouldn't you, lad? he thought sharply. You wouldn't shed too many tears and that's a fact.

'There's nothing wrong with me a good cup of tea wouldn't fix, lass.' He purposely kept his voice light but he was aware of his grandson's eyes on him as he sat down in one of the easy chairs, and it was all he could do not to meet the look with a glare. But he got nowhere with David like that, he'd learnt that much through the years. In fact he could swear his grandson enjoyed their mutual dislike and mistrust, relished it even. Oh, he was a queer blighter and no mistake. 'You have a good holiday, then?' His face showed polite interest, nothing more, when he raised his head.

'Fair to middling.' David was speaking to him but with his eyes on the door through which Jenny would come. 'Nothin' special.' Come on, come and sit down where I can see you. His thoughts narrowed his eyes at the door. That's not too much to ask, is it?

'What you get up to, then?'

'This 'n that.'

When Jenny came through with the tea-tray David rose before George could move, taking the tray from his sister and setting it down on the table in front of the deep-cushioned sofa. 'Any problems while I've been gone?' he asked softly.

'Problems?' She glanced at him briefly as she knelt down on the thick lambswool rug on which the table stood. It was the only place to pour the tea from, other than the settee, and she didn't want to sit there as to do so would bring her into close proximity with her brother. None of this was clearly thought out in her mind but merely instinct. If she had known that was how she felt she would have been disconcerted, shocked even, at the implications such a thought would hold. 'Why would there have been problems? Everything is fine. Did you have a good time?'

'Aye, fair.'

'Only fair?' she asked, glancing up at him.

'Fair's good enough. There's nowhere like home, isn't that what they say?' He smiled at her but she didn't respond, lowering her eyes to the tray.

'And Frank? Did he enjoy himself?'

'As far as I know.' His voice was now the voice of a man showing patience with what he considered inane questions from a woman.

George had said nothing during this exchange, accepting the cup of tea that Jenny offered him as she talked and beginning to sip it slowly as he watched their faces. Dammit, but they were a good-looking pair, aye they were. The same thick blond hair and grey eyes, but there was something, something in David's face that caught at him now and again, like that feeling, *déjà vu* did they call it? Where you felt you'd been there before, where something nagged at you. Aye, *déjà vu.* He was blowed if he could sort out what it was but it was there all right. If he could just put his finger on it . . .

'What was the guest-house like, then?' Jenny asked quietly.

'Adequate. You'd have liked the landlady. According to local gossip she was something of a gangster's moll when she was younger and even at seventy odd she's a wily old bird. We had some laughs with her . . .' As David continued to talk his face was open and pleasant, his body relaxed. He knew how to relate an amusing story and as Jenny laughed at something he said, her eyes warm on him, he knew a moment of deep passionate satisfaction. She was his, she would always be his, hadn't they shared the same womb, fought for life together? There was a bond between them that was unbreakable. Oh, she might not admit it in so many words but it was there all right. And the old man couldn't last for ever . . . His eyes moved to his grandfather for a brief moment and then back to Jenny's beautiful face. And when he'd gone he would persuade her to share a place with him, aye he would. He could do it, if he was careful how he went about it, and he wouldn't ask for more than just seeing her, being with her . . . As he finished talking he leant back in his seat and gestured towards his empty cup. 'Any more tea?'

'Of course.' Jenny was still smiling as she poured him another cup. She loved him when he was like this, like the old Davie. She had no need to worry – She caught herself sharply at the thought. She wasn't worried. Not about Davie. These . . . feelings that surfaced now and again when she was with him were her fault, of course they were. He had never done anything to hurt her, she knew that, *of course* she did. It was just that sometimes her mind seemed to have a life of its own. What had that doctor, the psychiatrist, called it? A long name . . . Oh, she couldn't remember but she knew what he had meant. He'd thought she was neurotic, a silly woman who imagined problems. It had been in his face and manner when she hadn't been able to explain what kept her awake at night or where her fears were coming from. She had only gone to him three times and on the last visit, when he had suggested group therapy, she had found it difficult to be civil. It was at that point she had thrown away the sleeping pills, preferring long nights of walking round the flat or sitting reading to the thick muggy sleep, frequently punctured by vivid disturbing dreams, that the pills induced.

'Would you like something to eat?'

'No, lass, no.' George had jumped in before David could reply and as his grandson's gaze slanted towards him George kept his face blank. 'I got some steak in special so we'll get off now, leave you to it.' He rose as he spoke and again that exhausted feeling seemed to swamp him before he pushed it aside. 'No doubt we'll be seein' you in a few days.'

'Goodbye, Jenny.' David too had risen but his face was blank now, the jocular manner gone as his eyes had hardened. He'd have his day with that old so and so, aye he would. All he had to do was wait, time was on his side. He'd noticed the change in him and he'd only been away a week and Jenny had commented on it too. Still, there was no way he was going to encourage him to see a doctor if that's what it needed, and he knew his grandfather would never willingly step through a surgery door. Aye, all he had to do was wait and he was good at that . . . Timing was all important. He could make the future what he wanted it to be, he could feel the power within himself at times. A home with Jenny, and Tinsley Street to see to the other side of things . . . The thought warmed him and his expression caused George to wonder what he was thinking as they left the flat.

Once alone Jenny didn't immediately clear away the tea things but found herself walking on to the balcony and looking out over the street to the parkland beyond, where the path snaked and wormed its way between neatly dug flower beds, devoid now of plants, and illuminated by the odd strategically placed lamp. She hadn't liked the look of her grandfather tonight, he seemed to have got so old suddenly, in the last few weeks, old and tired. She would have to persuade him to get down to see Doctor Penn in the next few days, but it hadn't been right to broach the subject with David sitting there. Had David noticed anything? Her brow wrinkled as she gazed unseeing at the park. He wouldn't say anything if he had in case it worried her, she knew that. Her face softened as she thought how her brother had made her laugh. He could be so amusing when he wanted to be and he was undeniably good-looking, handsome even. Why hadn't he married? She shook her head slowly. When she thought of all the girls who had set their caps at him and gone away disappointed . . . But perhaps he just wasn't the marrying kind? Anyway, she was hardly one to talk, was she? But that was different somehow . . . She leant her forearms on the cold iron balustrade, her face pensive. Yes, it was different. Because she had wanted to be. She had wanted to be so much – The thought brought the familiar ache in her chest and she straightened abruptly.

The years had mellowed the keenness of Peter's loss and she could now think of him with some semblance of peace, but even as she had found herself adapting to her new life as a working girl with a home of her own the sense of deprivation about all that had died with him had grown. Children, a partner she could go through life with, someone to share the mountain top experiences and be with her in the dark valleys, they had all gone with him. And she felt guilty now when she perceived it was the loss of these things that was still hurting rather than her grief at losing Peter, the man. But they would have been happy together. She shut her eyes tightly. And she wouldn't allow anyone else ever to take his place. Not ever.

Chapter Nineteen

'Excuse me, but don't I know you?' Jenny had known him the minute he had walked into the shop but had never dreamt she might be recognized by Lawrence Maine. 'I can't quite recall where . . .'

'It was in Kent.' She forced herself to smile and speak quietly even as her heart thudded a tattoo against her rib-cage. *Lawrence Maine*, of all people! What on earth was he doing round these parts? 'My family stayed in Holstone for a time when I was a child –'

'I remember.' He came close to the counter now and stared at her, much to the interest of old Mrs McNabb, who happened to be deliberating over whether her Tibbs would prefer chicken or tuna cat food for supper. 'It was the day of the Sunday-school picnic and you were wearing white.'

'I –' Now both her poise and speech had completely left her. *He had remembered her dress?* Lawrence Maine had remembered her dress? 'Can I help you? I – I mean, you want to buy something?' She was making the most awful fool of herself, she would have known that without the open-mouthed stare of Mrs McNabb, but his eyes were kind as they met hers and they were the same deep brown that she remembered, heavily shaded by long dark lashes that should have looked effeminate on a man and didn't.

'I went to the dance that evening but you weren't there.' He smiled slowly. 'I remember feeling most disappointed.'

'I – Did you?' She groaned inwardly as she prayed for composure. This was ridiculous. She wasn't a young starry-eyed teenager any more and he wasn't the lord of the manor. Well, he might be, but not this manor.

'I have carried the image of a beautiful young girl in a white dress around for some time,' he continued quietly. 'It seemed the very essence of summer to me.'

Her face darkened when she remembered what had happened to that frock. She had ripped it into tiny little pieces and burnt each one, slowly and painfully. Her eyes were cool now as she held his gaze, and slightly hostile. He was dressed in the understated way only the very rich can dress, his light-grey trousers immaculate and beautifully cut and his sports jacket in fine worsted tweed denoting an exclusive designer label. The hand that was resting on the counter had a fine, solid-gold watch at the wrist and more gold, in the form of a ring, gleamed on one finger. Of course. He would be married. He had been going to marry into the nobility if she remembered rightly. She had been unaware of the play of emotions across her face but to the tall dark man watching her so closely she was fascinating.

'That was a long time ago, Mr Maine.' The hard-won cloak of self-possession was firmly pulled into place and she spoke with a calm aplomb she was far from feeling. 'Now, how can I help you?'

'Have I said something wrong?'

The directness was unnerving and she hesitated for a moment, her eyes flickering as they left his. 'No, of course not.'

'Because I would be most perturbed if that were the case.'

'No.' Please, buy the wretched cat food and go, Mrs McNabb, she thought desperately as she felt the other woman's eyes boring into her face. This would be all over the street tomorrow. 'That Jenny Longbridge, her in the corner shop? Well, you wouldn't believe who was visiting her the other day, a right toff, he was. Old friends, they are, from what I can make out.' Oh, she could just hear Mrs McNabb right now. The elderly widow lived to set tongues wagging. 'Have you chosen the cat food, Mrs McNabb?' She took the bull by the horns but the old woman was having none of it.

'Oh, don't you worry about me, Jenny lass,' she said complacently, her eyes as round and bright as a magpie's. 'I'm in no rush. You see to your gentleman friend.'

She saw Lawrence Maine's eyes move from her to the old lady and back to her again but he said nothing more, merely purchasing a large box of chocolates, his face expressionless, and leaving with a formal thank-you that made her sigh with relief.

'Friend of yours, is he, love?' Mrs McNabb went into action before the door had closed behind him. 'Lovely-lookin' fella, isn't he?'

'He's an acquaintance my grandfather worked for when we lived in Kent,' Jenny said coldly. 'I haven't seen him in over fifteen years.' It was the wrong attitude to take but she couldn't help it. This woman was vitriolic with her gossip and Jenny had always disliked her. It was said that during the war her tittle-tattle about the goings-on of her neighbours had caused more explosions than Hitler's bombs.

'Fancy . . .' Mrs McNabb looked at her thoughtfully and it was plain she had formed her own opinion about 'the gentleman'. 'Remembered you though, didn't he? You must've stuck in his mind for some reason.'

'So it would seem.' She wasn't making matters any better but suddenly she didn't care. For one reason or another she had spent all of her childhood, and a good deal of her adult life, having to explain exactly whom she associated with and why to all and sundry and everything in her rebelled. 'Now, can I help you, Mrs McNabb?'

The old woman blinked a little, opened her mouth to say more and then closed it at the look on Jenny's face. Her mouth a pursed tight line, she banged a tin of cat food on the counter with considerable force, followed a moment later by a fifty-pence coin, pocketed the change without speaking and left the shop, her back straight and the tilt of her head indicating the extent to which she had taken umbrage far more eloquently than any words could have done.

'I don't care.' Jenny spoke out loud as she gazed round the empty shop, the space from floor to ceiling filled with every kind of item imaginable, foodstuffs making up about a half of the shop's merchandise. 'Spiteful old bat.' And she had sent Lawrence Maine away with a flea in his ear, she hadn't even been civil. She sat down rather suddenly on the stool behind the counter. And he had only been trying to be kind. What would he think? She put her hand to her mouth as she considered exactly what he would think and then groaned. She knew he hadn't been throwing a line, not Lawrence Maine of all people, but he didn't know she knew that, and he'd think she had such a high opinion of herself. Oh . . . She squirmed on the stool and for a moment she was a young girl again gazing at the young god who had just turned to look at her. What *had* he thought?

She found out exactly what he had thought when she was lowering the blind on the inside of the shop window an hour later. She had just raised her hand to drop the latch on the door when it opened abruptly and there he was. 'Oh!' She stepped back a pace and stared up at him. Somehow her memory hadn't had him this tall, and he had been leaning on the counter earlier when he talked to her. But close to, and they were close, he was a good nine inches taller than her.

'I'm sorry. Did I make you jump?' He didn't smile.

'No. Well, yes, a little.' She stared at him uncertainly, her eyes wide. 'I – is there anything wrong with the chocolates?'

'The chocolates?' It was as though she had spoken in a foreign language. 'Oh, the chocolates. No, no I don't think so. I'm sure they are delicious. No, I was just passing and –' He stopped abruptly. 'This is ridiculous, I am being ridiculous. I wasn't just passing, Miss . . .?'

'Longbridge. Jenny Longbridge.'

'I wasn't just passing. Actually I have been sitting waiting in my car across the street for the shop to close so I could have a private word with you.'

'You have?' Her hand went to her throat and now he did smile, raking his hair back at the same time.

'Please, don't be nervous. I can assure you you are quite safe.' His voice was beautiful, she thought inconsequentially, deep and clear and resonant, and although it was obvious he had had a good education he didn't speak with a plum in his mouth like his father.

'I'm not nervous.' He didn't reply to that but moved back on to the threshhold, which was indicative of how he viewed her denial.

'May I talk with you a moment?'

Her heart was beating like a sledge-hammer now but she knew all she had to do was make a movement to shut the door again and he would leave. His action had made that clear. And although it was crazy, ridiculous like he had said, she couldn't bring herself to do it. He couldn't possibly be interested in her, she knew that, but she also knew she would regret it for the rest of her life if she didn't listen to him. She couldn't quite find the words she wanted so she stepped to the side and waved him through, her eyes uncertain. And as he inclined his head and moved past her she caught the slight whiff of what she instinctively knew was a very expensive aftershave and again her stomach turned over. This was Lawrence Maine, *Lawrence Maine*, what on earth was she doing? He was rich and married and – Her thoughts made her speak before she considered her words. 'Where's your wife?'

'My what?'

'Your wife.' She made no move to shut the door but stood watching him, her hand still pressing the base of her throat. 'You were going to be married, when we were in Kent, I remember – I remember my friend telling me.'

'And she was right.'

Oh he was good-looking, she thought weakly. Quite alarmingly good-looking and – and he shouldn't be here.

'I was married for four years,' he said softly, without taking his eyes off her face, 'but my wife was killed in a riding accident shortly after her twenty-third birthday.'

'Oh, I'm sorry, I had no idea . . .' She glanced helplessly round the shop and lowered her eyes, her cheeks scarlet. 'I –'

'It's perfectly all right, please, don't be distressed.' The deep pleasant voice brought her eyes back to his face and she saw he was neither smiling or straight-faced but there was something in his expression that made the sledge-hammer start thudding again. 'There were no children, which in the circumstances proved a blessing.'

'Yes.' She bowed her head as she shut the door and dropped the catch, her movements automatic. What was she going to say to him or, more to the point, what was he going to say to her? How did you have a normal conversation with someone who was born to live in a different world to you?

'May – may I call you Jenny?' The slight hesitation brought her eyes snapping to his face and she realized, with a feeling of utter amazement, that he wasn't quite so self-assured as he seemed. But he couldn't be nervous, not of her. Not Lawrence Maine.

'Yes, of course.' She forced a smile.

'Is this your shop?' he asked quietly after another short pause.

'My shop?' She did smile now, a real smile. 'Good gracious, no, I just work here.'

'Then you don't live on the premises?'

'No.' She still hadn't moved from just in front of the door and remained there staring at him, wondering what he was getting at. 'I have my own flat. I live alone.'

'In that case I wonder if you would perhaps consider having dinner with me this evening?' he asked quietly. 'I'm in the district on business for one night only and although you are probably otherwise engaged I just thought I'd ask. I mean –' He paused again and this time it would have been perfectly clear to a blind man that yes, indeed, Lawrence Maine was nervous. 'I know it is very short notice –'

'I'm not doing anything else tonight.' Her voice was clear and direct and they stood looking at each other for a good thirty seconds before he seemed to straighten his body with a imperceptible sigh and smiled widely.

'You aren't? Good, good. And I must apologize for

embarrassing you earlier. The lady who was in here is something of a gossip, I presume?'

Jenny nodded, her smile self-conscious. 'Very much so, even when there is nothing to gossip about like now.' There, she had said it. She hoped he understood what she was trying to say, that she hadn't presumed –

'Oh dear. I realized too late that I had been less than tactful. You would have thought having been born in a village I would appreciate such things, wouldn't you?'

Born in a village? She thought back to the gracious mansion set in its acres and acres of prime land and the deference with which the smallest wish of the Maine family was treated by the villagers. Born in a village, my foot, she thought wryly, but it was nice of him to try and put it that way.

'Perhaps you would like to go home first to freshen up before we go out?' he asked quietly when she still didn't speak. 'My car is just outside.'

She made a small assenting movement with her head as panic filled her throat again, making speech impossible. She should have refused his invitation, she should, what on earth was she going to talk to him about all evening? And why had he asked her out in the first place? It couldn't be because he . . . Not Lawrence Maine. And then something of the feeling Peter had tried to instil in her through their brief courtship came to the surface, the sense of self-worth he had endeavoured to develop. She was as good as Lawrence Maine or anyone else for that matter, of course she was, and wasn't she being an inverted snob to think like this? Well, she wouldn't. If he wanted her company for the evening, she would enjoy it as a step out of her predictable routine and that was all. She wouldn't think any more, she would just *go*. She thought too much as it was, wasn't that what the doctor had said to her? Well, in that she had to admit he was right if nothing else.

As Lawrence followed her out of the shop, waiting at her side while she locked the door, she felt a definite sense of unreality take over which heightened still further when he gestured towards the opposite side of the road to a beautiful, gleaming dark-blue Bentley. 'Shall we?'

'That's your car?' It was a stupid question, she knew it. Who else round these parts would own such a magnificent vehicle?

'Yes.' He glanced down at her as they crossed the street but made no move to take her arm or touch her. 'Do you drive?'

'Me? Oh no, no.' She shook her head to emphasize the point. 'I couldn't drive.'

'Of course you could.' His eyes narrowed as they reached the car and he unlocked the passenger side first, opening the car door for her and then shutting it behind her once she had slid into the leather-upholstered interior. As he joined her a moment later she was aware that every muscle in her body had clenched but there was absolutely nothing she could do about it. 'Now, where are we going?' He turned his head to smile at her as he turned the key in the ignition and she found herself smiling back even though her stomach trembled at the enormity of what she was doing. And yet girls, women, did this all the time: had dates, went out to dinner, to the cinema, the theatre.

'I live in Woodpark Avenue on the way to Totley, do you know it?'

'No, but I'm sure we'll find it together.' Again there was a smile but this time she couldn't respond, bewildered by events and by her own feelings of excitement and joy, which were causing the blood to pound furiously through her veins.

She could never remember, later, what they talked about on the way to Woodpark Avenue but she glanced at him as they turned in to the pleasant wide street and was aware of the surprise, quickly smothered, on his face and in his voice. 'What a charming part of the city. You must be very happy living here.'

'Yes, yes I am, although it has its drawbacks,' she said quietly, 'one of which is that some of the residents have certain airs about them, mostly the ones who haven't been forced to convert their houses into flats. Quite a large number of us thought it would be nice to give the children a street party on the Queen's Silver Jubilee two years ago, but due to opposition from certain quarters it all fell through. Fortunately several streets combined in the end to hold a big party in the park.' She waved at the parkland opposite, its black expanse relieved by the lamps lighting the path. 'The children had a marvellous time.'

'I'm sure they did.' As she indicated the house he drew to a smooth stop outside, cutting the engine before opening his door and walking round to open the passenger door. As he helped her from the car the naturalness of his impeccable manners was further emphasized by his next words. 'I'll wait in the car while you freshen up, and please take your time, there's no rush.'

'Wouldn't you like a drink?' She knew he had sensed her nervousness and was trying to put her at her ease but it was doing the very opposite. The thought of him sitting outside in this beautiful car while she got ready was unbearable. 'A cup of tea?'

'Very much but if it would make things difficult –'

'Oh no, not at all. The plus side of living here is that

everyone minds their own business. I think really it's because they don't particularly care.' She glanced up at him and smiled wryly. 'But I don't suppose you can have it all ways.'

'No, I don't suppose you can,' he said quietly, his face blank as he walked with her up the gravelled drive with its border of shrubs and trees. Once in the flat he said nothing, following her as she pushed open the lounge door and motioned him through, and then turning to face her as she shut the door behind her. 'May I ask you something? You may think it presumptuous on my part.' She was aware that he hadn't even glanced about him and also that although his voice was gentle the tone was serious.

She said nothing, inclining her head towards him.

'Have I – In the past did I offend you in some way?' he asked carefully. 'I feel you are defensive and I'm not sure if it is me or whether you are normally so reserved. I'm aware you may think me audacious –'

'No, no, it isn't you, not exactly,' she said as a flood of embarrassment made her face hot. 'It's just –' She paused, unable to continue. 'I really don't think I can explain,' she finished helplessly.

He took his time in speaking, his eyes searching her face for a good thirty seconds before he smiled suddenly. 'Perhaps when we know each other better?' he said softly as he turned and glanced round the room, which was mellow and glowing. 'Your home is quite beautiful.' His gaze returned to her face. 'Quite beautiful.'

'Thank you.' She nodded her head but again she couldn't smile.

She was reading far more into this than was warranted, she told herself determinedly as she changed quickly into a warm smart dress of navy-blue wool in the privacy of her bedroom and then sat gazing at herself in the dressing-table mirror. He was at a loose end on some business trip or other, he had told her that, and any company was better than none in such circumstances. He probably looked at every woman of his acquaintance like that, it would mean nothing. She contemplated her hair, fastened in a thick curled knot on the top of her head, and on impulse loosened the pins and combed it out into soft waves on her shoulders, adding a light touch of dusky-pink lipstick before leaving the room, her stomach churning. Calm down, calm down, she told herself firmly just before she opened the lounge door. He probably viewed her as a woman of the world and was looking forward to a quiet relaxing evening before he left the town and her life. An evening filled with good conversation, good food and probably a good wine to boot. If anyone would know the right wines it would be a Maine. She just hoped he wasn't going to be disappointed.

'Ready?' He glanced at his watch as she entered the room and rose to his feet immediately. 'Ten minutes to get ready? You really are an extraordinary woman.'

'Hardly.' She knew her smile was strained but she couldn't help it. Was he making fun of her? She really wasn't sure, she wasn't sure about anything all of a sudden and the thing she was least sure about was having dinner with this tall dark man standing in front of her. He probably thought she had known lots of men, and would know how to behave, to play the social scene, and she was naïve, gauche, stupid –

'Jenny.' He moved across the space between them and took her hand before she could demur, holding on to her wrist when she would have turned away. 'I need to tell you something, confess something actually.'

'Confess?' So his wife was still alive? He had married again? He was engaged to be married? He –

'This evening, when I said I was here on business for one night? Well, that is true but – but I have to tell you I had a previous dinner engagement, with some friends who live in the area actually. The chocolates were for my hostess.'

'They were?' Her mind raced as she tried to make sense of what he was saying. 'But – then how can you take me out to dinner? What –'

'I telephoned my friends and told them I had met someone I had lost contact with years ago and had always been hoping to meet again,' he said simply, 'and they understood my dilemma. I find that if you tell the truth people usually try to understand. And it is the truth, I just want you to know that. I have always carried a picture of you in my mind. Oh –' He shook his head with a deprecating gesture. 'That sounds insincere even to me.'

'And is it?' she asked candidly.

'No.'

'Then I suppose that's all right.' He had let go of her hand now and she stared up at him, unblinking, and as their eyes met she smiled, and he smiled, and then their combined laughter cemented something into place that had had to wait nineteen years to come to fruition.

CHAPTER TWENTY

'Well? What's up? And don't say nothing 'cos I won't believe you.'

'I wasn't going to say nothing,' Jenny said quietly. 'I've been trying to get you by yourself for weeks now but you know what your lot are.'

'Don't I just.' Connie grinned her endearing grin. 'An' you'll never guess what the latest is with our Brian. He's got it into his head he wants to be one of these punks, like his best friend Adam. I ask you, at eleven years old. Mick went up the wall when he came home and found out he'd come back from Adam's with his hair spiked and dyed green, and the next day Brian's teacher sent him home from school with a note to say he wouldn't be let back in until something was done about what she called his amazing choice of hairstyle. She's a sarcastic old swine, that Miss Peters. Anyway, Mick did no more than take him down the barber's and get 'em to shear it all off, the lot of it. He's got a stubble now, that's all, but he doesn't care. He always bounces right back. He's a right little rebel that one.'

'And who does he take after?' Jenny asked with a lift of her eyebrows.

'All right, all right. I get enough of that from Mick. Come on, then.' Connie settled herself on the stool in her kitchen, which was as neat and shiny as the rest of her small terraced house, and peered at Jenny over the top of her coffee mug. 'Let's hear it. What's been happening with you?'

As Jenny stared at her cousin she felt for a moment she had gone back in time. The years since Peter's death and three children, the eldest of which, the said Brian, kept his parents well and truly on their toes, hadn't aged Connie at all. She still looked like a young girl of seventeen, eighteen, her hair cropped and her figure as trim as that of a teenager. Her expressions hadn't changed either, especially the one that was screwing up her face with burning interest at the moment.

'I've met someone.'

'You've . . . Who? When? Does anyone else know? How often have you seen him?'

'Connie, Connie . . .' Jenny raised her hand at the barrage of questions even as she laughed. 'It isn't anyone you know. It's – yet it's someone I used to know in Kent,' she said softly.

'Kent? Someone you used to know in Kent? What, one of the villagers?'

'Well, not exactly *know* . . . My grandfather used to work for his family.'

'You're joking!' Now Connie seemed about to fall off the stool. 'Not the Maines? The ones that used to be friendly with Doctor Mead before he died?'

Jenny nodded, staring at Connie over the expanse of the marble-imitation breakfast bar.

'Flaming hell . . .' Connie sank back on the stool and let out a long slow whoosh of air between her teeth. '*The Maines?* Flaming hell, Jen. I don't believe it. I just don't believe it. All these years and all the blokes who've been after you and you don't look the side they're on, and then you go for the nobility.'

'He's not really.' Jenny swallowed hard. 'It's just his family who have . . . connections, you know. But he's just a plain mister.'

'A plain mister who's worth a small fortune,' Connie said shrewdly. 'I don't believe it . . .'

'Stop saying you don't believe it and tell me how I'm going to break the news to . . . everyone.'

'How – how, you know, serious is it?' Connie asked now. 'I mean, do you have to tell anyone? If it's going to be just one of those things . . .'

'I don't know.' Jenny felt like twisting on her seat but kept perfectly still, resisting the impulse to squeeze herself round her middle. One of those things? She'd die if it was only one of those things. She had never thought she would feel like this again and yet – this wasn't like it had been with Peter. Then, everything had been like a whirlwind that had swept her up and carried her along almost without her comprehending what was happening. Now she was more mature, more . . . vulnerable. Yes, she was. However much she denied it to herself. Because she knew what it felt like to lose the one thing you wanted in all the world, to see it snatched away and be left with nothing, a nothing that still had to be worked in, lived in, existed in.

'You must have some idea?' Connie slid off her stool and came to stand at her side, touching her arm hesitantly. 'Jenny? He must have said something?'

'Connie, he's a grown man of forty-one, forty-two. He's been all round the world I don't know how many times, he's been married, widowed and had umpteen other women since then I should think. He's cultured, wealthy, runs his own business, a market-gardening concern with several different outlets dotted around England. He lives in a huge great house in Lincoln with stables and everything else. He's said – He seems to want to see more of me but how do I know what a man like that is really thinking? I just don't know . . .'

'How long have you been seeing him?' Connie asked, her voice low.

'We met ten weeks ago, when he came into the shop to buy some chocolates.'

'Have you told him about Peter?'

'Yes.' Jenny stopped swirling the dregs of her coffee about her cup and glanced up. 'The first night I went out with him actually. I don't know . . . We just talked and talked and I explained the circumstances of us leaving Kent, you know, that boy Steve Baker, and then I told him about Peter and Grandma. It just seemed right.'

'What did he say?'

'He was understanding, gentle, but then he's like that anyway. He's very tender-hearted. Perhaps that's one of the reasons he keeps seeing me? He feels sorry for me?'

'Jenny!' Connie's voice was scathing now as she frowned at her cousin. 'Doesn't your mirror tell you anything? I know full well why he is seeing you, and it isn't just your looks either. You have something, I don't know, a drawing power of some kind, I suppose I'd call it. Whatever it is it's very attractive. And you must get vibes from him? You must feel he likes you?'

'I do.' Jenny shook her head slowly. 'I do, but then, then he doesn't follow through . . . Oh, I don't know. Perhaps it's me. Perhaps I'm reading too much into this.'

'You probably made him feel he's got to go inch by inch,' Connie said perceptively, 'telling him all that's happened. The poor man probably thinks he's got a timid little flower by the stem and that it's going to break if he doesn't handle it with care.'

'There hasn't been any handling . . .' The two women fell against each other suddenly, their arms round each other as they became convulsed with laughter, and it was like this that Mick found them a moment or two later when he came through the kitchen door, dragging an indignant, red-faced Brian by one ear.

'You'll never guess what I found this little blighter doing –' He stopped abruptly at the sight of the two women, whose faces were wet with laughter. 'Oh, hallo, Jenny, lass, I didn't know you were here.'

'I never get a minute to meself.' Connie drew herself up, glaring at her husband. 'And you were supposed to be at your grandma's,' she said sharply to the small boy who was looking up at her with a head that still carried a faint green tinge. 'What you doing here? And where's Colin, and Christine?'

'They're still with me mam,' Mick cut in as his small son wriggled in a determined attempt to escape. 'But I couldn't leave him there, Connie, not after he put a toad in me mam's bog just afore she went out to do the necessary. It's scared her witless –'

'It wasn't my fault. Mam, it wasn't my fault.'

'Did you put the toad in your grandma's lav?'

'Yes, but –'

'No buts. Did you?' Connie asked sternly.

'It was lost.'

'Lost?' Both parents spoke in unison, their voices high.

'I found it in the backyard, it must've got out of someone's pond or something. Mr Piano's got one, the man who speaks funny three doors down –'

'It's Mr Piento and he doesn't speak funny, I've told you, he comes from a different country,' Connie said severely.

'Well, anyway, I reckon that's where it'd come from. And it needed water. They do, they need water –'

'Not your grandmother's lavatory water,' Connie said grittily, her voice harsh. 'And where is it now? You haven't left it in there?'

''Course not.' The small boy bestowed a glance of pure scorn on his mother and at the same time he produced from his trouser pocket a large and very much alive toad, which promptly leapt for freedom once the small fingers had loosened their hold and nearly landed down the front of Connie's dress. The resulting chaos was loud and fierce and Jenny just managed to make it into the street before she collapsed against the wall in helpless laughter for the second time that morning. Oh, that Brian, he might look like an angel with his big blue eyes and curly blond hair, when he had hair that was, but that's where it ended.

But Connie was lucky. The laughter was cut short and she straightened slowly from the wall and began to walk the five hundred yards or so to her grandfather's house three streets away. She had children. Children who loved her, who called her Mam, children she could tuck into bed at night, love, laugh with. And a husband who thought the world of her. She wished, oh, she wished Lawrence was just an ordinary man, someone from round these streets, who ground out a daily living pound by precious pound and to whom a bank balance was a foreign language. Because she would have felt just the same about him if he was, she knew that now, and it frightened her. Because he wasn't ordinary, he was far from ordinary, and the feeling that he had aroused in her had no future, it couldn't have. She knew that really. She hadn't needed Connie to spell it out for her but in a strange kind of way she acknowledged she had confided in her cousin because she needed to hear someone say it was hopeless. Then maybe her heart could accept what her head had been telling her for the last ten weeks.

She only stayed a short time with her grandfather, although she was perturbed at the sight of him. He had lost a considerable amount of weight over the last few weeks and his colour wasn't good, his eyes taking a distinct yellow tinge of late.

'No David?' Her brother was usually around on a Saturday morning when she called in.

'Darts match,' George answered briefly. 'They've gone by coach to Scunthorpe.'

'Oh, right.' She wanted to tell her grandfather about Lawrence, and yet she didn't. She knew exactly what his reaction would be, for a start. He was of the old school where there was no mix and match between religions, nationalities and especially between social classes. He would be shocked, anxious for her, convinced Lawrence was playing her along, the lord of the manor with the peasant girl type of mentality. And she – she wasn't sure he wasn't right. She bit her lip hard and forced a smile as she turned from the fish and potato pie she had prepared for his dinner to face him. 'I can't stop today, Grand-dad, things to do.' And David? She would never be able to tell David. But as Connie had said, it probably wasn't necessary anyway if it was going to be . . . just one of those things.

She was oblivious to anyone around her on the bus journey home. Lawrence was calling for her just after two to take her for a drive out of town, the late March weather having been unseasonably warm for the last few days, more like the mild days of late summer. That was another thing she found disconcerting, she thought to herself as her brow wrinkled against the knowledge. He had never pushed to meet her grandfather, David or Connie, although she had spoken about them all many times. The suggestion of a drive out of town was indicative of his whole attitude regarding her anxiety about her family discovering their relationship. It could be that he was considering her feelings on the matter, waiting for her to intimate a right time or it could be – It could be that he just didn't care one way or the other, she thought dismally. She had met several of his friends now and also his older brother, who had inherited the estate in Kent on their parents' death some years ago, and had found them all surprisingly easy to get on with once the initial hurdle was over. But – Oh, this was ridiculous. She would drive herself mad before long. She took a deep breath, straightened her back and squared her shoulders, but her heart was heavy as she stepped off the bus some minutes later and she didn't rush to enter the house to get changed but walked slowly and sedately along the pavement and up the drive, her head bent in thought.

And the reflective, almost apprehensive mood continued all afternoon despite her outward gaiety. It was as they sat in the peaceful garden of a little country pub in the twilight that Lawrence reached across and took her hand, drawing her eyes to his. 'What's wrong?'

'Wrong?' She smiled brightly. 'Nothing is wrong.'

'Jenny . . .' He shook his head slowly, his dark eyes tender. 'We have seen enough of each other over the last two or three months for me to know when you are telling less than the truth. This *joie de vivre* doesn't fool me.'

'This what?'

He let go of her hand now, leaning back in his chair and shrugging his broad shoulders before he spoke again. 'Your jollity, vivacity . . . There is something wrong, isn't there? Don't you trust me enough to confide in me?'

'It isn't that.' She stared at him miserably. 'I can't – It isn't anything specific.' She would be thirty-two years old tomorrow but she hadn't told him it was her birthday. Thirty-two, and her body had never known a man, never ripened with the bloom of being loved.

'Specific or not, if it is troubling you then I would like to know about it.'

'*Joie de vivre*'. That was what was troubling her. He spoke a different language, lived in a different world, belonged to a different set of people. She must have been mad –

'Jenny?'

It was as she opened her mouth to make some throw-away comment, an excuse, that her gaze became transfixed just over his left shoulder. And as he turned, following the line of her eyes, he saw a coachload of young, and not so young, men staggering off the large bus that had just parked in the small car-park at the side of the garden and immediately he noticed a tall blond man whose likeness to Jenny was extraordinary. But it wasn't that which had claimed his attention. It was the look on the younger man's face. He couldn't quite describe it, never having come up against naked malignant hostility before, but he knew enough to rise swiftly, his hand under Jenny's arm, as the man walked across the car-park, through a small gate and into the garden, closely followed by a smaller, dark-eyed little man.

'Hallo, David.' Jenny met her brother's glare without flinching although she felt she would collapse but for Lawrence's hand firm and warm under her elbow. 'Fancy seeing you here.'

He didn't answer, his eyes moving from her face to take in Lawrence's suddenly tense countenance. So this was the brother, this handsome hulk of a fellow. Well, well, well. And if he wasn't much mistaken, David was as enamoured with him as he had been with her first suitor. Lawrence held out his hand but his face was cold as he spoke. 'I understand you are Jenny's brother? I'm pleased to meet you.'

'What are you doin' here?' David's voice was harsh as he addressed his sister without even the barest acknowledgement of Lawrence's outstretched hand.

'What do you mean, what am I doing here?' As Lawrence's arm fell to his side Jenny knew a moment's piercing rage that raised her voice. 'What does it look like I'm doing?'

'David –' Frank's voice was a quiet warning to go carefully but it was doubtful that David even heard him.

'I could tell you what it looks like but I won't.' The words were spat through clenched teeth. 'Now I'll ask you again, and polite, like. What you doin' here with him?'

As Jenny opened her mouth to reply, her face white now, she was steered with an almost imperceptible movement of Lawrence's arm into the protection of his body, and it was Lawrence who spoke, his voice cool and controlled, and with a certain note in its depth she had never heard before. 'Is your sister married, Mr Longbridge, or committed to any sort of relationship?'

'What?' David's burning gaze transferred itself to Lawrence's face, which was stiff and haughty with disdain, and his eyes narrowed at the other man's clear refusal to be intimidated.

'I asked you if your sister has an obligation of some kind that I know nothing about.'

'What? – Look, don't you come the clever talk with me.'

'I will take that as a denial.' The words were biting.

Don't take that tack with him, Jenny thought desperately. It'll only provoke him, make him more enraged.

'And in that case, your sister being well over the age of consent, I think it is her own business who she does and does not see, don't you? Now, I presume you have come here to have a drink with your friends?' Lawrence's eyes moved briefly to Frank who was standing to one side, his mouth hanging open in surprise. 'So why don't you do just that and we can discuss this matter some other time if you wish.'

'*If I wish?*' It was clear David had been drinking heavily but he was sober enough to grasp the fact that he was being put in his place by an expert, and his growl of rage gave Lawrence just enough warning before the younger man's clenched fist drove at his face. When, in the next instant, David was looking up at them all from a prone position on the ground his face held the bemused expression of a fighter after the knock-out blow.

'Lawrence?' Jenny moved back from where he had pushed her just before he had swung his leg in an arching kick, his arm fending off David's attack.

'T'ai chi, it's a martial art,' he said briefly.

'Oh, Lawrence . . .'

'Come on, I think it's time we were leaving.'

'I can't –'

'You can, Jenny.' He turned her round, holding her shoulders as he looked down into her face. 'Do you understand me? *You can*. You'll see to him?' His glance moved as he spoke to Frank who nodded sullenly before his eyes flickered down to David at their feet who clearly didn't know what day it was.

'Uncle Frank –'

'Get along, lass.' Frank raised his gaze to Jenny's swimming eyes and it would have been difficult for anyone to understand the expression on his face. 'I'll see to 'im, you know that, and it'd be wise for you to go afore he gets 'is bearings.'

He blamed her, she knew that, and as she walked out of the pub garden she was painfully aware of the covert glances and muted conversations aimed in their direction.

But Frank didn't blame her. As he watched his daughter leave, and he thought of her as his daughter in a way he never had Connie, his guts twisted and burnt until it was a physical pain. He could understand his lad, aye he could, for you couldn't choose where you loved, more's the pity. But the lass was a grown woman now with a mind of her own, didn't she have his blood running through her veins? Like her mother before her she bore a strong resemblance to Martha, damn his wife's eyes . . . *His wife*. The slut, the conniving slut. But he'd made her pay for what she'd made him do, what she'd driven him to. Aye, he had that. He knew she was frightened of him, more than frightened, and this fact alone sustained him through days and nights that had become a subtle unrelenting torment of mind and body. She'd have gone to that filthy stinkin' great numbskull years ago if she hadn't believed he'd kill them both, he knew it. Would he have killed them? As David stirred and attempted to rise the answer was immediate. Of course he would. And taken pleasure in it too.

'Frank? . . .' David reeled a little as the older man helped him up. 'Where – Has she gone? Where are they?'

'They've gone, lad.' There was no condemnation in Frank's tone and he felt none. Society might consider that David's feeling for his sister was wrong but men like them weren't bound by society's laws, they made their own. His eyes narrowed as he watched David absorb the fact that Jenny had left. He'd have liked 'em to have set up together, aye he would. Hadn't he steered David in that direction for some time? It would have driven Martha mad now that she knew, an' George too. He knew enough about human nature to know that George was uneasy about his grandchildren's feelings for each other. What would the thick oaf do if he knew he was the father of the bairns? The thought gave Frank such a vicious dart of pleasure his eyes turned into slits of black light. One day, one day he'd tell him, but when he was unable to do anything about it . . . He'd wished a stroke on his brother-in-law more times than he could remember. Oh, that'd be sweet, aye, it would that, poetic justice . . .

'Did you know?' David's voice brought Frank's eyes to his face and he shook his head slowly.

'What do you think, lad?'

'No, I didn't mean – Sorry Frank.' David shook his head, squaring his muscular shoulders, which bulged like great plates under his thin shirt. 'I'll kill him . . .' He swore, the language foul and of the worst kind as he stared unseeing into the distance. 'Who the hell is he?'

Lawrence had kept hold of Jenny's arm until she was seated in the Bentley, whereupon he had walked round the bonnet and slid into his own seat without speaking a word. The encounter had shocked him. Not because he had been unaware of the essence of the problem: unknown to Jenny his own quiet and careful enquiries, plus an understanding of the subtleties of human nature had given him an insight into the conundrum he was facing weeks ago. But up until a few moments ago there had been a feeling of pity, of sympathy even, mixed with the frustration and irritation he felt at being forced to move at such a slow pace with the woman he loved simply because her brother wouldn't approve of her having a man friend. Man friend? Man friend be blowed, he thought grimly. He was more than a man friend and it was time Jenny and the rest of her family knew it. This was more than an overdeveloped sense of brotherly protectiveness. He could have understood that with the atrocious luck she had had so far. No, this was altogether something more sinister and all the more dangerous because she was unaware of it. Or was she? . . .

He manoeuvred the big car out of the car-park as his thoughts moved on. He had thought it strange, with her devotion to her grandfather so strong, that she had chosen to live alone, but it was becoming clearer now, as was the reason why her grandfather had encouraged the idea. She might explain away her need for independence, and the real reason was probably buried so far in her subconcious that to try and bring it into the light would cause untold damage, but somewhere, somewhere deep in the layers of her psyche, there lurked a knowledge of the truth. Damn it all . . . His mouth stretched into a thin line. Had the other fellow known, this Peter? He must have. And fate had played right into her brother's hands when the fellow had been murdered . . . His eyes widened as a sudden thought occurred to him but almost instantly he dismissed it as fanciful. It was one thing to suspect the man of coveting his sister but quite another to lay a charge like that on him. Besides, Jenny had told him a young lad had been convicted of the murder although he had maintained his innocence throughout. But this was a bad business . . . As with Peter before him the urge to get her out of the situation was strong.

He reached across and took her hand from her lap as

he steered with his other hand. 'Come on, my dear, it was a storm in a teacup.' Perhaps it was the jerk of her fingers as he touched her, or maybe the knowledge that he had been a damn fool in pussyfooting about so long, but whatever, the next minute he had swung off the road into a gated pull-in and taken her in his arms even before the sound of the engine had died away. And as she trembled against him, her face streaming with tears, there arose in him a conviction that now was the time.

'Jenny?' She was still quivering when he moved her gently from him, taking her hands and looking deep into her eyes as he spoke. 'I love you. I think I've always loved you even before I saw you that first day when you were a young girl in a white dress. There's always been a void in me that remained unfilled whatever I was doing and whoever I was with –'

'Lawrence –'

'No, let me finish, please. I know now I should have followed through on the impulse I had that day to seek you out; it was sheer cowardice that prevented me. I was engaged to be married, it had been arranged for some time and both families were exceedingly pleased . . . Oh, many things that have no significance now and had little then if only I had known. I was foolish, very foolish, but I don't intend to be foolish for a second time.'

'But you can't –' She stopped abruptly as she shook her head. 'You could have anyone, anyone, and your family – They'll expect you –'

'My family will expect nothing of me as I expect nothing of them,' Lawrence said quietly. 'Have you ever wondered why my second brother lives abroad? It is simply that he couldn't stand my parents when they were alive. He escaped, to lead a life of utter decadence following his aspiration to paint in a little hidey-hole in Spain.'

'Really?' She stared at him, amazed.

'Really. And although Charlie and I were less sensitive than Edward we could understand why he felt the need to disappear. Oh yes, we could understand it well,' he added quietly, before raising her hands to his lips. 'I want you to be my wife, Jenny. I know now I've always wanted it.'

'People will think you've married beneath you –'

'Don't.' His grip on her hands tightened. 'Please, don't say that. No one who is worth knowing could possibly take that attitude.'

'They will.' She tried to smile but it was beyond her. 'And none more than my own folk, the people who have known me all my life. Neighbours, friends, they will all smile and wish me well, at the same time as resenting the fact you have chosen me.'

'But you will have chosen me too.' He smiled slowly to hide the fact that her perception amazed him. 'If you do choose me, that is?'

'You know how I feel, you must do –'

'Only because I feel the same,' he said softly.

She stared at him, quite unable to believe that this cultured, wealthy and handsome man was asking her to become his wife.

'Jenny, what is it?'

How could she explain? How could she make him understand how it felt to be born with the niggling, unspoken knowledge that you were somehow different? To have it confirmed in the most brutal way possible? *Bastard*. The word had haunted her before she had heard it expressed and for years afterwards, producing this feeling of inferiority that had sapped her faith in herself despite the enlightened age in which she now lived. She had fought against it, and she knew David had too in his own way, and that thought, as always, had the power to touch her heart.

'David –'

'Will be glad for you.' He interrupted her swiftly. 'He will, Jenny, once he understands.' Believe me, he told her silently. Believe me and I will make it come true. Somehow. Either that or I will engineer that we go so far away that his wrath and bitterness will make no impact on our lives. But that would come later. First he had to persuade her that her life was tied up with his and he knew of only one way to fully convince her.

Later, as they drove home in the rapidly cooling dark night, Jenny felt a warmth that was nothing to do with Lawrence's lovemaking. He loved her, she knew now that he loved her. What it was that had made two wonderful men, first Peter and now Lawrence, feel such deep emotion for her, she couldn't begin to comprehend, she never would, but she wasn't going to miss this second chance of love. If she had married Peter she would have been happy with him for the rest of her life. But it hadn't worked out like that and now she had been given a second chance, which happened to few. A second chance . . . She hugged the thought to her as Lawrence's Bentley drew up outside the house.

'I wish you would reconsider.' There was a note of concern in Lawrence's voice. 'Stay a few nights with me, just until David has had a chance to adapt to the idea. What if he –'

'Lawrence.' She placed a tender hand on his arm. 'He's my brother, he won't hurt me, and I can make him understand far better if we are alone. Please, I know him. I'll see you as arranged Monday evening but I want the day tomorrow to tell my grandfather and Connie . . . Please?'

'Very well.' He took her in his arms again and she clung to him for a long moment before he opened the door and walked round the bonnet to help her from the car.

'You go now.' She touched his face as they stood together on the pavement. 'And stop worrying, it'll be fine. Everything will be fine now.'

'Jenny –'

'Go on.' She laughed softly as she pushed him towards the car. 'I mean it, go on.'

She was still waving as the car disappeared into the distance and her face was bright as she turned to walk towards the house, but in the next instant, when a large bulky shadow moved from the bushes at the side of the drive, her hand was to her mouth to stifle the scream that had sprung from her throat.

'David . . .' She relaxed the next moment, when she recognized her brother. 'You scared me half to death.'

'Who is he, Jenny?'

'His name is Lawrence.' She stood uncertainly for a second and then forced herself to walk towards him. 'Are you coming in?'

'Too true I'm comin' in.'

'Look, don't take that attitude, David. You've got no right –'

'No right?' His voice was thick, low and deep. '*No right?* The hell I haven't –'

'We will be thirty-two years old tomorrow, David.' She unlocked the front door as she spoke, her voice automatically lowering as they entered the wide square hall and began to walk up the stairs directly opposite the front door. 'And frankly I can look after myself.

I'm sorry about the incident in the pub but that wasn't his fault, you asked for that –'

'An' what has he asked for?' As she opened the door to the flat he pushed her in with his hand in the flat of her back and she swung round, her eyes blazing.

'And you can stop that right now.'

'What *has* he asked for, then?' It was as if she hadn't spoken and as he kicked the door shut with the sole of his boot she wondered, for the first time, if she had been wise to allow him in.

'Don't be coarse,' she said flatly as she walked into the lounge.

'*Coarse?*' He swore, the profanity harsh and ugly. 'Oh, we're the lady now, are we? Tryin' to keep up with that little upstart who talks like he's rollin' in it. Don't you know when you're bein' had, girl? It's all an act, that upper-class accent don't mean nothin', he's likely got his eye on this place –'

'Don't be so stupid –'

'Oh I'm stupid now, am I? An' of course you'd know. You who's been about here, there and everywhere and seen all there is to see. Real woman of the world, aren't you? 'Course you'd recognize a trickster right off.'

'He's not, I tell you.'

'An' how would you know?'

'Because – because I've known him a long time, known of him, that is.'

'Known *of* him?' He eyed her grimly. 'What does that mean when it's at home?'

'If you will sit down and start behaving reasonably I'll explain –'

'Oh, you'll explain all right.' He moved until her face was only inches away from his and she forced herself not to shrink away but face him boldly, her eyes staring straight into his. 'You'll certainly explain.'

'It's – He is Lawrence Maine.'

For a moment David's face remained the same and then as the eyes widened and his mouth opened she spoke quickly.

'You know, the youngest son of the Maine family. He – I met him a few months ago by accident, he came into the shop –'

'*The shop?*'

'Yes, yes.' She swallowed rapidly. 'He was here on business and needed some chocolates and – And that's how we met. He asked me out to dinner and –'

'I knew I recognized him from somewhere.' For a moment she was almost fooled into thinking he was pleased, relieved, by the quietness of his voice but then the heavily lidded eyes blazed as his head jerked in a hard, angry nod. 'Lawrence Maine, Lawrence Maine. An' what could a man like that want with the likes of you, as if I didn't know? How many times? *How many times have you done it with him?*'

'What?' She was transfixed by him, her eyes wide and staring at the expression on his face.

'You heard me, you little –'

'Don't you dare talk to me like that!' Suddenly the frustration of years exploded and the surprising action of her body, strained towards him and tight with rage, and her face red with unmitigated fury, stilled his voice for a moment. But only for a moment.

'Talk to you?' His voice was a low snarl and as she glared back at him the thought came to her that he was mad. He had to be. Because the look on his face wasn't human. 'I'll talk to you how I want and when I want –'

'*You won't! You won't!*' She was aware she was

screaming but the combination of fear and panic and red-hot rage had taken over her voice as well as her body, and when in the next moment his fist had hit her full in the face and she found herself flying backwards across the room she still continued to shriek.

'Jenny, Jenny . . .' When her head stopped ringing she found he was kneeling at her side and now a new fear took over as she felt his touch on her sprawled legs. 'Oh, Jenny . . .'

As her body shot up, she surprised him for the second time in as many minutes. Her arms thrusting his away, she leapt across the room, propelled by a fear that briefly made her superhuman. She had reached the front door and wrenched it open before he had taken more than a step and she flew down the stairs, banging on the door of the flat below, into which a young couple had recently moved. It opened immediately as if the occupants had been waiting for her knock, which their next words subsequently confirmed.

'What is it? We could hear you shouting and –'

'Please – Please can I come in?' They had pulled her into the flat and shut the door even as she heard David thundering down the stairs, but then everything became a blur when the pain in her head suddenly exploded into every nerve and sinew of her body, and as she began to fall she was vaguely aware of the young man reaching out to her but then all was rushing blackness as unconsciousness blanketed her bruised senses.

CHAPTER TWENTY-ONE

'You're crazy, Jenny, you know that don't you? Stark, staring, flamin' daft. Why on earth aren't you going to tell it as it is?'

'You know why.' Jenny raised the cup of coffee to her lips and then winced as her sore mouth made contact with the hot rim. 'Grand-dad isn't well and this would send him loo-lah. Oh please, Connie, we've had this conversation in various ways non-stop for the last few days. Let it rest.'

'Let it rest.' Her cousin snorted with disgust. 'Let it rest, she says. There's you too scared to go home and you're telling the world you fell downstairs. I'm surprised you had the sense to get that young fella to bring you here Saturday night –'

'I'm not too scared to go home.' Jenny shook her head but carefully. The last few days had told her all the movements she made with her head had to be slow and restrained if she didn't want it to feel as if it was about to fall off. 'Now you know that, so don't try to get me going. It was you and Mick who insisted I stay here for a few days –'

'Too true. Look at the state of you.' Connie stood back on her heels, her arms crossed, and surveyed her cousin's bruised and swollen face, which was turning a range of colours, from navy blue to sickly yellow. 'How he didn't knock your teeth out beats me. They were certainly loose enough when you first got here. He could've killed you, Jen, and you don't seem to be aware of it. And Lawrence doesn't believe you, you know, he hinted as much to me.'

'I don't care what he hints at as long as he doesn't

know for sure. Can you imagine how it'd be if he went round there to see David with Grand-dad so ill? It'd finish him off, I'm telling you, Connie. He's worried enough as it is and he thinks I've only fallen down the stairs.'

'You'll have to go and see him soon.'

'I can't.' Her face whitened at the thought. 'I can't, Connie. If David was there . . .'

'Well, what are you going to do then?'

'I'll wait till the weekend. This'll be a bit better by then,' she touched her swollen face gently, 'and David's away for the day with your dad on one of their darts matches Saturday. There'll be no danger of running into him then. And I'll go back to my place Friday. Your Christine must be dying to get her own room back.'

'Oh, she doesn't care.' Connie grinned wryly. 'She loves it in with the boys. She's always moaned 'cos she's on her own anyway. And I love having you here. You can stay as long as you like as far as I'm concerned. With Mick down the Labour Party place every second he gets, I'm glad of the company.'

'Well, that'll finish Friday too,' Jenny said quietly, 'once the general election's over. I can stay the extra night to save your mam babysitting if you want, you know.'

'No, she likes to get out of the house.' They both knew what Connie meant, but neither commented on it. 'And I've already asked her to stay over, we're bound to be late one way or the other. If the Tories get in, Mick'll want to drown his sorrows and if Labour pull it off, they'll drink themselves silly. Either way it'll be a good night.' She pushed Jenny as she laughed. 'I half feel inclined to vote for Maggie Thatcher meself, you know, I wouldn't dare tell Mick.

She's said she's going to look after the housewives if she gets in and she is a woman after all. That's got to mean something.'

Jenny smiled but said nothing. The general election was the last thing on her mind. Since that awful night five days ago every waking moment had been filled with a continuous replay of her fight with David. When the young couple had brought her to Connie's house in the early hours of Sunday morning she had been sick with fear that he would come and find her but that had diminished, along with the stark terror that the incident had called forth from the depths of her being. Because he couldn't have intended what she had felt, for one frightening moment, he had, and she was wicked, sick, to think he could. She was, she was. He was angry when he had no right to be and she wouldn't stand for it, she still couldn't believe he had actually hit her, but the other thing . . . No. She had been mistaken there. To think anything else would send her deranged.

'Well, I'm off to the shops. You comin'?'

Jenny shook her head slowly. 'No, I don't think so. I might have a couple of aspirins in a minute and have a lie-down. You go.'

'You sure? I don't like leaving you –'

'Now it's you who's being daft.' Jenny smiled to soften her words. 'I shall be back home in a couple of days and you can't nursemaid me there. You need another baby, that's what it is.'

'Oh you . . .' Connie laughed as she grimaced her distaste at the idea. 'I've had my fill of dirty nappies and broken nights, thank you, I'm going to leave all that to you in the future.'

'I hope so, Connie, oh I hope so.' There was a note in Jenny's voice that caused her cousin to hug her tightly before she left the room, and once alone Jenny sat for a long time without moving. Since Saturday night a lethargy had fallen on her which was all out of proportion to her physical state. The fact that she was suffering from delayed shock was only a small part of it. If anyone had told her that she lived in mortal fear, deathly fear, of history repeating itself in some way, she would have denied it strongly so adept had she become at burying her deep terror at the thing she called fate. But nevertheless the spectre of doom was forever with her and never more so than in the last few days. It was a deep-rooted fear that had caused the weight to fall off her since she had met Lawrence, giving her beauty an almost transparent fragility, and now as she walked across to the kitchen mirror and peered at herself her eyes stared back at her out of a face unnaturally thin and pale, the bruises standing out in vivid contrast to her bleached skin.

When the doorbell rang a moment later she almost jumped out of her skin, and she hugged herself tightly for a moment to steady her racing heartbeat. Who was that? It couldn't be . . . No. David would be at work, of course he would be. She walked out of the kitchen and into the light, white-painted hall and felt such a flood of relief when she recognized her grandfather's form through the glass in the front door that for a moment she clear forgot he was ill and supposed to be in bed. As she opened the door wide and saw his grey face, though, she remembered. 'Grand-dad? What on earth? Oh, you should be in bed, you know you should. What are you doing?'

'Just shut up and help me in, lass.' It had taken all of George's strength to walk the three streets to Connie's house and now he was breathing hard, his chest labouring as he struggled to get air into his failing lungs.

'Oh Grand-dad, Grand-dad . . . You shouldn't have come. What were you thinking of in your state? Connie said how bad you were . . . Oh Grand-dad . . .' She continued to fuss about him while she got him settled in the small living room in an easy chair, and then sat watching him anxiously as some semblance of colour returned to his gaunt face and his breathing stabilized. 'I'll get you a drink –'

'In a minute.' George raised a hand to prevent her leaving and she sank back down on the small pouffe she had pulled close to his chair, watching his watery eyes roam over her face. 'Well, me bairn, of the two of us I'd say you look the worse,' he said gruffly after a long moment.

'I'm all right –'

'You look it.' He shook his head slowly. 'An' there's no way you fell down no stairs, lass. I might be on me last legs but I'm not senile, not yet. Who did it?'

'I –' She stared at him as her mind froze. She couldn't tell him, she didn't dare think what he would do and how David might react. 'I did. I fell – '

'Your young man came round to see me last night,' George said flatly, 'an' we had a nice long chat. Now fortunately David was out, you know what I mean?' She continued to stare at him, her eyes enormous in the whiteness of her face. 'Lawrence told me David saw you and him together last Saturday, the night you fell down the stairs, an' yet the lad's said nought to me. You don't think that funny?'

'I –' Lawrence shouldn't have gone. He should have told her –

'I'm not blamin' you for keepin' quiet about Lawrence, Jenny. If I hadn't seen and heard him with me own eyes, I doubt I'd be for him now, but I am.'

'Oh, Grand-dad –'

He checked her when she would have thrown herself at him and something in his face kept her still. 'Now Lawrence Maine is no fool, Jenny, he's travelled far and seen plenty, and he knows what's what. He's gonna settle with David if I don't because he wants him seen to, you understand me? Your brother's not said a word about seeing you and it don't take the brain of Britain to put two and two together and make four. Are you goin' to tell me or do I have to drag it out of you?'

'It *was* David.' Jenny's head was bowed as she spoke and she didn't see the flash of emotion sear her grandfather's face. 'He was waiting at the flat when I got home Saturday.' Now she did raise her head, her eyes swimming. 'But don't do anything, Grand-dad. Can't you see it'll make it worse? I've told him. He knows what's what and I'm not going to let him alter anything. Lawrence has asked me to marry him and I'm going to, so he can't do anything.'

'An' he belted you one?' It was as though he hadn't heard the rest of her words. 'He raised his hand to you?'

'He lost his temper.' Jenny shuddered as she spoke, the incident still too raw in her mind to have lost its horror. The violence . . . She had never come up against such violence. Even that with Steve Baker had been different somehow because he hadn't been part of her. She hadn't cared about him, loved him. But David – She couldn't bear this agony that had her wanting to vomit if she tried to eat, that had her curling up in a tight little ball in bed at night as she tried to fight the pain. 'He didn't mean it, Grand-dad.'

So it was going to happen again . . . As he looked at Jenny it was David's face he saw, and as a veil lifted from his eyes he knew his grandson had killed both Steve Baker and Peter, and that it had been premeditated, cold and calculated, at least in the case of young Peter. He had always known. *He had always known* . . .

'Grand-dad?'

'I'll have that cup of tea now, lass.' George let his head drop on his chest, shutting his eyes, but when, after a moment, he heard her rise and go into the kitchen his eyes snapped open and he took a deep long pull of air. By all that was holy . . . How long had he known that his grandson was two quite separate people? One was the David that worked and slept and ate, enjoyed his darts matches and his Friday nights and appeared quite . . . normal. And the other? The other was frightening, terrifying . . . How often had he read in the papers about these people who weren't supposed to have known that their loved ones had committed the vilest of crimes, read and scoffed at their naïvety, at the same time as feeling a sickening thread of something deep in his mind that he had chosen to ignore? Damn it all . . . His heart was thudding violently and he felt the pain grip him again like a knife turning deep in his chest and back. Well, he knew what it was, he hadn't needed the doctor to confirm it, had he? But he had to keep going long enough to see her settled, safe . . . But how, *how?* Because she wasn't safe with that madman about and Lawrence Maine less so. But if he told her it would destroy her peace of mind forever, she'd never get over it, and yet he couldn't stand by and see further bloodshed. No, either way his lass would lose out.

He rubbed his hand across his face, beads of sweat standing out on his brow. When the pain was bad it made him sweat although them there pills the old doctor had given him helped, aye they did that, but they made him woozy into the bargain so he hadn't taken any before he left, damn fool that he was. He breathed slowly and steadily, forcing the pain back until it became bearable by sheer willpower, and when Jenny returned with the tea he was able to smile at her and pat the pouffe beside him. 'So where were you Saturday when David saw you? Your young man never got as far as telling me that.'

He listened to her talk as he sipped at his tea, although his mind wasn't really on what she was saying until she mentioned her uncle's name.

'Frank? Frank was there? An' how was he in it all, then?'

'All right.' Jenny bit her lip uncomfortably. The hatred between the two men was deep and strong, she knew that, but Frank *had* been all right when she thought about it, and she couldn't say less than the truth.

'He didn't have a go at Lawrence, then? Mouth at him?'

'No.' She shook her head quickly. 'No. He was . . . reasonable.'

Was he? George's eyes narrowed. Then this could be the answer, unpalatable as it was. The only person on this earth who had any sway with David was his uncle, and if he would be prepared to talk to him, persuade him to see sense? He leant back in the chair as Jenny went to refill his cup. It'd mean he'd have to go to his hated enemy cap in hand. Could he do it? The answer walked in the room and knelt down by his side, kissing his cheek as she handed him the tea. 'You shouldn't have come, Grand-dad, but – But I'm glad you did,' she said softly. 'I hated not telling you about

Lawrence but I wasn't sure how he felt, if it would come to anything. And then, when David –' She couldn't say hit me, she just couldn't. 'When I saw David at the flat I knew you'd be upset. I was going to tell you, later.'

'I know, lass, I know.' The pain in him couldn't have been worse if he'd been disembowelled, but it wasn't the cancer that was eating him up. No, he could deal with that on a physical level. It was the sick agitation, the morbid feeling that he'd been here before, that had given him a sleepless night despite the heavy drugs he was on and was now twisting his insides like a red-hot poker. And that one. Sleeping just the other side of the wall. He didn't know how he'd contained himself when he'd heard David come in last night. It was only the fact that he didn't know for sure that he had been to see his sister that had stayed his hand. He shook his head now as he rose, his movements slow and careful. 'I'm off back to bed, lass. I just wanted to see you for meself.'

'Grand-dad? Promise me you won't say anything to David, please?'

'I can't, lass –'

'*Please?*' She wet her lips and swallowed. 'Please, Grand-dad. It will all sort out, I know it. Please?'

Aye, it'd all sort out all right. And he knew who would engineer the sorting out. When he thought of that young man and the injuries he'd witnessed on his lifeless body that day he'd been called in to identify him, his landlady collapsing in a dead faint before she'd even set foot in the morgue, he couldn't believe that flesh of his flesh could be responsible, but the time for burying his head in the sand was past. His own days were numbered, according to that doctor they were in weeks not months, an' that being the case he had to sort this thing out now. Somehow. *But Frank Malley?* He'd never thought to see the day when he'd be asking a favour of that swine.

'I won't say nought for the present, does that satisfy you?' He pushed his lips outward, his eyes narrowed. 'But I'll only stay me hand so far, Jenny. If he tries another number like that –'

'He won't, he won't.' She was gabbling in her relief and stopped herself with a feeling of self-disgust. 'He won't,' she added more quietly.

'Aye, mebbe . . .' George touched his grand-daughter's face with the palm of his hand, his eyes tender. 'Cheerio, me bairn.'

That was twice he'd called her that, Jenny thought with a dart of worry, and she hadn't heard him say it for years. And he looked so ill. This was more than a touch of bronchitis. 'Grand-dad? These pills the doctor has given you?'

'They can't give you pills for old-age, love, and that's all that ails me, that and a touch of the old chest trouble.'

'But –'

'No buts. Now all I want you to do is to get better. When you goin' home? Back to your place?'

'Friday night.' She forced herself to smile. 'Connie and Mick are going to make a night of it, with the general election and all, so Aunt Martha is going to come and sleep here and see to the kids. I said I'd stay but she wants to come, so . . .'

'Right.' He nodded slowly. That fitted in with what David had told him that morning, that he was staying the night round Frank's on Friday in order to get away nice and early on Saturday morning for this here darts match. He'd thought it strange Martha would tolerate the lad under her roof, but if she wasn't going to be there that explained it. 'Well, you look after yourself, lass, you hear me?'

He had to concentrate very hard to get home and once in the house he sank down on a hard, straight-backed chair for some twenty minutes before he could move again. Once he had swallowed his pills he felt better, but he was conscious that the medication was losing its ability to repress the pain more and more each day. The doctor had said that that was the point he should consider going into hospital and he'd answered him he'd rather die first. He smiled grimly to himself as he remembered Doctor Penn's reaction to his black humour. He wasn't afraid of dying. Maybe he should be, all things considered, but he wasn't. He'd always thought he believed there was nothing once you breathed your last, that the finish of the body was the finish of everything, but the last few months, since he'd got ill, he'd felt Mary near more than once, so what did that mean? He was blowed if he knew. No doubt the psychoanalysts would have a fancy name for it, they did for everything else.

In the afternoon he slept a little in the easy chair in front of the fire and awoke with the conviction that Mary was trying to tell him something, something important. He told himself it was the effects of the medication, of the half-world he seemed to inhabit more and more these days, but still the gnawing sense that he had missed something, something vital, persisted, and when David came in later it stilled his tongue under the certainty that for whatever reason Mary had told him to speak to Frank first. He fought against it. Just looking at David was like a red flag to a bull, but the conviction that he had to wait and see Frank was so strong he bowed beneath it.

'You out later?' he asked David quietly.

David looked across at his grandfather as he spoke and although their eyes only met for the briefest of moments George could recognize satisfaction when he saw it, and that told him he looked as bad as he felt.

'Mebbe, mebbe not. There's no dinner on, then?'

'No, there's no dinner on.'

'Huh.'

The one word, spoken as it was with a wealth of contempt, brought George's teeth grinding together but he lowered his head to his chest and shut his eyes, feigning an exhaustion that wasn't altogether sham. No. He wouldn't be provoked, but depending on whether David went out or not he'd either go round to Malley's tonight or wait till tomorrow afternoon when he could catch him coming in from work. He didn't want David to know what he was about, and the pair were like Siamese twins the last few years, you'd think they were brothers instead of merely related by Frank's marriage to Martha. Martha . . . As he allowed himself to think of her his head slumped still more and David, watching him from the doorway, gloated in the change in the old man.

It was all coming his way now as he had known it would, he'd only had to be patient. His teeth moved over his bottom lip as he relished the thought. His grandfather's days were numbered, look at him sitting in that chair like a dirty bag of bones, he was finished, done for. *And that other one?* He moved from the doorway, walking into the kitchen and taking a beer from the fridge as he flexed his shoulders ruminatively. Thanks to Frank no one was aware where he'd been the day. He'd covered for him, saying he was stripping down a machine in another of the factories. He was a good bloke was Frank, the best. And Lawrence Maine? Aye, it was a grand place he had, grand. And he'd learnt enough to know that he went for a ride most mornings. Well, he was gentry, wasn't he! *Gentry* . . . He saw red for a moment and then forced the thundering in his ears to subside as he gripped the edge of the draining board. The swine, the clever-talkin' swine. He'd bought her with his fine talk and money, that's what he'd done. She was no better than one of the girls from Tinsley Street, flauntin' that ripe little body and all her charms for payment in kind. And she'd fooled him, aye she had. He'd still thought her as pure as the driven snow. But he'd fix her, and him.

He ground his teeth softly. Because accidents happened in stables, everyone knew that. Horses were unpredictable creatures, given to kicking and prancing about when you least expected it. Aye . . . He could picture it now. They'd find Lawrence Maine's body to one side of one of the great beasts, wedged in one of the stable boxes he'd managed to scout round on the quiet today. What had that girl in the shop down the road said? The one who'd been so helpful? Oh aye, his first wife had died being thrown. Well, if it was good enough for his wife . . .

He'd go down early of a morning next week on Frank's Honda. Frank'd cover for him if he was late in, and when he got the opportunity – He brought his clenched fist into the palm of his hand. All the money in the world wouldn't help Lawrence Maine then. He laughed thickly. And the beauty of it was that a lump of wood would do the trick, something that could be disposed of on the way back.

The shuffling sound in the doorway brought his head up and such was the look of glee on David's face that for a moment George, surveying him without speaking across the room, blinked uncertainly. 'What's up with you?'

'Me?' David rose slowly, his face straightening into an insolent sneer that was unmistakable. 'There's nothing wrong with me.'

'No?'

'No.' David drank the last of his beer slowly without taking his eyes off George and, after placing the bottle on the table, wiped his mouth with the back of his hand before sauntering from the room with a smile on his face.

Nothing wrong with him? *Nothing wrong with him?* George stumbled to a chair and sat down. By his reckoning the lad should be breathing fire and damnation, not looking as if he'd just won the pools. He shivered as a wave of nausea swept over him. The sooner he got himself round to see Frank the better, because as sure as hell was hot that maniac who was his grandson was planning something, he could smell it coming off him in a surging swell of malevolence that would sear anything he touched. How could his Jenny, his sweet Jenny, have given birth to anything like that? He didn't want to think there was anything of him in that big good-looking frame, which was so putrid and filthy on the inside. He shut his eyes tightly as his thoughts caused the pain to intensify. And yet his grand-daughter had none of that corrosive depravity in her, he knew she didn't. Somehow, when they were conceived, everything that was good had gone into one child and everything bad into the other, and now it looked as if he would die without knowing who had fathered them. The thought still had the power to twist his guts. Because he blamed the father for David, every nerve and sinew of him did. A man that would take a young bairn down, and no one would ever convince him different but that his daughter had been raped, he had to be sick, perverted . . . And those genes had been passed on to his grandson. His *grandson* . . . Blast 'em all, his grandson . . .

David didn't go out that evening and the night hours seemed endless to George as he lay awake waiting for the first glimmer of light. He heard his grandson rise just after seven and get ready for work, and when he left the house a few minutes before eight George fell into a light doze for most of the morning. He had his first two lots of pills but not the third and left the house just after four after drinking several cups of tea, although try as he might he was unable to force any food down.

'George?' Martha's voice was high with surprise as she opened the door and then her gaze became still as she took in the change in him. 'George?' Her voice was softer now, weak.

For answer George said one word: 'Frank.'

'Frank?' She was horrified, shocked, at the transformation of what once had been a tall, big, proud man into this gaunt, thin figure in front of her but she strove to hide it and stood aside for him to enter. 'He's not home yet, come and sit down a minute.'

'Aye, I will if you don't mind.' Mind? She ought to mind. The way she'd been treated by him she ought to do more than mind but somehow the sight of him, the pity it had invoked, cut through the last years of bitterness and resentment as though they had never been.

'I don't mind, Georgie, but Frank . . . Well, you know how he is, an' you say you want to talk to him?' He hadn't, but why else would he have spoken her husband's name like that? 'You think that's wise?'

'I have to, Martha.' He hadn't been able to reply until he was seated and now the few words took all his breath.

'Sit still. I'll get you a cup of tea.' He didn't want a cup of tea but he didn't say so, his eyes following her as she busied herself at the stove. He was a fool. He'd always been a fool. Aye, all his life. He shut his eyes slowly.

They didn't speak for at least ten minutes, Martha joining him quietly at the kitchen table as she placed the cup of tea in front of him, sipping at her own without glancing his way. And it was like this that Frank found them when he came in the back door that led straight into the kitchen, and the surprise on his face equalled that which had been on his wife's when she first saw George.

'What –'

'Hallo, Frank.' George's voice was quiet but he made no effort to rise, he couldn't have. The short journey from his house had taken his limited reserve of energy down to zero.

'What the hell are you doin' here?' Frank's eyes were hard and black and glittering as they moved over the sick man and there was something in their satisfied, contemptuous gaze that rang a bell in George's tired mind but as yet he couldn't formulate the thought.

'I want a word with you –'

'A word with me?' Frank slammed the door shut as he spoke and glanced at his wife. 'Get out.'

'Don't you dare talk to me like that –'

'I said get out.'

'This concerns Martha too, in a way,' George said tightly, gripping the cup in his hand hard to prevent the hot words burning his tongue from being said. By, he hadn't changed. He hadn't changed one bit.

'Does it indeed?' Frank's mean little eyes flashed, surveying their faces now and George spoke quickly, before any more was said.

'It's about David. David and Jenny.'

'Oh aye?' There was a stillness about the thin face in front of him that narrowed George's eyes. Frank couldn't know what he'd come for. He'd only known himself yesterday. But then, as his gaze moved to his sister-in-law he saw an essence of the look in her blue eyes which puzzled him further.

'He's all fired up about this new boyfriend of hers an' I understand you saw the pair of 'em last Saturday.'

'So?'

Although Frank didn't move a muscle he caught the sigh that escaped Martha's lips and the imperceptible slump of her shoulders. 'So, I don't want him to do anythin' silly, you know what I mean?'

'No.' Frank's eyes were black slits now. 'No, I don't. You'd better explain yourself.'

'Dammit, man, I shouldn't have to –' George caught himself abruptly. Steady, man, steady. 'You know how the lad is about his sister,' he said quietly now. 'How he's always . . . looked out for her. He won't like her having a man friend.'

'That's between them, don't you think?'

'No, no, I don't think,' George shot back angrily.

'George –' Martha came into the conversation for the first time, her voice soft and her eyes steady as she glanced his way. 'What exactly are you here for? I'm sorry, I don't understand . . .'

'The lad thinks a lot of Frank.' His eyes moved from Martha to Frank while he spoke. 'You know he does. If you had a word with him, calmed things down, like –'

'Me? Me have a word with him? An' what would that word be?' Frank asked slowly, his mouth twisted in a sneer as his neck strained out of his collar.

'You know what I'm askin' –'

'Oh, I know what you're askin' all right.' Now Frank moved towards him until he was leaning palms down on the kitchen table, his face thrust out and inches from George's. 'You expect me to tell David to leave the lass and her fancy man alone, is that it? Is it? Well, I can tell you now what his answer would be if I was stupid enough to try that, an' I don't blame him. If you're so worried about what he might do, why don't you tell him?'

'You know full well he won't listen to me –'

'No? Is that so? An' you his grandfather too . . . Well, well.'

'Don't, Frank –'

'An' you! You keep your clap shut, else I'll shut it for you.' He had swung round at the sound of his wife's voice with such ferocity that for a moment George was stunned, but only for a moment.

'That's enough of that, Malley, you leave her alone. I shouldn't have come –'

'Aye, you're right there, dead right.' The frustration and bitterness of years was in Frank's voice and body now. 'But that's just like you, ain't it? You've got no guts, no real guts. Instead of sortin' out your own problems you take the easy road, you always have. Well, this is one time the tab ain't being picked up by no one else. You do your own dirty work, you hear me? An' you can leave me wife to me, I know how to handle her. She's used to my little ways, ain't you, Martha love?' He laughed slowly, a thick low unnatural laugh. 'Did you know she tried to do away with herself a few years back?' he asked George in an almost conversational tone. 'I came home unexpected like, to find her with her head in the gas oven. The silly . . .' There followed a string of obscenities that brought

George to his feet and Martha shrinking into a corner of the kitchen with her hand to her mouth. 'But she didn't try that little trick agen, not when I told her what I'd do to her precious daughter if she did, and them there brats she's spawned. I won't be crossed. Frank Malley won't be crossed. That's where you made your big mistake.'

For a moment George really thought he was hallucinating again, as he had been wont to do once or twice lately with the effect of the pills on an empty stomach, because he couldn't believe the sheer unadulterated evil that was flowing out of Malley's crouched form, but then Martha turned agonized eyes his way and he knew it was no hallucination. Frank was mad. He had to be stark staring mad, like – His brain stopped and then raced like an express train. Like his grandson. Like David. *David* . . .

'It was easy, takin' your Jenny down,' Frank continued in the same conversational tone he had used talking about Martha, and George remained in a frozen tableau staring at the man who had taken on the likeness of the very devil. 'She knew I'd wanted to marry her aunt Martha, I'd told her often enough, made a joke of it, like, to win her confidence. An' then one day I said Martha'd been took bad an' her mam had sent me to fetch her. She came like a lamb –'

'You –'

'I wouldn't try anythin', George.' Frank's voice took on a venomous scathing quality as he let his eyes run up and down the gaunt frame of his adversary. 'One good shove and you'll be six foot under, and not afore time –'

'You knew?' George turned to Martha. 'You knew and you never told me?' The pain was slicing into him, cutting his breath.

'I couldn't.' She shook her head miserably, her eyes beseeching him to understand. 'What good would it have done? You'd have gone for him, likely ended up in jail, and there were the twins –'

David and Jenny. He felt a constriction in his chest that made him feel faint, and willed himself not to pass out. 'Does he know? David?'

'No.' It was Frank who answered.

'An' you're not worried I'll tell him? Tell him what type of dirty scum his father is –'

'He wouldn't believe you.' Frank stared at him, his black eyes unblinking. 'He wouldn't take your word agin mine, not David. An even if I told him the truth I've laid enough in through the years about the whore who gave birth to him for the blame to be lifted off my shoulders. She was anybody's, that's what he knows, anybody's –'

'*You!*' The hate that transformed George from a beaten, dying old man into a raging madman with enough power in his limbs to fell a horse took Frank completely by surprise as George suddenly sprang at his old enemy's throat. His fingers tightened, his face demented by grief and rage and loathing, but when in the next instant Frank's fists drove into his stomach George doubled up with the pain, stumbling backwards before falling over in a sprawled heap on the floor.

'You! You think you can beat me?' Frank was frothing at the mouth in his frenzy. 'You're nothin'! You've always been nothin' but she's been too blind to see it! An' now you've got somethin' to chew over haven't you? Aye, an' I hope you choke on it. Comin' here cap in hand expectin' me to help you out with David. He's mine, do you hear me? He's always been mine. Blood's thicker 'n water at the last count.' As he moved forward, intending to kick the writhing figure on the floor, Martha was there before him, her body crouched as though she too would spring at his face.

'You leave him. You touch him again and I'll kill you.'

'You?' There was an insolent pitying knowledge of how easily he could make her cringe in his words but this time the intimidation he used as such a formidable weapon didn't make her cower. Her eyes merely narrowed beneath his, her mouth a thin straight line.

'Aye, me.' And all the hate, the abject loathing she felt for this man was in her face when she ground out the next words. 'You've heard of the worm turnin'? Well, this is it, me lad. You touch him again and I swear I'll kill you, Frank Malley. You've treated me as less than human through the years and I've stood it, more fool me, an' for the reasons you made plain to him.' She nodded at George, who had now eased himself into a sitting position, leaning back against the formica cupboard, his face as white as lint. 'You're a pervert, a dirty, low, disgusting little pervert, an' you aren't fit to lick his boots.'

'*You –*'

'You try it, just try it and I'll tell the whole town what you and that filthy son of yours are. I know more about you than you think, aye I do. All them extra jobs you arrange for the work's lorries to do and you taking all the profit? An' that scrap deal you've got with Millett's. You think I don't know about that 'n all?'

'Keep your mouth shut, woman.'

'And that's besides your sexual habits. I'm sure there's a few leading lights in the steelworks who would find them interesting. All told, you'd be out on your ear quicker 'n you could say Jack Robinson and the name Frank Malley would be a by-word –'

'I'm telling you –'

'No, I'm telling you. You think you've got it all your own way but I've got plenty on you, Frank Malley, plenty. You could go down the line for the pies you've got cookin', and the only thing that's stopped me speakin' out in the past is how it'd affect Connie and the bairns, 'cos they'd get tarred with the same brush, I know this town. But I don't care any more, I swear I don't. You touch him again and I'll be down the cop shop so fast me feet won't touch the ground.'

'You're barmy, woman, barmy. They'd do you an' all.'

'I don't care! Get it through your thick head, I don't care!'

Their voices stopped when George raised himself from the floor, brushing aside Martha's hand as she reached out to help him, and he stood, swaying slightly and looking into Frank's tight face. 'There's scum and scum, Malley, but you're the dirtiest I've come across. What you've done –' He stopped, unable to continue for a moment as he laboured to pull air into his lungs. 'But I'm going to have you, I promise you that, an' to rid this earth of you would be like riddin' it of a foul, putrefyin' disease, 'cos you're filthy, rotten to the core.'

'George –'

As Martha reached out again to take his arm he pushed her away for a second time, not roughly but with a proud refusal of her help that cut her like a knife, and she knew he was blaming her for not telling him. But what good would it have done? she wanted to shout. Can't you see it wouldn't have done any good? She'd done it for the best, she had.

'Get out.' Frank's voice was more blustering than

angry now. 'Get out. You come round here shoutin' and carryin' on –'

'I'm going.' George forced himself to walk upright although the pain in his stomach where Frank's fists had met his flesh was crucifying. He'd done some damage, that much was for sure. Could you burst malignant growths? He didn't know, dammit, but pray God he wouldn't go before he settled this lot. If there is a God, hear me now, he prayed silently as he left the kitchen. Let me last a little longer till I've finished what Frank started thirty-two years ago. *Please* . . .

CHAPTER TWENTY-TWO

'David?' It was six o'clock on the same day and as George was making his way slowly home his grandson was knocking on Connie's front door, washed and shaved after his day at the steelworks, with his grey eyes soft and smiling and his blond hair neatly combed.

'Is Jenny here?' David continued to smile at Connie, and that fact alone told her something was afoot. In all the years she had known her cousin he had never once consciously smiled at her, not unless it was with scorn or contempt anyway.

'Yes.' Connie kept the door half-closed and her face straight.

'Can I see her?'

'No.'

'There's no need to take that attitude –'

'There's every need.' As Connie went to shut the door David's foot stopped her. 'And you can pack that in for a start. Mick's here and –'

'Mick!' The word carried a wealth of contempt. 'I'm shakin' in me shoes.' The smile had slipped and with it the charm. 'Now look, I don't know what she's told you –'

'The truth, and that was more than enough.'

'I'm going to see her.' Now the grey eyes narrowed.

'Not here you're not –'

'Connie, it's all right, really.' As Jenny appeared at her cousin's side she touched her arm gently. 'It's probably better we talk. Look, you go and finish your tea and I won't be long.'

'Jenny –'

'Please, Connie.'

'Well, all right, but I'm keeping the kitchen door open.' The last was directed at David, who smiled and bowed his head as though she had just given him a compliment, and the two exchanged a look of heart-felt dislike before Connie walked back up the passage and into the kitchen where the rest of the family were eating.

'She doesn't like me much, does she?' David looked up at Jenny as he spoke and as always his guts twisted at the sight of her.

'That works both ways. I've never known you to exactly put yourself out to get on with her either.'

Both the tartness of the words and the tone in which they were spoken surprised him but he forced the smile to remain in place, mellowing it to a soft, remorse-ful tremble of his lips when she didn't respond. 'I haven't slept since Saturday night, Jen, I've been goin' mad thinkin' about what I did. I can't believe I hit you, I can't . . .' He bowed his head. 'I've felt like killin' meself –'

'Don't be stupid.' But he could sense the uncertainty now.

'I mean it, I'm not jokin''. You see, I thought he was one of these fly boys havin' you on at first, and then when you said it was one of the Maines I thought he was messin' about with you, I didn't know how things were.'

'You didn't let me explain –'

'I know, I know.' He still kept his head bowed, it wouldn't do to let her see the light of satisfaction in his eyes. A few words and she was eating out of his hand. He knew he could do it. *He knew*. And he needed to get things sweet again 'cos who else would she turn to for comfort when fate repeated itself but him? And it would repeat itself. Come next week this nice little world that she'd made for herself without him, *without him*, would come toppling down about her ears. He felt excitement stir in his chest, causing the adrenalin to flow. 'I'm sorry, Jen, I can't tell you how sorry I am. If you want him and he's goin' to treat you right, then of course I'm for it, I love you, don't I?'

'Oh, David . . .' Her voice was soft and the softness took possession of his whole body, so that he had to wait a moment before he looked up. 'David, I want you to like him. I know you will. I couldn't stand it if we weren't friends –'

'Of course we are, if you can forgive me, that is.'

'Yes, yes, of course I can. I know you were only thinking of me, you always are, but you forget I'm a grown woman now.'

Forget it? There wasn't a minute of the day or night he forgot it, he thought grimly as he recalled endless nights of tossing and turning in spite of the expert services of Tinsley Street. She was like a fever in his blood, always there, sometimes more hot than others but always there. Why had it happened like this? For a brief moment he cursed against fate but then as he looked at her face he knew he didn't want it any other way. He made no attempt to touch her. He knew when he could trust himself and when he couldn't, and after a week of being starved of her presence . . . And he'd frightened her that night after she'd fallen, he knew he had, and he'd kicked himself ever since in spite of all his curses and self-justification. He had to win her trust again but the seeds had been sown and she'd always been putty in his hands . . . 'I'd better be goin', then.'

'You don't want to come in? I can get you a cup of tea –'

'No, no thanks, not right now.' He needed more than a cup of tea. A few whiskies and an evening at Tinsley Street should do it, and anyway, he didn't trust himself to hold his tongue round that Connie, the slut. She'd looked at him as though he was lower than dirt under her feet. But he'd have his day with that one, aye he would. There were more ways to skin a rabbit than the obvious. She thought the world of her Mick, didn't she? And the gormless idiot thought the world of her too. But a few little rumours dropped in the right ears, about how easy it was to be somewhere else when you were supposed to be canvassing and working at the Party headquarters, and madam wouldn't be so high and mighty. And he knew a few who would make waves, and didn't need proof. In fact, proof was the last thing they needed to spread their tittle-tattle. Aye, he'd teach her. He could get them at each other's throat all right.

Connie was waiting for her when she walked back into the kitchen, and she wasn't smiling. 'Well?'

Jenny saw Mick raise his eyebrows at his wife's tone but he said nothing. 'He came round to apologize,' she said flatly.

'And you believed him?'

'Believed him?' Jenny was surprised. 'Of course I believed him, why shouldn't I?'

'You don't think he's just trying to get in with you again?'

'*Connie.*' Now Mick did raise his voice. 'I think Jenny probably knows her own brother better than you do, don't you?'

'No. No, I damn well don't.' Connie put her hands on her hips as she glared at him. 'And if you weren't such a thick numbskull you'd know that without me having to tell you. She's got a blind spot where David is concerned, always has had, always will have.'

'Connie, he was trying to be nice,' Jenny said urgently as Mick's face darkened at being called a numbskull by his better half. 'That's all. And I'm glad he came. I don't like being at odds with him.'

'No, I know that,' Connie said more quietly now. 'And unfortunately so does he. Oh, Jenny, Jenny, I'm sorry . . .' She walked across to her cousin and hugged her before turning to the sink. 'But I don't trust him, that's the be-all and end-all, I suppose. I don't trust him and I don't like him – Oh, I suppose that makes me as blind as you in a way. I don't know, I don't really, but I suppose you're old enough to follow your own star, girl.'

'Can I have a star, Mam?'

'What?' They all turned to look at eight-year-old Christine who, along with her brothers, had been listening with avid interest to this adult conversation, of which they didn't understand a word.

'A star. You just said Aunty Jenny has got her own and I want one. I never get one from Miss Wilson at school, she's a snotty old bag, she is –'

'Christine!' As both parents joined voices, Christine shook her long blond plaits defiantly.

'Well, she is, 'n she don't like me 'cos of him.' She gestured with a small thumb to Brian who was thoroughly enjoying being out of the firing line for once if the grin on his face was anything to go by. 'She says we're as alike as pigs in a poke 'n I don't think that's very nice being called a pig, do you, Mam?'

Connie looked at her small daughter, then at her eldest son who was smiling widely now, and lastly at little Colin who, at five, knew when to keep quiet and make the most of an opportunity and was busy surreptitiously spooning strawberry jam out of the jam-pot on the table and straight into his sticky mouth, a practice that was strictly forbidden. 'I give up.' She looked at Jenny and Mick who were shaking with silent laughter. 'I do, I give up.'

When George got home he realized immediately he entered the house that David had been and gone, even before he saw the pile of dirty clothes flung in a heap on the kitchen floor by the side of the washing machine, by the smell of aftershave that pervaded the air. Once in the kitchen he sat for a long time fighting the nausea that was threatening to overwhelm him before going into the backyard and vomiting blood into the lavatory pan, kneeling on the cold stone floor of the small toilet. He felt like death. He sank back on his heels after some minutes and wiped his clammy face with the back of his hand. It was just as well David wasn't here, he'd have loved this, seeing him reduced to this.

When, after a few more minutes, a semblance of strength returned to his shaking limbs, he made himself rise and go back into the house, making a hot drink before mounting the stairs to his bedroom. He took his pills before getting undressed and climbed into bed, lying back against the wooden headboard with his eyes closed and his body limp.

Malley. Frank Malley. All these years it'd been under his nose and he'd been too blind to see it. He ought to be feeling crazy now, consumed with rage and bitterness and hate but strangely he felt calm, all of him felt calm and drained, the calm that comes before the storm. Because he knew now what he had to do. All he had to work out was how to accomplish it. He reached out for the hot milk liberally laced with brandy at the side of the bed and forced himself to drink. He had to take something in. He needed to keep going, just a bit longer.

It had hurt him that Martha had known and not told him, but somehow that too was lost in this still quietness that had taken him over. But he would set her free as well as Jenny, yes he would. It wouldn't make up for the wrong he had done her but at least she would have some years with Connie and the bairns and end her days without fear.

It was two o'clock in the morning before David came home and when he heard his grandson's footsteps on the landing outside George found himself calling to him, although he had made up his mind he would say nothing. But something, something deep and primitive and fundamental urged him to make sure about what he was going to do, told him that it was necessary, imperative, at least where his grandson was concerned.

'What's up?' David had opened the door but still stood on the dark landing. 'You feelin' bad?'

'No.' And he wasn't, in comparison to how he'd felt earlier. 'I want a word with you. Come in a minute.'

'I'm tired.' As David went to shut the door, George's voice rang out with a touch of its old authority.

'I said, come in a minute. You don't want me to have to shout so's next door can hear, do you?'

'Don't matter to me one way or the other.' But he came into the room now, staring at his grandfather through narrowed eyes in the dim light from the bed-side lamp. 'Well? I ain't got all night. Be sharp about it.' It was intended to get under George's skin and David's eyes narrowed still more when there was no visible reaction from his grandfather. So he'd found out. He'd found out he'd raised his hand to Jenny, that was what this was about. Well, he'd been expecting it, hadn't he? He'd known Connie would let the old man know sooner or later. His mind didn't question but that it was Connie who had done the deed. He knew Jenny wouldn't betray him, not his Jenny. Especially now.

'You got somethin' to tell me?' George asked quietly, his voice flat again.

'Tell *you?* Why would I want to tell you anythin'?'

'Perhaps it'd help if I told you about the visitor I had the other night. You've already made his acquaintance, I understand. A Mr Lawrence Maine?'

'Jenny's fancy man? Aye, I've seen him. What of it?' The cool tone fooled George for a moment until he looked him in the eyes and then he saw their greyness was blazing.

'You didn't think to tell me your sister has a man friend, then? Why?'

'Why should I?' David stretched with contained rage, his chest swelling as he remembered how that scum had felled him to the floor in front of Jenny. And he'd come here. *The scum had actually had the nerve to come here*. Oh, he'd enjoy seeing to this one.

'I'd have thought it obvious. Or perhaps it was because you paid a visit to Jenny later that night and caused her to . . . fall down the stairs? Is that it?'

'Why ask the road you know?' There was a sneer on his lips now as he looked at the frail old figure propped up in the bed. 'An' what's it to do with you anyway? It's atween Jen and me –'

'Oh no, it's not!' For a moment George sounded like his old self but then his voice dropped back to its flat quietness. 'No, it's not, lad. Not by a long chalk.'

'No?'

'No.'

'So you're gonna tan me backside? Is that it? Tell me what a bad lad I've been? Well, you can go to –'

'Are you going to leave 'em alone?'

'What?'

'You heard me, David. I asked you if you are going to leave Jenny and Lawrence alone.'

David moved a step nearer now, his eyes searching the lined old face as he wetted his lips. 'What does that mean?'

'I don't need to spell it out an' you know it. I didn't altogether blame you over Steve Baker, although it was against every law known to God and man, but Peter, Peter was somethin' different.'

'You're sayin' I had somethin' to do with that?'

'Didn't you?' They stared at each other for a full minute without speaking, George quiet and calm and still and David with his jaw thrust out and his hands clenched into great hammers by his side. 'Didn't you, David?' George said again at last. 'I'm not gonna shop you, lad, it's too late for that now and I've got no proof, nothin', and who's gonna take the word of a dying old man stuffed full with pills against that of a young whipper-snapper like you anyway?'

'What game you playin'?'

'No game.' George didn't take his eyes off the big frame in front of him in much the same way a hunter doesn't relax his guard when he's got one of the big cats in his sights. 'I just want to know if you are going to leave Jenny and her fella alone, that's all. You know he wants to marry her –'

'*Marry her?*' His voice sounded like the crack of a whip as it spiralled upwards. 'Marry her? You sound just like her, the stupid, interferin' old cow, that's what she said when I found her pokin' and pryin' about. "He loves her, David, he wants to marry her".'

His voice was shrill in a macabre imitation of a woman's. 'It didn't matter what I wanted, what I'd done to keep her safe, untouched. All those years, all those years when I thought Gran was on my side and then that fancy little schoolteacher came sniffing round Jen and it was, "He wants to marry her, David, marry her." She encouraged Jen, that's what she did, damn her! Well, it was her fault, do you hear me? She deserved what she got. She shouldn't have let me down, double-crossed me, but she found out, she found out I can't be beaten in the end. I fixed her –'

'What are you sayin'?'

'And you think I'd let that lily-livered scum have Jen? You really think I'd let him have her? You still don't see, do you? You don't understand. But you will, you will. I can't be crossed, you'll see I can't be crossed.' There was a froth on his lips now, and although he was staring at him George was sure his grandson wasn't seeing him in that moment before he turned and left the room, shutting the door with an unnatural gentleness behind him.

Mary? *Mary!?* He'd done for Mary? No, no, it wasn't possible. He sat staring into the murky shadows as the small clock on the bedside table ticked away the minutes. But it was, it was. And it wasn't until he felt the salt on his lips that he even realized he was crying.

CHAPTER TWENTY-THREE

'I'm sorry, lass.' Martha reached out a weak hand to Connie. 'I don't like to let you down at the last minute.'

'I've told you, don't worry, Mam.' Connie stood by the side of her mother's bed as she shook her head slowly. 'You don't half look bad though.'

'I've been up and down like a yo-yo all night since eleven. I was as right as rain afore that.'

'That's how these bugs are, look how bad our Colin was at the weekend, that's likely where you caught it from. Anyway, it's in all the schools and factories, they're going down like ninepins. Mick's worried to death it'll affect Labour's chances.'

'Oh, him and that blessed election . . .' Martha managed a weak smile although she felt totally drained from the virulent sickness and diarrhoea she had suffered all night.

'At least you've got the upstairs loo now,' Connie said brightly. 'I don't like to credit anything to Dad but that was one thing he did that makes sense. The last time Mick and I caught something off the kids we were in and out of the house like a fiddler's elbow. That's the next thing we're doing for sure. At least then when you feel your cheeks are being sucked out of your backside you can sit in comfort.'

'Oh Connie, don't make me laugh . . .'

'I'm gonna nip off home now then, if you're comfortable. I don't want to be here when Dad comes in.'

'No, I understand, you go, but I am sorry to let you down –'

'*Mam* . . . For goodness' sake, you aren't. Jenny had said she'd stay the extra night but I said no 'cos I thought you were comin', but she won't mind. She was gonna go after tea tonight when Lawrence comes for her, but they can stay and babysit at my house instead of goin' back to the flat. What they were going to do there they can do just as well in my front room, eh?'

'You're a bad lass . . .' Martha pushed at her with her hand as she smiled again, but she was already asleep when Connie left the house a few moments later, falling into a deep dreamless sleep of exhaustion that was both physical and mental.

'Of course I don't mind.' Jenny smiled happily. She didn't mind about anything. Everything was working out, just as Lawrence had assured her it would. She'd told her grandfather, or to be more exact Lawrence had told him, and he hadn't minded. Indeed, he'd been all for their association. And David had come round, thank God, thank God. She said the last in the form of a quick prayer. And Mr Slater had been kindness itself when she told him today that she'd be leaving to get married in a few weeks, making all the right noises about being sorry to see her go but assuring her no one could have had a better employee for the last few years and that she deserved her happiness, every moment of it. People could be so nice . . .

'You're sure?' But Connie was already in her best clothes and as Jenny grinned at her she smiled back, a trifle shame-faced now. 'Well, you said earlier you didn't mind –'

'And I don't, I don't, so get on with you . . .' She pushed at her cousin with the flat of her hand.

'Lawrence will be here in half an hour at eight and we can have a nice quiet evening in front of the telly. I'll tell him I'm moving back home tomorrow, OK?'

'Thanks, Jenny.'

'No, thank you.' Jenny's voice was soft now. 'I don't know how I'd have managed without you over the last few days, I tell you straight, Connie. Now, you go and join Mick ready for the big count and I'll be here in the morning when you get back.'

'I'm not really bothered about going but you know what Mick is, he'll expect me to be there, although if Labour doesn't win I'd rather be anywhere else, frankly. They all take it so seriously, Jen.'

'Well, no one could ever say you were a political animal, Connie.' The two fell against each other in a wave of laughter for a moment, and as she had done many times over the last few years Jenny blessed the presence of this irrepressible individual in her life.

'Give my love to Lawrence when he comes, won't you?' It had pleased Jenny how Connie and Mick had taken to Lawrence and he to them. 'An' Colin and Christine are already in bed and Brian's in the bath. I've told him eight o'clock is his deadline for being in bed, Friday or no Friday, and then he can read for an hour. I don't know what time we'll be back, Jen –'

'Just go, will you?' She pushed her cousin into the hall and towards the front door as she spoke. 'I'll see you tomorrow.'

Once alone she had the strangest desire to ring her grandfather but Connie had no phone and she didn't like to leave the children to walk to the nearest phone box at the end of the street. She had insisted her grandfather have one installed when she had left the house, her flat already possessing one, and when at home she rang most evenings to check he was all right, especially in the last year or so, since he had reached seventy. Still, he would be OK, of course he would. David would let her know if anything was wrong. But the feeling persisted, getting stronger over the next half an hour, and she met Lawrence at the front door when he arrived with something like panic in her chest.

'Hi . . .' He gathered her up into his arms in a bear hug as his mouth swooped down on hers and for a long breathless moment she forgot everything but him.

'Cor, that was a whopper.' Lawrence let go of her so suddenly she almost fell backwards and then they both peered up at Brian, who was sitting at the top of the stairs looking impossibly angelic in blue pyjamas with little brown dragons on.

'Brian . . .' Jenny's voice was a warning. 'What's your mother told you about eavesdropping?'

'I wasn't.' The childish voice was most indignant. 'I come to see who was at the door and to ask you if I can have me glass of milk and biscuits now. Mam said she'd left 'em in the kitchen till I'd finished me bath, else our Colin and Christine would have ate 'em. I wasn't eavesdropping.' He looked straight at Lawrence now as if appealing to a higher authority. 'I wouldn't have let you see me if I was, would I?'

'I suppose not,' Lawrence said gravely. Jenny knew that of the three of them Lawrence had a soft spot for Brian, and Brian, ever one with an eye to the main chance, had sensed this immediately.

'Well, you go and get in bed now and I'll bring the milk and biscuits up in a minute,' she said firmly without smiling. 'And you don't get out of bed again, do you hear me?'

'I shall have to afore I go to sleep.' Brian looked at them both solemnly. 'For a jimmy-riddle, you know.'

As Lawrence turned away and walked very quickly through to the kitchen she forced her face to remain straight. 'Well, not till then anyway. Now, go and get in bed.'

When she joined Lawrence in the kitchen she saw his eyes were wet with laughter. 'He's a little monkey, isn't he?' It was said with approval. 'I wouldn't mind if our first child turned out like young Brian.'

'Well, I would.' She stared at him indignantly.

'How many children do you want?' His voice was soft now, soft and warm, and she shivered as he reached out and drew her into his arms.

'Hundreds.'

'Me too . . .' They laughed and clung together for a long moment before her earlier anxiety reasserted itself and she pushed herself from him.

'Would you mind taking Brian his milk and biscuits while I pop down to the phone box?' she asked a trifle breathlessly. 'I want to ring Grand-dad and make sure he's all right.'

'Of course not. Why don't you pop round and see the old fellow? It wouldn't take you more than a few minutes.'

'No, no, I'll just phone. He's probably already in bed and now he's got the extension in the bedroom he likes a chat when he's in bed and it'd only disturb him if I went round.'

'Go on, then.'

As he picked up the milk and biscuits for Brian she looked at him for a second, loving him, wanting him, and suddenly desperately afraid of something she couldn't put a name to. She felt . . . unexpectedly strange tonight, and it had happened when she had been feeling so happy, too . . .

'Grand-dad?'

'Hallo, me bairn.'

'How are you feeling?'

'Fine, lass, fine.'

'You always say that.' She paused for a moment. 'How are you really feeling?'

'Fair to middling, fair to middling . . . How is that handsome young man of yours?'

'He's hardly young Grand-dad, he's forty-one, nearly forty-two.'

'At my age that's young, lass.'

'Are you in bed?'

'Aye, all settled down with the evenin' paper and a glass of stout, if you want to know, cosy, like.'

'I'm glad to hear it.' They talked for a few minutes more in the same light vein but when Jenny put down the phone she realized she felt no more reassured than when she had picked it up. Oh, she was stupid, she was. If there wasn't something wrong she invented it! She was going to go back to Connie's and have a lovely evening with Lawrence and forget all these strange fancies. She nodded her head determinedly and then stopped abruptly when she realized a little old lady was peering through the phone-box glass at her.

'You finished, dearie?'

'Yes, yes, of course.' She left with her cheeks glowing. Her grand-dad was fine. Lawrence was fine. David was fine. *Everyone was fine*. She had to stop imagining things.

George put the phone down quietly and continued to

stare at it for a few minutes before his glance moved to the two tins of paraffin in the corner of his bedroom. That was probably the last time he'd hear his granddaughter's voice, in this world anyway. 'Am I doing the right thing, Mary lass?' He spoke out loud. 'I can't let it happen again, can I, girl? And you know it would, aye, it would.' He screwed his eyes tight. He was fully dressed and had been since he had gone out to buy the paraffin just before midday, but once home he had stayed in his bedroom with the door locked, just in case his grandson should take it into his head to come home before he went round to Frank's. But he hadn't. And now it was getting on for nine o'clock and he still had a few hours to wait before he went out again. He had taken all his pills today, he dare not risk his health failing at the crucial moment, and by the time he was ready to go, the dizziness they induced would be fading. He'd done all he could, and now the time was approaching, the urgency to carry his plan through to fruition was strong. He couldn't fail, he mustn't, too many innocent lives had been lost already.

Innocent? The word caught in his consciousness and held. Had Steve Baker been innocent? No, no he couldn't really say he had. And Mary? She'd been a party to that first killing but through love. Could you put murder and love in the same breath? He shook his head slowly. He didn't know. But Peter, Peter had been a different kettle of fish. His back straightened against the headboard as he thought of the young man he had liked so much in the brief time he had known him. That had been the cold-blooded, sadistic slaughter of a young man who had been blameless, and only a blood-thirsty butcher could have carried out such carnage. What had David got in mind for Lawrence? George expelled air through his teeth in a long hiss.

Pray God he'd succeed tonight and never know. Or should he be praying to the other side for what he'd got in mind? His head swam with his thoughts. Could God countenance the extermination of evil when it meant the taking of human life? Life created in his image? *Stop thinking*. He forced himself to relax against the headboard. He knew what he had to do and no amount of analysing would make it any different. And there was Frank Malley . . . The calm was still holding but through it now was threaded a trickle of the red-hot anger and urge to savage and destroy that had gripped him the night before. All this, the devastation of his family that had begun when their Jenny was raped, all this could be laid at this man's door, all the heartache, the searing pain and agony of loss, all the misery . . . Frank Malley. *Frank Malley*.

He forced his racing heartbeat to slow, taking long deep steadying breaths, and then stood up, walking across and picking up the two cans before going quietly downstairs and into the front room where he switched on the television. He needed to keep his mind in the little bubble of isolation it had sought refuge in twenty-four hours earlier, and he couldn't do it if he started to think.

He sat on, alternately dozing and watching the first few election results begin to trickle through in the early hours, the commentators getting excited as they began to predict an overall landslide for the Conservative Party. Had he really cared about all this once? Aye, he had. In his own way he'd been a militant Labour man, fighting tooth and nail for what he'd believed in. No doubt Lawrence Maine was a dyed-in-the-wool Tory? The thought didn't bother him at all. Politics, the state of the country, they paled into insignificance against what was going to happen in the next few hours. He would wait till four o'clock, that was the time he'd arrived at. Even if David had paid one of his visits to that certain part of the town he was never later than three, and knowing he'd got to get up early in the morning for this coach trip he'd probably gone straight home with Frank after their customary visit to the pub on a Friday night, but he wasn't going to take any chances of running into him. No, he'd wait till four. It was still early enough then for the streets to be empty and dark enough for concealment, and Martha wouldn't be back from her overnight stay at Connie's for hours. She'd probably stay and have a bite of dinner with them if he knew Connie's persuasive tongue. And this had to be done right, it couldn't go wrong.

His chest felt raw, he'd vomited blood again earlier, but at exactly fifteen minutes to four he eased his old working jacket over his shoulders, pulled his flat cap on his head and lifted the cans, one in each hand. At the front door he placed the cans on the floor, opened the door quietly and peered into the deserted dark street, which was cold with an early morning drizzle that chilled the air. Almost immediately he started coughing and as he pushed his handkerchief into his mouth to stifle the sound he held on to the edge of the door stanchion, his body shaking. The linen was stained bright red when he pushed it back into his pocket but he didn't even look at it, moving the cans on to the doorstep before shutting the door behind him.

His mind was blank as he walked towards Frank's house. He had been worried his strength would fail him at the last minute but amazingly he felt stronger than he had in days, weeks, as he trudged the wet pavements, and then he was at the end of the thin lane between the backyards of the houses. Somewhere close by a dog barked, the sound mournful and lost, and then all was quiet again, the rain becoming a steady downpour that drummed on his cap and splattered on the top of the cans in his hands.

He opened the gate into the backyard noiselessly and walked quietly into the paved enclosure, and it was at that point he knew a moment's panic. The lavatory, the netty, where the hell was it? For as long as he could remember both Mary and Martha had always left the spare key at the back of the cistern in the lav in case of emergency, but now the small backyard was neat and empty of everything but a border of small shrubs and a large bird-bath dead centre. Of course, they'd had this modern bathroom installed upstairs, hadn't they? He shut his eyes tightly for a while as he leant back against the wall of the house, the cans slack in his hand. Why hadn't he come this way yesterday? He'd have seen, then. *Dammit*. Damn Frank and his ideas of getting on. From what Martha had flung at him it would seem most of his money came from shady deals on the side . . . He caught his rambling thoughts. Concentrate, man, concentrate. If he knew Martha, old habits died hard. He'd like to bet there was a key out here somewhere. If not, well, he'd have to do the job through the letterbox round the front, but he hadn't wanted that. Apart from the risk of being seen he'd wanted to make it look like an accident. It was important that, for Jenny's peace of mind after. If she ever suspected –

The thought galvanized him into searching but the small garden yielded nothing and then, just when he was preparing to leave and walk round to the front of the house, his eyes fastened on the large cork doormat outside the back door. No. It was too obvious. She wouldn't have. She had. The key beckoned to him, bright and shining, just under the corner of the matting. Martha . . . He grinned in the darkness. Good lass, good lass.

He let himself into the kitchen stealthily and there it was, the old paraffin stove he'd noticed the day before, tucked in a small alcove and surrounded by numerous pairs of shoes. He'd have to move it, it had to look as though somehow it had been tipped over . . . It was heavier than he'd expected and the strain brought on a coughing fit that nearly turned him inside-out in his endeavour to muffle any sound.

He sat for several minutes, dreading the sound of footsteps overhead, but there was nothing and after a while he breathed easier. Carefully, very carefully, he positioned the stove to one side of the door leading into the hall and then tipped it on its side. There was a thin dribble of potent-smelling oil but that was all, barely enough to wet the lino. Still, he'd expected as much. He unscrewed the lid of the first can and then paused for a moment. What was he doing? *What was he doing?* He was going to murder two men and one of them his grandson . . . And then the words Malley had snarled at him in this very kitchen just twenty-four hours earlier came back in all their malevolence.

'You've got no guts, no real guts. Instead of sortin' out your own problems you take the easy road, you always have. Well, this is one time the tab ain't being picked up by no one else. You do your own dirty work –'

'Aye, Malley, you're right.' George looked upwards as though he was speaking to the man asleep in the bedroom above him. 'And it *is* dirty work, I'll give you that, but necessary, aye.' He cast his mind back down the long, painful years and now there was no hesitation as he let the paraffin trickle from the can in a thin toxic stream that followed the slight incline towards the door and began to seep into the hall carpet. He placed the second can in the alcove with the lid still screwed tightly in place. It would look better that, as though they used it all the time, he thought grimly. Then he opened the door leading from the kitchen into the hall as he soaked the carpet still more until it was thoroughly drenched.

And now, as he stood in the stillness with the stink of the paraffin all about him, it wasn't of the two men asleep upstairs that he thought but of the women in his life, the women who had been made to suffer in their different ways for their association with Frank and his son, *his son*. David was his grandson no longer but Malley's son. There was his Jenny, his beautiful daughter, raped at barely fifteen and dead eight months later. Mary, Mary who had nearly gone mad in her grief and then thought to bury it by unknowingly stimulating that seed of obsession in David that had had its roots in the genes of the man who had sired him. And the second Jenny, his grand-daughter, barely less tragic than the first. But he could change that and he was going to. His bairn was going to have her chance at love and life, the chance her mother never had. When Frank Malley had taken his daughter down, forcing his poisonous seed into a body that was still little more than a bairn's, he might as well have killed her because that was the point when she stopped living.

He wiped his hand across his face, his eyes watery, but only from the effect of the oil fumes. All the emotion in him seemed to have transformed itself in the last few minutes into a burning desire for justice, albeit his sort of justice, which was sitting on his chest like a live thing, tearing at his vitals.

And Martha? Martha . . . It was Frank's obsession with her, every bit as deadly as David's with Jenny, that had started all this thirty-two years ago. Would she guess he had had a hand in tonight's business? And if she did, would she give him away? He didn't care if she did as long as she kept her mouth shut about his grand-children's paternity, but she would, she would, he could trust her in that. Martha . . . Strangely the name was just a name now, not the pivot of his existence. Of all four women it was her who gripped his mind least and yet he had loved her for years, countless long years, thought he would go mad for the pain and yearning that had consumed him minute by minute, hour by hour. It just showed . . . He shook his head slowly. But he could end the torment she'd suffered at the hands of that maniac, was still suffering. Aye, he could do that one last thing for her and he'd do it gladly. Would she hear the fire engines where she was at Connie's? Maybe. But at least she'd be clear of any danger there. That's why he had to do this tonight: there might not be a second chance with her out of the way, not with his strength failing so rapidly the last few days. An' if she heard the sirens she wouldn't know they signified the end of her life sentence, her life sentence tied to a madman. But she'd be all right, Martha would be all right. If he knew Frank Malley the house would be insured and the money would come to her. No, she wouldn't lose out. He blinked his eyes rapidly. Get on with it, man, stop your mind from a-wanderin'. Do it now.

He threw the lighted match into the hall at exactly half past four, leaving quickly by the back door, which he locked behind him before returning the key to its resting place under the mat, and by twenty-five minutes to five the bottom floor was billowing lethal black smoke. At twenty to five the house was a blazing inferno and Martha's life sentence, along with her life, had just run out.

'Damn and blast it, damn and blast it . . .' George found muttering the profanities helped him to put one foot in front of the other as he stumbled homewards. He couldn't collapse now, not out here in the street, in the open. He had to get home, wash his clothes and shoes clear of all traces of the paraffin and then get himself into bed where he would be found . . . later. But his chest and stomach, already weak from the tenacious hold of the cancer that was consuming them, were making the going difficult.

He saw no one except a solitary milkman sitting high on his milk float some way in the distance as he reached the top of Crown Street, and then when he was halfway down the deserted pavement the far-off whine of fire engines met his ears and the encroaching clamour, as it got louder and louder, gave him the shot of adrenalin he needed to get into the sanctuary of the house.

He almost fell against the front door, shutting it behind him and stumbling, fighting for breath, into the kitchen where he collapsed in a chair for a long time, how long, he didn't know. 'Come on, lad, you've work to do yet.' The words fell with a dull thud into the emptiness but it was another full ten minutes before he could rouse himself, and then he slowly stripped off his clothes down to his bare skin and bundled the whole lot into the washing machine, setting the controls with a shaking hand and hearing the machine whir into action with a deep feeling of relief. 'So far, so good, lad.' He found talking to himself helped and shook his head at his own absurdity. 'Now the next bit, keep at it.'

After taking his dressing gown from the back of the kitchen door where he had hung it earlier in the day, he scrubbed his shoes in the deep wide sink before taking them outside in the backyard and dirtying the soles and toes. Once he was satisfied with their mucky condition he placed them on the doorstep outside the door where soon even the faint odour of the paraffin had evaporated in the cool thin air.

When the washing machine ground to a halt, its job finished, he placed the damp clothes neatly on to an airer in a corner of the kitchen, and now his footsteps were leaden and his heart thudding like a piston as he climbed the stairs, which seemed like Mount Everest.

Once in the bedroom he sat again for several minutes in a pain-filled daze, his head sunk on his chest as he lost all track of time, and then forced himself to rise and open his wardrobe, taking a full set of clothes and placing them on the chair by the bed, ruffled and untidy, as if they had been discarded the night before.

That accomplished, he placed the previous day's evening paper on the bed along with a magazine or two, put on his pyjamas slowly, very slowly, and then climbed thankfully into bed, the blood thundering in his ears and the pain in his body excruciating.

It was a relief to unscrew the top of the bottle of sleeping tablets and he tipped the contents, about twenty-five in all, on to the counterpane of the bed before pouring himself a full tumbler of whisky from the bottle on the bedside table and drinking it straight. The neat spirit burnt like fire and his eyes streamed with the effect of it, but he poured another glass and began methodically to swallow the tablets one by one until there were fifteen or so left on the bed, which he carefully tipped back into the bottle before placing it next to the whisky after pouring yet another full glass. He had listened intently to what the doctor had told him about these particular tablets. The maximum dosage in any twenty-four hours was four tablets, and never with alcohol, so the amount he had swallowed would do the trick. It had to look as though he had become muddled, taken too many after getting slightly drunk. Jenny mustn't suspect the truth.

It was done. It was finished. He drank the third glass of whisky quickly, leaving just a small amount in the bottom of the large tumbler before relaxing with a sigh of satisfaction. 'I've done all I can, lass.' His head was already beginning to swim. 'It's out of me hands now.'

Within five minutes his head was nodding and he settled deeper into the banked pillows behind his back as the lethal combination of drink and pills banished the pain completely for the first time in weeks, and a deep thankfulness that Jenny and Lawrence were safe flooded his heart.

Had he done the right thing in the eyes of God? He shook his head slightly. He didn't know. But perhaps the Almighty alone could understand the depth of the evil he had annihilated. One thing was for sure, his Jenny would never have been able to have a life of her own while her brother lived, and David would have sent Lawrence the way of Peter. And Martha too had been slowly suffocated by something he couldn't bring himself to term as love, and if she'd tried to do herself in once she might try again if she got desperate. This way, his lass was safe, really safe, and Martha could spend the years that were left to her with Connie and her grandchildren, free from Frank's sick depravity. No, he had no regrets and he wouldn't condemn his soul further by being a hypocrite. He would leave his judgement to God . . . What was he saying? He opened his eyes briefly but the effort was too much. All his life he had been what Mary had called an unbeliever, so what had changed?

He was still pondering the question as he slipped into that last sleep from which there is no awakening, and the glass, which had been held loosely in his hand, tipped sideways, its contents spreading out in a small brown blood-like stain as it soaked into the white candlewick cover.

CHAPTER TWENTY-FOUR

'That sounds near.'

They must have fallen asleep in each other's arms in front of the flickering television screen, Jenny realized dazedly, coming to as Lawrence struggled upright. 'What?'

'That noise, it sounded like a fire engine. Didn't you hear it?'

'No.' She smiled sleepily. 'What's the time?'

'Almost five.' And then they both stiffened as the noise sounded even nearer now. 'There's some trouble somewhere, and if I'm not mistaken that's more than one vehicle.'

'Well, it's not here so I don't care.' She smiled again as she raised her hands to him. 'Come and sit down again and I'll get us a cup of tea in a minute.'

'Very tempting but I ought to be going, my dear.' Nevertheless he joined her again on the settee, taking her into his arms as he kissed her lightly on the mouth. 'I'll be back here in a few hours anyway to take you to the flat.'

'So why not stay and have breakfast? Connie and Mick'll be home soon anyway.'

'And what will master Brian think if he finds me still here when he wakes up?' Lawrence asked with a wry grimace. 'That boy is very perceptive –'

'Don't be silly.' She shook her head at him, her eyes soft. 'He won't think anything, he's only a little lad. Anyway,' she paused as she let her gaze run over his unshaven face. 'I've never made you breakfast before.'

'Oh well, in that case . . .' He smiled at her but his eyes went to the window again. 'You know, I really think that fire must be in the next street or two, Jenny. Perhaps we ought to –'

'Perhaps we ought to do nothing.' She wrinkled her nose at him as she sprang to her feet. 'Now I'm going to make us a nice cup of tea and you can tell me how the election is going, and then I'll do breakfast. Do you like a full English one?'

'Normally, but at this time of the morning toast will do.' He groaned as he flexed the arm against which she had been lying. 'You're a ton weight, woman. I never guessed that slender little frame was so heavy.'

'Does that mean the wedding's off?'

'What do you think?' His voice was soft, full and soft, and she smiled again before walking to the kitchen. She seemed to be doing that all the time lately, smiling, and today she felt more like it than ever. That funny feeling of the night before was completely gone and she felt lighter, freer in her mind than she had in, oh . . . Her eyes widened as she considered. Than she ever had, really. It was as though some restraining force, some weight, had been lifted. She shook her head at her nonsense. But it was. She couldn't really explain it.

She placed several slices of bread under the grill and as she did so she heard yet another fire engine scream in the distance, the sound drawing nearer and nearer as the bread browned. There was certainly a big fire somewhere, and she hoped no one had got hurt.

'Another one.' Lawrence appeared in the doorway.

'Yes, I heard.' She didn't want to think about anybody else's misfortune this morning, not this morning. 'How's the election going?'

'I think Margaret Thatcher has got it canned.' He grinned at her. 'Mick is going to be less than thrilled.'

'Oh dear.' She laughed with him and then waved

her hand towards the front room. 'You go and sit down and I'll bring a tray through, OK?'

'Yes, ma'am.'

He looked gorgeous like that, all unshaven and ruffled, Jenny thought happily as she turned back to the toast, buttering the golden slices and placing them on a plate before reaching for the marmalade and jam and mashing the tea. Gorgeous . . . She couldn't believe how lucky she was, it was as if her life was only just beginning. And a woman Prime Minister in England. She hugged the thought to her for a moment. And not before time. A woman would understand the real issues so much better than a man, be softer, more sensitive to people's needs rather than just saying what she thought the public would want to hear and then doing something completely different. Yes, a new era was beginning, and not just for her alone.

She carried the tray through and they ate in a companionable silence as they watched the television, Lawrence demolishing the slices of toast as eagerly as Brian would have done. Oh, she loved him, she did. She laughed at him now as his hand reached for more toast to find the plate empty. 'I'll get some more.' As she walked back into the kitchen she heard Lawrence open the front door and several pairs of running feet thudded on the pavement outside.

'What's happening?' She heard his deep voice and then a shouted reply that brought a quick dart of sympathy to her breast.

'There's been a terrible fire, mate. Three of 'em bought it the night.'

Oh, the poor things. She put more toast under the grill and moved to peer out of the kitchen window into the square of sky visible between the surrounding roof-tops, her mind returning to the thing that had consumed her thinking for months, years. She had been wrong about David. Thank God, oh thank God. He had been glad for her after all and that other . . . fear, it had been her imagination, all in her imagination. How could she have ever thought he would hurt her, how could she?

Even as the thought surfaced she pushed it back down deep into her subconscious, where it was to remain. He was her brother and she loved him, she always would. That was probably why she was feeling so liberated today, as though she had been let out of a cage like a small bird given its freedom, because David approved of her relationship with Lawrence and she could really look forward to the future. Because if he hadn't, well . . . She would never have admitted it to Lawrence or any living soul but the guilt would have begun to strangle her, she knew it. It was ridiculous, illogical, but that's the way it would have been.

She breathed deeply. But David had told her himself he was all for it, and she should have known he would feel like that when he had had a chance to think about it. After all, he was her brother, her twin brother, and who else loved her quite like he did?

Epilogue

On 20 September 1981, the following announcement appeared in *The Times*:

> Mr and Mrs Lawrence Maine, of The Manor House, Lincoln, are pleased to announce the safe arrival of a son, David George, born on 18 September 1981.
> The couple wish it to be known that the child was named after his mother's late brother, David George Longbridge. 'May your spirit live on.'

SIGNET

Published or forthcoming

FIRST BLOOD

Claire Rayner

An American in exile, Dr George Barnabas, forensic pathologist, never imagined that she would exercise anything more than routine professional skills in her new post at the Royal Eastern Hospital, London. Events prove otherwise. Not that the death of a rich, indulged man in late middle age – or a second on a dangerous building site – should necessarily indicate foul play.

But George has learnt not to take events at face value. Launched on a murder investigation, she finds bloody-minded feminine intuition an excellent weapon with which to play the police at their own game. And, of course, the murderer.

SIGNET

Published or forthcoming

A KISS BEFORE DYING

Ira Levin

Dorothy, Ellen and Marion: three attractive sisters with a very rich father.

Dorothy meets a handsome young man with an eye for her inheritance while she is at college. They are to be married and her life will be blissful; but Dorothy is pregnant and her fiancé's plans are ruined, for Dorothy will be disinherited if her father discovers the truth.

So the young man provides his bride-to-be with some pills that will solve the problem. Soon there will be no baby – and perhaps no Dorothy either …

SIGNET

Published or forthcoming

ROSEMARY'S BABY

Ira Levin

When the truth is more sinister than imagination ...

Rosemary and Guy Woodhouse's new apartment in the Bramford was everything the young couple wanted. Yet as soon as they'd signed the lease Rosemary began to have doubts.

The neighbours were quaint but friendly. Too friendly. Especially after Mr and Mrs Castavet learned that Rosemary was planning to have a baby.

'A darkly brilliant tale of modern devilry that induces the reader to believe the unbelievable. I believed it and was altogether enthralled' – Truman Capote

'This horror story will grip you and chill you' – *Daily Express*

'Diabolically good ... the pay-off is so fiendish it made me sweat' – *Sun*

'A terrifying book ... I can think of no other in which fear of an unknown evil strikes with greater chill' – *Daily Telegraph*

Published or forthcoming

Private Scandals

Nora Roberts

Television journalist Deanna Reynolds is a rising star at CBC news. With her warmth, intelligence and beauty, she has all the talent to succeed in the glamorous, high-powered world of network TV.

Yet even she has something to hide, and competing against her is rival talk-show celebrity Angela Perkins. When Deanna is confronted with her own private scandal from the past, both her career and her love for the wildly attractive and impulsive Finn Riley are threatened. And as the attentions of an admiring fan spill over into obsession, Deanna is faced with a terrifying choice ...